THE POINT OF NO RETURN

"Not now," he whispered, placing his hands on either side of her face. He stared at her. Erika's eyes were huge and confused. Between them, something was happening and he didn't know if he wanted to stop it, or even if he could. Michael lowered his head and brushed his mouth over hers. Her lips were full and soft, yielding. This could be his undoing. He didn't want just any woman. He wanted her.

It wouldn't take much for him to crush her against him, devour her mouth, peel this red suit from her brown body and take her on the bed only a few feet from where they stood.

He wouldn't do that. He couldn't do it. There was something about her that told him she was fragile and could easily break into a million pieces. He kissed her tenderly, cradling her head between his hands. She returned his kiss with equal gentleness, opening her mouth to his enticing persuasion, accepting the fullness of his tongue as it swept inside and tasted the sweetness of her being.

Michael tore his mouth from hers. He stared down at her, both of them breathing raggedly. "Make no mistake about this, Erika," he said in a voice thick with emotion. "I want to make love to you." She started to say something. "Shhh . . ." He put his finger to her lips.

Her tongue darted out and licked his finger. Michael nearly lost his power of speech. A spiral of emotion fissured through him.

"Erika, this isn't part of our agreement. We're awfully close to stepping across a line that hasn't been defined. There is a point of no return."

LEGACY

Shirley Hailstock

ARABESQUE
BET BOOKS

BET Publications, LLC
www.msbet.com
www.arabesquebooks.com

PINNACLE BOOKS are published by

Kensington Publishing Corp.
850 Third Avenue
New York, NY 10022

First Printing: July, 1997
10 9 8 7 6 5 4 3 2

Printed in the United States of America

To William D. Bennett, who taught me math and chemistry but left me with a legacy that can only be expressed in words, if accompanied with friendship and happy tears.

Prologue

"Money, Erika, like poverty, is one of life's true burdens."
Carlton Lipton-Graves fell back against the pillows. He was
pale white and small, never having stood more than five-feet,
five inches, even in his prime. Now a withered, old man in
his nineties, he looked like a dwarf in the huge bed, its head-
board stretching nearly as high as the ceiling. Erika St. James
sat on the white coverlet, watching him die. She'd been doing
it for nearly a year, and the strain took its toll on her energy
level. "Some want to take it from you," he continued. "Swin-
dle it from you, con you out of it, even steal it. They'll try
any means." He slapped the bed weakly with his fist. "Some
want you to *give* it to them, as if somebody gave it to you."
He muttered the last. "Others criticize you for what you do
or what you don't do with it." He closed his eyes and took a
deep breath. His small rib cage expanded and contracted. Erika
thought he'd dissolve into wracking coughs as he'd done in
days past, but surprisingly he remained calm and coherent.

"Carlton, what are you talking about?"

"It's no favor I've done you, Erika." His gaze was steady,
although his eyes were faded and aged. "You or Michael."

"Michael?" she frowned. "Who's Michael?"

"I'm sorry, Erika. I'll tell you that now." He continued as
if she hadn't spoken. "It'll probably do him good. Get him
off that damn hill. Been up there too long. Time for him to
join the living, not the dying."

Erika thought it a strange comment from a man who probably wouldn't last the night. She berated herself for thinking such a thing. She and Carlton had been friends since she was a child of eight, for twenty-six years. He was sixty years older. Together they had formed a special friendship. A bond existed between them that only the very young and the very old can understand. She had lived in California for the past eight years, and her visits were frequent, but never had he mentioned anyone named Michael. When had he met him? For a moment Erika thought Carlton might be senile, but quickly abandoned the idea. At ninety-four, Carlton had a mind as sharp as it had been when she first met him. He was rambling, but he was entitled, and she was obliged to listen, tired or not. Tonight was possibly his last night on earth. He could do whatever, say whatever, he wanted. Erika didn't mind. Tears gathered in her eyes. Carlton had called her a year ago, almost to the day, and asked her to return. She knew he was ill. There had been nothing to keep her in California, certainly not Bill Castle, her former fiancé, a man who'd run off and married another woman without the courtesy of breaking it off with her first. Carlton's request was a blessing, a chance to escape the sympathetic eyes and hushed whispers that had followed her entrance into a room.

Bill Castle, an entertainment lawyer, was invited to the best celebrity parties, and Erika joined him in his high profile lifestyle. His abrupt marriage had left her reeling and emotionally stung. He was no better than her mother. When Carlton called, needing her, she came here—home. The only place she'd called home since they'd met.

Carlton closed his eyes. She remembered the day she'd met him. She'd been running from some horror, long since forgotten. Without thinking, she'd run through the hedges and over the lawn. There wasn't a gate then. Nothing had impeded her need to get as far away from her mother as possible. She ran through the front door and smack into him. He wasn't as tall as her father had been—he was only half a giant—but his strange white hair and scowling expression put fear in her heart and closed her throat, even to the scream that lodged there. Then he laughed. Not a booming, from-the-belly-laugh, but a happy laugh. She hadn't relaxed even then. Grown people often began with a laugh, but ended being angry. Carlton hadn't. He invited her to tea. They drank it in his garden, a wonderful place full of flowers and smelling of sunshine and fall. She remembered that smell to this day. He invited her to come back whenever she was free, and she'd left smiling. Only her father had ever treated her like that.

Erika came back to the present. Carlton lay quietly, his eyes closed, his breaths even. Brushing a nostalgic tear away, she moved to get up. She wouldn't leave him. It was her duty to stay, a duty she considered more an honor than a command. Erika had resigned herself to the fact that he wouldn't recover from his illness. It had been diagnosed as heart disease, but his body was simply giving out from use. Another tear escaped her.

He stopped her. "Where are you going?"

"I thought you were asleep," she said, resuming her position on the spread.

Erika wore a satin robe. It was a luscious green and contrasted with the white spread. Carlton had given her the robe for her last birthday.

He took her hand. His fingers were thin and felt bony against her flesh. "I won't sleep again. I know that now. When I close my eyes it'll be for the last time."

Tears sprang to Erika's eyes. She didn't contradict him. The doctor had said to keep him comfortable, agree to anything he said, and give him whatever he wanted. Medical science had done everything it could. It was up to a higher authority now.

"I did want to see Michael again, but . . ."

Erika thought he was talking more to himself than to her. Who was Michael? Maybe she could call him. Have him come as quickly as he could.

Carlton interrupted her train of thought. "I guess you'll have to tell him for me."

"Tell him what?" she whispered. "Who is Michael?"

"My grandson."

Grandson? This was the first she'd heard of him. She knew Carlton had had a son. He died three years before Erika met Carlton, the same year her father had died. The commonality gave them the foundation for their alliance. It was rare for the old man to mention his son. Erika thought about him. She understood. She hadn't been able to explain her pain after her father died. But a grandson!

"Where is he?" Erika asked, unable to keep an incredulous note out of her voice. "He should be here." She had known Carlton for twenty-six years. How old was his grandson? Thirty? Thirty-four? He had to be at least as old as she was. What had happened to him? Why had he never come to see his grandfather? Why, when Carlton knew he was dying, had he called for her, and not his own flesh and blood? Of course she'd been glad to come back. Not just because Carlton was her friend, but because her life in Los Angeles had gone sour. Bill was no longer a consideration. Her position as Vice President of Marketing for a manufacturing company that made polyurethane products and sold them, mainly to the fantasy factories of Hollywood, meant nothing, and she was fed up with the shallow personalities of the west coast.

Returning to Philadelphia to help Carlton had seemed a perfect reason to leave the stares behind and begin anew. But even knowing Carlton was ill hadn't prepared her for his dying. She knew she'd have to help him at Graves Enterprises, and she'd looked forward to the opportunity. Carlton had been her teacher more than any of her college professors at UCLA. When applying for jobs, she'd stood heads above other candidates in her ability to analyze a market and understand the dynamics of trending and competitive advantage. From the time she was a small child, Carlton had taught her how to run a diverse business.

"He should be here. Doesn't he know . . ." She stopped, realizing what she was about to say—did he know his grand-father was dying? "I'll call him, Carlton." Erika leaned for-ward. A phone sat on the nightstand next to Carlton's bed. The ancient black instrument sat incongruously among brown plas-tic bottles of prescription drugs and a silver pitcher of water. The ice inside caused droplets to form on the shiny surface. Erika noticed a drop slide down the side to disappear into the white cloth at its base.

"No phone. He's stuck on that mountain and no one can get him off." Then Carlton looked at her. His eyes cleared and he stared as if he was seeing her for the first time in years. "Maybe *you* can, Erika. I'm counting on you. Get Michael to come back."

Erika felt manipulated. She wouldn't promise a dying man she would do something she wouldn't. She couldn't. Promises were the most sacred things one person could offer another. She'd had enough of them made to her and broken. No matter what Dr. Mason had said, she was not going to promise Carlton anything having to do with his grandson.

"Carlton, I didn't even know you had a grandson."

"He needs someone, too," Carlton said.

Erika swallowed. She knew exactly what Carlton meant. When she was eight she'd needed a friend and Carlton had been there. Erika, at thirty-four, knew that need didn't go away with adulthood.

"Promise me, Erika?"

She hesitated. "Carlton—"

"Promise me," he interrupted, grasping her hand in his bony one.

Erika peered into his eyes.

"Promise me!" He raised his voice, a shuddering, weak imi-tation of the voice she remembered from childhood.

She nodded, hating Carlton for forcing her to do something she didn't want to do.

"Get me the book." Carlton pointed toward the large, ornate

desk in the corner of the room. It had been used by generations of Graves since the 1800s. Erika went to it. She didn't see any book. "In the drawer," he whispered, his voice weak.

Erika pulled a drawer open and found file folders, each neatly labeled by Carlton's secretary. She closed it and opened another. "Bottom," he said, raising himself up on his elbows as if the effort cost him all his energy.

She found it, a leather-bound photo album with the name Michael Lawrence Lipton-Graves embossed on it in gold letters. It was obviously old and well-worn. The leather was soft, with small creases from being opened and closed.

"Bring it." He reached toward the album.

Erika took it back to him and placed it within reach. He lay back against the pillows, clutching it to him as if holding something precious. His eyes softened and clouded for a moment. Erika had never seen him look so vulnerable. She'd seen him weakened by age and pain, but this photo album had added a weakness that only love could cause.

Erika only barely remembered that kind of love. She never got it from her mother, but her father had loved her unconditionally. She knew Carlton, too, loved her, but not with the same passion as for someone whose bloodline was the same as his and flowed in his veins. Michael Lawrence Lipton-Graves alone held that distinction. When Carlton left this earth, left behind him would be a piece of himself.

Carlton opened the soft leather album, using his gnarled, arthritic fingers, which must be in pain. Turning the book toward Erika, he pointed to a photo. A small black child of about ten years old looked up from the time-encased shot.

"Michael," Carlton said . . . and died.

One

Michael woke with a start. It wasn't the dream this time—but the crate against his back had fallen away. He lay on the small wharf next to the rowboat. The bobbing had relaxed him and he'd fallen into a light sleep. Pulling the crate back into place, he repositioned himself. The August sun warmed his face, but fall came early in the mountains and winter's snow would soon follow it. Michael liked winter. He liked the freshness in the air, even when he'd lived in the city. Winter days were fresh, biting sometimes, but always clear enough to get his mental juices flowing. Maybe this winter he'd finally get rid of Abby's image.

Michael looked up. Birds, in the standard V formation, flew southward in the sky overhead. Trees swayed in the light breeze. It was quiet, relaxing. Yet he felt disturbed. He'd dreamed of Abby last night, and since then hadn't been able to shake the helpless feeling that he should have done something. Over and over he'd replayed that dream in his head. He couldn't have done anything, didn't have time to react before everything was over. Yet she haunted him from time to time. Just when he thought she was going away, she'd show up again.

A movement from the side caught Michael. He saw her. For a millisecond he thought Abby had stepped out of his dream, but watching her come forward he realized she was just another lost tourist—tourist or weekend camper coming up to the mountains for the weekend who couldn't find the campgrounds. Why did they think camping meant going to a park and plugging in all the amenities they had at home?

She came toward him, one hand raised against the sun. She wore pants, not jeans like most of the tourists but slacks like women wore to offices, and shoes, not tennis sneakers. Her blouse was white, long-sleeved, and soft. The breeze pressed it against her breasts. Her gait was confident and purposeful. Despite her shoes, she didn't tiptoe over the stones that defined the path to the jetty where Michael had a small rowboat. Something stirred inside Michael. For the first time in a long while he felt the beginnings of arousal. Michael gauged her gait. She walked as if she knew where she was going. She reminded him of a fast car, dark and sleek, with underlying power. He'd had a car like that once.

She had to be from his office. Although he'd never set eyes on her before, somehow he recognized that corporate control, that I-can-do-the-impossible attitude.

Stopping in front of him, she studied the mountains in the distance as if she were assessing the place, looking it over with thoughts of buying it. It wasn't for sale.

"Are you Michael Lawrence?" She asked the question without looking at him.

He eyed her, not moving from his position. She had long legs and short hair. If he stood up she'd probably come to his shoulder. He was six foot two. That made her tall for a woman. Her skin was flawlessly smooth and as richly brown as a thoroughbred's coat. No one had come looking for him in the year he'd been here. Except for the last week, when a car had come three times to deliver telegrams he hadn't bothered to open, he'd seen only lost tourists. Now this woman had come specifically for him.

"Who are you?" he asked. His voice came out gruff. He didn't want to be found. He wanted to be left alone.

"I'm Erika St. James."

The name meant nothing to him, and she hadn't said it as if it should. "Do I know you?"

"No." She shook her head. Wispy curls were caught and kissed by the wind. Michael frowned at the thought of how that hair would feel. "I sent you three telegrams about your grandfather."

Michael didn't move, but he eyed her closely. So she'd sent the telegrams. "You've got the wrong guy. I haven't got a grandfather"

"You're Michael Lawrence?"

He nodded.

"Carlton Lipton-Graves told me you were his grandson."

"Not to my knowledge." He shrugged. The name meant nothing to him. Both his sets of grandparents were dead. He'd never known any of them. He squinted. What was she doing here? She knew his name. Why did she think this Carlton was related to him?

Her eyes captured his attention. They were brown, huge, and fringed by dark lashes. He wanted to keep looking into them, but forced himself to look away.

"You didn't read the telegrams?" she asked.

"I have no use for telegrams, newspapers, TV, telephones, or fax machines, for that matter. Whatever you've come here for, I'm sorry it was a wasted trip. Good day, Ms. St. James."

He went back to his position against the crate, closing his eyes, dismissing her. She didn't leave. He would have heard her footsteps on the gravel. What was she waiting for? He opened his eyes. She was standing in the same position, her hands on her hips, her breasts rising and falling with controlled breathing. From his position on the wooden wharf his gaze was drawn to her.

"Is there something else you have to say?"

"Yes . . . no," she corrected.

"Then have a nice trip back to the city."

She turned away, then stopped. Michael could see her hands curl into tight balls. Every line of her body was stiff as she stood still. A moment later she looked back at him. He thought she was about to say something, but changed her mind. She turned again, starting up the slight incline that led back to his cabin and eventually to the road. Michael watched the sway of her hips as she moved away from him. It had been a long time, he thought since he'd wanted a woman, but God, he could want her. Closing his eyes, he shifted his body to relieve some of the tightness in his loins and went back to himself.

He should have asked how she knew his name, and why she thought his grandfather was still alive, but he hadn't. He didn't want to. He didn't want to talk to anyone. Since he'd come here he wanted only solitude, and up to now he'd had it. When the telegrams arrived he'd thought they were from his office or his mother, or Malick, his old friend. Only they knew where he'd gone when he left the city. He'd dropped the telegrams in the drawer with the unopened letters he'd received shortly after coming here. He wasn't going back then, and he wasn't going back now. No telegram would get him off this mountain.

Erika turned back and checked over her shoulder. Thank God she'd known he was older than that picture Carlton had shown her. The album was full of pictures of Michael at various stages of his growth and development. She'd gone through the whole album before embarking on this trip. Carlton had captured the high points of a man's life to this point: his school days, sporting events, graduations, law school acceptance—a mini-world inside the pages of a hundred-page book.

Michael, she estimated from the pictures, must be in his mid-thirties. He fascinated her. He hadn't moved. She knew he could still see her, yet his gaze was as fixed as if he were the only person on earth. He'd made her angry. She had nearly told him right then and there. Before the words tumbled out she'd caught herself, though, thought better of it. She remembered her mother telling her that her father was dead. She hadn't thought to soften the blow. She'd just blurted out the words. "He's dead. Your father's dead." They'd hit her like sharp rocks.

Michael had made her angry enough, but she held her

tongue. Since he hadn't read the telegrams, he didn't know. Obviously, there was bad blood between Carlton and his grandson. Denying that he existed was only a defense mechanism. It was probably tied to the reason he was hiding out at this place. She'd wondered what he was doing here during her drive into the Maryland mountains, but she hadn't thought to ask the attorney about it after the will had been read. She was too stunned. First she'd found out Carlton had a grandson, and on the heels of that she'd been confounded by the terms of his will.

Still, no one deserved to hear of the death of a loved one without concern for its impact. There would be time for that later. It wouldn't be dark for another four hours. She had made a reservation at the only motel she'd seen in the last seventy miles. She had some time, but not that much. It had taken longer to negotiate the narrow, winding curves to find him than she expected. She didn't relish the idea of driving down this mountain without the benefit of daylight. Once she'd talked to Michael, she could go back there and spend the night before driving back to Philadelphia.

She had hopes of him returning with her, but now that she'd come up against his hard exterior she knew he'd need time to get used to the idea. Hadn't the general store owner, where she'd stopped to ask directions, told her he came in to pick up food, spoke sparingly, and kept to himself? She could see how his attitude could put people off.

His look reminded her of the old mountain men—dark, unkempt beard, broad shoulders that spoke of hard work despite the heavy, plaid jacket he wore. His denim-clad legs were long, and she couldn't help notice the strength of his thighs. His hair was long, and his clothes were covered with paint, oil, and something else she didn't want to define. Yet his eyes made her breath catch. Deep set and ringed with signs of lack of sleep, they were light brown mirrors that spoke of great pain. It was probably his eyes that pulled at her compassion. They also stirred passion in her. She had no doubt of that.

After Bill, though, she'd have nothing to do with a man for a long time, even if she wanted to.

Erika looked at the cabin as it came into view. She glanced at the clear, blue sky and took a great gulp of clean, mountain air into her lungs. When she was in grade school she'd dreamed of living in a cabin like the pilgrims did, fishing in the nearby stream and cooking her own food. This place seemed to have everything her youthful mind had thought of. Then she got closer, and her dream shattered. It looked as rustic as Michael did, made of logs and covered with a rusty tin roof. She wondered if it leaked during rainstorms, and was glad she wouldn't be here to find out. The perimeter of the small structure was cluttered with old tires and junked auto parts. She wondered how long they had been there, since the only vehicle in the area was her Bronco. Everything had a rusty, discarded look about it as if things were dead, things with no hope of returning to useful life. Weeds overran the path to the door. What could have happened to Michael Lawrence to bring him to this kind of life?

At the Bronco she picked up her phone from the front seat and dialed the office.

"Erika, thank God it's you," Jeff Rivers, her chief financial officer, greeted her after his secretary put her through.

"Is everything all right?" she asked, climbing into the seat.

"For the time being. The stock market closed at three, so nothing more can be done until Monday."

"How was activity?"

"If I said brisk I'd be putting it mildly," he told her.

"It will calm down, Jeff. The market needs to get used to the idea of me sitting in the CEO's chair."

"You've been in that chair for over a year now."

"I know, but Carlton was always there to lean on, and the market knew it."

"I think we still need to keep an eye on this."

"I agree. We don't want any surprises."

Erika could almost see the financially savvy brain spinning in Jeff's head.

"I'll get to work on it. Meanwhile, what did you find out about Michael Lawrence?"

Erika took a deep breath and turned to look back toward the lake. She couldn't see Michael from where she sat, but she assumed he was in the same position he'd been in minutes ago. The news of Carlton's grandson had gone through corporate headquarters like a tornado over flat ground. Morale dipped to an all time low, and she was responsible for raising it.

No one at Graves Enterprises knew Carlton had a grandson, and they were naturally nervous to suddenly find he held their fates in his hands. They looked to her to protect them.

"So far I haven't been able to talk to him," she went on to explain. "He didn't read any of the telegrams I sent."

"Does he even know Carlton is dead?"

He doesn't even know Carlton's his grandfather, she thought, but didn't say. "I don't think so."

Jeff let out a long breath. Erika could hear it through the cordless phone. "I don't envy you."

"How long do you expect to be there?"

"I figure I'll wait around and talk to him, then spend the night at a motel where I made a reservation. In the morning I'll drive home."

"If I find out anything else, I'll leave a message on your answering machine."

"Thanks, Jeff."

Erika pushed the off button and snapped the antenna down. Someone was trying to unseat her, gain control of Graves Enterprises by a hostile takeover, and they hadn't been able to find out who or why. Jeff Rivers was a good man, and she knew he was loyal. If anyone could find the true culprit, it was Jeff.

Carlton had left Michael and her more than enough stock for control of the business, but someone coming in could ruin her plans, force a seat on the board and, with enough influence and charisma, sway the other board members.

Erika was confident in her position at Graves. She knew what she was doing. Carlton had taught her the business from the ground up, but his death, a possible stock problem, an unexpected grandson, and the morale issue were more problems than she wanted to deal with.

Erika wished she were at the office helping Jeff. There had to be something she could do. They should be searching out this problem together. Graves Enterprises was her company. Yet Carlton had forced her to come up this mountain and talk to his grandson.

Erika shivered. Without heat, it was cold in the Bronco. Maybe she'd wait in the cabin. Michael needed time to think about why she'd come looking for him. He'd know she hadn't left if he didn't hear the Bronco motor start up and the sound die away in a fading Doppler effect. When he came in, she'd tell him. In the meantime she was starving. Maybe she'd fix him something to eat. She'd promised the general store owner she'd deliver his groceries. She hoped he wouldn't mind her sharing some of them with him.

Erika got two heavy bags from the back of the truck and elbowed the cabin door open. She stopped suddenly, stepping backward and propping her shoulder against the doorjamb as she tried desperately to hold onto the bags. Breath left her body. The place was filthy. The main room of the cabin was littered with dirty clothes and the remnants of food in various stages of decay. Erika wrinkled her nose as the odor of filth and sweat assaulted her.

"Oh my God!" she gasped, grateful it was too cold for flies.

The urge to turn and run gripped her. Waiting in the truck seemed infinitely more appealing. Then she remembered Carlton. Michael was his grandson, and she'd made a solemn promise to comply with his wishes. From what she could see, after a five minute conversation with Michael Lawrence, he needed family support. At the moment she was as close to family as he could get. She was obligated to Carlton to at least tell him about him. She also needed his help to carry out Carlton's wishes.

Erika hoisted the bags a little higher and went inside. How could he live in this filth? The place had two rooms. There was an area that served as a kitchen and another with a sofa she would have called a living room, except no living creature should enter it. Along one wall was an open door. An unmade bed sat inside.

Pushing aside the debrís, she set the bags on the kitchen ta-ble—if it could be called that. It was four foot square, and every inch of it was covered with some kind of crud. Erika frowned, refusing to even think of what it could be. Two spindle-back chairs sat on one side of it. All the spindles were missing from one, and only two remained in the second. Their seats were both covered with a sticky goo.

She tried to remember how long Carlton had said Michael had been on this mountain. Hadn't he ever cleaned this place? She went about opening the two windows in the main room and the front and back doors. She didn't enter the bedroom. Cold air swept through the place, ridding it of some of the smell.

Erika had left home at sunrise. She'd had an almost inedible tuna sandwich and a cup of oily coffee at a truck stop, her only meal of the day. Facing her was a teeth-gnashing trip to the motel. She wasn't about to do it on an empty stomach. Despite the state of the place, she was still hungry.

Wrinkling her nose, she picked up one of the open contain-ers of old food between two fingers. Holding it out in front of her, she went to the trashbasket. It was overfilled with gar-bage. Dropping the container inside, she pulled the plastic bag up and tied the ends before going in search of a replacement. She found a dust-encrusted box of bags under the sink. With her face in a perpetual frown, she went about picking up the containers of decayed food and dropping them in the trash. She couldn't cook, let alone eat, in a kitchen this dirty.

Starting with the open containers of food, she raked each of them into the trash bin. When she finished the kitchen area she continued, searching for more trash in other areas of the single room. Returning to the kitchen she stacked the full trash bag next to the other one. Then she attacked the kitchen, washing dishes, wiping down counters and scrubbing the table and chairs. Why she was doing this, she didn't know. Something seemed to drive her. Carlton had been more than a friend. He'd treated her like a granddaughter, and she looked on him as a relative. From the way people treated her at the funeral and afterward, she knew they saw her as a part of his family, too. Erika wiped moisture away from her eyes. Carlton was her final link to a loved one. Accepting that she was alone in the world was taking a toll.

Erika scrubbed harder at the stain on the table. She called it therapy. In the week since the funeral she'd been too busy writing notes and seeing to Carlton's affairs. The long drive had afforded her some time alone, time to think—until she started the ascent to the cabin. Now she needed to be unemotional when she talked to Carlton's grandson. She couldn't show her grief or loss. She couldn't dissolve into the tears that had been close to the surface of her emotions since she'd been called back from California. Keeping her hands busy was a way of controlling her thoughts.

Memories of Carlton came to her, anyway. For twenty-six years they'd shared a friendship that transcended their races. He'd been more a parent to her than her own mother. He'd taught her, consoled her, and praised her accomplishments. The only secret he'd kept from her was about Michael and the contents of his will. How was she to know he'd left her a fortune, but she'd only get it if she and Michael could work together?

Time passed and Michael did not return to the cabin. Hunger overcame Erika. She went through the bags the grocer had given her. Everything was in a can or a box, except for the two steaks and four sweet potatoes he'd thrown in with a wicked wink when she'd offered to deliver the food. Obviously,

Michael never had visitors, and the old man in the store was surely matchmaking. Little did he know she wasn't there due to any romantic interest in the man she'd found by the water's edge.

She tried the gas stove but it didn't work. She could hear it, but nothing came through. She was sure nothing worked properly here. Did Michael ever make himself a meal? The open cans she'd picked up looked as if he'd eaten directly from them. *Well, not today,* she thought. Pulling the stove units free, she dropped them in the pan of soapy water she'd changed three times in her effort to make the place habitable. Ten minutes later she used a pipe cleaner to free them of the dirt preventing the gas from flowing properly.

By the time the kitchen was spotless Erika's stomach growled with anticipated hunger. She ached for the microwave oven sitting among the possessions she'd stored when she left California. With it she could have a meal cooked in minutes. As it was, instead of baking the potatoes, she cut them up and dropped them in boiling water. When they were nearly done, she put the steaks on, prepared broccoli, and brewed a pot of decaf coffee. From the look of Michael's eyes, he didn't need caffeine.

Using chipped plates and silverware that must have been forged in a munitions plant, Erika set the table. Michael had yet to make an appearance, but it was time to eat now. She would wait no longer. If she wanted to get down the mountain by nightfall she'd have to leave within the next hour. Smoothing her hair back, she turned toward the door. She'd go get him.

As she reached the door Michael came through it, practically bumping into her. Surprise registered in his eyes. Erika jumped back and her heart thudded and her breath left her. She gasped, filling her lungs with air a moment later.

"What the hell are you doing?" he asked.

"I've made coffee," she told him, recovering. She kept the emotion out of her voice. "I've prepared something for us to eat." To keep herself from having to endure the intensity of his stare she went to the stove and checked the food. "We need to talk."

"I don't want you here." He came toward her.

Erika sidestepped him. She moved to the sink and picked up two mismatched cups and saucers. Her heartbeat accelerated, but she kept quiet. She'd promised Carlton.

"What are you doing?" Michael followed her.

"I'm sure you can see what I'm doing."

"Is there something wrong with you?" He grabbed her hand, taking the cup and stopping her actions. "Don't you know when you're not wanted?"

She snatched her arm away, taking a step back and staring at him. She certainly understood when she wasn't wanted. It had been drummed into her since she was very young. Quickly she snatched the cup away from his hand and turned back to the table, making unnecessary adjustments to the knives and forks.

"Look," he said. "I'm sorry. I didn't mean that. It's just that I don't want . . . could you stop that?" After a moment he added. "Please?"

Erika straightened and faced him in the only clean area in the place. She forced herself to remain still. He looked older than she had thought at first. When she'd seen him by the river she'd thought he was asleep, but judging by the look of him he hadn't slept in weeks. He had large bags under his bloodshot eyes. The episode at the door had brought her close enough to smell alcohol, if there had been any on him. She hadn't smelled it, so she attributed his state to some form of insomnia. She didn't know if it was voluntarily or not. His eyebrows were thick and bushy. By the stream she'd seen defined muscles, but now his clothes appeared baggy, hanging on his body as if he'd lost a lot of weight.

"Say what you want to say and leave me in peace." His voice jarred her. "I don't want you cleaning my house, and I don't want you cooking meals for me."

"You certainly look like you need someone to do it. How can you live in this filth?" Her gaze swept the room. Michael's didn't follow it.

He put his hands up, palms facing out, to stop her when she would have gone on. Erika saw him weave as if he wouldn't be able to stand up for long.

"Are you all right?" Involuntarily, she took a step toward him.

"I'm fine. Just go!"

She jumped at the force of his voice.

"Sit down." She took another step toward him but stopped when his head came up and his look pinned her in place. He staggered to the sofa, now devoid of extraneous clothing, and sat down.

"When was the last time you ate? Or slept, for that matter?"

"I'm not your responsibility," he shouted. "My rituals are none of your business." His hand went to his stomach, rubbing it as if he were in pain. Erika recognized hunger.

"You ought to be somebody's," she muttered. "You obviously haven't eaten in way too long." The food was ready. She made the plates at the stove and placed them on the small table. She called him, instinctively knowing he'd hate it if she came to help him.

"Would you like to eat there?" She hadn't done more in that area of the room than remove dirty clothes to get at the decaying food. She wanted to talk to him, but she preferred the cleanliness of the kitchen area.

Michael didn't want her here. She was too much a part of another world. He'd left that world behind and wanted nothing more to do with it. He didn't want her food, either. Even though it smelled like a piece of heaven and he hadn't eaten in longer than he could remember, he wanted to be alone. The aroma made his stomach juices churn, protesting the fact that he had not given them proper attention. He was weak with the need to taste the food that smelled so good. She was smart, though. She wasn't going to come and get him. She was asking him to give a little. The carrot she was hanging over him could be considered cruel and unusual punishment.

Michael stared at her. Something about her stance told him she wasn't leaving until she'd talked to him about this grandfather she claimed he had. He wasn't in the mood to fight with her, and he *was* hungry. He could eat with her and then send her packing.

Michael had never set eyes on Erika St. James, yet she knew how to broil his steak to perfection. She'd made delicious potatoes. He'd never cared for broccoli, but hers was covered in a liquid cheese sauce that added a wonderful taste to the crunchy vegetable. Even the iced tea tasted heavenly. He'd helped himself to seconds and thirds. Pushing his plate aside, he felt much better. He'd forgotten what a home-cooked meal tasted like. For a moment he considered how quickly he could get used to meals like this. Then he remembered they entailed returning to the city, and he'd vowed he wouldn't do that.

Erika took his plate away and washed the dishes. He watched her without comment. She wasn't his type of woman—too tall, her features too sharp. Yet there was something about the way her waist curved in and her hips flared out that drew his gaze and had him shifting in his chair.

The sun set in the August sky and twilight settled over the cabin. It had a generator for the electric lights, but he hadn't used it in the year he'd been there. The yellow glow of kerosene lamps he'd never noticed bathed the room, and Erika, in a soft hue.

"Can we talk now?" she asked, placing the wet dishtowel over the sink and bringing the coffeepot to the table. Pouring two cups, she set the pot on the stove and returned.

"Who is Carlton—" Michael raised his eyebrows in question.

"Lipton-Graves. Carlton Lipton-Graves," she supplied.

"Are you related to him?" In the back of his mind Michael wanted to know. If she proved a relationship between him and

Carlton Lipton-Graves, would there also be a blood connection between the two of them? Ironically, he hoped not.

She shook her head. "He was my friend. He practically raised me." She smiled and Michael thought her memories must be happy.

"Was?" he asked.

She hesitated, taking a breath. "Carlton died ten days ago."

"I'm sorry," he said. She didn't bow her head or lower her gaze from his, but he could see her eyes fill with tears. She blinked only once and the tears receded. Michael took a drink from his cup, feeling at a loss for what to say. "What do you want with me?" he asked.

"Before he died," she said quietly, "he told me you were his grandson."

"He had to be talking about a different Michael Lawrence."

"He showed me your picture."

"He's wrong. I have no grandparents. They all died years ago." Michael remembered wanting grandparents. Every other kid had them. They had programs at school when he was a child that involved inviting them. Some kids went to stay with their grandparents, and some of them got presents. Michael had wanted that, longed for it, but he'd never said a word to his parents. It wasn't to be his—he knew that—not then, and not now.

"What does a picture prove?" he asked. His picture had been in the papers for months. Cameras flashed in his face all the time. Anyone could have taken a picture.

He looked back at Erika. Why didn't he show her the door? Why did he feel as if there was something intriguing about her, something she wanted to tell him and he wanted to hear? Darkness fell fast on the mountain and the roads were steep and unlighted. It would be hospitable for him to invite her to stay the night, but he didn't want her here. If she planned to get anywhere tonight, she should leave soon. He should remind her of that. Why didn't he?

"Carlton's lawyers had a file on you—birth certificates,

blood test results. There is no mistake. Your father was Carlton's son, Kevin. He married Edith Edwards thirty-eight years ago on May seventh. A year later you were born, and before your first birthday Kevin Lipton-Graves died in a plane crash."

"My father's name was Robert Lawrence. He taught Honors English at the local high school in New Brunswick, New Jersey, where I grew up. He died of a heart attack when I was seventeen."

"Robert Lawrence married your mother when you were three years old. He adopted you, had your name legally changed to Lawrence, and raised you as his son."

Michael didn't believe her. His mother wouldn't keep this kind of secret. She would never have done anything like keep information away from him. Erika St. James had either concocted this elaborate practical joke, or she had the wrong man.

"You don't believe me." She stated it as fact.

"My parents would have told me."

Erika thought of her mother. Mothers didn't always do what they should, what was expected of them. "They should have," Erika said quietly.

"You have the wrong man."

"There were blood tests, DNA matches." She shook her head slowly. "There are no mistakes."

He frowned. "When were these tests done?" Michael knew blood tests were used to identify paternity. DNA matches were like fingerprints; no two were the same. He'd used them himself, to get child support payments for children.

"Right after your father died."

"Why?"

He already knew the answer, but he waited and let Erika swallow while she formulated the words.

"Apparently, someone wanted to prove Kevin Lipton-Graves was your father."

"Maybe they wanted to prove he wasn't." He smiled, slipping easily into the role of prosecutor.

Erika gasped. Her eyes opened wide. Michael couldn't stop the immediate response that gripped him when he surprised her. She obviously hadn't thought of any other reason for the tests.

"Does it make sense?"

"I—I don't know," she stuttered, then recovered. "If Carlton wanted to prove you weren't his grandson, why would his dying words be of you?"

Michael thought about that. He didn't have any idea what he should feel. Carlton Lipton-Graves meant nothing to him. He tried to think of what he'd feel if his mother died and her last words were of him. Suddenly Abby's face crowded in on him. What had been her last thoughts before she died? Had she called her children's names? He couldn't remember.

He got up and walked to the door. The sun was completely gone. Stars dotted the sky like silver glitter. The air, cold enough to penetrate his shirt, caused goose bumps on his skin. He thought about what Erika had said. Why should he even consider it? Could she be right? Was there any truth to what she'd said? Had his mother kept this secret from him for the past thirty-seven years? Had his dad not been his real father? Were his brothers only half-brothers? He'd known he was different from them. While the three of them were unmistakably related, he hadn't looked like them at all. He looked like his mother. That was the explanation he'd given himself, never voicing a question except in anger, as all children do. Erika's story would support his . . .

He stopped. It wouldn't. She'd given him a suggestion and he was letting it push its way into his thoughts. His grandparents were dead. He'd seen pictures of them, both sets of them. He remembered thinking his genes had to reach back further than their generation. Believing her would explain why he looked so different from those on his family tree, why he could see none of his father in his own face. Michael closed the door and turned back. She was wrong. She had to be.

"It's dark now. I think you'd better finish up if you plan to get off this mountain before morning." He was angry. She'd thrown his equilibrium off the moment he'd seen her, and now that he'd been in her company for over an hour, he found he liked talking to her, hearing her voice. There was something about her, something deeper than the face she showed to the outside world. It was power, like in his car engine, underlying and apt to break free with the slightest touch of his foot on the accelerator. He wondered if she'd respond in the same manner. Where was her accelerator? Then he didn't want to know. He wanted her gone. He wanted to be alone, to extinguish the lamps so he couldn't see the places where she had been. Somehow he knew that even when she no longer sat at his table, no longer stood at his sink, he would be able to see her there.

She stood up, glancing toward the window over the sink. "I made a reservation on my way up. I need to get there before too long."

"Where?"

"A motel, a few miles back."

"The closest motel is at least a two hour drive down this mountain. You stopped there?" His eyebrows were raised in surprise.

"No, I saw the sign and called."

"Phone in the car?"

She nodded. "You're right. I should be going, and I'm not looking forward to the drive." She took a breath. "Michael, it's important that you believe what I've told you."

"Why?"

"I need your help. Carlton's will left everything to us."

"What! Why? He didn't even know me."

"You're his grandson."

"I'm not his grandson. I have no grandparents." He stopped, taking a long breath. "I've enjoyed talking with you tonight. I liked your food. But you've done nothing to convince me that Carlton Lipton-Graves and I have anything in common."

"I've told you about the blood tests and the DNA. What do you want?"

"You said he practically raised you. What does that mean?"

She smiled. Michael leaned forward. He liked the way her cheekbones made a picture of her face. Her eyes lit up.

"I went to Carlton's every day after school from the time I was eight years old. He helped me with my homework, taught me values, refused to let me hate or love too quickly."

She looked down as she said the last part. Michael wondered what that meant, but didn't interrupt her.

"He met my boyfriends when I began to date and treated me as if I were his grand—"

She stopped.

"He treated you as a granddaughter, but he never once came to see me. Why is that?" He took a step toward Erika. She moved back.

"I don't know. We may never know the answer to that, but I can tell you, he was the kindest man I've ever met."

"You said he was your friend. Are you a distant relative? The daughter of a cousin or an old maid aunt, or even an old war buddy?"

Erika shook her head. "We're not related in any way."

Michael stared at her for a moment. Erika felt as if she were on the witness stand. "You are in no way related to Carlton Lipton-Graves, yet you're the person who shared his life, acted as his granddaughter, presided over his house and funeral, even administered his will?"

"It's not like that," she began.

"But I am his grandson, according to you. I am a blood relation who has no knowledge that he even existed. When he was dying did he call for a relative? No, he called for you." Michael stopped a moment, then continued. "I don't believe anything you've told me. If I had a grandfather alive, my mother would have told me about him. And even if she hadn't, what prevented him from coming to me? It's not like I'm an impressionable child. I'm thirty-seven years old, certainly capable of understanding the information."

"I can't explain Carlton's actions. I only know that he told me you were his grandson, the lawyers confirmed it, and he left his estate to us."

"Well I don't want it. Now you've delivered your news. You can take it back to his lawyers and tell them to leave me alone."

"You mean you won't help me?"

"Exactly." He came to stand directly in front of her. "I'm not sure about you. I haven't decided if you're telling the truth or if you have another reason for being here."

"What other reason could I have for driving all the way up this mountain?"

"You could have been sent by my firm or my family to get me to leave here. They've tried everything and nothing has worked."

"I don't know anyone in your family other than Carlton. It is my purpose to get you to leave here," she confirmed. "I'd hoped you'd return with me."

Erika thought he must make a worthy legal adversary. He even looked different. Gone was the gaunt looking man she'd fed. In his place stood a strong opponent.

"Michael—" She took a step that brought her within arms' reach of him. Her hands came up. She'd been about to touch him when she saw what she was doing. Stepping back, she brought her hands down. Her eyes locked with his, and for the space of a lifetime they stared at each other.

Michael cleared his throat, breaking the bonds that held them suspended. Erika turned to face the sink and let her breath out.

"If you're planning to get to that motel, you'd better leave." Michael was behind her, but close.

She turned back, looking about confused as if she couldn't find something. When she arrived she'd left her jacket in the truck. It was still there.

"Please think about what I've said." Her voice was weak to her own ears. "Carlton's will has some terms that are a bit strange. No matter how I questioned his attorneys they remained adamant about the conditions."

"Conditions?"

She swallowed. "Carlton left us in control of his company. We must work together for a year to keep his business—"

"Stop," he said. "So that's it. That's what this is all about. Another ploy to get me back to the firm. Who is it really? My mother? The firm? Who hired you to act this role?"

"No one." She looked genuinely startled.

"I won't do it. I like it fine here, and I'm not leaving. I'll bet there is no Carlton Lipton-Graves. You're here on behalf of my brothers. They want me to come back to the firm. Well, you can climb in your little truck and hightail it back to wherever you came from and tell them your acting was good, but not good enough."

"I'm not acting. Carlton did leave us his estate."

"Even if he does exist, he cared nothing for me in life. Why should I suddenly adhere to his wishes?"

"You get half the estate at the end of a year."

"I don't want or need his money."

Erika looked around. Suddenly the cabin he'd rarely ever noticed looked rundown and shabby. It was little more than squalor, except for the section she'd cleaned.

Michael let out a breath. "I think you'd better leave."

Erika hesitated, then walked to the door. She opened it. The stars were close enough to touch. Their nearness startled her, but she stepped into the night, anyway. She went to the Bronco and yanked the door open. Pulling herself into the driver's seat she started the engine, then quickly killed it. Next to her sat the album she'd brought. Grabbing it, she went back inside.

Michael had dropped into a chair at the kitchen table. He looked up when her shoes made a noise on the bare wooden floor. "What now?" he asked.

Without a word she walked to where he sat. He looked at her as if at any moment he might get up and bodily remove her. She dropped the album on the table. Opening it, she pulled

a large manila envelope out and placed it on top. Turning, she
left the cabin, and Michael, to himself.

Michael pulled the envelope and album to him after he'd
heard the crunch of gravel the tires had spun up when Erika
made her angry getaway. Pushing the envelope with a legal
return address aside, he pulled the heavy book onto his knees.
His name was embossed on the cover. It fell open at a page
that revealed him in full smile. His arms were spread wide.
He smiled at the memory. It was his graduation from law
school.

How had she gotten this? Where could she have been to
take this without his knowledge? Michael looked at the door
as if she were still outside.

"Damn," he cursed. She had to be wrong.

Two

The road curved tighter than Erika had anticipated. She was speeding a little too fast for the Bronco to master the turn. Her heart leapt to her throat as she fought for control of the truck. It careened toward the edge of the mountain. She prayed it would stop in time. Things seemed to speed up and slow down in the same instant. The rail came frighteningly closer to her. Gravel crunching under the size fifteen tires and the music of Whitney Houston coming from the CD changer were combined in a discordant symphony.

An inch short of the guardrail, and a three thousand foot drop, the Bronco came to a stop. Erika let out her breath and rested her head on the steering wheel. Switching off the engine, she sat in the dark breathing through her mouth.

Michael had made her angry. Why had Carlton put her in this position? Why, in the last twenty-six years, hadn't he once mentioned a grandson? Why did he leave them everything? And why now, when she needed to be in her office, was she running around a mountain after a man who couldn't care less about Graves Enterprises?

Well, she'd done what Carlton asked her. She'd come up here and she'd tried to get him to return. He refused—refused to help her, and refused Carlton's requests. She couldn't be held responsible for his actions. The lawyers would certainly understand that.

She'd return to Graves Enterprises and resume the position she'd held since she'd come back from California. After all, she had run things. She had taken care of all the problems and kept Carlton informed of her decisions. They had discussed everything for a while, but Carlton's strength ebbed. More and more he'd told her to handle it in her own way. She had. At night she hadn't wanted to burden him with the details of the day, so she'd sat with him and read or talked about the world. She'd let him remember his wife and his son. Yet in those states of memory he'd managed to keep Michael Lawrence a secret.

Michael's face came into her mind. How long had he been here? Carlton had said it was a long time. By the look of him, he needed care, and the way he'd eaten she thought he was going to make himself sick. She hadn't told him they had only thirty days left to begin the terms of Carlton's last will and testament. If she couldn't persuade him to leave this mountain and return to Philadelphia, she'd lose the company.

She sat back and stared through the dark window. She had a long drive ahead of her. She had wanted to head home tomorrow, but now it looked as if she'd have to return here and see if he was more willing to talk. She'd left the album and a copy of the will. If he looked at them, he might be willing to listen to reason.

Erika started the engine. Suddenly the door of the Bronco was yanked open. She screamed as she turned to face her assailant. Michael stood, angry, in front of her.

"We need to talk," he said.

"I have been talking," Erika told him. She slumped back against the seat. While she wanted to tell him everything she knew, she was tired. "Tomorrow," she sighed. "I'm absolutely drained now." She closed her eyes for a moment, feeling the effects of nearly going over the side of the mountain. "It's a very long drive to the motel."

"One you'll never make. Move over."

Michael pushed her, but her seatbelt kept her in place.

"I beg your pardon," she said, resisting his effort.

"You can't stay at that . . . motel." He grinned.

"Why not? I have a reservation."

"I'm sure you do, but it's probably gone by now."

"Why?"

"Move over." He again tried to climb into the cab, and she again pushed him back "You can stay at the cabin," he told her.

Keeping him at bay, she said, "You think that's an enticing advertisement for me to return? I'm looking at clean sheets and the absence of a man who thinks I'm a liar. I should give that up for—"

"It's not a motel," he interrupted her.

Erika turned toward him as if he'd lost his mind.

"It's not a real motel."

"I supposed I imagined it," she said. "I suppose I imagined the man I talked to on the phone, too."

Michael shook his head. Erika could see a faint smile on his face. She wanted to encourage it. She hadn't seen anything but a scowl since she found him by the water.

"It's a guest house, Erika."

"And I'm a guest."

"A tourist home—a place you rent by the hour, not by the night." He paused. "Don't you know what a guest house is?"

Her eyes must have grown as wide as dinner plates. Realization dawned on her. She hadn't heard of a guest house since she was in high school and her first boyfriend tried to coax her into having sex with him. He knew where there were guest houses in Philadelphia, places where they could go to have sex and no one would question their ages or the fact that they signed the register as George and Martha Washington.

"Seventy miles *is* a long way to drive," she said helplessly.

"I guarantee you there won't be an empty room in that house."

Her shoulders dropped. "What am I going to do now?"

"You can stay at the cabin. You can have the bed. I'll sleep on the couch." Michael looked down a second. "I apologize, but I do need to talk to you." He paused. "Please."

Erika stared at him for a long time. His eyes, though still bloodshot, had a life to them. She knew she needed to talk to him, and she didn't look forward to making this drive twice tomorrow. But, as she'd told him, the prospect of spending the night in the cabin with him was no enticement. She couldn't say she'd stayed in worse places. She didn't know if he was lying about the motel being a guest house, but if she drove seventy miles only to find he'd told the truth, she'd have no place to go. Sleeping in the Bronco wasn't something she wanted to do unless she was prepared for it.

"I'll drive," she said, making a decision.

He hesitated a second, then slammed the door and went around the back to climb in on the other side. Erika backed away from the guardrail and turned up the mountain.

"How did you get here?" she asked.

"I knew you wouldn't get far in the dark and I know these hills. I cut through the trees. My heart nearly stopped when I saw you heading for the guardrail."

Erika wanted to smile. Her heart swelled at the thought that he was concerned for her safety. Then she remembered the album. He was interested in how Carlton had gotten those pictures, and admitted to herself, she was his only source of information.

Michael closed the album. The name on the cover was his, at least part of it. He'd looked through the book three times and still found it difficult to imagine a grandfather. The pictures were definitely of him. He remembered the situations; high school basketball games and the parties they'd had after them, graduation, the class trip, his first day of law school, and his last. Michael couldn't help smiling at the happy memories. Erika sat across from him at the table she'd cleaned, and on which he'd had a meal.

"He took these?" Michael asked.

"I don't know. Until a week ago I'd never heard of you."

"He never mentioned my name?"

"Not until the night he died." She spoke softly, reverently. "We must have been growing up at the same time. Since I was thirteen I lived at Carlton's house. He travelled a lot. It wouldn't have been difficult for him to attend one of these events without me knowing about it."

"Tell me about him?"

Erika got up and went to pick up her purse. She took her wallet out of it and slipped out a snapshot. She handed it to him. "This is a picture of Carlton Lipton-Graves."

Michael took it. It was a Christmas shot. Erika, in a red dress with white fur collar, sat on the floor in front of a man in a winged chair. Behind them was part of a decorated tree and a roaring fire.

"We took this last Christmas." She swallowed hard, reseating herself. "It was our last."

The man was small. He looked directly into the camera, giving Michael a clear view of his face. "This is Carlton?" Michael asked.

Erika nodded.

"This man cannot be my grandfather." Michael stood up.

"Why not?"

"He's white. I can't have a white grandfather."

"Surprise, Michael, but we don't get to pick our parents . . . as much as we might like to."

"But—"

"Look closer at the picture," she interrupted. Reaching across the small table, she touched his hand and pushed the photograph a little closer to him. "Can't you see the resemblance between you and him?"

Her touch was soft and warm. Michael wanted to grasp it and hold it for a while. He had to concentrate on performing the action she'd requested. When her hand left his he did as she asked.

"When I saw you by the stream, it was like seeing Carlton again, before age and illness took his strength."

"We might have some of the same features," he agreed. "But everyone can find a resemblance if they look for it."

Erika sighed. She was tired and he knew it, but she'd come to him with these "facts" and he wanted to know the truth.

"What was your association with him?"

"He raised me. We met when I was eight. When I was a teen, he kind of adopted me. I guess I've been kind of a granddaughter to him. I knew he had a son, but he died before I met Carlton."

"How old are you?"

"Thirty-four," she said.

"I'm thirty-seven. Why didn't he ever come to see me? If he took all these pictures, attended the events that were important in my life, why did he never let me know he existed?"

"I can't answer that. Knowing Carlton, I do find that a bit strange."

"Why is that?" Michael asked.

"Carlton insisted I visit my mother. I'm surprised he had a grandson whom he never acknowledged."

Michael didn't reply. Erika had mentioned her mother. Michael needed to talk to his. If even a bit of what Erika said was the truth, Ellen Lawrence had some explaining to do.

Michael gasped in the humid air. It was heavy and hard to breathe, pressing against his chest like an invisible hand. He ran up and down streets he'd never seen. His lungs threatened to burst from exhaustion, yet he trudged on. Every breath burned. His legs, like iron appendages, weighed him down.

Disorientation gripped him as he whirled around trying to find something familiar; something that would tell him where she was hiding. He started running again, pulling at the tie around his neck. It came loose. He sucked air into his lungs. It didn't relieve his distress. The hand on his chest pressed harder.

"Abigail!" he called. "Abigail! Where are you?"

He stopped, listened . . . nothing. He ran again, seeming to get further behind with every agonizing step.

Then he saw her. She was frightened, screaming, running away from him, and away from *Frank*.

"Frrraannnnkkkk, nooooo!" she screamed, her face contorted, her words drawing out several syllables as if she were speaking in slow motion.

Frank Mason chased Abigail, a gun in his hand. Michael dragged his heavy legs in pursuit. Frank pointed the gun at the scared woman.

"Noooo . . ." he shouted. The shot rang out. "Noooo . . ."

Erika sat up straight. Someone was screaming. For a moment she didn't know where she was. Then she remembered the cabin, and Michael. Pushing the blanket aside, she ran barefoot into the cabin's only bedroom.

She went straight to the bed. Michael fought her as she tried to calm him. His face was bathed in sweat, and his arms flailed madly in the air.

"It's all right, Michael," she said, keeping her voice calm. "Stop, Michael."

"Abbyyyyy," he called. His legs raced under the sheets as if he were trying to run lying down.

Erika didn't know who he called, but she decided the only way to get him quiet was to let him have his wish. "I'm here, Michael." He still fought his unseen demons. His strong arms batted at them. She grabbed for them but missed. Several times they played an air game of arms missing arms. Erika reached again. Michael's fist connected with her jaw, knocking her to the floor. Pain reverberated up her face, through her ear, creating a flash of light before her eyes, then blurring them with tears. Holding her jaw she waited, watching him thrash about in the sheets as if he fought the devil himself.

Testing her jaw, Erika opened and closed it several times. The pain abated but did not go away. She went back to the bed, resting her knee on the mattress and grabbing at Michael's arms, careful to keep her face sufficiently away from his wild throws.

"Michael!" she shouted. "Wake up. It's me." She was about to tell him, "It's Erika," when she remembered the woman he'd called. "It's me, Abby," she said. The name calmed him this time. All the fight left his arms, and they grabbed her, pulling her down on top of him and burying his face in her neck. Erika lay weakly against him. His sweat soaked through her shirt. She felt the heat of his body. Hers warmed in response. His hands massaged her back and held her secure. His ragged breathing pumped air through her short hair and around her ear. Erika let him hold her. She didn't move. She was too afraid. She lay like that until his breathing quieted. She raised her face to look at him. Michael's even breathing told her he was asleep. She let her breath out in a long sigh. Trying to pull herself free, she moved, and her attempt caused his arms to tighten around her.

Biting her lip, Erika went still. The pain in her jaw made her relax her muscles. She didn't want Michael to wake up and find her in this position. She didn't want the feelings running through her to emerge. He was nothing like her ideal man. She wanted someone educated, with a good job, a sense of humor, and a ready smile. So why was her body going soft and warm over a bearded mountain man who couldn't take care of himself and had horrible dreams about a woman called Abby?

Erika breathed in slowly. She was sure the thumping of her heart would wake Michael even if his nightmares didn't. Despite the state of the cabin and Michael's clothes, he smelled like clean air and sunshine.

Reaching behind her, she caught his arm and pulled it. His hand banked over her buttocks, and sparks rushed up her spine. Involuntarily she arched her back, bringing her into closer contact with his nearly naked body. The pain in her jaw was no competition for the pleasure that flowed through her under his hands. Groaning she rolled off the bed. Holding her stomach, she hobbled to a chair, where she supported herself, forcing herself to breathe in and out. What had happened to her? She'd come in here because Michael was having a bad dream. How had she ended up sprawled across his body, and why did such emotions riot through her? She never felt like this with Bill, and she'd been engaged to him.

She had to get hold of herself. She'd come through more than one bad relationship and she knew she didn't ever want to be involved in another one, no matter how her body reacted. He'd been in pain. She'd come inside because of her compassionate nature. She hadn't counted on the raw sexuality he'd aroused in her.

Weak-kneed and breathless, Erika pushed herself away from the chair and went back to the sofa. She was sure she'd spend the rest of the night in open-eyed terror. She didn't want a relationship with Michael. She never wanted a relationship again. Hadn't her mother written that epitaph for her long ago? Relationships weren't her forte and she wasn't even attracted to Michael Lawrence. So why had she reacted as she had? Erika would be glad to see daylight come. She couldn't wait to get off this mountain and away from Michael. She bit her lip at the paradox of her thoughts. It Michael didn't agree to return with her, she'd lose the company. If he did, she'd have to work side by side with him for the next year.

Would these feelings erupt again? Erika swung her feet to the side of the sofa and sat up. She was certainly capable of controlling her feelings and the situation. She'd been in his bedroom, in his bed. That would certainly not happen again.

Why had Carlton done this? There was no reason to give her an overseer for a year. She was capable of running Graves Enterprises alone. She'd done it for the past year with a degree of success.

What was Carlton's purpose in making a will that forced them together, and what was her part in it?

Michael turned over. Light streaming through the window cut across his eyelids. He smiled. He felt refreshed. He'd had the dream—he remembered that—but then he'd slept well, better than he had in months.

The smell of coffee wafted through the morning air. Where was it coming from? Then he remembered Erika. She'd stayed the night, refused his bed, and slept on the sofa in the next room. He listened to her movements. He wondered what she looked like this morning. Was she grouchy before her first cup of coffee or was she easy to talk to? Michael sat up, pulling his jeans on and walking barefoot to the door. After last night's dinner, his stomach growled at the smell of an anticipated breakfast.

Erika stood at the stove, her back to him. She no longer wore yesterday's clothes, but had on navy blue stirrup pants. Her blouse had been replaced with a long white sweater. A wide blue line angled across the back, beginning at her shoulder and crossing her back to her hips. Her hair had less curl on the top, and the sides were straight and ended in sharp points, yet he wanted to run his hands through it.

"Good morning." She smiled, turning to face him.

He swallowed, thinking how lovely her smile was and that he'd like to see it more often. His insides started a slow melt, and he wished he'd put on more clothes than a revealing pair of jeans, which he had only zipped part of the way up.

"Would you like some coffee?"

He came into the room and took the cup she offered.

"I found some syrup and enough ingredients to make pancakes. I had to use dried milk, powdered eggs, and water, since there's no refrigerator. I don't think they taste too bad. Of course, there was no bacon or ham."

She put a plate in front of him. It smelled wonderful. She sat down, her own plate before her.

"You look a lot better this morning."

"I slept well," he told her. She had no way of knowing the dreams that tortured his nights, how he'd wake in the middle of the night and not be able to get back to sleep. Michael took a fork and dug into the plate of food. "How about you? Did you sleep all right?"

"Most of the night," she said, bringing the coffee cup to her lips. Her eyes almost closed as she looked down to the cup. Michael noticed her long lashes.

"You should have taken the bed."

Her hands shook as she placed the cup on the scarred table. She checked her watch.

"I have to leave soon." Her lip twitched slightly. "Are you sure you won't go with me?"

She wasn't looking at him. Her gaze was trained on the broken cup handle. Her fingers played with it. Michael found it unnerving. He could talk to her better if she looked at him. He'd been trained to make eye contact, to stare at his opponent on an even scale and deliver his message. With Erika looking down he had only her body language to respond to, and it told him she was disappointed in his reply.

"I'm sorry," he said. "My returning to Philadelphia won't accomplish anything. I'll get in touch with the lawyers and turn everything over to you."

"You know that won't work. We're talking about a will. Carlton's lawyers are as adamant as he was. They'll make sure the terms of that will are followed to the letter. If we don't do as requested, all Carlton's money goes to the defense fund of someone named Frank Mason."

Michael stopped eating. The fork in his hand stopped halfway to his mouth. Erika stopped talking. Time on the planet ceased. The only thing that moved was the thumping of his heart, which threatened to jump out of his chest. That damn old man Graves. The sonofabitch, who'd never seen him face-to-face in life, would try to manipulate him in death.

Swallowing the mouthful of food he hadn't chewed, Michael scraped the chair back and stood up. He went to the door and out of it. His bare feet stepped onto the cold ground outside the cabin and he went into the woods toward the stream.

He didn't know how long he stood there, the past running

through his head like a old movie. Erika came to stand next to him. She remained quiet. He couldn't talk to her. He couldn't tell her that after the dream and after the first peaceful night he'd had in months, that some unknown relative he couldn't care less about was trying to force him to return to a life of defending people like Frank Mason.

"Who is he?" Erika asked quietly.

Michael turned to her. He liked Erika St. James. He wished he could meet her sometime in the future when he'd made peace with the demons, if that ever happened. She had an underlying compassion about her. He wouldn't invite her into his nightmare, though.

"I won't return, Erika. I'm not sure Carlton Lipton-Graves was my grandfather. My life is here, and here is where I stay." He took her hands in his and looked at them. They were cold. She had long, slender fingers with a strength that was evident in them. "I think you'd better go now." Impulsively he pulled her forward and kissed her on the mouth.

Erika closed her eyes. It was the lightest feather of a kiss, yet she felt as if he'd lifted her off the ground. Her body trembled with reaction. She put her hands up to take hold of his bare arms, but he pushed her back and released her. Her eyes came open. The world was back in place, exactly as she had left it, yet she felt as if something about *her* had changed. She'd stepped over some imaginary line which she could never again retreat across. She stared at Michael, looking for some sign that he felt the trauma that had gone through her, but he'd turned away. His body was stiff, impassible. She knew nothing she could say or do could change him. He was no longer in her world. He'd retreated into the one he'd been in when she arrived a lifetime ago.

Erika placed her fingers on her lips. They still tingled from the memory of Michael's kiss. She was nearly back to the main highway. His short kiss remained at the top of her thoughts. Not even the swerving mountainous roads or the need to get Michael to return to Philadelphia could replace the feel of his mouth against hers. Why hadn't she stopped him? She'd seen it coming, but wanted it. Since she'd found him in the throes of the nightmare, she'd wanted to kiss his hurt away.

The sensation was new to her. She'd never wanted to mother anyone, to fight anyone else's battle. She had too many of her own to fight to take on a stranger's. Yet Carlton had told her about Michael. She'd promised him she'd try to get him back to the city. He'd said Michael had been on the mountain too long. Had he thought she could get him off of it? Well, she'd failed in that, too, just as she'd failed in everything else she'd ever tried except running Graves Enterprises. Her mother had been right. She was no good at anything, and no man would ever want her.

Suddenly Bill Castle's face came into her mind. What was he doing now? It had been almost two years since he'd abruptly married Jennifer Ahrends, her secretary. Just before she'd boarded the plane leaving California she'd heard Jennifer was pregnant. Her baby should be born by now. Erika's eyes were dry, her body numb. She couldn't imagine herself with a child, a baby. She'd loved Bill, but she couldn't see herself as the mother of his children. She couldn't see herself as a mother at all. Some women just weren't cut out for nurturing, she told herself.

Then she remembered Michael's nightmare. Her mouth tingled again. Her tongue darted out to wet her lips. She raised her hand to touch them. Michael's mouth had been soft, undemanding, warm, and tasting of the morning coffee she'd brewed in the ancient coffeepot.

Why could she still feel it? Why could she still taste him? And why did a feeling deep in her belly tell her she wanted more than a taste?

* * *

"Damn!" Michael cursed as he pulled the starter cord for the ninth time. What was he doing? It wasn't going to start. In the last three hundred and sixty odd days he hadn't once tried to get this generator to work. He'd never felt the need for electric light. Yet tonight he wanted to flood the cabin with it. He'd already cleaned the chimney and started a fire in the seldom-used fireplace. The glow was yellow-gold, and he needed more light. He needed these damn electric lights to work. Why didn't he light the kerosene lamps? A voice inside his head spoke to him. *She lit them, that's why.* He didn't want to think about her or the way that yellowed light cast golden shadows across her face.

As he tried the cord again the mechanism groaned, then died completely. Michael pulled one of the spark plugs, dusted it on his pants legs, which were black with the soot of the chimney, and replaced it in the generator. He grabbed the cord and yanked. His index finger caught between the frayed nylon cord and the metal casing, ripping through the skin.

"Ouch!" he shouted, sticking his finger into his mouth. He tasted soot, dirt, oil, machine grease, and rust. Quickly he snatched it from his mouth and inspected it. He'd live, but it was her fault. If she'd stayed away from here he wouldn't have to be reminded of the world below the mountain. He wouldn't have to remember Abigail Mason.

Michael glanced one more time at the generator and grabbed for the cord with his uninjured hand. Stubbornly the mechanism refused to perform its intended purpose. It was the belt. The machine needed a new one. The one there was cracked and brittle, and refused to hold the required RPM's to begin the generation of electrical power. *Mr. Hodges would have a belt,* he thought. Mr. Hodges, over at Hodges General Store and Mercantile, stocked everything from aspirin to cure a simple headache to supplies to fully outfit a mountain climber.

The walk was at least two miles uphill. Michael stared at the road—the same road that Erika's Bronco had taken when she left that morning. He took a step. The walk would do him good. A climb up the mountain would be better, but it was dark and that made it dangerous. He'd get his exercise on the way to the store. He hoped the walk would keep his mind off her and that kiss.

It didn't. His mind replayed it over and over with each step he took. Why had he done that? Many woman tourists had come by in the last year. He'd never wanted to kiss any of them. But he'd wanted to kiss her the moment he'd seen her in the afternoon light. And later, in the cabin, when he'd come upon her by surprise, his heart had jumped in his throat at the way she looked with the gold, autumnal effect of the kerosene lamps. When she'd followed him to the stream he could no longer resist. She was leaving. He never expected to see her again. It was his request that she leave. Then he'd looked at her, with the sun behind her, her brown hair showing highlights that framed her head with a red-gold aura. His head had just tilted. His mouth touched hers softly and the shock of heat which attacked him—he couldn't think of another word to describe the sudden impact on his body—had told him to run—quick and fast. If he didn't, she'd have him back where he didn't want to be, down the mountain, in a dark suit with red suspenders and a white shirt. She'd have him seeing clients and going to court, and he'd be right back where he was before he'd ever heard of Abigail Mason. And that's exactly where he never wanted to be again.

Michael unbuttoned his jacket. He was warm despite the cool mountain air. Late August in the city would produce warm nights, but on the mountain it was cold. He wondered if it was warm where Erika had gone.

The air here was cool and crisp, but he was sweating. He told himself it was from the exertion. The store was just up ahead. He could see the roof of the building. It was no more than a rustic log cabin with a wide porch. The overhead covering protected barrels of various seasonal items. In summer one of them was filled with pickles, with dill seed and spices floating in the dark water around them. Winter saw barrels of salt to control the ice that seemingly grew on the steps leading to the door. Since it was August he was likely to find the last remnants of summer seed packets and trays of vegetables.

He wasn't disappointed. Michael smiled to himself for being right. Also present were wooden cases of sweet potatoes, string beans, and fresh broccoli. Michael remembered last night's dinner, and the way Erika had draped his vegetable with melted cheese. She was back—in his mind. His walk hadn't produced the desired effect.

"Hullo, Mr. Lawrence." Gerald Hodges came toward him with an outstretched hand. Michael took it and shook hands.

Michael had little contact with any of the full-time residents on the mountain, but he had met Gerald Hodges and knew that he'd lived all his life on this mountain except for a two year stint in the Army during the Vietnam Era.

"She found you, I take it," he said.

Michael looked blankly at him. How could he know about Erika?

"The Lipton-Graves heiress," Gerald went on to explain. "She come in here looking for you a couple of days ago. I gave her your order. Didn't you get it?"

"The food, yes," Michael told him. "She brought it."

"She's quite a looker."

He had to agree with that. Although she wasn't beautiful, not the way Michael liked his women, there was something about her. Something that had made him kiss her.

Abigail Mason had been beautiful. When he'd first seen her he'd been struck by her beauty. With Erika there was something more than beauty, some deep inner loveliness that touched him deep inside. The word *compelling* came to him. She compelled him to remember her.

"I never met an heiress before," Gerald was saying when Michael brought his attention back. "At least not one with as much money as she has. I did meet Milton Hershey's grandson once, but I don't think he—"

"Would you have a generator belt?" Michael interrupted. If

he let Gerald go on he'd be there until closing. Talking was the only thing Gerald liked more than listening to gossip. Michael knew that whatever the inhabitants of Highland Hills, Maryland, population 140, knew about him they'd gotten from Gerald Hodges.

"What kinda belt?"

Michael suddenly felt like a fool. He'd been so intense in his thinking about Erika he hadn't even looked at the make and model number of the generator. "I don't know," he said.

Gerald checked the ceiling as if it knew the answer. "Let's see, I believe ole man Nelson bought that generator back in . . . must be ten years ago." He brought his gaze back to Michael. "Don't worry, Michael. I have one." He turned to leave, presumably to go and get the item, then stopped. "I've been saving something for you," he said. Going to the counter he pulled a newspaper from beneath it and pushed it across to Michael. "I thought you'd enjoy reading about her."

Michael picked up the paper. Gerald smiled, nodded, and went toward the back of the store. Michael studied the grainy photograph of Erika St. James. Again her eyes captured him. Even from the paper she called to him. Next to her was the photograph of a man. William A. Castle was written under the picture. A streak of anger sliced through Michael. It came unbidden and unwanted, but was there nevertheless.

"Erika St. James, longtime friend of Carlton Lipton-Graves, will walk away with the lion's share of the corporate giant's estate," Michael read. *"The thirty-four-year-old former vice president of La Canada Manufacturing Corporation near Los Angles returned to Philadelphia last year and took over the operation of Graves Enterprises from the ailing owner."*

Again Michael lifted his gaze to the photograph. It pulled at him, forcing him to look into those eyes. He looked away, checking the back room to see if Gerald appeared. Michael was alone, except for the presence of Erika. Michael bent his head back to the paper, whose date was two weeks old.

"Ms. St. James was engaged to William A. Castle, noted entertainment lawyer, also of Los Angeles, in September of last year when (in a surprise move) Mr. Castle married his fiancée's secretary, Jennifer Ahrends."

She's been engaged, jilted, Michael thought. He looked at the photograph of William A. Castle, irrationally disliking the man. How could he hurt her so? The man was a coward, running off and marrying someone else, without the backbone to tell her. *In a surprise move,* he read again. How often had he seen those words? They were lawyer's words. Michael was a lawyer, too. No wonder Erika St. James looked so sad. She probably also hated lawyers. *Good,* he thought, but his heart wasn't in it. He had been a lawyer once, but not anymore, and he'd never be one again.

The rest of the article detailed Erika's education and qualifications. It also touched on the direction of Graves Enterprises and ran a few quotes from Erika. His name wasn't mentioned, but it did allude to some details of the will which had not been disclosed.

Yeah, Michael thought, *like he was an equal partner in everything Carlton had left behind.*

Gerald startled him when he came in. "Sorry to keep you waiting, Michael. It took me a while to find the thing." He held up a hard rubber oval partially hidden inside a faded cardboard rectangle. The word "generator" could easily be read through the watermark circle, indicating it was nearly as old as the one on the dead machine back at his cabin.

The bell over the door rang. Michael and Gerald turned to see a young woman come into the store. She smiled at Gerald and came over.

"Hi, Gerald," she said, but kept her eyes on Michael. Suddenly he wished he didn't look so much like a bum. He'd been working all day, dirty work, and his clothes showed it.

"Amy Foster, this is Michael Lawrence."

"Please excuse my appearance," Michael said.

"You're at the old Nelson cabin," she said.

Michael nodded. Twenty-four hours ago he would have called it a house, but the moment he found Erika there he knew it was only a cabin, meant to be used for weekends, for city people coming up for a back-to-nature weekend before they returned to the world of modern conveniences.

"You planning on staying a while?" Amy asked.

He'd been there over a year, but he'd learned that a while meant different things in different parts of the county. Here it probably meant a lifetime.

"A while," he said. Turning to Gerald, he asked him to put the generator belt on his bill. Gerald sent a monthly invoice to the offices of Lawrence, Barclay, West, and Lawrence. His brothers made sure they were paid. He nodded at Gerald and said goodbye to Amy. At the door Gerald stopped him.

"It's about dark, Michael. Why don't you let Amy drive you back to the cabin?"

"It's no trouble," Amy said before Michael could refuse. Twenty-four hours ago he would have refused and thought nothing of it. Now he felt the need to explain.

"Thank you, but my clothes would leave a permanent mark on your car," he said.

"Don't worry about that." Amy smiled, waving her hand in a nonchalant gesture. "You should see the stuff Jake brings in."

Michael didn't ask who Jake was.

"Now, Amy," Gerald asked. "What can I get you?"

Michael waited by the door and followed Amy out of the store when she'd bought milk, bread, ice cream, and diapers. On the short ride back to "the old Nelson" cabin, as she called it, he learned she was married and had a three-month-old at home. Jake was her husband and he loved to hunt and fish.

Michael thanked her at his driveway and walked the short distance back to the generator and his thoughts of Erika St. James.

Three

The twin bed, with no head or foot board, was slightly over an inch longer than Frank Mason. He folded his body into the fetal position whenever he slept, which wasn't often. Tonight he lay on his back staring at the cracked ceiling. He'd read about people who did that, prisoners with nothing to do night after night but count the cracks in the ceiling. He'd counted two hundred and sixty-seven. He'd done it nineteen times, with never a variance. Exactly two hundred and sixty-seven cracks. His bed had fourteen lumps in it, seven of which were in the spot that cradled his back.

Light filtered in from the hall. He knew Smiley Curtis was on the desk. Smiley came every night at exactly eleven forty-five. He was never a second later. As the chime on the clock in the distance outside his window went through its rendition of St. Michael's Serenade in twelve notes, Smiley Curtis would come through the door. Under one arm he carried the early edition of tomorrow's newspaper. To this he added a cup of coffee and a wide smile. By midnight the exchange of duties had been accomplished. Smiley knew who had taken their medicine calmly, and who had fought against the small white pills the patients had to take. He knew who had spent a pleasant day and who had been a royal pain for the past sixteen hours.

At five minutes past midnight Smiley would make his rounds, speaking to the insomniacs and smiling at the sleepers.

Then he'd settle into his chair, switch on the wall-anchored color television and open the paper.

Frank had watched this routine, sometimes pretending to sleep, sometimes acting as if he couldn't. With Smiley it never wavered. He was there on time and he left promptly at the end of his shift. Frank waited. Sooner or later his chance would come, and he figured it would be during Smiley's shift. During the day there were too many people there, too many nurses and doctors, too many patients wandering in and out, for him to remain unnoticed for any length of time.

He'd been here three months. First the jail cell, then the mental ward of the prison, and now this hospital. He grunted in the darkness. This was no hospital. It was a prison. Frank knew a prison when he saw one. The walls might be sheet-rocked, and the windows covered with curtains, but there was nowhere he was allowed out without an escort. He couldn't take a walk alone. Everyone had to have a "buddy." He was thirty-seven years old. What did he need with a buddy? But he didn't expect that to take much longer. He'd be out of here soon. He'd planned it and soon he'd be home. Home with Abby.

A blue moon. There really was such a thing. Michael had always associated blue moon with the cliché, with thoughts of going back to the city and returning to his firm. Now he looked at the shining disk and thought of Erika St. James's eyes. He stared at the silver-blue color as he walked along the road for the second time in as many days. Cloud formations hugged the sky; flat, grey bottoms supporting a puff of gold-tinged cotton, turning the road into a black ribbon meandering through the landscape.

This should be a leisurely walk after dinner, but it wasn't. Michael had only half eaten his meal. Erika had left the will along with the picture album, and what he read there had led him to this road. He held himself stiffly, his hands stuffed in his pockets, shoulders hunched, his gait determined and purposeful. He needed a phone. He needed to call his mother. Find out if there was real truth to Erika St. James's story. He'd told her he didn't believe her. But he did. Now he wanted confirmation. He wanted his mother to tell him the unguarded truth; that she had been married to Kevin Lipton-Graves, and that he was the product of that marriage.

He wanted to call his brothers and have them investigate Erika and her claims, but he knew better than to involve them. There was only one person he could ask to confirm her story— Malick Wainscott.

Michael's breath congealed in the cold air. He dug his hands further into the pockets of his parka and continued his uphill climb. The trees were mere dark images along the side of the road. Michael's attention wasn't on the trees. He was thinking of Malick. Their friendship went back to his law school days. Malick had been his professor, his mentor, and later his friend. Separated in age by twenty-five years, Michael and Malick had formed a strong bond. Malick ran a practice in Philadelphia and taught Criminal Law at the University of Pennsylvania. He'd help him. All Michael had to do was ask. Michael had tried all day to forget the will, forget Erika St. James, and return to his quiet existence, but neither would leave him alone.

He'd climbed the mountain this morning, keeping his concentration on his ropes and spikes and conquering the task before him.

Now he walked up this ribbon of road on his way to Hodges General Store and Mercantile to use the phone. With each step his anger mounted instead of abating. The will stated he'd have to return to Philadelphia and share the legacy Carlton Lipton-Graves had left him with Erika St. James. That legacy included a house and joint management of Graves Enterprises. The name was vaguely familiar, but it meant nothing to Michael. What stuck in his craw was the contingency. *If either of the main parties fail to adhere to the terms of this will, barring death or catastrophic injury, the entire estate bequeathed jointly to Erika St. James and Michael Lawrence will be awarded to Frank Mason.* . . . The words had been unwittingly committed to memory. If he didn't adhere to the terms of the will the entire estate would go to Frank Mason.

Michael's hands balled into fists at the thought of Frank and what he'd done to Abby and her children. Reaching down, he picked up a stone and threw it as far as his pitching arm would let him. Why Frank? Had Carlton known Frank? Did he know what he'd done to Abby? Or was he just a manipulative old man trying to get his way, even from the grave?

Michael could see the light ahead. Hodges General Store and Mercantile had the only streetlamp Michael had seen since he'd come to Highland Hills. He stopped a moment, staring at the pool of light cutting into the engulfing darkness. Tiredness seemed to rush into him. It had been a long day. He'd worked hard today, not just with his hands but with his mind, trying to keep it off Erika St. James and trying to forget the terms of the will lying on the clean wooden surface of the table where he'd eaten only this morning.

Why should he go back? He'd fought his fight and lost. He never wanted to see the inside of a courtroom again. He never wanted to return to a world where people like Frank Mason could say one thing and do something as frightening as—.

Michael stopped the thought. Forcing his feet to move, he continued toward the store.

"Malick, this is Michael," he said several minutes later when he'd completed the walk to the store and Gerald had let him use the private phone in his office. Around him were order slips, stacks of cases with vegetable names written on them; corn, peas, lima beans, string beans. The general clutter reminded Michael of his desk back at Lawrence, Barclay, West, and Lawrence.

"Michael!" The surprise in Malick's voice was clearly evident. "It's good to hear your voice. When are you coming back?"

Malick never beat around the bush. Each time Michael had

spoken to him, all three of them, in the last year, he'd begun the conversation in the same manner.

"My plans are unclear," Michael told him, and that was the truth. If he could confirm the validity of the will, he would either return to the world beyond the hill or let Frank Mason walk away with whatever estate had been left to him.

"Do you need anything?" Michael heard the concern in his friend's voice.

"I'm fine, Malick. My health is excellent." Except for his weight, he was as fit as he'd been when he arrived. And even with the dreams, his state of mind had improved. "I want you to do me a favor, something I want to keep quiet."

"What is it?"

Michael could almost see the older man sit forward in his chair, pulling a yellow legal pad close, as he crunched the phone between his ear and shoulder.

"Ever heard of a woman named Erika St. James?"

"Who hasn't?" Malick said. "She's been all over the news since Carlton Lipton-Graves died two weeks ago. A real Cinderella story. The press is eating it up. How do you know her?"

"I don't," Michael replied, then thought of her warm mouth opening under his. Quickly he clamped the lid on that area of memory. "She came to see me."

"Why?" Malick's question came out on a long, incredible breath. "The press has been trying to interview her, but so far she's been behind closed doors. Every newscast ends with 'Ms. St. James was unavailable for comment.' "

Michael groaned. He wanted no part of the press. He'd had enough of them a year ago, when they'd made his life unbearable. Now he might have to return to the same game.

"Malick, I need you to make some discreet inquiries about her and Carlton Lipton-Graves."

"Exactly what are you trying to find?" Malick asked, his voice as dry as sandpaper.

Michael explained the conditions of the will Erika had left with him and the alleged parentage.

"She claims there are DNA tests confirming this. I need to know if it's the truth."

"Why would she lie?"

"I don't know. I don't know if she's even the real thing. Her picture was in the paper, but that can be faked."

Malick described the photo he'd seen and Michael had to agree it was the woman who'd spent the night on his sofa.

"Why don't you do the obvious thing, Michael? Call your mother and ask her."

"I plan to. I just want to know that I have the facts straight before I do that."

"All right," Malick sighed. "Can I reach you through the store?"

"Yeah," Michael told him.

"Give me a couple of days."

Michael knew he could count on Malick. He'd put an investigator on it in the morning and by dinnertime he'd have a report on the heiress to the Lipton-Graves millions. He smiled, replacing the phone. *Millions. He should be so lucky.* He'd never heard of Carlton Lipton-Graves. It wasn't like he was J. Paul Getty or Howard Hughes, dying and leaving a fortune. Malick *had* said the press was carrying the story. He knew the press. They carried anything that sold papers and commanded air time.

If Carlton Lipton-Graves had left a fortune, Michael wouldn't know it. He admitted he'd been single-minded when he practiced law. He'd resided in New Brunswick, and he hadn't concerned himself with much outside of the law and court. If Erika had inherited millions she would surely be courted by the press. Even if she hadn't, her elusiveness would be enough to make them hound her. The more she remained unapproachable the longer the story would play out. Secretly Michael hoped the whole thing would blow over. Then he pictured her, saw her standing by the stream in the misty morning light, staring at the mountains in the background. She looked as if she loved the stone facades, as if she belonged on the hill as much as the evergreen trees and the deer that kept a discreet distance from him. Too bad he hadn't taken their cue and stayed away from Erika.

Erika tapped the head of her pen against the marble-edged blotter on her desk. She should be working. She should be doing something about the takeover. But her mind wasn't on it. She glanced at the phone again. It must be the hundredth time today she'd thought of calling Michael Lawrence. It had been a week since she left him; a week for him to read the will, to get used to the idea of Carlton being his grandfather.

She knew it had to have been a shock to him. She'd grown up with Carlton. He was her friend, and like a good friend she'd grown used to him. Finding out that the man you thought was your father wasn't, that in his place stood a man who didn't even share the same heritage, had to be a revelation that he needed time to assimilate.

She checked her watch. It was only a few minutes past six. The office was quiet, so no one would disturb her, and she was sure Mr. Hodges would still be minding his store. She could call and leave a message for Michael. She could ask him to call her, and then they could discuss the future.

Lifting the receiver, she punched in the number she'd printed on one of her business cards. *Maybe Mr. Hodges isn't there,* she thought when the phone went through its third ring.

". . . bye, Ed. Say hello to Helen."

She heard his voice as he picked up the phone without ending his conversation. She had the feeling that Mr. Hodges was always in the middle of a conversation with someone.

"Hello," he said, speaking to her.

"Mr. Hodges, this is Erika St. James. You may not remember me."

"Not remember an heiress? They'd pull my friendship license if I forgot a beautiful woman like you."

Erika laughed. A little of the tension which held her shoulders stiff lessened, and she relaxed.

"I wanted to leave a message for Mr. Lawrence," she began.

"Sorry, he's gone."

"Gone!" Her grip on the handset tightened. "Where did he go?"

"Said he had some things to see to. I suppose he'll go back to the city. Newcomers never last long up here. He lasted longer than most."

"How long ago did he leave?" Erika interrupted.

"Yesterday, about four o'clock. Dropped by to tell me to rent the cabin if I wanted to."

"He's not coming back?" Erika found her heart sinking. How could she find him if he'd left the cabin?

"He'd didn't say. He left me an address in case you called."

Her heart lurched. He'd assumed she would call. He knew she would.

"Here, I've got it." She knew he was holding it up as if she could see it.

"Would you read it to me?"

Seconds later a frown changed her facial expression from elation to incredulity. Mr. Hodges read Erika's own address, to her. For a moment she thought it was a joke. He knew she'd try to reach him again, and intentionally he'd given a false address. If he'd been coming to see her, he would have arrived late last night or early this morning. The house was full of servants. If Michael had arrived, one of the maids would surely have called to let her know.

She didn't have any idea where he'd go. Maybe he went to talk to his mother. She thought that might be the normal thing to do, if his mother was still alive. Would he get the information he needed? An image of her own mother came to mind. Erika knew Alva Redford would be the last person she'd go to for confirmation of something important in her life.

"You got it?" Mr. Hodges asked, calling her back to the phone she held in her hand.

"Yes, Mr. Hodges. I have it. Thank you very much."

"You're welcome. Come back and visit us when you're out this way again."

She smiled. She liked the old man. "I'll certainly do that, Mr. Hodges."

Erika replaced the receiver in the cradle. She faced it for only a second before punching in the numbers to her own house. As expected, the maid informed her no one had come looking for her all day. Erika thanked her and hung up.

Pushing herself back, she faced the windows and watched the sun drop on the distant horizon. Where was he? She had to know. Her time was running out. There were barely three weeks left. She turned back and looked at her office. Remnants of Carlton's presence haunted the room, but she was also there. Her desk was a huge structure of carved mahogany. She felt comfortable behind it. The walls had pictures she'd chosen. The étagére in the corner held several of her awards and a collection of crystal figurines she'd been collecting for years. The desk held a new computer, something Carlton couldn't stomach and she couldn't live without.

She loved it here, loved this company and her role in it. She'd loved it since her sixteenth year, when she applied for a job in the shipping department without telling Carlton. She hadn't wanted anyone to think he got her the job because of their friendship. She'd worked there for six months before he found out. She thought he'd be angry, but instead he'd begun teaching her things. She worked in every department from the ground up, and by the time she left for college she'd worked there three years.

Then she'd gone to California and stayed there, until Carlton called her home. She wanted to keep this company, run it the way she'd been doing since she returned. She wanted to keep it alive for Carlton. Of course, it offered her wealth, more money than she'd ever dreamed of having, and power. But beyond the wealth and the power, Graves Enterprises offered her the chance to prove that she could do the job. Now she didn't have Carlton showing her, sanctioning her decisions, or guiding her along as if she were his student. She needed to prove she could stand on her own feet. The only person she needed to help her was Carlton's grandson, and at the moment she was without clues as to his whereabouts.

Erika pulled herself closer to the desk and picked up the phone again. The clock on the desk read seven o'clock, but she knew Steven Chambers would still be in his office.

"Chambers," he answered on the first ring.

"Hello, Steven, it's Erika."

"Erika, what can I do for you?" His voice held the no-nonsense tone she was accustomed to hearing whenever she talked to the seasoned lawyer.

"I need to know more about Michael Lawrence."

"I afraid I can't tell you anything I haven't already." He sounded distracted, as if he wasn't really concentrating on her.

"Steven, stop whatever it is you're doing and listen to me."

She could hear his sigh. "All right, Erika. You have my full and undivided attention."

"Michael left the cabin he was occupying in the mountains and I don't know where he's gone. He told me his father died when he was seventeen. Would you know if his mother is still alive, and where she lives?"

"I'm afraid I don't."

"Can you find out?"

"I can put an investigator on it if that's what you want."

An investigator. She hadn't thought of that. "Yes." She seized the opportunity. "I need information fast. I only have a few weeks left."

She knew Steven was aware of that.

"Do you think this investigator can find out where he is?"

"If that is what you want him to do."

"I do," she said.

"All right. I'll have someone on it first thing in the morning."

"Thank you, Steven." Erika hung up again. This time she felt better. An investigator. Steven knew her dilemma, knew she would lose everything, including his enormous fees for services, if the estate fell into the hands of Frank Mason. Who was he? She wished she'd asked Steven to have his investigator find out something about Frank Mason, too. But finding Michael was more important. She could concentrate on Frank Mason later, if need be.

"How much did you say?" Michael asked. He stared at Malick Wainscott from across the dinner table at Bookbinders in central Philadelphia. He and Malick hadn't seen each other since the Mason trial. Always well dressed, Malick wore a dark suit over his custom-made shirt. His shock of white hair reminded Michael of the photo Erika had shown him of Carlton Lipton-Graves.

"You might have lost weight, Michael, but your hearing is not impaired. Carlton Lipton-Graves's personal net worth, including pending stock options, is over forty-seven million dollars. If you want to know about Graves Enterprises, the pharmaceutical division alone grosses four billion dollars in sales."

Michael lifted his brandy snifter and swirled the liquid before taking a drink.

"No wonder she wants me to exercise the will."

"I don't blame her—even if Frank Mason wasn't a contingent benefactor."

Michael's hands clenched at the sound of Frank's name. "Why did he do it?" he asked, almost to himself.

"Frank?" Malick asked.

"No, Carlton."

"Obviously, he wanted to get you off that mountain and this was a surefire way of doing it." Malick leaned forward, grasping his brandy in both hands. "He dangled a carrot in front of you, Michael. Granted, it's a forty-seven million-dollar carrot, but that much money can certainly change a lot of opinions."

"What do you mean?"

"If you don't comply with the terms of the will, and Carlton's lawyers closed every available loophole, Frank Mason becomes the richest convicted mental patient in the world. It won't be long before some lawyer, smart, and extremely well paid, convinces a medical board and a court that Frank was only temporarily insane and he should be freed, that he was not responsible for his acts and he's truly been rehabilitated."

Michael studied the window, staring at but not seeing the street outside or the neat rows of parked cars along both sides of it. His mind was on Frank. So much in his life had changed since Erika St. James walked into it, beginning with his father.

After his call to Malick he'd gone to see his mother. He hadn't wanted to ask her about Erika's claims over the phone. From her reaction, maybe he should have. He'd tried to hold onto the belief that Erika could still be wrong, that his mother hadn't concealed information from him his whole life, but the expression of horror on her face told him in the first five minutes that everything Erika had said was the truth. Robert Lawrence wasn't his biological father. His father was a man named Kevin Lipton-Graves, and his grandfather was Carlton Lipton-Graves.

"Why didn't you tell me?" he asked.

"Michael, I couldn't. It was so long ago and when I met Robert, he loved you. It didn't seem important."

"Not important, Mom? Not important that I had a family and you concealed it from me?"

"Michael, I wasn't trying to hurt you. Carlton didn't want me to marry Kevin. He didn't even believe you were his grandson. He had all those tests done when Kevin died. I hated him. I didn't marry Kevin for his money, and I didn't want anything from his father."

Well, Carlton must have wanted something, Michael thought

as he swirled the liquid in the brandy snifter. He'd wanted a part of Michael, even from a distance.

"Did he ever attempt to see me?" Michael had asked.

"A few times." Ellen Lawrence swallowed.

"You refused him the right." It was a statement. His mother nodded.

"You had a father," she said. "Our life was comfortable. There was no need to confuse you by introducing him into your life."

"Did his color have anything to do with it?"

Ellen hesitated. "Yes," she said. "I'd been married to a white man. I loved him, Michael, and I would marry him again if given the chance. But I know the horrors we went through, and I didn't want you to have to go through those things."

Michael wondered what that would mean now. The press had to find out about this sooner or later. A man leaving an estate worth forty-seven million dollars to a black man would have to be newsworthy.

"What are you going to do?" Malick's question brought his attention back to the restaurant.

"Do I have a choice?" Michael frowned. "There's no way I'm going to let a person like Frank Mason wangle an easy way out of jail."

"What about returning to the law?" Malick asked.

"Not a chance."

Born in St. Peter's Medical Center thirty-seven years ago. . . . Erika picked up one of the reports and stared at it. She'd received them weekly from the private investigator Steven had hired on her behalf. She knew facts about Michael Lawrence, but the facts didn't tell her where he was. She checked her watch again. It was after eleven o'clock on the final day, and though she'd gone to bed she couldn't sleep. She had returned to the library and these reports.

If Michael didn't show up in the next forty-seven minutes,

the entire estate went to Frank Mason. It looked as if Frank Mason would be a very rich man within the hour, and she would be homeless.

She knew he didn't know yet. Steven had told her Carlton's instructions stated that Frank Mason was not to be informed until the expiration of the time limit, a limit that hovered close by.

She'd tried, she told herself. She'd thought he would come. She also thought she'd have more time to try to make him help. But she hadn't figured he would leave without giving an address, or that he wouldn't call to let her know his decision. He knew her address. Carlton's law firm's address was printed on the papers she'd left with him. If he'd wanted to find her, he had all the information. He obviously hadn't.

Erika dropped the papers on the desk and stood up. She wrapped her satin robe closer around her, feeling cold even though it was warm in the room. Why had Carlton played this game, she wondered. He was usually quite up front with his requests and beliefs. She knew Michael had held a very special place in Carlton's heart. He told no one about him, yet attended his ceremonies and vicariously basked in his glory. For some reason Michael had retreated to the mountain, and Carlton wanted him off of it. This was one method of getting his way. Only Carlton wasn't here to see if his plan worked. He was leaving it up to her to resolve, and she'd failed.

"I'm sorry, Carlton," she said. "I tried." She just wished he'd told her what he was up to before he died. Erika felt beaten. Her shoulders drooped with the weight of the burden she'd carried for the last month trying to locate Michael, all for nothing. Tomorrow she would go to the office and make the announcement. Within a week she'd have packed everything, turned over the reins to the new president, and left.

She was a little angry at Carlton for tangling her with Michael, although he hadn't left her penniless. If Michael refused to comply, she would still have a trust fund that paid her $50,000 annually until she died.

It was enough to live on but it wasn't what she had, what she'd become used to and considered her own. She wanted Graves Enterprises, but that looked like something she wouldn't get.

Erika paced the room, feeling lost and disconnected. She should be concentrating on what she would do tomorrow and the rest of her life. But she couldn't. She was too angry. People didn't just disappear these days. There were computers, credit cards, the Internet. How could Michael Lawrence leave a rustic cabin on a Maryland mountain and disappear into thin air? Why couldn't Steven's investigator get his law firm and his brothers to tell him where Michael was? He had to be somewhere.

She walked back to the desk and slammed the file closed. Then, in frustration, she sat down. Ten minutes to midnight. The clock didn't make a sound, but Erika felt as if it were ticking her life away. Michael held her fate in his hands, and it meant nothing to him.

Erika put the file in the desk drawer. She reached for the desk lamp and extinguished it. The darkness closed in around her, but she didn't move immediately. She let her eyes adjust to the darkness, waited for the images of furniture and lamps to settle into place. Finally she pushed her chair back and stood up. She knew this room as well as she knew all the rooms, and she'd be heartbroken to leave it. She walked through the room, neither touching nor bumping into anything as she went toward the splash of hall light spilling through the entry door.

She noticed the time as she passed the grandfather clock on her way to the stairs. Three minutes to midnight. Stopping at the base of the huge staircase, Erika remembered sliding down the curving banister when she was nine. She remembered standing there to have her picture taken when she graduated from junior high school, and going through the front doors with a nervous date on her way to her high school prom. Tomorrow she'd leave a lot of memories behind.

Erika started up the stairs. On the fifth step she stopped,

sniffling, trying to hold back tears that were threatening to fall. At the top she turned toward her room.

"Is it all right if I use this part of the house?"

Erika whipped around, her heart thudding. The upstairs hall was long, branching off into two wings. The lights were off and she couldn't see anyone, but she'd heard Michael's voice. Her gaze searched the darkness. Did she really hear him? Was her mind conjuring him up? Then he stepped into the light.

"Any objections?" he asked. Not waiting for a reply, he turned and disappeared into the darkness again.

Her breath was expelled, and her vision blurred. *I'm going to faint,* she told herself. Her knees went weak and rubbery and she gripped the banister to hold herself up. The clock chimed behind her. Tears clouded her eyes as Erika waited, counting the number of gongs on the clock until it reached twelve.

Her body went numb. Mechanically, she started up the stairs. She occupied the third room on the left, next to the one in which Carlton had died. She opened the door and fell against the wood panels as it closed. Her knees give way, and she slid down along the wall to the floor.

He's here.

Four

The night passed. Erika remembered every hour of it as she filled her breakfast plate with eggs and toast. She'd wavered between elation and fear. He'd come. He had to be here to help her. There could be no other reason. What would he want changed? Would he try to usurp her position and take over the day-to-day running of the operation? He was a lawyer and they were presently looking for a legal counsel. Maybe he would be willing to take over that part of the business. Of course, the will said they shared everything. She would certainly discuss anything with him that he wanted to know about. She wasn't planning to exclude him from anything. Carlton wouldn't have forced her to share the company with someone he considered unqualified. Then she remembered the Michael she'd met at the cabin. He wasn't the same man she'd seen in the upstairs hall last night.

"Good morning," he said.

She started, hitting her coffee cup, but luckily it didn't spill. His gaze still went to that nervous act. She'd thought she'd be prepared for him this morning, but his presence sent her blood careening though her veins. He was clean-shaven and wearing a business suit. It fit his strong shoulders as if it had been custom-made. The haggard look about his eyes was still present, and in the shadow his eyebrows looked slightly sinister. Other than that, he was devastating, and every part of her body knew it.

Holding herself erect she said, "Good morning. The coffee's hot and I alerted the cook that you would be here for breakfast."

"That was nice of you." He went to the server and heaped food on his plate. "I take it I won't be enjoying any of your cooking while I'm here."

Erika felt her face warm as memories of the cabin flooded into her brain. A place setting had been set to her right. Michael slipped into the chair in front of it. The gesture was as comfortable as if he'd been doing it for the past twenty years.

"I suppose we should discuss just how long you plan to stay."

"According to Mr. Steven Chambers, this arrangement must remain intact for twelve months. Apparently my . . . grandfather thought you and I should carry on after his death."

So that's how he'd gained access to the house. Steven had given him the packet of information left for him, which included a key and the security codes for the front door. Unfortunately, neither of them had bothered to call her and let her know.

"I believe we are to share everything, including this house," Michael said.

"That's what it says in the will."

"Twelve months from today we have the right to do whatever we want with the companies, the house, and our lives."

Erika nodded.

Michael bit into a crisp piece of bacon. Erika dangled like a puppet.

"Have you agreed?"

"I signed all the necessary papers. I suppose you'll show me around the offices, beginning this morning."

"It would be my pleasure," Erika told him, but it was no pleasure. It took half an hour to get to the offices of Graves Enterprises. A company limousine picked her up each morning. She and Michael sat in strained silence during the drive to downtown Philadelphia and the corporate offices.

She showed him the office she'd picked out for him, which adjoined her own and had been recently decorated. Anything he didn't like his secretary would have redone. Michael looked around approvingly and followed her on the office tour.

"Graves Enterprises major business is pharmaceutical," she explained as they entered the accounting department. "We also own several cosmetics companies and a few hotels. We have our own fleet of cargo ships and use them to transport our products to manufacturing sites which are located in South Carolina, Georgia, Puerto Rico, and Germany. We have a full fleet of trucks that carry our manufactured goods to distribution centers all over the country. We also have marketing and sales organizations in twenty-seven countries around the world."

Michael listened attentively, asking questions, smiling and shaking hands when she introduced him to people in the departments they passed through. He was good-looking and charming. Without turning to look behind her, she knew people were nodding their agreement that he'd make a good addition to the family of companies.

"You appear to know a lot of people here," he observed when they were back in her office.

"I've been here a while."

"You never told me how you and my grandfather came to know each other." This time there was no hesitation when he referred to Carlton.

"I was only eight," she told him. "One day I ran through the hedges and into him." She smiled. "He invited me to tea and we became very good friends."

Erika didn't tell strangers about her childhood. Michael didn't yet qualify as a trusted friend.

"And he didn't tell you about me until—"

"Until the night he died," she finished for him. "He had me bring him the photo album. He pointed you out, called your name, and died." Erika swallowed the lump that formed in her throat whenever she talked about Carlton. "I thought you were a small child until the will was read. After that I looked through the album and found a full history of your accomplishments."

Michael watched her. She wasn't the same as she'd been in

the mountains. Last night when he found her in the hall, dressed in a peach nightgown, he'd wanted to scoop her up and carry her to bed. Today she'd receded behind a corporate uniform—navy blue suit, white blouse, low heeled shoes. He preferred her in the sweater and pants she'd left the cabin wearing.

"I went through Carlton's things." She swallowed. "Most of his clothes have been sent away. He left some of his jewelry, gold watches and rings, to the servants, but there is a box of things you might want to go through when you have time."

Michael could see her distress. He changed the subject. "How do you propose we begin this year of sharing?"

Erika took the seat behind her desk. "We are in need of a corporate counsel and—"

"No," he interrupted too quickly and loudly. "I'd prefer something else," he said in a lower voice.

"If you want to learn the business, it might be a good idea if you visited one or two of the plants, to see how the process begins."

Michael nodded. It was a good idea. It would take him out of town for a while. Yet strangely, he didn't want to go. "How about I do that later? Initially, I suppose I could just find my way around. You could explain what you do, and maybe I can help carry some of the burden."

He thought he saw a flash of fear in her eyes, but quickly it disappeared. "Of course," she said. "We can begin tomorrow morning."

"What's wrong with today?" He checked his watch. "It's nearly lunchtime. How about directly after lunch?"

Erika hesitated, then nodded her agreement. "Where shall we eat?"

"I'm afraid I already have a luncheon engagement."

To Michael's retreating back, Erika's mouth dropped open.

The day had been exhausting. After Erika returned from lunch, in which the discussion revolved around a competitive product that would carve into their hard-won market share, Michael had stuck as close as her shadow. She'd pulled up reports on her computer screen and shown him how to access data from the system. She'd explained their product lines, profit margins, and sources of information. Erika explained the rules to him and told him he had the right to request reports or gather information from any of the data sources in the company.

They'd returned to the mansion in the same car and she was now in her room, feeling the first sense of relief she'd felt in twenty-four hours. She showered and stood before her closet dressed in a terry cloth robe.

She'd been standing there for ten minutes, trying to decide what to wear to dinner, when it occurred to her she was trying to pick something that would impress Michael. What was wrong with her? She shouldn't care what he thought of her clothes. Closing her eyes, she reached inside the closet. Her hand came to rest on a black dress. She frowned when she opened them, then shrugged and began dressing. The dress clung to every curve she had and the bodice seemed a bit low, showing off her small breasted cleavage. Hooking a three-strand pearl choker around her neck and applying drop earrings to her ears, she stepped into her three-inch heels and left the bedroom.

Erika entered the salon where she'd always met Carlton before dinner. Michael had not come down yet and for a few minutes she had the room to herself. The grey September day had fallen into a dark night that reflected her appearance through the long windows that faced the courtyard at the back of the house. Across the stone patio the yard was ringed by a low brick wall that had made Erika feel safe when she was small.

She didn't feel safe now. In fact, since Michael's unexpected arrival she'd felt trapped—trapped in space that was her domain, places where she should have the advantage. Somehow he seemed to have taken it.

Leaving the window she went to the bar and poured herself a glass of wine, something she rarely did. Tonight she needed to relax. Except for the brief period at Penns Landing, while Michael attended his luncheon engagement, he had been her constant companion. She had to get through dinner and the evening with him in the house. It was strange, she thought, that all the while she lived here with Carlton and the staff she'd never felt the presence of anyone as much as she felt Michael's.

Lifting the glass, she sipped the chilled liquid. It was smooth, and warmed her as it went down. The door opened behind her and she turned. Michael stood there dressed in a black suit and a white shirt that contrasted with his skin, making him look like some handsome movie star. She was no teenage groupie, but at that moment she prayed her knees would hold her up, for she wanted to melt to the floor.

Finding her voice she said, "I should have told you. We don't dress for dinner."

"I didn't," he said, advancing into the room. When he stood only a step from her he replied, "We were so busy this afternoon I forgot to tell you I wouldn't be here for dinner."

"You have a date?"

"Yes," he said, flashing her a smile.

Something as sharp as an arrow pierced her heart and Erika fought to keep her expression noncommittal. She should be relieved. Only a moment ago she'd been telling herself she had to get through dinner and the evening with him. Why was she disappointed that the problem had been resolved?

"I see you're going out, too." Michael's glance covered her from head to foot. Then he moved around the bar and poured a glass of mineral water.

Erika looked down at her dress. "No," she told him. "I have no plans for the evening other than some reading."

"Then can I assume that lovely little number is for my benefit?" He raised an eyebrow.

Erika felt the blood heat her face and ears. "You're a lawyer, Michael. I'm sure you know what assume means."

Immediately she regretted her words. The playfulness he was having at her expense was suddenly gone. She watched the friendliness in his eyes disappear, replaced by something she thought must hurt him deeply. She wondered what it was, and why the mention of the word "lawyer" had changed him. This morning, when she suggested he take over the legal counsel position, he'd flatly refused.

"I apologize," she said.

"For what?"

"I don't know."

Her answer, though a statement, was an open question for him to answer, but he didn't, and he wasn't going to. He didn't want to think about the law and all the entanglements involved in practicing it.

He changed the subject. "You're quite comfortable at Graves Enterprises?"

She nodded. "I am."

"Rumor has it you've been there since you were a kid."

"I was sixteen and—"

"And what?"

"Afraid, like most sixteen year olds are, I suppose."

Michael didn't believe her. She'd been about to say something else when she caught herself. When he'd been sixteen he hadn't been afraid of anything, except maybe a girl turning him down for a date to the junior prom. He smiled, remembering that time in his life and wondering what Erika's had been like.

"You said you met Carlton when you were very young."

"Eight," she answered, her gaze level on him as if she were suspicious of his motives.

"How did you come to live here?"

"My mother gave me up for adoption and Carlton adopted me."

"When you were eight?" That was highly unusual unless a

child was being abused and the courts stepped in and removed the child. Then they tended to get lost in the foster care system, which changed them for life—and for the worse. He couldn't see Erika like that, but suddenly wondered if she had been abused. Some people were good at hiding bruises, but invariably they were revealed in some way.

"Your mother is still alive?"

"Yes." Erika's voice was as dry as a desert. "She is."

"She gave you up when you were eight?"

"I was fourteen, and can we stop with the Twenty Questions?" Erika turned away, going to the windows and staring out into the darkness

"Now it's my turn to apologize." Michael put his drink on the bar and went to her. He wanted to put his arms around her, but every line of her body told him not to touch her. "I didn't mean to pry."

Erika lifted her head and stared at him. Her eyes were enormous but dry. Somehow he thought she never let anyone see anything vulnerable about her. She was a tower of strength to the world, but Michael knew from firsthand experience that those kind of people hurt deeply in the confines of privacy. He didn't like to think of Erika hurting.

"You'd better leave," she said, interrupting his thoughts as she checked her watch. "You wouldn't want to keep the lady waiting."

Michael didn't move. There was that impulsiveness again—the action that had made him kiss her good-bye at the cabin, and the one now that nearly had his hands moving to take her in his arms. He lifted one hand and touched her arm. "Good night," he said with a gentle squeeze. "Enjoy your evening." With that he left.

As the cold, wintry air hit him Michael tried to tell himself Erika St. James was not his problem. The two of them had a one year agreement. After that they were both free to do what they would. His intention was to sign over Graves Enterprises to her, take his share of the settlement and walk away. He would return to his mountain or go to Timbuktu, but whatever his decision it had nothing to do with the walnut-colored woman inside.

Her heels clicked hollowly in the cavernous foyer as Erika closed the door and walked across the gleaming black and white tile. She thought she'd heard someone knock. Had Michael already forgotten the set of keys he'd been given? No one was there when she opened the door. Since Carlton died, there seemed to be a steady stream of people coming and going. By now she thought they would have gone on with their lives and forgotten about him, but she found that Carlton had more friends than she remembered. Tonight she wished at least one of them had dropped by. Her lonely dinner gave her time to think about Michael and who he might be having dinner with. How could he have a date so soon? He'd been here less than twenty-four hours, and already he'd met someone.

Ripping her attention away from Michael, Erika thought over her position in this house. Rarely had she ever thought about it. She'd come first here as an intruder, then as a friend. It was her refuge, her haven of sanity when her mother flew into her rages. Eventually, she'd clashed with her mother and run away so much that the judge allowed her to stay here permanently, visiting her mother on holidays for short periods of time. Carlton had insisted that she keep some association with Alva Redford. He said family was important, and when you lost family you could never replace them. She wondered about that now that she knew about Michael. Carlton had not done what he'd forced her to do.

People treated her as if she were a grieving granddaughter. She felt like a granddaughter, but she wasn't one. Carlton had a grandson. What had happened to keep them apart? Why did Michael not know about Carlton? Why had Carlton never mentioned Michael?

Erika slipped into the living room. The coffee service was

there and hot. She poured a cup and went to the sofa. Slipping out of her shoes, she curled her feet under her and settled into a comfortable position.

Her mother's house had been gloomy, not dark, but unfriendly. Here there had been no fighting and arguing, no screaming. She sipped the hot liquid, remembering her childhood. Carlton had helped her with her homework, and come to see her in school plays and assembly programs, programs she hadn't even mentioned to her mother. He was always there to talk to her, never too busy or too tired to take an interest in anything she had to say. Now he was gone.

Erika's heart felt tight in her chest. She'd forgotten the deep sense of loss that accompanied death. Balancing the cup on the edge of the sofa, she hugged herself as she shivered in the warm room.

Carlton had been her sanctuary when she was a child and when she needed to come home after Bill. No, she wouldn't remember, not tonight. She stared into the large fire burning in the huge grate.

She needed a vacation—an escape. This just wasn't the time. There was too much to do at work. She had a meeting scheduled with Jeff Rivers tomorrow and she expected it to last most of the day. Even though she'd been at Graves Enterprises permanently for the past year, Carlton's death had left morale low, and people feeling uneasy about a possible restructure. With Michael's arrival and a possible takeover looming, things would invariably get worse before they got better, and she couldn't leave in the middle of that. She needed to be there to show them they had no reason to feel nervous. Carlton was a visionary. She'd learned much in the past year about the pharmaceutical industry. She also had her past experience and the firsthand experience of working at Graves Enterprises. She planned to keep on the same track Carlton had begun. They were releasing a new product and they had a healthy pipeline. With the steady growth of market share in several divisions, they were sitting comfortably. She hadn't discussed conditions with Michael, but she could see no reason why he'd disagree with her.

Michael, she thought. Who was he with? He'd only kissed her, she told herself. He hadn't asked her to have his children. Maybe the way he kissed her good-bye was the way he said good-bye to every unattached female who slept on his sofa.

Erika smiled. Thoughts of him warmed her. Involuntarily her hand went to her mouth.

Erika lifted her cup from the sofa arm. The liquid was cold now. She got up and placed it on the silver tray. Reaching down, she lifted her shoes and headed barefoot for the staircase and her bedroom on the second floor. Before she reached it the doorbell rang. Instinctively, Erika checked the time on the grandfather clock.

Maybe she'd been right before, and Michael had forgotten his keys. If it was him, his date was rather short. She smiled at the thought that he might have not enjoyed himself.

Erika changed direction and started for the door. One of the maids came through the kitchen and met her in the hall. Erika signaled she'd answer it, and the woman left. With her shoes dangling from her fingers Erika went through the foyer. The heavy, carved wooden door had a beveled glass window in the top portion. Through the clear facets Erika saw the last person on earth she expected to find. Hesitating for a moment, she drew in her breath and pulled the door open.

"Mother!"

Alva St. James Redford stood under the portico, her body wrapped in mink, her red Mercedes sport coupe behind her. The light flatteringly bathed her skin tones. Erika's surprise at finding herself face-to-face with her mother took her power of speech.

"I never expected to cross this threshold again," Alva said, pushing past her daughter and entering the foyer. She turned back to Erika, her stance as dramatic as that of an actress from the old black and white movies. Gloria Swanson, with long black hair and a mole on her chin, came to mind. Alva pulled her mink coat closer around her as if the room were cold, instead of comfortably warm for this time of year.

"What brings you here?" Erika asked as she closed the door and started for the living room.

Alva paused at the entrance to the high-ceilinged room full of high, draped windows. The facing sofas shared a beige and rose color scheme and sat on a carpet that picked up the rose color. Erika watched her mother take in the room as if looking for something. After a moment she slipped out of the coat and dropped it on a chair by the door. Advancing, she came toward her daughter.

"Is there something I can get you to drink—coffee, a soft drink?" Erika wouldn't willingly offer her mother alcohol. She remembered all too well her moods after she'd bent her elbow on one too many scotches. "This is cold, but I can make a fresh pot."

"Why don't you ask someone to get it? After all the years you've lived here, haven't you learned how to have servants serve you?"

"The servants work a full day, Mother. At this hour they are afforded time to themselves."

She could see Alva Redford would never stand for this kind of treatment. Erika knew she should make the suggestion again, but sat down, putting her shoes back on and refusing to do so.

Alva sat on the facing sofa, stretching her arm along the back and studying her long, blood-red fingernails in a decidedly feline manner. "I see nothing much has changed here." She lifted her gaze to the life-size portrait of Carlton's wife, Loretta, which hung above the dying fire in the fireplace. She pointed to the far wall. "I'll bet you if I opened that chest over there, there will be a collection of Fabergé eggs and some precious stones."

Erika was obviously surprised at her mother's knowledge of

the house. Except for one incident, when Alva had stormed into the house demanding her daughter be returned to her, Erika couldn't remember her ever being here.

"This isn't my first visit," she said, as if she could read Erika's thoughts. "I've been here many times. I can even tell you the color of the wallpaper in your bedroom."

"That won't be necessary," Erika said. "You can tell me what you want, and then we can end our visit the way they always end."

"Erika—" She stopped. For the merest second Erika thought her name sounded strange coming from her mother's lips, as if the woman hadn't said it in so long she'd forgotten the sound of it. "Erika, I only wanted to make sure you were all right."

Erika stared her straight in the eye, looking for any hint of insincerity and finding none. *She's a good actress,* Erika thought. *Who is she playing today, and why?*

"After all," she went on, "Carlton died more than a month ago. All the people surrounding you must be gone. I wanted to see if you needed my help."

Erika stood up and turned away. The thought of her mother offering help was so ludicrous that she nearly laughed out loud. She turned back, her arms folded across her. "Mother, thank you for your concern. You've done your duty. I am not lonely, alone, or in need of your help."

"Erika, don't sound so angry. We are related, and family is the most important thing in the world."

She'd heard Carlton say that. It was the reason he insisted she visit her mother at times. Erika remembered the visits, the arguments over how she looked, what she wore, how she combed her hair, or made up her face. In Alva Redford's eyes, her daughter was a sore disappointment.

"I think I'll have that coffee now," Alva said.

"Mother, you didn't come here for coffee." Erika raised her hands to prevent her mother's protests. "And you aren't here to inquire about my state of health."

Alva rose from the sofa as if she were Cleopatra about to deal with a disloyal subject. "Why, dear, am I here, then?"

"You're here about the money." Erika was rewarded with a small gasp from her mother. "I know about the checks Carlton had been paying you. Just what service did you provide that afforded you that kind of payment?"

"Don't be disgusting!"

"I'm not, Mother. My mind and my conscience are clean. Can you say the same thing about yours?"

"Why, you inconsiderate little wretch! You're just like your father, stubborn and—"

"Leave Daddy out of this. You can't go on blaming him for everything that's happened in your life. And you can't blame me, either."

"Forget your father."

"I'll never forget him, but you certainly have. You probably drove him to killing himself."

Erika knew she'd gone too far. Her mother's hand was suddenly in the air, and the slap that swiped across her cheek stung like an entire hive of bumblebees.

"Hey, what's going on in here?" Michael stood in the huge archway. Both women started as he spoke, and turned toward him. Neither of them answered him. Michael walked into the room. Erika blinked, trying not to let the tears her mother always drew from her spill over.

"Michael," Erika found her voice. It was tight and formal, but she got the words out. "I'd like you to meet my mother, Mrs. Alva St. James Redford."

Michael turned to the older woman and nodded. Alva smiled as if she were sizing up a new conquest. Erika's stomach wrenched and she swallowed the bile in her throat.

"Mother, this is Carlton's grandson, Michael Lawrence."

Alva laughed, a throaty sound. The laughter escalated and went on and on while the two other occupants of the room looked on.

"You . . . you," she said, hesitating, using her fingertips to wipe tears from the corner of her eyes. "You must have been a real surprise to Carlton . . . and Erika." She stopped and pointed toward Erika as the smile on her mouth wore away. "A grandson. Wait until the reporters find out about this one. They are going to have a field day."

Erika had a sudden mental picture of her mother being interviewed by the *Philadelphia Inquirer.*

"Mother, I warn you." Erika spoke through clenched teeth.

"Darling, daughters should never warn their mothers. It's not done." She sauntered toward the door, where her coat lay on the chair, but stopped in front of Michael. She looked up into his eyes for a long moment. Then she went to the chair and pulled on her coat. With an exaggerated flourish she turned back to Michael, delivering her parting shot with the best Gloria Swanson imitation Erika had ever seen. "Erika told me she wasn't alone . . . or lonely."

Five

This time Michael didn't think about what he was doing. His legs took him across the room and he turned Erika into his arms. She resisted only a moment before giving in to his comfort, but she didn't cry. Her arms went around his waist and she buried her face in his shoulder, but no sobs came from her. She needed to hold onto someone. Michael understood that. How many nights had he awakened in a cold sweat and wanted someone to hold him?

He didn't say anything, and didn't expect her to do anything more than cling. After a while he walked her to the sofa and sat down, keeping her cradled against him. She was soft and smelled of a sweet perfume. He swallowed at the sensations she aroused in him.

"Do you want to talk about it?" he asked.

She shook her head against his shoulder. Michael cradled her closer and she settled against him. Invariably his thoughts went to Abby, and the time he'd comforted her in almost the same way. Turning his head, he brushed his mouth against Erika's hair. He didn't like to see her hurt, and her mother had hurt her. When he'd walked into the room he knew the only thing keeping Erika from breaking down was sheer will. He thought she was holding something back. With her mother throwing daggers at her, Erika inherently felt something for her. In her eyes had been a raw plea for love. Michael had seen it before—once, in Abby's eyes. But it hadn't been for him.

Michael looked down at her. She breathed easily and he knew she'd fallen asleep. He thought of her sleeping at the cabin, her face clean of any makeup and wearing a flannel nightshirt. Here she was a queen, always on duty. Michael pulled his arm free and slid away from her. Easily he let her fall backward until she was stretched out on the sofa. He turned the lights off in the downstairs rooms and checked the doors. Coming back, he lifted her into his arms and started for the stairs.

"What are you doing?" Erika jerked awake when his foot touched the first step.

"Shhh," he said and continued up the stairs. She was thin in his arms, light and warm. He enjoyed holding her, smelling her perfume and soap. She rested her head on his shoulder. He forced himself not to put his head on top of hers. At her door he let her slide her feet to the floor. "Are you all right?"

She nodded.

"Good night," he said, then lifted her chin and kissed her lightly on the mouth. Before either of them could respond further he broke contact, turned, and walked toward his own wing.

She called to him. "Michael." Her voice was low, quiet and sexy. It surrounded him, stopping his retreat. He didn't want to stop. He knew if he turned back her eyes would be dewy and inviting. Why had he let himself kiss her? Why did she stir feelings in him that to date he'd been able to control? "Michael." Her voice cracked as she said his name. He turned to look at her. "Thank you," she said. "I mean, thanks for coming." Michael shrugged and turned again.

That night the dream came again, stealing into his subconscious and robbing him of the ability to rest. Michael ran, panting, following Abby and Frank up the hill, toward the building. His lungs burned as they tried to contract and expand. A fiery pain swelled in his chest until he knew his lungs would burst. Yet he kept going. He had no choice. He had to get to Frank, get the gun, and keep him from—.

Michael bolted upright, his teeth clenched, his muscles tight, hands balled into fists. Sweat poured down his face and over his chest. The room seemed hot and stuffy. For a moment he was disoriented, wondering where he was and where Abby had disappeared to. Then he let his breath go and sagged against the pillows. He hoped he hadn't screamed out in his subconscious rage. Pushing the covers aside he left the bed, which looked as if it had been an unwilling participant in a prizefight. Going to the window, he opened it. Leaning against the frame, he sucked in the cold September air, letting it cool his fevered body.

Taking a chair when his breathing returned to normal, he wondered when the dreams would end. Tonight after leaving Erika he would have welcomed dreams of her, but Abby and Frank had invaded his dream state and devastated his ability to relax. When this happened at the cabin he'd do something physically exhausting—chop wood, row the boat, or climb the mountain. There was a full gym here. He could go there and work out. Then he remembered the pool. Dressing in a pair of trunks and hooking a towel around his neck, he headed for the indoor pool. He felt better already. This would be a pleasure. In college he'd been on the swim team, and never tired of the sport. With a pool inside he could swim in any weather and at any time of the day or night. Tonight he intended to exhaust himself until he could do nothing other than sleep.

The water glowed green and inviting under the lights of the Greek style bathhouse. Michael entered the room, smelling the chlorine and feeling the eighty degree heat, and stopped. Erika cut through the water with sure, easy strokes. She swam effortlessly as a water nymph, at one with her environment. Michael wondered if she'd had a bad dream, too. She reached the end of the Olympic-size pool, ducked under the water, and pushed off toward the end closest to where he stood. Her reversal had all the skill and elegance of a choreographed dance. She raised her head out of the water to breathe at regular intervals, but she didn't see him, not until his shadow fell across her and she stopped, finding him directly in front of her.

"Couldn't you sleep?" he asked. The argument he'd interrupted between Erika and her mother came back to him. It pushed his own sleeping problems to the back of his mind.

She angled herself out of the water, wiping her face and smoothing her hair back. Michael noticed how big her eyes looked and how her nearly naked body curved. She wore a royal blue, one-piece suit that had him wishing he'd worn a robe.

"Whenever my mother and I fight, it ruins my sleep. I thought I'd come here and exercise for a while."

"Do these fights occur often?"

She picked up a towel and began drying her face and arms. Michael couldn't stop his gaze from following the towel as she stroked it against her skin. "She and I usually try not to cross paths, but it *is* a small planet."

Michael smiled. He knew a fighter when he saw one. When she'd arrived at Highland Hills he knew she'd be a worthy adversary. She'd come to the cabin to take him on, when no one else had been able to make him budge. Tonight he'd seen her in action. Yet the emotional drain took its toll on her subconscious. He wondered at the methods they each chose to solve their problems.

He wanted to ask her more questions, but decided against it. He'd told himself he wouldn't get involved with her or anyone else. And he was sticking to that rule, despite what his body told him. Despite the fact that when her mother left he'd kissed her and he wanted to kiss her again. Right now.

"How's the water?" he asked, glancing over his shoulder and dragging his attention away from the fact that she looked beautiful soaking wet. He hoped the water was cold. He needed it to be cold now.

"I'll race you to the deep end," she said.

Frank panted, breathing through his mouth. He never thought it would be this easy, and during daylight, too. He knew he'd escape during Smiley's shift. He'd planned it, studied Smiley's routine until he could follow it as well as Smiley could. Then the unthinkable happened. The gate was open—not wide open, just a little ajar, not even noticeable. It was visitors' day. Outsiders, the normals, crowded about the place. Frank never had visitors. He usually spent these kinds of days sequestered in his room. The day staff didn't bother him on these days.

Leaving would be no problem. He already had clothes. They were hidden in a tree at the north end of the compound. He'd collected them a piece at a time and taken them to the tree. He knew he'd need them when he was finally free. And today was freedom day.

Frank waited. The nurse at the station stacked folders on the counter. He nearly smiled at what he knew was about to happen. His heartbeat accelerated, and he consciously willed it to return to normal. He'd practiced his escape, knew every detail of it. All he had to do was remain calm and his plan would work. Finally, as Frank expected, the folders reached critical height and tumbled over. The nurse cursed, then stooped to retrieve the mess she'd made. At that point, Frank eased through the door. Carefully he pulled it closed, listening for the slight click as it locked, while his gaze remained on the white-clad nurse. She was trying to make order out of the chaos when he turned and walked down the hallway, taking the first turn to keep out of her view. He knew the way to the yard. Frank reached it without incident. Outside, he appeared to be one of the patients returning to his weekly visitor. Frank walked easily, smiling at people he'd never seen before.

He kept his gait short and easy. He didn't want anyone to notice him. Following his usual route, he kept going until he reached the clump of shade trees in the distance. He stopped, taking a moment to look back and see if anyone was looking at him. All was calm. *This is just too easy,* he thought. He wondered how long it would be before someone noticed he was missing. Visitors came and went all afternoon. Lunch ended before the visitors arrived. It could be dinner before they thought to check on him. By then it would be dark and he would be miles away from here.

Frank checked the ground. He saw no footprints. The ground varied between pine needles and packed earth. The warm, dry air of the past few weeks acted as an unwilling accomplice to his escape. Frank found the tree where he'd hidden the clothes, and climbed. From inside a hollow knot he pulled a green plastic bag. Refusing to take the time to change now, he forged ahead. The trees became denser and darker until he reached the wall.

Thirty feet high, made of solid, tan brick, it looked as impenetrable as the locked door. Frank knew there was no such thing as a locked door. If you wanted to get through it bad enough, all you had to do was find the key. He looked up, his gaze stretching from tree branch to tree branch. Out here maintenance wasn't performed with as rigid a regimen as it was near the front gate. No sentry held duty here. The guards were more nurses than wardens, and the height and breadth of the wall was a deterrent in itself.

Frank had stood in harder places than this. Often he stepped aside when dividing the men and boys, and he rarely came upon a problem without a solution. Frank moved back several yards and exchanged his hospital whites for jeans, a sweatshirt, jacket, and sneakers. He looked like any other visitor now. No one would notice him. Putting the hospital clothes inside the bag, Frank hooked it onto his beltloop and climbed the first tree.

He went as high as the branches would hold him. Then, using moves that could kill him if he fell, he jumped to the next tree and the next, and one more. Finally, he was one tree from the wall; six yards from freedom. With his arms spread out like a tightrope walker, Frank balanced himself; step by step he moved along the branch until he could reach the next tree. He grabbed the branches. They were coarse against his hands and swiped at his face like scratchy fingers. Holding his breath, he pumped the branch and swung his weight to the last tree. He prayed this would hold him and he wouldn't die from a thirty foot fall over the side of the wall.

Frank crouched for the final trial. Crawling backward along the dark wood, he moved with care. The branch dipped under his weight. Frank held his breath. For the space of a lifetime it dipped downward. Frank squeezed his eyes closed, expecting to hear the snap of wood and know his life would end in seconds as he fell to his death only a few feet from freedom. Finally it stopped. Frank hung over the side, his hand slipping along the leafless branches, his feet fighting for footholds along the smooth wall.

Finally he stopped. His heart beat so fast he thought it would surely stop soon. Frank closed his eyes and waited a moment. Then he looked down. It must be twenty feet to the ground. Vertigo attacked him as the ground bobbed back and forth before settling in place. Frank took a breath. His hands slipped again. The skin on the inside of his right hand tore, and blood dripped into his face as he looked up at it. It was time, he thought. Taking one more deep breath he let go of the branch and fell the remaining feet to the ground. The impact bent his knees and he landed in a sitting position. The branch snapped back into position. It waved for a second, then settled into place as if no human had ever hung from it.

Frank looked up and down the road that followed the outside wall for any sign of trouble. He saw nothing. The other side of narrow strip of blacktop held another clump of trees. Frank went into them and waited. If luck was with him, he'd hop a ride on the first truck or van that came up this road.

He didn't have to wait long. The first car was a low compact job, its rear bumper so low to the ground that Frank would have had to drag himself. He waited. The next vehicle was a minivan. He could have jumped on that, but the driver traveled so fast Frank would have killed himself trying to get a grip on the back.

A quarter hour passed before another car came by. This time

there were four in a row, and no time to come out without someone seeing him in a rearview mirror. Frank settled back to wait. Then he heard it. One of his night sounds. The engine labored on the hill, out of sight. He knew it was the bus. The bus that brought patients to the hospital and sometimes transported visitors to the facility. It didn't run on a schedule, and came at odd hours. During the day, with other noises, it was difficult to hear it until it turned into the driveway. At night, with the crisp air magnifying the sound, Frank could hear the engine missing as the driver shifted well-worn gears.

The blue and white bus had long ago lost its fresh paint job, and the mirror on the passenger side had never been replaced after it was broken.

Frank waited for it to completely round the curve before he left his hiding place. Jumping on the back fender, he held on, his fingertips in the crease created by the rear door. Frank rode along the road, following the wall until it ended. When the bus turned onto the connecting road and stopped, Frank jumped clear. He walked to the next road and hitched a ride with a tractor trailer driver.

He was free.

The steady and monotonous droning of cold rain awakened Erika the next morning. Despite her lack of sleep and the promise of a grey, dreary day, Erika felt wonderful. She had enjoyed swimming with Michael. Yesterday she had dreaded his company, been unsure about his presence on a daily basis. This morning she knew everything was going to be all right. She had help.

Carlton must have known that when he wrote the will. She smiled, pulling a red suit from the closet and dropping it on the bed before heading into the shower.

Several minutes later Erika walked into the breakfast room to find the table set for one. She wondered where Michael was. Wasn't he having breakfast this morning?

"Tess, isn't Mr. Lawrence having breakfast this morning?" she asked when the maid came in to bring coffee.

"Mr. Lawrence ate earlier and left, Ms. St. James."

Erika didn't ask why, or when he had told them he was leaving. She felt a little awkward that Michael hadn't told her. They'd swum for nearly an hour, then talked a while before going back to their rooms. The clock had chimed three o'clock as Erika put the light out. Had Michael still not been able to sleep? Had he gone for good? Erika nibbled on her toast and sipped her coffee, trying to remember if he'd said anything to let her know he wasn't satisfied. She could think of nothing.

At Graves Erika checked his office. It was empty, and no one had seen him that morning. She shrugged, still not understanding, but then the pressures of the day required her attention and she didn't have time to dwell on Michael's absence. She found herself thinking of him over and over. Why hadn't he told her he wouldn't be in today? Why had he acted so friendly last night and then disappeared this morning?

At three o'clock, as she prepared to go to a meeting, Erika knew he wasn't going to show up at all. She phoned the house and was told he had not returned or called. Earlier she had been angry, but that was slowly turning to concern. Had something happened to him? He could have been involved in an accident, and no one had notified her.

They hadn't been partners long enough to be responsible to each other. They had set no rules about accounting for their time. It was truly none of her business where he was. However, he was supposed to share this business with her, and during business hours she didn't consider it too much of an imposition to expect him to tell her when he would, and would not, be available.

Erika gathered her folder and walked to the door of her office. She opened it and stopped. The room was full to capacity.

"Ms. St. James, is it true you share this company with the man who won the custody battle for the Mason children?" a woman in a grey suit asked. Flashing camera lights blinded her. Questions hit her like bullets. She'd been through this before. Bill Castle came to mind, and she wanted to shrink back into her office and slam the door.

"Ms. St. James, where is Mr. Lawrence?"

"Ms. St. James, is Mr. Lawrence in Philadelphia?"

"Ms. St. James—"

Erika didn't hear any more. She turned to her secretary. "Call security," she shouted. "And call the police. I want this office cleared."

"Michael! Michael Lawrence!" June Ferrell unplugged her headset and came around the receptionist's station at Lawrence, Barclay, West, and Lawrence. "How have you been?" she asked, catching him in a bear hug.

"Fine, June," he told her. "It's good to see you." June Ferrell had been receptionist at the law firm since Michael and Evan Barclay began it only three years after graduating law school. Michael liked her immensely. "I see you've changed—lost weight, less grey hair. There must be a man in your life."

June laughed. "Don't I wish?"

"Is my brother in?"

She nodded, going back to her station and plugging into her board. "Won't he be surprised?"

"Don't call him. I *want* to surprise him."

June smiled conspiratorially. "Go on. I'll see you soon."

Michael passed his own office on the way to his brother's. Several people gaped at him in open-mouthed surprise. He smiled and waved, but didn't stop to chat. As he approached his brother's secretary he put a finger to his lips to keep her from calling his name.

"How have you been, Margaret?" he asked when he was within whispering distance.

"I'm just fine. But look at you. You've lost weight, but you still look good enough to eat. Are you coming back?"

"No." He laughed, shaking his head. "I just need to talk to Bobby."

As if on cue a soft buzz sounded from her phone. They both looked toward the desk.

"He's calling me," Margaret said.

Michael smiled and went through the door to his brother's office.

"Margaret, I need the Bennett file. I just talked to him and he'll be in tomorrow at four." Bobby hadn't looked up when the door opened and closed. He'd continued making notes on the yellow pad and begun giving instructions. "Also, would you call Mrs. Anglender and ask her the status of her Case Information Statement? We'll need to get that into the judge's office by the end of the week. And I need—"

Michael interrupted his list. "I don't think I'll be able to help."

"Michael!" His brother shouted and jumped up from his chair. The two hugged, patting each other on the back, then shook hands and smiled. Bobby wasn't prone to outbursts of emotion. He was the calm, controlled lawyer, able to quickly analyze the situation and act. What Michael had just witnessed was a side of his personality he generally hid from the world. Bobby must be truly glad to see him.

"I'm so glad you're here. You're coming back," he stated. "We've been so busy since you left. It will be good to have another hand to carry the load."

"Bobby," Michael stopped him. "I'm not returning. I have something else to do. Maybe after it's done I'll consider coming back."

Bobby's shoulders dropped, the exact same way their father's had when he was disappointed. Michael stared at his brother. He could see a lot of his father in Bobby. He'd never liked to compare how much they looked like their parents. However, when Erika entered his life, she caused the foundations on which he lived to crumble.

"How long is it going to take? We could really use you here."

A pang of guilt ripped through Michael. "It's a year contract." Apparently, their mother had said nothing to her second son. Otherwise he'd be aware of where Michael was living, and the details of the will that had been left by his grandfather. "How about hiring another lawyer if there is work to keep another one busy?"

"Actually we have been discussing that, but so far we haven't really had time to interview anyone."

"You will," Michael assured him. "I really came by to talk to you and Peter. I had hoped Mom would be around."

"She's up visiting Aunt Irene in Boston. It was a spur of the moment thing. She called about a week ago and left the next morning. I asked if everything was all right. She said she hadn't seen her in a while and wanted to go."

Michael well knew why. His mother didn't want to deal with him. He'd seen her once when he confronted her about Carlton Lipton-Graves and his true parentage. After that she'd obviously packed her bags and headed north.

"Can you spare a few minutes for lunch?" Michael asked. "Peter's agreed to meet us at The Pub." Michael checked his watch.

"I suppose I can spare time for a brother I haven't seen in a year."

Bobby got up and pushed his arms into his suit jacket. He took a moment to let Margaret know where he was going while he slipped into his overcoat. Moments later they were on the street, walking toward the restaurant. Peter met them at the door with a friendly handshake and a wide grin.

The more outgoing of the three, and certainly the best looking, as he liked to tell them, Peter worked for a local cable company in the newsroom.

The Pub was an old building in downtown New Brunswick. The inside was dark and the seats wooden and hard. The tables had the marks and indentations of the names of hundreds of college students who'd attended Rutgers University, only a few blocks away. Miniature trains ran around a track mounted overhead. Their father used to bring them here as children on Saturday afternoons for lunch. Michael remembered those times.

When they were seated and the waitress had taken their order Michael asked his first question. "Have either of you talked to Mom lately?" None of them lived with their parents any longer. Bobby was married and Peter lived with his girlfriend. Before Michael had left for Maryland, he'd lived in his own condominium in East Brunswick.

"I talked to her this morning," Peter said. "She seems fine, enjoying Aunt Irene's cooking."

Michael looked at Bobby. "Last Sunday," he said. "We called her."

"Did she mention anything about me?"

The brothers looked at each other, then at Michael. Each shook his head.

"Have either of you ever heard of a man called Carlton Lipton-Graves?"

"Sure," Peter said. "I reported the news of his death about a month ago." Peter anchored the New Jersey News. On weeknights at six he could be seen on WNJN. "His substantial holdings in this state prompted the station to do a story on his passing," Peter went on to explain.

"How about Erika St. James?"

"I believe she was Acting CEO while the old man was alive." Peter paused, seeming to pull his memory into focus. "If I'm remembering correctly, she walked off with the lion's share of Graves Enterprises."

"The pharmaceutical company?" Bobby asked.

"That's the one," Peter told him.

"I remember this now," Bobby said. "What's all this got to do with whether we talked to Mom recently?"

The waitress arrived with their lunches. Michael waited for her to set the plates out and leave before answering his brother. "What I'm about to tell you I've already told Mom. I thought she might have let you know, but I will admit when I left her I was pretty angry. I wanted to put as much distance between her and me as possible. Later I regretted it, and returned to apologize."

Peter and Bobby stared at him. He wasn't making much sense.

"Michael, what are you talking about?" Bobby asked.

Michael took a sip from his water glass and began. "About a month ago a woman came to see me. Her name is Erika St. James."

"You let *her* on that mountain, when you wouldn't let any of us come and talk to you?" Bobby asked.

"You haven't met Erika." Michael remembered the picture of her that day, straight, tall, and representing a past he didn't want to confront. Her words and the will she delivered had taken his choice away from him, and he was back. "I didn't let her come and talk to me. She took that initiative herself."

"What did she have to say?" Peter asked. His attention was fastened on Michael, and the playfulness of his tone was completely gone.

"What she told me has a direct effect on all of us." Michael stopped assessing their expressions as he would a witness in court, memorizing what the look was like so he could compare it to the look that would come when he finished his interrogation.

"Come on, Michael," Peter said. "Stop keeping us in suspense."

"Yes," Bobby agreed. "What does the Lipton-Graves heiress have to do with us?"

"Erika St. James isn't the sole heir to the Graves legacy," Michael said.

"You're not going to say he left part of it to us?"

"No," Michael smiled, feeling a little of the tension leaving his body. He went on to explain the exact terms of the will and the news of his true parentage. He told them everything, from Erika's first visit to his day at corporate headquarters.

When he finished, his two brothers hadn't eaten a bite, and were looking at him in amazement.

"Mom knew this?" Bobby asked.

Michael nodded. "I told her about the will a couple of weeks ago."

"In all these years she never said a word to you? Never told you you had a living grandfather?"

"She said it didn't seem to matter. My real father was dead. I had no memory of anyone other than Dad. So she just let it go." Michael paused. "I don't blame her. What would have been the reason to tell me? She'd never received anything from Carlton in the way of support, emotional or financial. From what she told me, Carlton didn't believe I was his true grandson. He had unauthorized blood tests performed in an attempt to prove I wasn't part of his bloodline."

"That must have gone over well with Mom," Peter said.

Michael nodded, knowing his mother's explosive nature when one of her children was in danger. She'd have gone up against Carlton Lipton-Graves and his millions if the need had come, but apparently it hadn't.

"You said he had a photo album of you," Bobby said, unconsciously retreating to the confuse-the-witness technique that all lawyers use. "Where did he get these pictures?"

"I don't know. According to Erika he could have been there, taken them himself."

"What do you think?" Peter asked.

"I'm not sure. I don't think he would have left me half his estate if he'd never laid eyes on me."

"Did Mom say anything about him wanting to see you?" Bobby asked.

"He'd asked to see me a couple of times. Her reasons for refusing made sense, but he never demanded any familial rights, and he never acknowledged that I was his grandson."

"At least, not until the will came to light," Peter commented.

"Mom thought it best to put everything behind her and go

on, and there was Dad, providing everything we needed, never treating me any differently than he treated you two."

Michael thought of his father. He could never replace Robert Lawrence with the figure of any other man. He'd loved him as a son, and even the knowledge that he had not fathered him didn't change the important part of his life that he'd given him—time, guidance, emotional support. Looking at his brothers, he knew his father would be proud of them all. He didn't know what he would think of Michael's retreat to the mountains, but he would certainly be supportive of his decisions.

"Michael," Peter said. "What are you doing about the conditions of this will?"

"I've given up the cabin in Maryland," he began. "I'll have to stay in Philadelphia for a year and co-manage the companies Carlton left."

"After that, you become one of the most eligible bachelors in the United States and you're free to do as you wish?" Peter had sized up the situation

"Yes." Michael nodded. "Only *you* would put it like that."

"Why hasn't this been reported in any of the papers?" Bobby asked.

"All the details of the will were not disclosed, but I have reason to believe they might be soon." He remembered Erika's mother and her veiled threat to go to the papers. But even without her as a motivation, he thought his brothers should know. They had grown up as family, and he didn't want them to find out through the local news.

"Damn," Peter said. "I feel bad.

"Why?" Michael asked.

"All those times I said you weren't my brother. Now I find out it's true."

Peter's words were refuted by the wide smile that creased his face. Bobby joined him with a grunt that turned into a laugh, and soon the three brothers were laughing, hilariously.

"It doesn't change anything between us," Bobby said when they could speak again.

"So tell us about *her*," Peter said. "According to the reports she'd worked at Graves Enterprises for years and had been running it solely for the last year. How did she take to you suddenly having a say in things?"

"We haven't clashed over anything yet," Michael hedged. "We're working out which one of us is responsible for what, so we can make this a good relationship."

"Is she beautiful?" Peter asked. The smile on his face showed definite interest. "Even the newspaper pictures were good."

"Why should you care? You have a girlfriend."

"Not any more," Bobby told him. "Peter and the beautiful Cassandra parted company six months ago." He paused to glance at his brother. "Our dear brother here is on the loose."

Peter smiled. "Maybe I'll come stay with you for a while."

"The commute to make the six o'clock news might be a little steep," Michael told him.

The three of them laughed like old times. Michael was glad. By some trick of fate he'd been given the best family in the world. He knew that, and he never wanted it any other way.

"How's Catherine?" Michael changed the subject to Bobby's wife.

"Pregnant," he said. "She should be delivering in the next two weeks. You're going to be an uncle."

"Congratulations!" Michael said, reaching across to shake his brother's hand. "You will call me when the baby is born?" Michael grabbed a napkin and wrote the address and phone number down. He passed it across the table, but Peter took it.

"Isn't this where Erika St. James lives?"

Michael suddenly remembered his brother's uncanny ability to hold details in his head.

"We share the company *and* the house. It was a condition of the will."

Peter's eyebrows went toward the overhead trains.

"She has her wing, and I have mine," he explained, but Peter didn't seem to understand that, from the smirk on his face.

For a moment the three of them didn't say anything. Then Peter sobered and commented, "I suppose that mess in California is all behind her now."

What mess? Michael wanted to know but didn't ask. He knew about her engagement to William A. Castle. The newspaper Gerald Hodges had saved him detailed a little of her association with the entertainment lawyer—that Erika had been in Los Angeles, that she'd worked there before returning to Philadelphia. What had happened that his brother knew about? He didn't want to ask, to reveal he didn't know, and if it was something Erika wanted to forget, he could respect that. Michael knew everyone had secrets. Erika was no different.

He had the sudden urge to talk to Erika. He'd enjoyed their time last night by the pool. They didn't know each other very well, but maybe they would by the end of the year and she would trust him enough to tell him about California. He might trust her enough to tell her about Abby.

"Michael, you didn't answer me. Is she really as beautiful as her pictures?" Peter asked.

Michael couldn't tell him how beautiful she was. A picture of Erika in her blue bathing suit crowded into his mind, and Erika smiling, Erika talking to him in the pool area, Erika at the cabin, her hand raised against the glare of the sun. "Yes, she's beautiful," he finally said.

Suddenly he wanted to leave. He wanted to see her, wanted to go back and have dinner with her. Michael stood up. "I have to go," he said.

"Michael," Peter stopped him. "When do we get to meet her?"

"I'm not sure I want her to ever meet you," Michael teased his youngest brother. He actually felt a tingle of jealousy. He felt more for Erika than he'd realized.

"How about bringing her to Thanksgiving dinner?" Bobby was saying when he brought his attention back. "It's at our house, but Mom is cooking."

"I'll let you know."

Michael left them. He didn't spend time thinking about his brothers and what they would discuss after he left. He wanted to know what Erika was doing. Had she missed him? He wanted to stop the car and call her, but he didn't. He drove straight to the house. It was too early for her to be home from the office.

Michael went to his rooms and dressed for the pool. Within minutes he was swimming laps in the Olympic-size bathtub. His mind was free and happy, anticipating her coming.

He was on lap number fifty-seven when he heard something and looked up. Erika stood at the end of the pool where he'd stood the night before. She had on a red business suit and high heeled shoes. It appeared to be the right color—with her hands on her hips, every line of her body said she was angry.

"How dare you," she said, moving toward him. "You let that story hit the papers and you disappeared into oblivion, leaving me alone to answer the questions."

"What story?"

"That's good," she grunted. "Really good. You heard my mother last night, and today the story is all over the television. My office has been besieged by calls and reporters and you . . . you swim." She stopped as her voice cracked. "I thought we were supposed to share everything. Wasn't that how you said it, *everything?*" She imitated him. "Where were you today, while I was sharing your infamy?"

Six

"What are you talking about?" Michael caught up with her halfway down the hall. Grabbing her arm, he turned her to face him. "What's happened?"

Erika tore her arm from his wet grasp. "What do you think happened? I was assaulted by an army of reporters over your status, and you weren't there to help."

"I didn't know."

"Where were you? Why didn't you tell me you weren't going to be in the office today?"

He couldn't tell her. It would sound trivial. He'd been on the receiving end of battering by the press, and he knew he should have been there. Last night after their swim he had known he needed to see his family. He had to go and tell them the news before they found out from someone else. According to Erika, he'd done that only moments before it became common knowledge. However, he hadn't been there when she needed him. That he regretted.

He hadn't been there for Abby, either. The thought suddenly popped into his head without warning.

"Tell me what happened," he said, pushing the thought aside.

Michael and Erika stood in the hall. The water dripping from his body formed a wet splatter on the light-colored rug, but he refused to postpone the interview to go for a towel.

Erika took a deep breath and looked at him. "Somehow the complete details of the will were discovered today, and my office filled up with reporters like a war room. I opened the door to find lights flashing in my face. People fired questions at me so fast I couldn't possibly have answered them even if I intended to do so." She turned, pacing back and forth. " 'Where is Mr. Lawrence?' they asked. 'Is it true he owns half this company? Is it true Carlton Lipton-Graves was his grandfather? Is it true the two of you are living together?' "

She stopped and stared at him as if waiting for him to say something. Before he could, she came to stand in front of him, anger making her vibrate.

"And where were you? Out somewhere, completely oblivious to the chaos going on in the office?" She answered her own question. "What do you think this is, some cabin where you can decide not to work if you don't want to? Well, Michael Lawrence, this is not the Maryland mountains. Your word means something here, and when you make a promise I expect it to be kept."

Michael stared at her. For some reason he had the impression she wasn't talking about something that had happened today, or even when Carlton died. Erika was angry, angry over something that happened far longer ago than this afternoon. He wondered if it had anything to do with what Peter had mentioned? Something that happened in California.

Michael folded his arms across his chest and waited for her to finish. "What did you do?" he asked quietly.

"I called security and had my secretary calling the police if they didn't vacate the building."

Michael hid his smile. He knew she was a gutsy woman, but she was frightened, too. He wanted to find out what was behind the anger, what had caused it, and he knew her day at work was only a catalyst that brought back painful memories.

"Why didn't you tell them the truth?"

"Truth!" she exploded. "They're not interested in the truth. They want sensationalism." Her hand flew up in disgust.

"They want a few words so they can misquote you and print lies because it makes better copy and sells more newspapers."

"Is that what they did to you?"

As if she'd turned to stone, Erika stopped. All motion about her ceased, and she stared at him with ice in her eyes. For a long moment she held his gaze. Then, turning on the balls of her feet, she strutted away from him. Michael watched for a moment, then followed her. He hadn't intended to deliver another blow. Obviously she'd had a bad day and he'd fueled it trying to find out something about her. It was an unfair tactic. How easily he'd done it didn't surprise him. He'd been trained to rout out concealed information, to find the truth wherever it lay, and without thinking he'd done that to Erika.

Erika started up the stairs at a trot, but she wanted to run. She wanted to dash up them at full sprint. She wanted all the reporters to leave her alone and she wanted to put distance between her and Michael Lawrence. Going straight to her room she slammed the door closed.

"Erika!" he called.

Disregarding her privacy Michael charged in after her.

He'd brought it all back. The memories of Bill Castle and the incessant press. Cameras pointing at her, flashes lighting in her face. The questions, the neverending, embarrassing questions that had her hiding in her own house. Everywhere she went people recognized her, whispered behind her back, until she could no longer stand it. If Carlton hadn't asked her to come home, she would have left Los Angeles, anyway. She'd held herself straight, refusing to let them get the better of her.

It was happening all over again. She'd thought the initial news of Carlton's death and her inheritance had come and gone, lost behind more sensational news than the passing of a rich old man. She didn't realize there was something about Michael that would have them hounding her again. Something about Michael and Frank Mason.

"Erika," Michael called again.

She turned to face him, her arms at her sides, her face blank and unreadable.

"When I left they were in the parking lot, waiting," she began. "They followed me home. I assume they're at the end of the driveway, probably with a full television crew, waiting until we come out and give them what they want."

Michael glanced through the window over her shoulder as if he could see the reporters from here. They were out there somewhere, on the other side of the beveled glass door, down the winding driveway and outside the wrought iron gate.

"Where did you go?" Erika asked him. Her voice had softened. She stared at him with hurt in her eyes. Michael felt guilty. He hadn't intended to have her take the full brunt of what he knew would happen. His heart constricted, and he knew he was going to take her in his arms. In a second he'd crossed the room and pulled her against his bare chest. His arms were around her, and with only a minimal amount of resistance she relaxed against him.

"I went home. I needed to talk to my brothers."

"Mother!" she pulled back, concluding this awful day had been the results of her mother's threat. "I forgot all about her. I've got words for her that will turn her roots grey." She went to pull out of his arms, but he stopped her.

"Not now," he whispered, placing his hands on either side of her face. He stared at her. Her eyes were huge and confused, but her gaze was direct. He understood—he was as confused as she. Between them something was happening and he didn't know if he wanted to stop it, or even if he could. Heat swirled around them, drying his skin and cocooning them in a world where only they existed. He lowered his head and brushed his mouth over hers. Her lips were full and soft, yielding. A sound crawled in his throat at the pleasure of her touch. He continued the easy, brushing motion. This could be his undoing. He'd been without a woman for a long time. And Erika wasn't just any woman. He didn't want just any woman. He wanted her. She'd been on his mind since the moment he saw her. Even without the motivation of thwarting Frank Mason, Michael wasn't sure he wouldn't have come to Philadelphia just to see her again.

It wouldn't take much for him to crush her against him, devour her mouth, peel this red suit from her brown body and take her on the bed only a few feet from where they stood.

He wouldn't do that. He *couldn't* do it. There was something about her that told him she was fragile and could easily break into a million pieces. He kissed her tenderly, cradling her head between his hands. She returned his kiss with equal gentleness, opening her mouth to his enticing persuasion, accepting the fullness of his tongue as it swept inside and tasted the sweetness of her being.

Her arms circled his waist, her hands spreading about his naked back with a silkiness that made him shiver with need. His body was warm, hot, melting, and hard. His lack of clothing left her in no doubt about his state of arousal. She was aroused, too. He felt it in the boneless wonder of her arms as their mouths left each other's and her head sank to his chest.

Michael had never experienced a kiss like this before. He'd known plenty of women. He understood passion and sex, uncontrolled and wild, but the tenderness she evoked in him was a new experience. With her in his arms he wanted more than kisses, more than sex. He wanted to be tender. He wanted to know her, understand her hurt and her compassion. She was different from every other woman he'd ever met. He wanted to understand how she could drive him crazy with her look. He wanted to protect her from the reporters outside and from the world that threatened her.

He'd thought he wanted to escape from the world, not interact with mankind or the entrapments that contact invariably caused, but with Erika he wanted to be her champion. She mattered. Why, he couldn't say. He hadn't known her long, but somehow her good opinion of him meant something.

He lifted her chin. Her eyes were full of passion and he knew he'd put it there. His body wanted hers. He wanted to bury himself inside her and make love the rest of the night. They could forget the reporters, forget their pasts, however bad they had been, and only live for the next few hours. But Michael wouldn't do that.

He would kiss her again. That he couldn't stop. Her look pulled his head down, and his mouth took hers. This time the passion he'd held in check fought for release. He kissed her hard, sliding his arms around her waist and pulling her body into close contact with him. His mouth devoured hers as his hands rode low on her hips, pulling her into intimate contact with him. He wouldn't make love to her, but he wanted her to know he could.

He heard the throaty sound of pleasure that escaped from her mouth into his, and he felt her body mold itself around him. He was losing it. In seconds he'd forget his vow and have her naked on the bed. Michael tore his mouth from hers. Her arms tightened around his neck, and he held her for another agonizing moment before pulling free.

He stared down at her, both of them trembling, both of them breathing raggedly. "Make no mistake about this, Erika," he said in a voice thick with emotion, "I want to make love to you." She started to say something. "Shhh . . ." He put his finger to her lips.

Her tongue darted out and licked his finger. Michael nearly lost his power of speech. A spiral of emotion fissured through him.

"Erika, this isn't part of our agreement. We're both rational people and we're awfully close to stepping across a line that hasn't been defined. We might want to think clearly before doing something we could both regret."

Erika sat in her office the next morning, one hand holding her head. For two nights straight she'd had little or no sleep. Her other hand gripped the coffee cup as if it were a lifeline. She drank the hot liquid, black. Usually she added sugar and cream, but this morning she needed something to cancel out the men with sledgehammers inside her head.

Michael hadn't been at breakfast today, either. Erika didn't know whether she should be glad or sad about his absence. He'd only postponed their next meeting. It had to take place sometime. The will pitted them together for the next twelve months. They'd only been together for forty-eight hours, and already they'd been only a hair away from being intimate.

They were strangers, she told herself. How could she act like this? She knew better, knew it was disastrous, but in his arms she didn't think . . . that was the problem. If she were to go on with this for the next year, she had to think clearly, and that meant staying away from him.

Michael was right. The agreement didn't call for them making love, and they certainly would have if he hadn't stopped them. She couldn't believe the way she'd acted. He'd kissed her and the only thing she'd been aware of was the dark heat of his skin, the smell of the dried water, and the contours of his chest. She pictured herself close to him, kissing his male nipples and removing the only barrier he wore between the world and his nakedness.

Erika shook her head. What was she doing? She needed to concentrate on sales levels, on strategy for increasing their market share ratios. But her concentration was gone. Just as it had been last night. One minute she was arguing with Michael over the reporters, and the next she'd been trying to climb inside him.

This time there was no doubt in her mind about his motive. On the mountain he'd been saying good-bye, and the other night he'd been comforting her, but last night, last night was raw, unleashed, sexual excitement, and she'd wanted him to take her to bed. She wanted him to make love to her. The urge was stronger than she'd ever known it could be. But he'd told her he'd regret it, regret making love to her.

Rejection! She knew it when she saw it. How many times would she set herself up for this kind of disappointment?

Hadn't she learned anything? Hadn't the trauma with Bill taught her to tread lightly? Or the years with her mother, a woman who didn't want her and had never done one thing but push her away? Obviously, she hadn't, if it took so little provocation and even a smaller amount of resistance on her part before she was lost in Michael's arms.

"Erika?"

She heard her name. Heard Michael's voice. Her head snapped up. He was standing in front of her desk. Erika clenched her teeth. She'd hadn't heard him come in, but a quick glance at the door connecting their offices told her he'd opened it and come inside. How long had he been there?

"Are you all right?"

"I'm fine," she said, trying for a smile. She looked at him. Unlike her, he appeared fresh and rested this morning. A flash of anger went through her. The kiss they'd shared had to have some effect on him, but he must know how to handle the situation better than she did. She admitted she didn't have much experience. Barring Bill, there had only been three other men in her life, and she'd handled none of those relationships well.

"I called a press conference for ten o'clock this morning."

"You what!" She stood up so fast her chair careened backward and hit the wall.

"We can't let them hound us. I know what it's like . . . and hiding doesn't work. It only intrigues them more. If you're not up to it, I'll handle it alone, but I'd really like to have you there."

Erika stared straight at him. She hated the press. There were things Michael didn't know. If she went to that conference they'd drag her through the Bill Castle story again. She'd have to sit there and go through the humiliating questions. She'd have to remember that her fiancé married another woman. Bill Castle was as famous as some of the rock stars he represented. His name was a household word. How could the press let her get away without asking for every intimate detail of her relationship with him?

"Why can't we just issue a press release?" she asked, knowing it wouldn't be enough to satisfy the hungry mob.

"If I thought that would work I'd suggest it, but after seeing them as I left this morning I know that won't keep them from following us around. The only way to get rid of them is to give them what they want."

"They want blood!" she told him, anger stealing into her voice. *Mine,* she added to herself.

"It's not going to be easy," Michael said. "They're bound to bring up Frank Mason."

Frank Mason was nothing compared to William Castle. Erika let out a sigh. When Carlton died she'd avoided the press, but it didn't deter them. They'd hounded her until she finally granted an exclusive interview to a lesser known reporter whom she figured wouldn't have the gall to ask her about Bill.

She'd been wrong.

"More than likely, they're also going to remember your California incident."

She stared at him. "You know about that?" Her throat was dry. A pain lodged in her chest.

Michael shook his head. "My brother mentioned it yesterday. I let him think I knew what he was talking about."

He waited for her to explain. She'd only heard a few questions yesterday about Michael and Frank Mason having a history together. She didn't know the truth of it. But he was asking her to tell him why she'd left California.

"I was engaged to Bill Castle." She checked to see if he recognized Bill's name. Anyone who knew popular music knew of Bill Castle.

"I've heard of him," Michael confirmed.

"He ran off and married my secretary," she said without emotion. Her stare never left his face. She couldn't see any change in his features—pity, concern, or judgment. "The press followed me everywhere. I became a prisoner in my own house. Every time Bill made the news, someone tried to interview me." Erika dropped her gaze to the desk, remembering the hounding nature of the unrelenting press. "They'll ask intimate questions, pry into my life as if they had a right. I'm not sure I want to go through that again."

Michael admired her. She didn't say she couldn't go through it, just that she didn't want to. He didn't want to go through it again, either, but he knew neither of them had a choice. The press was an estate unto itself. Like the army, it would continue to come. The longer the two of them avoided the media, the more people would be assigned to find out the truth.

If they didn't want a small story to escalate into front page news, they had to go through the bad and get it over with.

"This time you won't be alone, Erika," Michael said. "Carlton left us everything to share. We can begin with the press."

She looked at him with a hardness in her eyes. Michael held her gaze until it softened.

"Neither will you," she said.

Michael squeezed Erika's hand as they stood outside the seminar room where the reporters had assembled.

"Let's get it over with," she said.

He took a deep breath and nodded. Michael wasn't looking forward to this, either, but he'd run away before and he refused to do it again. He knew they'd ask questions about Frank Mason and Abby. As much as that would bring back memories, he had to get through it.

Erika grasped the doorknob and turned it. The door swung inward and she walked through. He followed her. Conversation, which had been at a thirty decibel level, deceased to zero. For the space of a moment no one said a word. Then they all tried to speak at once. Michael couldn't make out any questions, but he could hear his name and Erika's being shouted from the sea of suits, cameras, and microphones.

Without a word he and Erika took seats in front of the crowd and waited for them to be seated. The room returned to order and Michael spoke.

"Good morning." He cleared his throat, adjusting the microphone. "I'm glad so many of you could make it on such short notice." A ripple of laughter went through the room.

He glanced at Erika. Her expression was professional, giving nothing away as to how she really felt—which, Michael knew, was scared as a kid on her first day at kindergarten. He felt much the same way, knowing that behind more than one of the many faces in the audience lurked the questions he didn't want to answer.

"I'd like to say something before we answer your questions," he went on. "You all know the terms of the will, if today's papers can be believed." Another ripple of laughter. "I have confirmed to my satisfaction that Carlton Lipton-Graves was my grandfather." He expected a reaction, but all he saw was the nodding of a few heads. "His legacy to Ms. St. James and myself is that we share the running of Graves Enterprises. We have discussed this." He looked again at Erika. Her gaze met his this time. She nodded her confirmation. Somehow he thought her actions reflected a well orchestrated script. Maybe she was relaxing. "Ms. St. James and I plan to fulfill the outstanding contracts of Graves Enterprises and to lead this corporation into the twenty-first century."

Erika turned to look at him. Questions were in her eyes. Michael didn't have anything more to say. He knew he should defer to her, but he wasn't sure she was ready, especially after the way she looked at him. He'd called this conference. He had time to prepare for it. She'd only had ten minutes before she had to go on.

"I'd like to add something," she said, surprising him. He kept all expression off his face, as if they had decided beforehand how to handle the press. "Mr. Lawrence and I have not completely worked through all the details of responsibility, but like any growing organization we'll find the right fit."

She's a trooper, Michael thought. Her voice was controlled, authoritative, and calm. She spoke as if she gave orders, and knew how to get results.

"Now, if there are any questions concerning the business and our roles in it, we'll be glad to answer them."

He almost smiled. She was good, cunning. She'd told them to stick to the point. Of course, he knew they wouldn't, but it would give them a way of deflecting unwanted questions. For as much as she'd feared this arena, Michael somehow didn't think Erika was.

She nodded at a man with his hand raised.

"Did you and Mr. Lawrence really inherit over forty million dollars?"

Erika smiled, a wide grin that reached her eyes. The first question generally set the tone for the rest of the meeting. Michael was grateful to the man.

"Our lawyers are still determining the exact amount of the estate. However, I'm sure the company is in sound financial condition. The third quarter reports will be available to you in a few weeks, and we're expecting to post a profit for the year."

Deflection One.

"Mr. Lawrence, you're a lawyer. Are you taking over the legal affairs of the company?"

"While there is a position available for a general counsel, the requirements are those of corporate law. My expertise in law is in another area."

Michael thought he did well, but he knew there was a gaping hole in his answer. If there was a smart reporter out there, he or she had a perfect opening to ask him the Frank Mason questions.

They didn't come. For half an hour the questions were business oriented, and Michael began to feel they were going to pass this without running into any problems.

Then a man rose from the back of the room. "Ms. St. James, did you know that Bill Castle's marriage is on the rocks, and he's mentioned you in several recent interviews?"

"I haven't spoken to Mr. Castle in over a year." She paused. "And, as you probably already know, Mr. Castle didn't keep me informed of intentions when we were . . . an item." Many in the room laughed, and Erika cut the reporter a look that said he should not pursue that line of questioning.

Unfortunately, the door had been opened, and the entire room seemed to pour through it. Question after question dragged out details Michael was sure she would just as soon forget. But she kept up with them, never flinching, answering the questions with wit and professionalism, managing to keep them from making her look like a fool.

"Were you surprised to find Mr. Castle had married your secretary?"

"No, Mr. Lahey." She obviously knew this reporter. "I usually discuss the marriage plans of my fiancés when they decide to marry other women."

Uproarious laughter spread through the room. Erika also smiled. Michael wanted to laugh out loud, but he controlled it.

His turn came as soon as the laughter abated. A pretty, young reporter in the front row rose and looked directly at him. He could tell. She was the smart one he'd thought of earlier.

"Mr. Lawrence." She looked directly at him. He held her stare, knowing this was his turning point. He'd either get through the rough part or he'd crash and burn right here. "Did Frank Mason know he was a contingent beneficiary?"

"I have no idea," he answered truthfully.

"Have you had any contact with him?"

"Not since that last day in court."

"Frank Mason vowed to make you and everyone else pay for sending him away."

"I heard that," Michael said. "I never saw Frank in person after his children . . . died." Michael couldn't help the slight catch in his voice.

"We're getting a little off the mark," Erika interjected. "Could we bring the discussion—"

"Did you know," the woman interrupted Erika, "that Frank escaped his prison and is on the run?"

Michael's heart missed a beat. How could he escape? He was psychotic. Why wasn't he watched every moment, awake or asleep? He appeared normal, logical, even rational, but he wasn't. He was the most dangerous man Michael had ever come across, and he'd met some beauties. He'd been in and out of court with some of the lowlifes of society, men who beat their wives and girlfriends, women who abused or neglected their children. But when he'd met Frank, he'd thought the man was sincere. He'd taken his custody case, because he appeared to be genuinely in pain at the loss of his marriage and the forced estrangement from his children. Michael had fought hard for Frank and he'd won, but Frank had duped him in the worst way, and now four people were dead. He'd told him lie after lie, and Michael had drunk them in like a smooth cognac. The man seemed sincere, charming, but it was an act. His true colors were shown two weeks after Michael had successfully petitioned the court to give him full custody of his three children. He'd taken them away from his crying ex-wife, and at their first visitation meeting he'd put bullets through their heads. Weeks later, in a state of depression, Abby had taken her own life. Michael was left to deal with the aftereffects of his actions.

How the hell could Frank have escaped?

Seven

Champagne, caviar, crystal wineglasses, diamond rings—the accoutrements of the rich and famous. Well, the rich and famous died exactly like the poor and destitute. Frank Mason refilled his glass and dropped the empty bottle into the brown paper bag next to him. He sat on the boardwalk, far away from East Brunswick, where he'd completed his task. The place was deserted, the T-shirt, souvenir, and food stores closed for the season. Frank was alone, remembering the Gilfords. Angela and Jason Gilford. Angela had been Abby's lawyer. She'd said some pretty horrible things about him, brought out all the terrible things that had happened in his marriage. He couldn't forgive her for that.

She'd pleaded for her life, begged him. Frank smiled. She'd been wearing a purple sweater, looking regal and aristocratic, just as she'd looked in court. Well, she'd gotten hers, and that husband of hers, too. They both lay in their East Brunswick house with the high ceiling and walls of glass in the entryway, dead as scared mice, while he sat here, drinking their champagne and eating their caviar.

He dropped the crystal glass into the bag. It clinked against the empty Dom Perignon bottle and broke. Frank pushed the paper bag down until the plastic one covered it completely. Then he tied the end of the plastic bag and stood up. He'd throw the bag in a river. It was already weighted down with stones. The ocean wasn't as good as a river. A river didn't have waves, or adhere to the changing tides. The ocean could throw it back, wash it ashore, but in a river it would sink for all time. And even if it were found, he'd be safe. He knew fingerprints were mostly water, and that water would wash them away, but he hadn't left any. There was nothing in the bag to connect him with Angela and Jason Gilford.

He headed for his car and his next target.

"Who's Frank Mason?" Erika asked the moment she and Michael left the conference room. She recognized his name as the contingent beneficiary, and had made a note to find out who he was while she was trying to find Michael last month. When Michael had shown up she'd forgotten about Frank.

"I'd rather not talk about him," Michael said.

Erika glanced sideways as they walked back to her office. Michael had visibly stiffened when the reporter interrupted her and told him Frank had escaped. She hadn't known Michael very long, but she recognized the tight posture of a man who was retreating into himself. She didn't want that to happen.

Who was Frank Mason and what did he have to do with Michael? Where had he escaped from? What had happened in court?

At the door to his office, Michael left her without a word. She watched him enter. He was tense, as if every nerve in his body had coiled into a tight spring. Erika wondered if she should go to him. She thought he needed someone to talk to, but she didn't know if she should interrupt or let him work it out himself. It would have helped her if he'd told her what he and Frank Mason had in common.

Erika opened the door to her own office. Inside she called Carlton's attorney, Steven Chambers.

"Steven." She smiled when his voice came over the line. "It's Erika St. James."

"How are things going?"

She knew he was asking how she and Michael were getting

on. "We're slowly becoming comfortable with each other," she lied.

"Then what can I do for you?"

Steven was great at coming to the point. He didn't have time to waste, not even on clients who paid him well.

"I wonder if you could hire that private investigator again."

"What for?"

"I want to find out about Frank Mason."

"Frank Mason?" he repeated.

"He was the contingent beneficiary in Carlton's will," she said, hoping Steven would know something and volunteer the information she was seeking. "Do you know who he is?"

"I was surprised when Carlton wrote him into the will, especially after what happened."

"Steven," she said, trying to keep the agitation out of her voice. "What happened?"

"Michael Lawrence was Frank's attorney in a child custody suit. The case went on for weeks, and was quite notorious in this part of the state." Steven went on to relate the events of the case. Erika listened in open-mouthed horror as he related the reasons that had caused Michael to escape from the world and retreat to the Maryland mountains.

"So you think the will was Carlton's way of getting him to return to the world he'd rejected?"

"He never told me that, but what else can I infer?"

"Frank's escaped."

"My God!" he said. "When?" Steven was nearly as surprised as Michael had been.

"I don't know. A reporter told us this morning at a press conference. Michael didn't take the news well."

"I imagine he wouldn't," Steven said. "The press hounded him after the children were killed. Some of the not so ethical papers had blaring headlines blaming Lawrence for what happened to the Mason children, and to Frank's ex-wife."

Erika remembered her own moment of notorious fame. She couldn't blame Michael for retreating to the mountains. She'd done practically the same thing in returning to Philadelphia. Her return had been after the press stopped pursuing her, but she gathered Michael had bailed out before that.

"Erika," Steven said, calling her back.

"Do you still want me to hire an investigator?"

"No," she said. Steven had told her what she needed to know. "Thank you." She hung up the phone and stared at the door to Michael's office. The information she'd just heard told her a lot about the man behind that door. He felt deeply about what he'd done. So deeply that he'd turned his back on his profession and his family and retreated to a lonely mountain where he could be alone.

For a year he was there with only his thoughts and the nightmares. Since the storekeeper, Mr. Hodges, had told her Michael kept to himself, she knew today's news must have hit raw nerves. In the mountains he'd been alone, but now he was on the other side of that door with his thoughts of Frank Mason and what his actions had led to, however indirectly.

Erika went to the door of Michael's office. Her hand curled around the brass knob, and she hesitated. Opening the carved oak door that separated their offices, she heard him speaking and realized he was on the phone.

"Is he all right?" Panic was evident in the voice she heard. While eavesdropping wasn't Erika's usual method of gaining information, she was concerned about Michael after the surprising news he'd received at the press conference.

Erika pushed the door open. Michael stood, clutching the phone, his back to her, his body stiff.

"Where?" he asked.

Rapidly he scribbled something on a piece of paper.

"I'll be right there." Hanging the phone up, Michael grabbed his coat and headed for the door.

"Michael?" Erika came forward. Something scared her. "Is everything all right?"

He faced her. "A friend of mine is in the hospital. I have to go."

Erika wondered who she was. A surprised streak of jealousy raced through her at the way he'd stood, and the way he was about to run out. She wondered if he'd run to her this fast if she were ill. Immediately she felt ashamed of herself.

"Is there anything I can do to help?"

The corners of Michael's mouth turned up slightly and he walked over to her.

"Thank you. I don't know how bad he is yet."

It was a he. She couldn't account for the relief that flashed through her.

"Will you call me when you know?"

A brief smile curved his lips again. His hand came up and touched her cheek. He nodded.

Erika put her hand where his had been when he left the room. Two scares in a short period of time. She wondered if he were really all right. First the trauma of Frank Mason, and then a friend suddenly taking sick.

Michael was certainly a complex man. She recognized the strained look on his face. He was worried—about his friend, or the press conference revelation?

She wanted to know him, but he pushed her back each time she got close to him.

Last night he'd kissed her so tenderly she'd thought her feet would never touch the ground again. Then he'd rejected her, walked away, leaving her alone, lonely, and without an understanding of what had just happened to them.

This morning she was more in control, and more confused than she ever thought she'd be. Sharing everything with Michael was light years more complicated than Carlton could have possibly known, if his only intention was to get Michael off that mountain. She wondered if Carlton had thought about her, about the effect Michael's personality and constant presence would have on her.

Had Carlton planned this? Was he trying to manipulate them both? Michael was off the mountain, and she—who'd vowed never again to fall in love—was falling in love with Carlton's grandson.

The University of Pennsylvania Medical Center housed a first class trauma center. A tan brick structure, built to be functional rather than aesthetically beautiful, it covered several blocks of prime real estate. Michael pulled into a parking space in the hospital garage and made his way to reception.

"How do I get to ICU?" he asked a young, blond woman in a pink and white striped jumper.

"Follow the blue arrows." She pointed to the wall on her left. Michael's gaze followed her finger. The pale yellow wall was bisected by a blue, green, and brown stripe which ran to the end of the room and disappeared through a windowed door.

Michael followed the lines on the walls through a maze of hallways that took him into another building before ending at a set of tan-colored doors.

Pounding in his ears, his heart seemed to stop as he scanned the beds for Malick Wainscott. Michael approached him slowly, breath coming in shallow puffs.

Malick lay under a white sheet, pale as kindergarten paste. His silver hair was tousled against the pillow. Michael stood stock still while tubes dripped clear solutions into his friend's arms and machines beeped around him, monitoring his vital signs. Oxygen tubing was wrapped over his ears and around his face to help him breathe.

"Malick?" His voice croaked. Malick didn't stir. Clearing his throat Michael called him again.

Malick opened his eyes and closed them. A second later he opened them again. A frown creased his brow and his eyelids closed. Michael waited, breathing easier now that he'd confirmed his friend was still alive.

Stepping forward, Michael leaned over the bed. "Malick," he called.

Malick opened his eyes.

"Michael, you made it," Malick said in a weak voice.

"What are you doing here?" Michael tried to cover his concern with a joke.

"I needed a rest." Malick returned his playfulness, but Michael could see the strain in his face and the effort it took for him to talk.

"Don't talk," he said. "Go back to sleep. It's probably good for you."

Malick didn't argue with him. He closed his eyes and was immediately asleep. Michael stayed for a few minutes, noticing the even breathing and the steady sound of the machines flanking his bed. Leaving the room, he went to the nurse's station.

"May I speak to the doctor in charge of Malick Wainscott's case?"

"Are you related to him?" the white-clad woman asked.

"I'm as close to a relative as he has."

"May I have your name, please?"

"Michael Lawrence."

"One moment, please." She dialed a number and spoke into the mouthpiece. When she replaced the receiver she said, "Dr. Washington will be with you in a moment."

Michael paced the floor, waiting for the doctor to arrive. He turned back, glancing into Malick's room. He slept undisturbed.

"Mr. Lawrence?"

Michael turned toward the voice. A black man about his own age faced him. He had dark, steady eyes, and kept one hand on the folded stethoscope in his pocket.

"I'm Dr. Washington."

"I'm Malick Wainscott's friend. He has no relatives. Could you tell me how he is?"

Dr. Washington walked toward the exit and Michael fell into step with him. They crossed the stenciled hall and went into an office. The doctor sat down behind the desk and Michael took one of the two chairs in front of it.

"In simple language, Mr. Wainscott has had a mild heart attack. That's an area between minor and massive. It's a serious condition. The walls of his heart are not damaged, but his stress factors are very high." He paused. Michael thought he was waiting for the familiar family reaction, which Michael held. He'd felt his stomach fall, his hands went cold, and he wanted to grip the arms of the chair in which he sat, but didn't want to admit that Malick might not recover. "We think with proper rest and less stress he will recover," the doctor went on.

Michael let go of his breath. "Thank God," he said wiping his hand down his face.

"We're keeping him in ICU for a few more days, just to make sure he responds to the medication and regains his strength."

Michael was relieved. Malick was a mainstay in his life. He'd never thought of him dying. They'd been friends since his days at Catholic University Law School where Malick had taught him Criminal Law. Michael assumed he would be around for a long time. Michael rarely thought about the differences in their ages. Malick was in his late sixties, still young by today's standards. This sudden attack let him know how mortal Malick was.

"Is there anything else I should know?" Michael asked the doctor.

"Not that I can think of. We're doing everything we can."

"Thank you." Michael stood, shaking hands with the doctor. He left the office and returned to sit with his friend. Malick slept for an hour while Michael waited. Nurses came in and changed his IV bag. The equipment continually monitored his condition with monotonous precision.

Michael thought of Erika and knew how she must have felt when Carlton was ill. He was helpless. There was nothing he could do to help his friend.

Malick woke just before dark. "Michael, is that you?" he asked. His voice was groggy and slurred. "You're still here."

He remembered he'd been there before. Michael took that

as a good sign. "I thought you'd want company when you woke." Michael achieved lightness this time.

"You'd better go home," Malick said. "Erika might need you."

He remembered he hadn't called her, and she didn't know which hospital he'd gone to.

"Erika is a strong woman. She can handle anything that comes her way." He was suddenly surprised by his character assessment. Erika *was* strong, and he knew she could handle things without him. Hadn't she proved that this morning, when the reporters had brought up her past? Then she'd stepped in and tried to bring the discussion back to business when the attack turned to him. She'd defended him, even when she didn't know the impact of the reporter's revelation.

When she'd asked him to explain he'd put her off. He glanced at Malick, who'd fallen asleep again. He needed to call Erika. He admired her, and right now he wanted to hear her voice.

Darkness had fallen and only a small lamp illuminated a corner in Malick Wainscott's ICU cubicle. Erika stood in the doorway, her body casting a shadow on the floor. Michael looked up and saw her.

He sat on the opposite side of the room in the darkness. In a single movement he was on his feet, but he didn't come toward her. She couldn't see his expression in the darkness, and uncertainty about invading his privacy caught her.

"I—I'm sorry," she stammered. "I thought you might need some company." When he'd left the office this morning on the heels of the press conference, she'd been concerned.

For an awkward moment they stared at each other. Then Erika took a step forward. Michael reached for her and she put her hand in his. His grip was surprisingly strong. Erika forced her gaze to the sleeping figure in the bed. Michael must be extremely worried about him if he'd stayed here all afternoon.

The man reminded her of Carlton. He didn't look like him, but he was small and white, and in a medical bed. This was the first time Erika had been in a hospital since Carlton died, and she had the feeling of death about her. Fear gripped her and she clamped her teeth down on her lower lip. She'd come here for Michael, to keep him from the feelings she'd lived with for the long year before Carlton's death. He'd had nurses in the house twenty-four hours a day and the staff was always present, but she'd felt alone. She'd come so Michael wouldn't feel lonely.

"How did you know where I was?" he asked, his voice nearly disembodied in the darkened room.

She glanced at him. "Your secretary told me. When the call came in they identified it as the ICU department at the University of Pennsylvania Hospital."

Michael nodded and continued to hold her hand.

"Is he a good friend?"

"He was one of my law school professors. After I graduated we kept in touch. He's my best friend."

Erika stepped closer and curled her hand in his. "Have you eaten?" she asked, already knowing he'd sat there since he arrived, keeping vigil.

Michael shook his head.

"Would you like me to get you something?"

Michael stared at her for a moment.

"We could go to the hospital cafeteria," she suggested. "I know you haven't left this room since you arrived. The walk will do you good, and you have to eat."

Michael slipped his arm inside her coat. It went around her waist and he pulled her to him. Erika went easily, turning herself toward his body. He needed someone to hold onto. She knew the feeling, and she was glad she was there. She put her arms around him and held him for a moment. She heard his sigh as warm breath against her neck. His arms tightened, and she felt as if he were a small boy needing his mother. Erika didn't mind. She let him hold her until he loosened his grip and stepped back.

"Something to eat might be a good idea," he said.

Minutes later they sat in the hospital cafeteria, a room with sterile white formica tables and blue and white tiled walls. Before them sat buff-colored trays with a hospital version of a turkey club sandwich, hot coffee, and a piece of apple pie. Michael ate in silence, finishing all the food on his plate.

"Talk to me, Michael," Erika said. "I understand what you're going through. I went through it with your grandfather."

He didn't answer immediately. The moment stretched on and Erika didn't think he was going to answer her. Michael got up and took her cup and his. He refilled them both and returned to the table.

"I suppose Malick was my Carlton. We met when I was in law school. I was a young, brash kid who thought I knew everything." He laughed at what must have been a memory of a younger Michael. "Malick quickly made me aware of how little I actually did know." Michael paused, his gaze staring through Erika as if he'd retreated into a past life. "After that he became my unofficial mentor and advisor. We spent hours discussing cases, present and past, politics, art, music. I don't think there's any subject we haven't covered."

Erika wondered if that included her.

"By the time I graduated I was renting a room in his house." Michael laughed and sipped his coffee. "I never actually paid for that room. It was kind of an agreement. I had a lease, but Malick never accepted the money. He said I was a poor law student and I should use the money to buy books."

Erika smiled at him. "Does he still teach law?" She knew from the investigative report Steven Chambers had given her that Michael had gone to Catholic University Law School in Washington, D. C.

"Yes." Michael nodded. "Five years ago he took a job here." Michael spread his hands, encompassing the room. "The University of Pennsylvania had tried to get him to come for years. Finally they made an offer he accepted."

"You must have been practicing by then."

"I was. My partner and I began our firm in New Brunswick. I'd go down to D.C. three or four times a year and stay with him, and we'd talk long into the night. He'd return the favor by coming to New Jersey. When Malick moved to Philadelphia, we met even more regularly."

"Is he going to be all right?" Erika asked the question softly. Michael leaned back in his chair.

"The doctor says he should recover."

Erika could hear the "but" in that statement. Impulsively she reached across the table and took his hand. He caught it and squeezed. "I'm sure he'll be fine," Erika told him.

As they walked back to ICU, Erika thought of the man next to her. This morning they'd sat before news media people, and tonight he stood vigil over a friend's bedside. She recognized there were many sides to Michael Lawrence, the man. Erika thought of the rude mountain man and tried to compare him with the tenderhearted one who held her hand. He had strength and compassion, and Erika had never met anyone like him.

Malick was awake when they entered the room. He looked tired, his eyes half open and his shock of white hair mussed by the pillow. Erika preceded Michael.

"You . . . must . . . be Erika." He spoke slowly and tried to smile. Erika returned it. Surprisingly, her eyes filled with moisture. "I am very pleased . . . to meet . . . you."

"How do you feel?" she asked.

"Better," he said, yet somehow she knew he wasn't telling her the whole truth.

"How are you and Michael getting along?"

Erika stopped herself from looking at Michael although he still held onto her hand. Michael had talked to him about her. She wondered what he'd told him. Did he know about their kiss?

"We're," she said, clearing her throat, "we're having growing pains, but I'm sure we can work them out."

"Growing pains." He grunted, trying to laugh. "Michael will do that to you," he said, as if talking about a child. "But hang in there. He's worth it."

Erika felt strange. Why had he said that? It sounded as if they were engaged. Erika wanted to pull her hand free, but it would look too obvious.

"Malick, you're embarrassing her," Michael said, dropping her hand to move closer to the bedside.

A nurse came in then and told them visiting hours were over. Michael was reluctant to leave.

"Go, Michael. There's no reason for you to sit here watching me sleep. You've been here for hours. Go home."

Malick sounded tired and Michael looked at Erika. He seemed to need her approval. She nodded.

"I'll come back tomorrow," Michael told him.

"It was good meeting you, Malick." Erika took his hand and squeezed it.

"She's prettier than her pictures," Malick said, looking at Michael.

Eight

Jilted Fiancée And Mason Children Lawyer Head Graves Enterprises. The headline greeted Erika as she set her briefcase on the polished surface of her desk the next morning. So much had happened last night that she'd nearly forgotten about the press conference yesterday morning. The story in the supermarket rag detailed just enough of the facts of her engagement to Bill Castle and of Michael's involvement in the custody battle for the Mason children to keep them from being sued. It wasn't that the facts were distorted that bothered her so much as the tone of the article, and the implication that they were incompetent to head the conglomerate.

Erika picked up the paper with two fingers and dropped it in the trash can as if it contained three-day-old fish. She didn't expect the papers to be kind to them. Her history didn't regard her kindly and reporters wanted to sell papers, just as the pharmaceutical division wanted to sell medicine. The difference was that her products were ethical. They had been developed, tested, gone through clinical trials, and approved by the Food and Drug Administration before being given to the public. Newspapers were supposed to print the truth, keep the public informed of the facts, but she knew in her case the facts had been distorted.

Erika looked at the letters on her desk. Most of them were marked *Personal*. She didn't recognize the return addresses. Taking a letter opener, she slit the first one and pulled out a single sheet of paper. It was a proposal. Someone actually asked her to marry him. How on earth had word gotten out so quickly? Then she remembered television. She'd never turned the set on yesterday.

The second letter was an attack on her and Michael. It was unsigned. The next one held another proposal, this time for Michael. She put that one aside to give to him. The mail didn't surprise her. She'd gotten the same kind of mail after Bill Castle jilted her. Proposals, attacks, people telling her she was the real winner in that triangle. Except for the ones addressed to Michael, she dropped them all in the trash and decided to go for coffee before reading the other newspapers.

The small kitchenette was crowded with people discussing the days' news when she walked in. Her entrance ended the conversations, each person suddenly remembering a previous engagement requiring their immediate attention. Filling her cup, she knew it was time to do damage control. Michael might not have wanted to go on a site visit, but it was time she left her ivory tower and returned to the trenches.

Back in her office, she saw the *Inquirer* had been kinder to her. *Financial Wizard Has Hollywood Past,* the banner over the two columns read. They'd put her story on the financial page, listed her training, her previous work experience, her history with Graves Enterprises, but had led with her broken engagement to Bill Castle. Michael's had been about the same as hers, with the exception related to his being Carlton's grandson. *Black Lawyer Heir Graves Enterprises* topped his story.

Sipping her coffee, she dropped that paper into the wastebasket, too, wondering if Michael had seen them yet. They seemed to be on different schedules. He wasn't at breakfast and she thought he might need the rest after spending yesterday at the hospital. He still looked tired and he was obviously worried about his friend. She wondered if he were still having nightmares.

A tap sounded on her door. She looked up as it opened. Michael strolled in, looking refreshed, better than she'd seen him since they met. He came straight toward her, a cup of coffee in his hand.

"Have you seen the papers?"

"Yes." she nodded, glancing toward the trashbasket.

"The stories could use some editing, but the photos were good." He made light of the misleading facts.

"You're in rare form this morning. I suppose you're going to tell me it'll pass in a few days."

"It will." Michael lounged in the chair. "Something else will come along and we'll be old news."

"I certainly couldn't tell by that pack of wolves that met me as I drove out of the gates, and the one that met me at the elevators."

Michael held his cup in both hands and drank, but his eyes were trained on her. Erika wanted to smile, but forced herself to keep a straight face.

She changed the subject. "How's Malick this morning?"

"He's wide awake and talkative."

Erika understood Michael's mood. Yesterday his friend had been close to death, but today Malick was recovering. She'd gone through the same stages with Carlton, but in the end Carlton had died. A sudden emptiness developed in her. She missed Carlton. Her talks with him were some of the best. Michael had the same kind of relationship with Malick Wainscott. She envied him.

"Are you leaving to go see him?"

"I'll go tonight. I thought I'd stay around here and settle in. I see my desk is piled high with books about the company."

"I hope you don't mind. I think it helps when you know the history of where we've been and where we plan to go."

Michael nodded.

"Because of the newspaper reports, I think it would be a good idea to take a stroll through the company. Would you like to come with me?"

By mutual consent they left Erika's office and began a slow process of walking through the various departments. Michael had met most of the vice presidents, but he didn't know the majority of the people who made Graves Enterprises a successful company. Erika introduced him to most of the people they came into contact with, taking time to answer their questions and concerns about what they'd read in the papers. This was so much more personal than calling a conference. Erika truly liked the people who worked for Graves. She knew most of them by name, and with some she even knew their families' names.

Michael was charming, answering questions in a quiet, non-confrontational manner. Erika noticed he had a wonderful memory for names. When introduced to a group of people, he managed to remember all their names and address them that way. She heard positive whispers each time they passed from one department to another.

The damage hadn't been as bad as Erika'd thought it might. The publicity department staff was doing a fine job of answering questions and issuing press releases about the direction of the company. Michael had calmed the fears of the people they talked to. All she had to do was keep a calm head, no matter how much she disliked being the center of media attention.

The tour ended in Jeff Rivers' area. The usually smiling face of the chief financial officer was grim this morning.

"I need to see you, Erika," he said after he'd shaken Michael's hand and introduced him to some of the members in his department.

Erika stared at him. His blue eyes had a nervous look. Erika walked into his office. Michael and Jeff followed her. They took seats at the conference table, which sat in the corner between two sets of windows. The day was bright and sunny, but Erika knew the coming news wouldn't be good.

"How many more?" she asked.

"Ten thousand," Jeff answered.

Erika stared at him.

"Ten thousand what?" Michael asked.

Erika turned to face Michael. "Shares of stock. For the last several months there's been increased activity in the number of shares of Graves stock trading the market. Jeff seems to think there could be a takeover in the making."

"Who's it registered to?"

"We don't know. The shares are made to companies that collapse, and then are transferred to another name. As soon as we find them, they move. It's as if someone is making a job of keeping us out of the loop."

"Do they have enough shares for control?" Michael asked.

"Not yet."

"Can you counter them by exercising options? I remember the lawyers saying something about that."

"We're locked out. Until our year is up we can't exercise any options, sell any current shares, or buy any more on the open market."

"I don't understand. Why would Carlton do that?"

"Money, Erika, like poverty, is one of life's true burdens." Michael looked confused.

"It was one of Carlton's favorite sayings," she explained. "He felt that too much money too soon didn't give a person enough time to learn how to handle it. By preventing us from using too much power, he took out our ability to amass large amounts of cash."

"It's also a safeguard," Jeff explained. "Carlton ran this company for decades. He knew his death could trigger all kinds of stock activity. To prevent you two from creating a decline in stock value, he took the options out until you were fully aware of the ups and downs of the market."

"Unfortunately," Michael said. "He didn't consider that by tying our hands he might make it easy for someone else to step in and take over, while we stand by helplessly."

"They won't be able to take over—" Erika explained, "between us we have control of the company—but unexpected activity can create either good or ill."

"How so?" Michael asked.

"An unwanted shareholder can force his way onto the board,

and once there create havoc by arguing against programs, swaying other board members, holding up discussion, being generally disagreeable," Jeff answered.

"But whoever it is can't really do anything?"

"That's correct," Erika said. "On the board he can't do anything, but the activity in the stock market could cause the stock to drop in price."

"Wouldn't it cause it to go up, if activity is suddenly increased?"

"Maybe," Jeff said. "The market is so fickle that it's difficult to predict what will happen. Even with the solid foundation Graves Enterprises has, people are still uncertain about its continued success since Carlton's death. Sudden activity in the market and rumor could cause our customers to begin buying from our competitors."

"So even if this phantom stockholder isn't trying to gain access to the board, he could erode market share and ruin the company."

"Exactly," Erika said.

"So what are we doing about it?"

"First, we don't even know if there is a real threat. If we're wrong, we want to be on the cautious side."

Michael nodded.

"We have a broker tracking the buying and selling," Erika went on. "So far the number of shares moved in one day clouds the fact that a single individual is buying in great numbers. We don't want the information to get out to the financial community, or it could create the very thing Carlton wanted to avoid."

"You're not going to be able to hide this for long," Michael told them.

"I'm surprised we've been able to keep it covered this long," Erika agreed. "Stock analysts are very astute. Graves Enterprises is no mom-and-pop operation. Like those reporters yesterday, there is some smart analyst out there tracking the buying and selling patterns, looking for his chance to be the next financial wizard on Wall Street. With the introduction of you, as Carlton's grandson, and me as . . . as part of the Hollywood scene, they're probably going to keep keen records on transactions as a measurement of our ability to run a company this large."

"How much time would you estimate we have?"

"Two weeks," Jeff said. "Three, if we're lucky."

The thought of a possible takeover was still on Michael's mind when he walked into the hospital later that day. He wanted to talk to Malick. SEC regulations weren't in Michael's area of expertise, but he knew that he and Malick could come up with a plan to uncover the culprit.

The arrows on the wall ended and Michael went toward the room where Malick had been the night before. He looked much better tonight. He was awake and sitting up when Michael came in. The clear tubing still supplied him with oxygen, and fluids passed through other tubes, to disappear under adhesive tape that covered his right hand.

"You look much better," Michael said, taking a seat in the chair next to the bed. "How do you feel?"

"Much better." Malick's voice was stronger than it had been the night before and his coloring, though still pale, had begun to return to the red, ruddy color that often made Michael think of people who try to tan their white skin in one day. Malick's skin tone looked even more striking against his silver-white head of hair.

Michael felt better today, too. He'd had a real scare when the hospital called, and now he felt as if Malick would recover.

"Have you talked to the doctor today?"

"He was here about an hour ago."

"What did he say?"

"The usual stuff they tell heart patients." He waved his hand as if it were nothing.

"What would that be?"

"That I need to take it easy, avoid stress, eat better, and get plenty of exercise. He even suggested golf would be good." Malick frowned. Michael well knew Malick's view of golf. It was too quiet for him. While he often went to the games in person, most of them he spent as a very vocal television spectator.

"That's good advice, Malick."

Malick stared directly at him. "I know it's good advice," he said harshly, but Michael knew he didn't mean it. "But who ever does what's good for them?"

"You're going to have to."

Malick sighed, then shook his head in agreement. Then he sized Michael up, and he suddenly had a cord of fear running down his back.

"What?" he asked.

"I need you to do me a favor."

"Anything," Michael said.

Malick raised his left hand, favoring the right one, which had the IV needle hidden in it. "It's a big favor."

Michael leaned forward. "Go on," he said.

"I need someone to take over my class—"

Michael was out of his chair. "Malick, you know I can't do that!"

"Why not?"

"I can't go back to the law. I want nothing to do with it." He'd sworn after the Mason children died he'd never go back. It was because of him they were dead. If he hadn't been there, the children would be here today, with their lives in front of them. Michael wouldn't, couldn't, go there.

"Michael," Malick interrupted his thoughts.

He could hear the fatherly nature of Malick's voice and knew what was coming.

"I'm not asking you to return to practice, just to train some first year law students. I have coverage for the day classes. It's only the one night class I need you to teach."

"It's too much." *Too close,* he thought. First year students were the most eager. They knew nothing, but argued every point as if they were before the Supreme Court. He didn't want to stand in front of them as they hung on his every word. And quite possibly they'd know about the Frank Mason case. Was there anyone in America who didn't know about it, with the possible exception of Erika? He doubted it.

"Michael, don't make a decision now. Think about it. Weigh both sides of the argument and make a decision then."

How often had Michael heard Malick say that to a class where he was the student? "I'll think about it," he said.

Erika preferred the library as an office to the upstairs study Carlton had used. As a child she'd spent hours in there doing her homework and reading. The leather-bound volumes along three walls had been her friends during many sleepless nights after she first arrived. Erika only occasionally suffered bouts of insomnia today.

She sat in the library, papers spread around her, as she waited for Michael to return from the hospital. She couldn't believe he'd only been here a few days. It seemed that so much had happened, and was happening—the press conference, his friend's heart attack, and the conglomeration of reporters that camped outside her walls. She stared unseeing at the pages before her—numbers of shares of stock sold in the past month. A graph of the amounts going to the top fifty purchasers lay in a blur on top of the desk.

Erika heard the door, then Michael's footsteps across the tile foyer. She smiled, recognizing the rhythm of his steps. Her heart thumped in anticipation of seeing him. She'd left the door open and the lights on. Standing, she waited for him to come into the room.

"How is he?" she asked when he appeared in the doorway.

"He looks a lot better and he says he feels better."

"Don't you believe him?"

Michael nodded.

"Then, why do you look like someone died?"

Michael slipped his overcoat and suit jacket off. Coming forward, he hooked them over the back of one of the leather chairs before the massive fireplace and sank into the soft cushion. Carlton had often sat there, and in this light Michael reminded her a lot of his grandfather.

She left her position next to the desk and came to perch on the end of the chair next to him.

"What happened?" she asked quietly, forgetting the stock papers on the desk and her own set of problems.

"I'd do anything for Malick," Michael said. He stared blankly into the unlit fireplace. "He asked me to take over one of his classes."

"Michael, that's wonderful!" Erika slipped onto the seat. "I taught briefly right after college and I loved it." Erika didn't think Michael shared her enthusiasm. "Are you worried about being away from Graves Enterprises?"

"It's only one class and it meets during the evening. There won't be any effect on Graves Enterprises."

"Then what's the problem?" She tried to keep her voice level and nonthreatening.

"It's teaching the law," he said after a long pause.

"Don't you think you know it well enough to teach?"

He looked into her eyes. She didn't see doubt there about the subject matter, but she did see fear.

"I can't teach law."

His statement seemed final, as if it were explanation enough. It wasn't enough for Erika.

"What does that mean? I think it's wonderful he has enough confidence in you to ask. He didn't impress me as a man who does things without giving them sufficient thought."

"You're right," Michael agreed. "Malick thinks through all his decisions."

"You should be honored he asked you."

Michael looked at her with no enthusiasm in his eyes. "You think I should do this?"

"I can't decide for you, but you did go to law school, and I can't believe you can turn your back and walk away from something you studied years to do and were apparently very good at." She paused. "And it will help Malick, take some of the worry away from him until he's out of the hospital."

"I told him I'd think about it."

Erika could tell he'd been thinking of nothing else during his drive back to the house. She wondered if the real problem was that he really wanted to return to the law, but had told himself he shouldn't. If he truly wanted no part of the law, why was he wrestling with Malick's request?

"If you really don't want to do it, you must know other lawyers who'd be qualified to take over one class. Why don't you suggest this to Malick? Either way, the pressure of trying to find solutions for things beyond Malick's control will be removed."

Michael leaned back in the chair and closed his eyes. He looked tired. "I'll think about that, too," he agreed. He changed the subject. "What did you find out about the stock?"

"Nothing," she said. She hadn't been able to concentrate, and nothing had been done tonight. The man they hired would probably find the answers soon. Erika thought she'd look over some of the papers, hoping a different set of eyes would see what might be hiding between the lines, but she'd seen nothing. She'd been too busy worrying about what Michael was doing.

"I think I'll go to bed," Michael said, getting up and folding his coat and jacket over his shoulder.

Erika stood, too.

"Coming?" he said.

For a moment the two of them going up the stairs together flashed into her mind. "No," she said. "I have to clean up here first."

Michael nodded and left her. At the door he looked over his shoulder. Erika had turned to the desk. He knew she was concerned about the problems at Graves Enterprises. She was also hiding something from him. He wondered if her supporting Malick's idea had anything to do with it. Quickly he dismissed the idea. She'd offered him another solution to teaching. He could find a replacement himself, or surely the university would find one. Michael didn't think he was the reason for Erika's secret. He remembered thinking there was something more to her when they were in the cabin. She needed this year. It was important to her. Michael didn't think it was the money. Not once during her day and night in the cabin had she mentioned the worth of the estate. And to date she hadn't mentioned its value. The numbers alone should have been enough to make anyone leave his home and come here. Yet she hadn't used the obvious trump card she held.

What was it Erika St. James wanted?

How long had he been running? Michael's legs felt like they were tied to weights. He went as fast as he could. His lungs pumped, breath congealing in puffs as he followed Abby up the hill. What was she doing here? She never came here. She always went up toward the building. There was no building here. She climbed, surefooted. How come she didn't seem to have a problem with the ascent? Why was she climbing the mountain? Where was she going, and what did she plan to do when she got to the top?

Michael saved his breath and pushed on after her. His legs and lungs screamed for him to stop, but he pushed on. Then he saw Frank ahead of him, between him and Abby. Fear stilled his heart for a beat, then forced him to push harder. He found it more difficult to breathe. Each time Abby checked over her shoulder he could see the fear on her face. Her long hair unfurled in the wind. Michael felt the wind's raw fury against his face.

"Abbyyyy!" he called. "Stopppp." The wind took his voice. He knew she couldn't hear him but he kept calling her. Frank pursued her with deadly intent. Michael knew Frank would reach her before he could. Either that, or she'd tumble off the other side of the mountain. There was nothing there, no gentle incline, just the sheer face of a cliff and an unrelenting drop. Three thousand feet of open air, then jagged rocks. Her body would be cut to shreds as it pounded into the stone. The mental picture made him run faster. He hoped he could reach Frank, and Abby would know there was nothing to fear.

Then he saw the gun! Frank stopped, took aim. The woman above him didn't know, hadn't turned to look over her shoulder. She was a perfect target.

"Noooo!" he shouted. "She's innocent, Fraaaaank."

Abby moved around a rock as the first shot rang out. In the wind its sound was blunted. Frank started moving again. Abby turned. She looked different. Michael tried to see her but Frank blocked his view.

Michael didn't think he would make it. His legs felt as if he were trudging through a rough sea at high tide. Suddenly Abby moved higher than Frank. Only she wasn't Abby. Michael's heart stopped. It was Erika!

Frank took aim again. The gun was pointed directly at Erika's back. In a second she'd be dead. The shot rang out, reverberating in Michael's head.

Michael screamed.

Erika heard him as she reached the top of the stairs. She knew Michael was dreaming again. Without thinking she headed for his rooms. The second scream sounded like a man in agony. She opened the door at the end of the hall and found him fighting the covers, the same as he had at the cabin. Erika remembered what had happened when she tried to subdue him.

Approaching the bed, she stayed clear of his flailing arms until she could grab them. With her knee on the bed, she wrestled with him for several seconds before he collapsed. Like the time in the cabin, Michael hugged her close. His breath was heavy against her neck, and she could feel his heart hammering against her breast.

Erika stayed, holding him long after he'd relaxed and fallen into a restful sleep. He lay heavily against her, and his head fell back onto the pillow. Erika stared at his sleeping form. He was a beautiful man, but he was made ragged by demons. She didn't know how deeply they were buried. He'd never be a full person until he exorcised them.

Erika knew about demons. She'd lived with them. Her mother had had demons, still had them. Alva St. James Redford had suffered with her enemies day and night. Her life was a living hell, and she'd made Erika's the same until Erika ran to Carlton and refused to ever go back there.

Standing up, Erika straightened the covers over the sleeping man. She laid the back of her hand on his forehead. He was warm but not fevered. She should go to her rooms now, but she felt a reluctance to leave. As tired as she should be, she felt like staying the night and making sure Michael slept comfortably through the remainder of the dark hours. She knew it wasn't the rational thing to do, but that didn't make it any less her wish.

She moved toward the door, thinking how much he had to contend with—the news media and their incessant dredging up of long forgotten stories, his friend being sick, his guilt over refusing to take over his classes, the added pressure of a new job, new people, and *her*. A man used to staying by himself, he must be going through several adjustment problems with her in the same house, albeit a big house.

She certainly knew she had adjustment problems with his presence, and not all of them were bad.

Nine

Michael cleared his throat and answered the question the student in the last row had asked. When he finished he checked his watch. Class was over. It had ended fifteen minutes ago and every student was still there. He'd forgotten the time, too.

"Thank you, class. We'll meet again Thursday."

People began putting their books away and filing out of the room. When they were all gone Michael sat down. It hadn't been as bad as he expected. In fact, it had been better than he could have dreamed. He loved talking to them, discussing the points, the logic of it all.

He was exhilarated. He wanted to rush home and talk to Erika, tell her how well things had gone. Snapping his briefcase closed, he drew on his coat and left the room. Chalk on his fingers reminded him of the class he'd just left.

Erika was in the library when he arrived. She wore a dressing gown and had her feet curled under her as she read. Michael liked the picture she made. It surprised him how much he enjoyed finding her waiting for him. He wanted to run to her, pull her into his arms and kiss her. He wanted to take her to his bed and make love to her.

He shrugged off the thought. They were together for one year to run Graves Enterprises, he reminded himself. Then it was over. They would both be free to go their own ways. Romantic entanglements could get messy.

She hadn't turned when he entered. Maybe he should leave her to her reading and go to his room. But he watched her.

The light highlighted her hair, giving her natural brown an auburn glow. Michael wanted to run his fingers through it, just as he'd wanted to that first morning when she stood above him.

"Hi." She smiled, looking over her shoulder. "How was it?" She uncurled her feet and stood.

Michael didn't know what to say.

"You liked it?"

"It was better than I expected," he conceded

"You *liked* it."

He paused a long moment. "I liked it."

Like a birthday girl getting a present, Erika ran to him. Instinctively he opened his arms and caught her. Whirling about the room, Michael felt as if *he'd* been given the present. When they stopped he just held her, knowing there was more he wanted to do, but he didn't trust himself. After a moment he stepped back. She was smiling.

"Tell me all about it."

She drew him to the sofa, where she pushed her book aside and sat down. Michael joined her.

"You can't imagine how scared I was walking into that room," he began. "It was like my first day in court—no, worse than my first day."

"But you relaxed," she prompted.

"After a while. Malick had wonderful notes and I started by following them, but shortly into the discussion the class seemed to take on a spirit of its own." Michael told her everything. He couldn't help talking. He'd had a great night. He felt like a kid bubbling over after a great day. Finally something felt as if it had a purpose. *He* had a purpose. He could do this, delve into the law and be safe, away from changing anyone's life.

When he stopped, Erika didn't move or say anything. She just stared at him with an I-told-you-so smile on her face.

"I'm glad you enjoyed it."

Michael actually thought she was glad. It made him feel

good. It had been a long time since he thought anyone really cared how he felt.

"It's late," she said.

They stood. Michael reached for her hand and drew it through his arm. Together they left the library and walked to the steps. At the top of the landing Michael let go of her. He didn't want to. He wanted to fulfill his fantasy of lifting her from the floor and carrying her up the remaining steps toward his rooms. Instead, he gently touched his mouth to her cheek and whispered a thank you before turning and heading toward his suite.

That night the dreams came back. This time they were different. He ran and ran, but couldn't reach Erika. Abby wasn't there. Frank Mason raised his gun and pointed it at Erika as she went up the mountain.

Michael shouted. He sat straight up in bed. His body was covered in sweat and his breath came in ragged gasps. Putting his feet over the side of the bed, he leaned his elbows on his knees and held his head in his hands. He tried to calm himself, calm his rapidly beating heart.

Why was Erika in this dream? This was the second time she'd been there. And it was more real. Often, he didn't waken. The dream would end and he'd fall asleep without ever fully awakening. Tonight, though, he'd been so sure Frank would kill her that he'd screamed enough to wake himself. He still had the feeling Erika was in danger.

Then he remembered that Frank had escaped. As much as he tried, Michael couldn't shake the feeling that Erika was in danger. Grabbing his dressing gown, he pulled it over his naked body and padded, barefoot, toward her suite. Michael didn't exactly know where it was. He'd only seen her go that way, not which door she opened.

He tried the first door on her side of the stairs and found the room empty. The second door must have been to Carlton's room. It was huge, dark, and austere. He couldn't image Erika living in there. The third door was hers. He opened it quietly and looked inside. The walls were light beige or yellow. There was a sitting room with a fireplace, and several sofas and chairs making a warm conversation area. The fire had been lit, but had died during the night. Only a few embers snapped on the hearth. Michael went through to the bedroom. Erika lay in the big bed.

Michael should have turned and left then, but he didn't. Her bed was a tall four-poster with swags of fabric giving it an air of openness. Her sheets and comforter were white satin, and she lay between them like a small child. Michael went across the room. Quietly he stood watching her even breathing. She was all right. Michael let go of the breath he didn't know he was holding. His dream had been just that, a dream. He should return to his own room. Why didn't he move? Why was he standing there mesmerized by the sight of a woman sleeping? What would he do if she woke up? Could he explain his presence?

He knew all the answers to these questions, yet he didn't move. He remained staring at the darkness of Erika's skin against the whiteness of the sheets. She was beautiful. She seemed to get more beautiful each time he saw her.

Erika moved. She turned over. Michael froze in place. When she'd settled herself, he let go his breath and stole out of the room.

Erika couldn't shake the feeling this morning that something was wrong. She showered and dressed the same as she did every morning, but today she felt uneasy, more so than usual. Maybe it was the past few days of stress-related incidents, Erika thought. She'd been under stress before, though, and never had the feeling that had awakened her during the night.

Maybe it was Michael. He was new in her life. Maybe she'd just imagined he'd been there. She shrugged, trying to shake off the feeling. As she left her rooms and headed for breakfast she hoped this feeling wouldn't persist.

Michael met her at the landing.

"Good morning," she said.

They fell into step together. "Are you ready for another day?"

Erika nodded. She wasn't her usual self and she wanted to ask Michael a strange question. She just had no way of saying it. She'd always had a good memory and sleep had only been a problem when she'd had a run-in with her mother, but since he arrived her routine had been disrupted. Last night had been . . . more *real,* was all she could call it, more real than ever before.

"I'd like to ask you a question," she began, needing to clear her throat.

Michael shrugged. "Go ahead."

Erika hesitated. They'd reached the bottom step and she still hadn't said anything.

"What is it?" he asked again.

At the door of the breakfast room Erika stopped and faced him. "Were you in my room last night?"

"Now there's a very interesting question."

The door swung fully open. Both Michael and Erika turned to face the person who'd spoken.

"Good morning, Mrs. Redford."

"What are you doing here?" Erika asked, anger dripping from her words.

"Obviously, I've come to protect my daughter." She looked at Michael. "Young man, did you sleep in my daughter's room last night?" She lowered her head and looked at Michael, like a schoolteacher peering over her glasses.

"No," he said decisively. "I slept in my own room."

"Too bad," she said, a smile showing her even, white teeth. "It might be just what she needs." Alva Redford threw a look at her daughter. Erika walked away and poured herself a cup of coffee. She didn't want her mother here this morning. She'd wanted to have a leisurely breakfast with Michael before they went to the office. After she'd asked Michael her question,

depending on the answer, she couldn't have predicted how leisurely their breakfast would be. Now she'd have to contend
with another of her mother's requests.

"What do you want?" Erika asked again.

Alva took her time. She strolled to the server and lifted a
plate as if she were the owner of the house. Piling it high with
food, she then poured a cup of black coffee and walked to
where Michael stood.

"Would you mind if I talked to my daughter alone?"

"You promise there will be no blood?" Michael glanced at
Erika.

Alva laughed. "I can only speak for myself, Michael." She
said his name with all the emphasis of a Southern belle.

Michael smiled and accepted the plate and cup. "I'll be in
the library," Michael said and left them.

Alva closed the door.

"All right, Mother. We're alone now. Why are you here?"

Alva returned to the server and made herself a plate of fruit
and croissants. She then took a seat in front of a cup that
already had her lipstick on one side. Obviously, she wasn't
going to speak until Erika sat down. Erika remembered this
and wondered why she'd let herself fall into her mother's trap.
Alva wanted the upper hand, and this was a small measure of
her showing Erika she still had the ability to make her cringe.

Erika took a seat opposite her mother.

"Score one for Alva St. James Redford," Erika said. "She
won the battle of the chairs. Now what do you want?"

"You know, Erika, Carlton and I had an agreement."

"What kind of agreement?"

Alva lifted her cup. The rings on her fingers shone in the
morning light coming through the open curtains.

"An agreement that I believe has been overlooked in the
period since his death."

Erika took a deep breath and placed her palms on the table.

"You're back about the checks."

Alva picked up a butter knife and began adding a film of

butter to her croissant. "Yes, darling, I'm here about the checks. Why are you holding them? They are mine."

"Mother, I've been running this company solely for over a year. Carlton never mentioned owing you anything. What were you blackmailing him with?"

"Not blackmail, Erika," Alva said sternly. "I never black-mailed Carlton."

"Then why was he paying you, regularly and systematically? It certainly looks like blackmail to me."

"Well, it wasn't."

"Are you an employee of Graves Enterprises?"

Alva didn't give an answer and Erika did not expect one.

"Did you sell something to Carlton?"

Again silence met her question.

"Did you lend money to Carlton, and this was his method of repaying you?" Erika stood up. She went toward her mother. "He'd been paying you every month for how long, Mother? Two years, three, twenty-five? Hasn't Carlton been paying you since I left your house and came to this one?"

"Erika, it's a trust fund."

"Why, Mother?" Erika asked, the menace in her voice made more terrifying by the restrained quiet evident in it. Erika leaned on the polished surface of the dining table, her face only inches from her mother's. "Why did Carlton, who had nothing to do with you, establish a trust fund to take care of you?"

It had been a long time since she felt like an adult in her mother's presence. Then Alva St. James Redford stood up, taking back all the ground Erika had won.

"All you need to know, Erika, is that the fund *was* established. Carlton's will did not restrict, limit, or dissolve it. It's there, and it's mine." She took a step, bringing her to within a foot of Erika. "I'll expect my regular and systematic check to be in the mail this afternoon. And furthermore, I expect a check each and every month, and without the need for me to arrange my day in order to join you for breakfast."

The two women stared at each other as anger remained the only force speaking in the room. After a second Alva turned to leave.

"Mother!" Erika stopped her. "There's one more thing before you leave."

Alva lifted her chin, facing her daughter as if she were an enemy.

"I'll give you the benefit of the doubt and not outright accuse you," Erika began, but she had no doubt that her mother was guilty. "The last time you were here, you intimated that you'd go to the press with Michael's story."

The smile that crossed Alva's face told Erika her mother knew she had the upper hand.

"Are you responsible for the reporters we're having to deal with?"

Erika couldn't read the expression on her mother's face. She had no idea what the smile meant. As the seconds ticked off and Alva offered no response, Erika realized she wasn't going to get one.

"Make sure that check is in the mail," Alva said, and left.

Erika had known she'd lose this fight. When her mother appeared suddenly at her door several nights ago, she'd known the woman had come to discuss her finances, but Michael had interrupted them. Erika purposely had not let the check be mailed. It sat in the drawer of her desk. She wanted to know the reason for the fund. It had been established while Erika was still a teenager. From what she could tell, it appeared Carlton had made some deal with her mother. Erika hated the thought that formed in her mind when she'd heard about the fund. Had her mother effectively sold her to Carlton?

Earlier and earlier, Frank thought, standing at the window watching the Christmas scene. It wasn't even Thanksgiving yet and the Christmas decorations were everywhere in the mall. Mounds of cotton, representing snow, adorned a scene of mov-

ing mice, dressed as people and sliding about on a track. Both adults and children smiled as they stood for a moment to watch the wonder.

Frank thought of his children. They would love to see this. Maybe when he was done. When all the people responsible had paid, he and Abby would bring the children and they would see the mice and the red-cheeked Santa. Frank would take them for pictures with the bearded old elf who sat at the center of the mall and asked every child what he wanted for Christmas.

Frank liked waiting to shop. He wouldn't buy anything today. He'd look, get ideas, make lists, and on Christmas Eve he'd buy his gifts. On Christmas morning they would get up and have a family event opening their presents, like when he was a child. His children's Christmas morning would be like his, complete with a warm fire and lots of presents.

All he had to do was complete his work. He'd be finished long before Christmas Eve. Even today's setback hadn't bothered him. He'd missed the judge. The man must be out of town. He'd camped out for three days waiting for him but he simply hadn't appeared. No mail was delivered, no garbage appeared for pickup, and no newspapers gathered in the driveway.

Frank wasn't concerned. He was a cautious man, a patient man. He had time. He could wait and plan until the time was exactly right. All of them would pay for what they'd done to him and his family. Then he'd shop for his children's presents.

Ten

The two women at the reception desk were different than the ones Michael had seen on his other trips to visit Malick. He passed them with a nod and a smile and made his way to Malick's room, which had been upgraded to a regular one.

Malick sat up in bed watching television. He switched the set off as Michael came in. He looked years better than he had only a week ago.

"How was class?" Malick asked without a greeting.

"I got through it," Michael said. He didn't want to tell Malick that he had been right, that he liked teaching. Erika had seen it the minute he walked into the room, but then he was coming directly from the classes. Tonight he'd had time to compose himself. He knew he'd tell Malick what he really felt about the class, but he didn't want his friend gloating too soon.

"I'm sure you did more than that."

"I didn't follow your plan very long. We began discussing The State of Pennsylvania vs. Adams but then other precedents were cited and we were off on a tangent. I thought it was an important path for the students to take, so I didn't stop them."

"Good," Malick said. "It's exactly what I would have done. What time did you finish?"

"What?" Michael said, trying to buy himself some time.

"Did you finish before the class ended, or was the entire class still there after the time they should have been gone?"

Michael knew why Malick was such a good lawyer. He'd

cornered him into this question and Michael could see where he was going with it.

"Only fifteen minutes," he said.

"Fifteen minutes beyond the time. I knew it! I knew you'd be good. Students are a hard lot and if you got them to forget the time, especially on your first night, they had to be interested in what you were saying."

"I suppose I'll be all right until you return," Michael conceded.

"If the press doesn't discover you're there."

Michael looked confused.

"I've been watching the news. You and Erika made the headlines two days in a row. How's she taking it?"

"She's weathering it." Michael remembered the haunting look on her face when he'd told her about the press conference. Yet once she got there she'd taken control and held it until the end.

"What about you?"

"I'm fine," Michael shrugged.

"Are you really? You've had a lot of stress points in the past few weeks."

"I'm all right, Malick. You don't need to spend your time worrying about me." Michael knew his friend had thought of him constantly when he'd gone to Maryland. Coming back could be just as stressful as the events which had sent him there. "Except for Erika, I'm the same as I was before I went to Maryland."

"You and Erika aren't getting on?"

Michael hesitated. He didn't know how to explain it. "It's not that we don't get along. Quite the opposite. We get along very well."

"Then what's the problem?"

"I'm not sure there is a problem."

"Is she all business? No woman under the business suit?"

Michael remembered holding her close. He shook his head. That was certainly not the Erika he knew. If anything, she was all woman.

"I know I was a little groggy, but she appeared to have a pleasing personality. Isn't that the case?"

"She's fine, Malick. I can't think of any faults or complaints to brand her with."

"Do you want to brand her with something else?"

"What do you mean?"

Malick started a smile that burst into a laugh.

"What's so funny?"

"Michael, you have all the symptoms of a fourteen-year-old, and you don't even know it."

Oh, he knew it—and that was his problem. He was falling for Erika.

"Michael, she's a beautiful and obviously intelligent woman. Why are you fighting the fact that you have feelings for her? I'd think you should question yourself if you didn't."

Michael hadn't come here to talk about his feelings for Erika. Yet he talked to Malick about everything else. Why should Erika be any different?

"It's Abby, isn't it?"

"I suppose everything comes back to Abby. I wonder what will happen to every woman I meet. Will I be the reason some man hurts her?"

"Michael, you can't keep blaming yourself for Abby's death. You didn't kill her."

"I know, but I'm responsible for her death."

"And just how did you manage that? Were you there? Did you provide her with the means?"

"No, just the motive. I'm as much responsible as if I'd poisoned her myself."

"Stop that!"

Michael's head snapped up at the anger in his friend's voice and the sudden crash of Malick's hand against the bed table. His plastic pitcher and cup danced, then settled.

"You didn't poison Abby. If anyone is responsible for her death it's her husband. Now, you get any thoughts like that out of your head and keep them out."

Malick's face was beet red, and Michael knew his blood pressure must be off the scale. If he didn't change the subject he'd be responsible for Malick returning to ICU.

"Let's not talk about Abby any more."

"Fine by me," Malick agreed, settling back against the pillows. "I really want to talk about Erika, anyway. I liked her. She seems like a very nice woman."

"You figured that out from a few groggy minutes in her presence?"

"She came back to see me."

"When?" Surprise made Michael raise his eyebrows. She hadn't mentioned it, but he had done most of the talking. She'd listened to him, shared his happiness.

"Last night while you were in class. We had a nice chat. She's a very interesting woman. Haven't you noticed?"

Michael couldn't have helped noticing. "What did you talk about?" He wondered if they'd discussed him. His feelings were mixed on the answer. Did he want Malick to tell Erika about him? Did she even feel enough for him to ask? She had to. She couldn't have kissed him the way she had, and feel nothing.

"We talked about the shape of the economy, what's happening to the youth of America, would the Phillies win the National Championships . . ."

Michael frowned. Malick obviously didn't plan to help him out.

"Malick?"

His friend stopped talking and looked innocently at him. "I think she likes you, too."

"Did she say that?" Suddenly Michael wanted to know the answer to that question.

"She didn't have to. I could read it in her eyes."

"Then you're better at reading than I am." He'd looked into Erika's eyes many times. Most often he'd gotten lost in the liquid brown pools.

"So you have looked into her eyes?"

Michael could have kicked himself. He'd set himself up for that, and Malick had an open court for his return.

"Where is this leading, Malick?"

"To a grandson, I hope, or the next best thing."

Michael's jaw dropped open. "What are you talking about? Erika and I are only friends."

"That sounds like something her ex-fiancé would have said."

"You know about him?"

Malick nodded.

"What do you know?"

"Don't change the subject. We're talking about Erika and you."

"There is no Erika and me. We're doing a job, and when it's over, we're over." Michael gave his friend a piercing look. "And I didn't miss that comment you made practically assuming we were engaged."

Malick laughed. "You could do worse."

"Malick, I'm not in the market for a relationship."

"Then what was all that talk about getting along and working together? You two wouldn't be the first couple who met on the job."

"Malick, when this year is up I plan to return to Maryland and never leave that mountain again."

Malick smiled. Not the reaction Michael expected.

"She's getting to you," he paused. "Well, Michael, I'm not a betting man." Malick stretched his arms over his head and rested them behind his neck. "Leastways, not outside the courthouse. But I'm willing to put money on you and Erika St. James."

"Then you'll lose your money."

Michael couldn't help staring at Erika. Even now, as they sat in a meeting of area vice presidents, all he could concentrate on was how great she looked. Malick had planted the seed in his mind and each time he looked at her he thought of *them,* a couple, a family unit. He'd shake himself to bring his concentration back, but it never did any good. The only time she wasn't at the top of his thoughts was when he stood in front of the eager faces of his law students.

Erika seemed to grow more beautiful with each passing day. Michael could hardly keep his mind on work with her in the same room. He smelled her perfume and he wanted nothing to do with business. She'd explain competitive action programs while he concentrated on keeping his hands from shaking.

Erika appeared not to notice. She continued to point to her charts and explain every aspect of the presentation. Even outside these meetings she would ask his opinion and keep him informed of every detail. He couldn't fault her. She wasn't trying to push him out of the company.

"Any more questions?" Erika asked. When none were forthcoming, she smiled. "Thank you," she said.

The meeting broke into small groups, each discussing something that had happened at the meeting. Little by little they all left the room. Erika gathered her notes and prepared to leave.

"Erika," he said.

She looked up at him. "Yes," she said, and took a seat.

He was looking at her again with those eyes that made her soul melt. She'd tried hard to concentrate during this morning's meeting, but it was hard with him looking at her. Sometimes he scribbled on his pad, but she knew he missed nothing.

"Are you free for dinner tonight?"

A date? Was he going to ask her for a date? It was the last thing she expected from him. They had dinner together most nights when he wasn't teaching. Even when he went to visit Malick she waited for him. It was the one indulgence she allowed herself.

"Yes," she finally answered. Her heart hammered in her chest. Why? She'd been asked out before, and she'd wanted to go before, but never had she wanted to spend time with a man as much as she wanted to spend it with Michael.

"Would you have dinner with me?"

It was business. He wanted to discuss something he didn't understand about the meeting. Then why couldn't they talk about it now . . . or in the dining room at home?

"Erika, you had dinner with me in the cabin. Is there any reason you won't go to a restaurant?"

"The reporters," she said, remembering, although there had been fewer of them lately. A large arsenal, discovered in the basement of a local business, and the bust of a high ranking official in the police department had pushed them off the front page.

"I think we're safe enough now."

"What brings this on? We have dinner together every night that you're not teaching or visiting Malick. This sounds like a . . . date." She had to swallow to get the word out.

Michael dropped the pencil he'd been playing with and lounged back in the chair. "It is a date."

"Why?" she whispered.

"There's too much going on. We both need a break. I thought going out would give us time to relax and forget about our problems for a few hours. How about it?"

Erika nodded.

"Is that a yes?"

"Yes," she said.

Erika's bedroom looked like an explosion in a clothing factory. She'd changed clothes five times and still she wasn't satisfied about her looks. It was just a date, she told herself. It wasn't like it was her first. Why couldn't she decide what to wear? She and Michael saw each other every day. Why couldn't she put something on and be done with it?

Picking up a green velvet dress, she slipped into it and pulled the zipper up. Barefoot, she stepped in front of the mirror and looked at her reflection. Frowning, she dragged the zipper to its base and let the dress slither to the floor.

Erika kicked it away in frustration. She was no further toward being ready than when she'd entered the house over an
hour before. Going back to the closet she pushed dresses aside
one by one, rejecting everything until she came to a grey lace.
She stopped, remembering the last time she wore it—the last
time she and Bill had gone out together. The day before he
flew to Las Vegas and married Jennifer Ahrends. Why hadn't
she thrown that out? Maybe she shouldn't go out with Michael.
How did she know he wouldn't turn out to be another Bill?
She knew she was already falling for him. If she went out
with him, socialized, got to know him, then the year would
end and he'd go off and leave her, too.

"This is the wrong decision," Erika told the dress. She
couldn't go out with Michael. Hadn't she learned anything in
the last thirty-four years? Didn't she realize these things never
worked out for her? The best thing she could do was to run
the company and forget about personal relationships. In that,
her mother had been right. She'd never find a man who'd want
her. She proved that time and time again, and Michael
Lawrence was no different.

Erika swatted the dress as if hitting out at a person. Grabbing a bathrobe, she pulled it over her underwear and left her
room. She'd decided and found no need to put off telling Michael. Marching to the steps that junctioned the house into
wings, she took purposeful steps down and then up the other
side. Michael's room was at the end. Going straight there she
stopped outside the dark wood panel door and took a deep
breath. Then, not giving herself time to think, she knocked.

Michael whirled toward the door at the knock. In the month
he'd been here no one had ever knocked on that door when
he was in the house. Tonight it could be no one other than
Erika. He'd assumed they'd meet in the library. And she was
early. *Why?* he wondered.

Quickly checking his clothes he pulled the door inward. She
stood there looking beautiful but a little frightened, and she
wasn't dressed.

"Has something happened?" he asked.

Erika's hand went to her throat as if she'd only just realized she was wearing a bathrobe. "No, it's just that . . ." she stopped, staring at him. He looked down. His clothes were fine. He looked back at her.

"Come in," he said, taking her arm and drawing her inside. He left the door open as he guided her to a chair near the massive unlit fireplace. "What's wrong?" he asked when she was seated. "Why aren't you dressed?"

Michael took the facing chair. He was physically separated from her, and knew he needed to be. He could smell the clean scent of the soap she'd used in her shower. Her hair wasn't perfect, the way he'd seen it in the past, and she wore no makeup, but she looked better than he could remember—except for that morning in the cabin when she'd come out to look at the mountain in the early light.

Erika looked at him and nearly lost her nerve. He had on jeans and a blue shirt, unbuttoned at the neck. His short cropped hair lay neatly in place, and he smelled good enough to taste. She had mingled with some of the most beautiful people in the world, at least those in Hollywood. Women trying to be the next soaring star. Men with looks, physiques and drive, but never had a combination affected her more than that housed in the rich, brandy-skinned body of Michael Lawrence.

"Erika?"

"I—" she stammered. Looking at him made her tongue-tied. "I can't go out with you."

"Why not?"

"I thought about it and . . ." Lying wasn't her usual way of getting out of things, but this time she had no choice. She couldn't start something with Michael when she was sure from the beginning that she would be the one hurt in the end. This time the publicity would be more than she could handle, since she knew her heart would be involved. "We're partners, and I think it's best if we kept our relationship a business one.

When our year is over we can go our separate ways with no entanglements."

"Tonight you believe we—" he pointed from her to himself, "we will become an entanglement?"

Erika was boxed in. She didn't want to answer that question. She was already tangled up with him and she didn't trust herself to keep the secret inside her heart. "Maybe not after one time, but there's no reason for us to begin something that can only lead—"

"Lead where?"

"I'm sorry. I didn't mean to say that," she said. She should have thought about what she'd tell him before she got here, but she hadn't and now she had to escape. She knew Michael would see through her. It was his profession to get the truth out of people, and she'd put herself in his path. Erika stood up. "I'll get something to eat from the kitchen." She moved toward the door. Michael stood up. "And I have some work that needs looking at." Erika moved away from him. She was nearly at the door when Michael stopped her.

"Erika." He was directly behind her. She could feel the heat of his body and wished she'd put on some clothes. "Tell me the truth," he whispered. "Why won't you go out with me?"

Erika dropped her shoulders, but she said nothing.

"I'm not Bill Castle," he said.

Erika turned around, then backed away. "I never thought you were Bill."

"Didn't you? Don't you still?" He came toward her. Erika backed up. "Don't you think every man who tries to get close to you will treat you like Bill Castle? Isn't that the reason you don't have any dates, don't even entertain the idea of having a man around? Isn't that why you run each time I get near you?"

"I don't run."

He took another step. She moved away.

"Don't you?"

For a long, long moment Michael held her stare. He could

detect no fear in her eyes, but he knew he frightened her. Bill Castle had done a first class job of making her afraid of another relationship. He'd sworn off women, too, yet here he was practically badgering her into going out with him.

He'd wanted to spend time with her, time alone, without Graves Enterprises between them, without thinking there was anything in the world that prevented them from meeting and talking, sharing a meal. Yet she'd had second thoughts. She'd opened the door to allow him to retract his invitation without complicating conditions. Why wasn't he accepting it?

You don't want to, a voice inside his head told him. It was all he needed.

"Don't move this time, Erika," he said. He took another step. She remained still, lifting her chin in defiance. Michael only looked at her. Her hands were at her sides. There was little tension in her features, yet he knew her knees were knocking. He wanted her. He was only a step away from getting what he wanted. If he touched her, she'd be his. Then he knew he couldn't do it. When he touched her, she had to want his touch.

He stepped back. Erika's breath came out in a slow sigh. He saw her shoulders move slightly, the only outward sign that anything had changed within her.

He went to the door and pushed it to its widest point. With his hand extended he offered her escape. "Good night," he said.

Michael closed the door after she'd left. The telltale smell of her soap lingered. He wanted to grasp it somehow, hold it a little longer than the air would allow, but it was as elusive as the depth of mistrust in her eyes.

She intrigued him more than any woman ever had. He enjoyed talking to her, listening to her. Yet she only wanted a business relationship. Well, he could give her one.

"One business relationship, Ms. St. James, coming right up."

* * *

Thirty-seven. Erika banked under the water, pushing off the deep end wall, and began her thirty-eighth lap in the pool. She hadn't been able to forget Michael's comment. The worst part was that he was telling the truth. She did avoid men. She hadn't wanted to trust anyone again. She knew relationships weren't for her but with Bill she had tried one last time, and that had resulted in chaos. She wouldn't try it again, even with Michael. She'd know from the beginning it was headed nowhere.

Thirty-nine, she counted, swimming harder and faster than she'd ever felt the need to before. She was right, she told herself. They should maintain a business relationship, and only that relationship. It would be the best thing for both of them, for their futures. Then why was she here swimming lap after lap instead of working on the papers she'd brought home or merely reading a book? Why was she battling this water as if it were her enemy?

Michael wasn't Bill. She knew that. He could hurt her a lot worse than Bill did. Her feelings had been mostly embarrassment when Bill jilted her. If she let herself fall in love with Michael her emotions would be involved, deeply involved, so deeply that when he left she would have no recovery.

He would leave. He'd told her that when he came. This arrangement was for a year. He wanted to prevent Frank Mason from inheriting Carlton's money. When the year ended Michael would have more money than he could possibly spend in a lifetime, and with it came responsibility.

Money, Erika, like poverty, is one of life's true burdens. How often had she heard Carlton say that? When Michael had his half of the estate, he'd have the burden of women, many women. Not that he didn't have that now. He was an attractive man. She was attracted to him. She'd seen the women in the office reacting to him, each one of them trying to get his attention.

Forty-three. She dipped under and reversed again. If they wanted his attention, she vowed, they could have it. Beginning tomorrow he would be her partner . . . and nothing more.

Eleven

Rain had drizzled over the city for the past four days. It was raining hard when she woke, and had continued through her shower. Erika had the feeling the heavens were crying for her. For two weeks she'd kept her vow of a business only relationship. Time should have made it easier, but it had become harder each day to maintain her distance where Michael was concerned.

Today was Saturday. As large as the house was, she was bound to run into Michael. She could go to the office, but there was no reason for her to be there. Going in would make it obvious that she was avoiding him. Maybe she could call a friend and suggest they meet for lunch. Suddenly she couldn't think of a soul she wanted to visit who wouldn't question her about Michael's presence, and in her state of mind she was apt to spill her feelings.

She could begin her Christmas shopping, but her heart wasn't in it. She never liked to shop before Thanksgiving, anyway.

She wasn't a coward, she told herself. She could certainly have a conversation with Michael that had nothing to do with business and didn't border on their personal lives. Leaving her bedroom, she headed for the breakfast room. Skipping down the stairs she realized she had on the blue and white sweater and stirrup pants she'd worn in the mountains. At the bottom of the steps she stopped. She'd been wearing this outfit when Michael first kissed her.

Erika grabbed the newel post. Maybe she was a coward.

* * *

Blood. The human body held between four and five quarts. Frank Mason released the leather belts he'd used to secure Judge Raymond Baldwin to the dining room chair. The last blood his heart pumped had squirted through the slits in his wrists twenty minutes ago. Frank had stood behind the judge, watching the arc of blood as it squirted, until it petered into a trickle.

The judge acted like the lawyer. He pleaded and begged, telling him he could help him. How could he help? He'd had his chance, and what had he done? Confined him to that place. He'd die before going back.

Look at him. The judge didn't look so tough now. He had no robes, no high chair above the rest of the crowd. He was just a man. Just a dead man.

And Mrs. Baldwin. She was tougher than her husband—she was still alive—but not for long. Frank pulled her straps free, and her bulk made her body fall out of the chair. Frank wouldn't touch her anymore. He wanted to be careful not to get any of the blood on him. He checked his white coat and shoes. He'd posed as a doctor and they'd trustingly let him in. As white as when he stepped across the threshold. Frank smiled at his handiwork.

"Good night, Judge Baldwin," he said. The smile left his face, replaced by a look of hatred. "See you in hell."

Michael looked at himself in the bathroom mirror. He'd slept in this morning, since most of his night had been spent listening to the silence after the dream. This couldn't go on. His eyes were red and the bags under his eyes would soon be as large as those of the Cowardly Lion from *The Wizard of Oz*. He looked as if he'd been on a dead drunk, but he hadn't. He simply couldn't sleep without nightmares of Frank Mason and Erika. She'd totally replaced Abby in his nocturnal mind. The dreams had become so frequent he would soon have to go to a doctor. Malick had noticed his state, but Michael had been able to attribute it to the strain of the office.

He wasn't far from the truth there. Since he and Erika had established their plan the strain of being close to her had intensified. Each time he saw her at meals or during the business day he'd wanted to convince her to change their plan, but he knew better. He knew a relationship between them was out of the question. He couldn't sustain it. Yet his body didn't quite agree with him. He wanted to touch her, hold her, feel her come to life in his arms as they both let the throes of passion lead them to the place that only a man and a woman can understand. Erika, though, was logical and strong enough to keep the conversations structured around Graves Enterprises.

They'd discussed the pharmaceutical division's product pipeline and new drug applications being filed. There was a lot of excitement about a new AIDS drug awaiting approval. The reports of the stock sales were still being watched, but the buying patterns seemed to have cooled.

The only thing that hadn't cooled was him. Pushing himself back, he entered the bedroom as the phone rang.

"So tell me, is she coming or should I find my own date?" His brother, Peter, laughed in his ear.

"Peter!" He was glad to hear him. "What's going on?"

"Not much. I was wondering if you were free for lunch and we could meet later."

Michael sighed with relief. He needed a method of leaving the house and Peter provided it. "Lunch will be fine."

"Good. If I invite myself there will I get to meet Erika St. James?"

He wanted to come here. Peter had mentioned Erika before, and he knew his brother. He probably only wanted to come to meet Erika. Suddenly he was jealous of his own brother, jealous of his easygoing manner and his ability to attract the opposite sex. They'd never been rivals before, but with Erika it was different. He remembered watching her sleeping and wanting to climb into bed and hold her, make love to her.

"Michael, are you still there?"

Michael cleared his throat. "I'm here."

"Well, how about it?"

"I don't know what Erika's plans are, but I'm sure she'd love to meet you."

"I'll see you in about an hour."

Peter hung up before Michael could say anything. His brother couldn't have picked a worse time to come. His relationship was strained. His physical appearance showed his lack of sleep. He knew Erika was attracted to him. Right now, though, they were at a crossroads and he didn't need a handsome TV personality showing up to tilt the scales.

Michael dressed quickly in jeans and a sweater. He needed to find Erika and let her know about Peter.

He found her in the library, ensconced in papers. She spent all her time working. What was it that drove her? She had to know she was doing a wonderful job. The stock had stabilized. They no longer thought anyone was trying to gain a hostile seat on the Graves board of directors.

Even with that, with market share showing a steady climb and a pipeline of products looking good enough to keep them profitable into the next century, Erika drove herself as if her last meal would be served if she didn't supervise everything herself. She let nothing get in the way of her and Graves Enterprises.

"Good morning," Michael said.

Her head snapped up. She looked tired, too, tired but beautiful. The light was subdued this morning due to the rain outside, but even without the highlights falling on her hair she was beautiful.

"Hello," she said. Her voice appeared unusually low and sexy. She put her pen down and sat back. Her body was stiff and businesslike. Michael suddenly wanted to haul her out of the chair and make her melt into the woman he knew her to be. But he did none of the things his mind told him.

"What are you doing?"

"Going over some of the reports I never get a chance to read in the office."

"Anything I can help you with?"

"You have the same reports. Have you read them all?"

He had read most of them but he still had a desk full of papers that needed his attention. Something about her eyes disturbed him. "Do you work all the time?"

"No," she said. He could see defensiveness creep into her body language.

"Why don't you date?"

"I don't think that's any of your business."

"It is if it affects your performance at Graves Enterprises."

Erika's eyes opened wide. "My dating or not dating has no effect on the company."

"I disagree. If you get out and socialize it makes you a more informed person, someone who understands what is going on in the marketplace, how real people feel. You can't get everything from a report." He spread his hands at the array of papers on her desk. Erika followed his lead.

"Are you trying to get me to go out with you again?"

It hadn't been his intention when he walked into the room, but the thought of her on his arm as he squired her about town—dinner, a show, conversation in a small jazz club—was tantalizing.

"All right." Erika stood up. "If you think the health of Graves Enterprises hinges on whether or not I date, then I'll find myself a date."

She moved to push past him. Michael caught her by both arms and turned her to face him. "That's not what I meant, and you know it." Then he did something he'd promised himself he wouldn't do. He pulled her into his arms and clamped his mouth to hers. She resisted for the merest second but he wouldn't let her go. He couldn't even if he'd wanted to. He'd wanted to taste her again since that first kiss, dreamed of her, pliant in his arms, and now that he'd maneuvered her into them he wasn't going to let go so easily.

Oh God! Michael thought, feeling her hands on his waist and then reaching around him as she pressed her body close. Her breasts, small and firm, pushed against his chest, sending a jolt of need straight to his knees, which threatened to buckle with the onslaught. He shouldn't have done this. He should have let her walk away. He should release her now, let her go and apologize, but he couldn't. He needed more. He wanted more. He couldn't settle for this one kiss alone. He needed massive doses of her, and preferably several times a day. He didn't know that he could survive without her now that the floodgates were open and the wave had swept them away.

Erika stopped her struggle and her arms climbed up his back. She refused to think. If she thought, she'd push herself away, and the way he made her feel she didn't want to be logical. She wanted to rip the thin barrier of clothing between them away and feel his hard nakedness against her soft skin. She wanted to remain in his arms, with his mouth sealed to hers, with his tongue deep in her mouth and the sensations rioting through her body like lightning fissuring through the unresisting sky.

Erika gave as much as she took. She went up on her toes to get closer to him. His hands raked her body, combed through her hair, cupped her face and hips, pressing her into him as if he could merge the two of them into a single being. No one had ever made her feel like this before.

Then Michael's hold changed. The passion in his mouth slowed, teased, and turned to reverence. He held her lightly, gently, as if his hands were too big, too rough, for her delicate features. Erika had never been held like this. His mouth slipped from hers, and his hands cradled her head. He pushed back to look at her face. His eyes were darker and filled with a passion that spoke volumes. Her breath caught and she couldn't speak.

Then she was free. Michael stepped back and the moment

was gone—gone but not lost. Erika didn't think she'd ever be the same again. When Michael looked at her for that half second she'd felt as if their souls had linked and she would never again be complete without him. No one had made her feel as if she were the single most important thing in the world.

But the man who had held her in his arms was gone. In his place was another Michael. He looked like the same man, but he was different. She felt as if she'd suddenly lost something, something important, and that she'd never have it again.

"I came in to tell you my brother called this morning. He's invited himself to lunch. He wants to meet you."

He was stiff and formal, as if the interlude in his arms had never taken place, as if the need she knew dwelled inside him had been arrested and placed in solitary confinement. A chill ran through her. She felt cold, as if a sudden wind had passed through her or someone had walked over her grave.

Peter couldn't have been more charming, and Michael had never wanted to strangle his brother as much as he did right now. Erika delighted in talking to him during their meal. She laughed at his jokes and asked questions about his job.

Could this be the same woman he'd held in his arms only an hour ago? The woman he'd seen dressed in only a bathrobe, without makeup, and dripping wet as she came out of the pool? She was confident, in control and an excellent hostess.

Michael felt left out. Peter dominated the conversation—but then, he always had. A ready smile and the right words were always at hand for Peter. And Erika was eating it up.

"Nut brown?" Erika's laughter tinkled when Michael brought his mind back to the conversation. "Really?"

"It's my color," Peter was saying.

"And you really let them put it on you?"

"The lights are very hot and the makeup artist is very good."

Erika looked at Michael. "Can you imagine Michael doing the news?"

Peter turned his attention to his brother. He shook his head. "Michael's much too serious. He'd want to fix all those problems he reported."

Michael tried to join the conversation. "Maybe not *all* of them."

Peter continued to talk about the methods of broadcasting the news and Erika looked genuinely interested in everything he had to say. Finally the conversation wound down and Erika pushed her chair back and stood. Peter stood up, too. She walked to where he was and offered him her hand. Peter took it in both of his. Michael noticed he did not release it.

"It's been nice talking to you, Peter, but you probably want to talk to Michael." She glanced at Michael. "I hope to see you before you go."

"I'm sure Peter didn't come all this way to see me," Michael said, hoping he could keep the jealousy out of his voice.

"Actually, there is something I'd like to talk to you about," Peter contradicted him, finally dropping Erika's hand.

Michael stared at his brother. A beautiful woman was about to leave the room and he wasn't pursuing her. Whatever Peter had to say must be serious.

"I'll leave you then."

Erika turned to go, but Peter stopped her.

"I've had a wonderful lunch, and mostly because of you." Michael couldn't believe these lines worked, but the expression on Peter's face was genuine and Erika looked as if he were telling the truth. "I hope to see you again on Thanksgiving," he finished.

"Thanksgiving?"

"Didn't Michael tell you?"

They both turned to look at him. He felt as if their questioning stares were tangible. He'd forgotten about Thanksgiving. So much was happening to him—the office, Frank Mason's escape, the dreams, Malick. He'd completely forgotten about the invitation. In light of his previous invitation, he doubted she would have accepted even if he had remembered.

"Michael was supposed to invite you to the family dinner."

"I suppose it slipped his mind," Erika said. "It was nice meeting you. I'll have your coffee and dessert sent in."

Quickly she left the room. Michael tried to catch her eye, but she purposely didn't look at him. She couldn't be hurt. She'd told him they should only have a business relationship. A forgotten invitation from him couldn't mean anything to her. Could it? She'd refused his previous offer of a date. He had to be wrong. She was just leaving the room as she'd planned. He wanted to go to her, but the maid came in with the coffee and poured it into their cups. When she left, Peter started to talk.

"People say this all the time and I never thought I'd find myself saying it, but she's much better looking in person."

"Back off, Peter," Michael said. There was no mistaking the warning note in his voice.

"So it's like that, is it?" Peter asked. "I've been trying to figure that out."

"It's like that."

"Then why haven't you invited her to Thanksgiving dinner?"

"I've had a lot on my mind," he answered weakly. "I forgot."

"You could forget a woman like that?"

"Peter, can we drop it?" His tone was harsher than he intended, but Erika had completely thrown his senses out of kilter this afternoon and he hadn't completely recovered them yet. "I apologize. I didn't mean to sound so—"

"Jealous." Peter supplied the word he'd been groping for.

When Michael started to protest his brother stopped him. "Don't worry about it. Jealousy is healthy." Peter added sugar to his coffee and drank. Setting the cup back in the saucer, he said, "I came to talk to you about something that looks rather odd to me."

"What's that?" Michael sat forward in the chair. His brother's expression had changed from happy-go-lucky to serious.

"How much have you heard about Frank Mason since he escaped from the mental hospital?"

"Only that the police are still looking for him."

"Do you remember what he said at his sentencing?"

Michael didn't think he'd ever forget the words, or the expression on Frank Mason's face as he turned in the crowded courtroom and stared him directly in the eye. "Peter, where is this going?"

"Frank Mason swore he'd make you pay for what you'd done to him," Peter said. "He swore he'd make everyone pay. And now he's on the streets."

"What are you saying?" Michael was intrigued, but he didn't have time for a feature-length story.

"Got a VCR handy? I have something I want you to see."

They both stood. Michael took his coffee cup and started for the door.

"I think you'll want to leave the coffee," Peter stopped him.

"What do you have, dirty movies?"

"Absolutely," he said. "The gruesome kind."

There was none of the usual playfulness in Peter's face. He looked like the serious newsman who sat at the anchor desk five nights a week and read the evening news.

Michael ran his hand over his eyes half an hour later, when the screen went blank. Leaning forward he hid the emotion that gathered in his eyes and made him want to cry. Except for the Mason children and Abby, he hadn't cried since he was a small boy, but seeing the pictures on the video tape—Judge Baldwin, Abby's attorney and her husband, the blood, the sadistic method of killing—he hadn't thought anyone could be that crazy.

"Where did you get these?" Michael asked. The emotion wasn't fully out of his voice. "These are police tapes."

"I have a friend on the force. I reported the mystery of the lawyer's death, but didn't put him together with the Frank Mason case until the judge's story broke."

"What are you thinking?" Michael stared at his brother, the bloody pictures still in his mind.

"I think Frank Mason is making good his threat, and you're in his direct line."

"Why should I be there? I was *his* lawyer . . . much as I regret it," he added.

"Michael, I don't think he's going to remember that. I think he's crazy. How could a man do what he did and be sane?"

Michael stood up, feeling the need to walk. He went to the windows and looked out on the brown grass. The rain hadn't let up. Michael felt the weight of Frank's crime on his shoulders.

"Peter, I'm safe here. This place has its own security force, and Frank Mason doesn't even know where I am."

"You've been well publicized. It wouldn't be hard to find you, especially for a person who wants to, and remember how persistent he could be."

Michael remembered. Many times Michael had suggested that Frank accept other terms to full custody of his children, but he'd been relentless and Michael had been his puppet, getting him what he wanted, only to have him betray the innocent children.

"There's also Erika."

Michael turned abruptly at the mention of Erika's name.

"Notice who he's killing," Peter began. "The wives, husbands, families of the victims."

"You think—"

"If he comes looking for you, she's in danger, too."

Michael's stomach knotted. He hadn't considered Erika. Frank was his problem, not hers. He needed to protect her.

"Michael, I think you should leave here. Go someplace else until Frank is caught."

He could hear the concern in his brother's voice. Peter was

afraid for him. "I can't leave," he told him. "Erika and I are bound by the terms of Carlton Lipton-Graves's will."

"Your life is in danger. I'm sure if you went to court and explained to the judge, he'd grant you special dispensation."

"He might, but I doubt it."

"Why?"

"Frank hasn't been caught, and according to you only circumstantial evidence connects him with the crimes. They could be coincidences. The perpetrator could be another of the judge's enemies. He need not be Frank Mason."

"It's still worth a try." Peter's face was drawn and Michael knew his brother was concerned about his safety.

"Even if I did go before a judge, there's still Erika. If Frank is looking for me and comes here, he'll find Erika. He could hurt her in order to find me. I can't leave her here alone."

"Don't you think she'd be willing to come with you?"

This was a huge house. Michael could see the two of them confined to a small apartment or hotel room. After what had happened this morning he knew being confined with Erika would be like throwing a match in a vat of nitroglycerin.

"I'll have security doubled, alert them to be on the lookout for Frank, and make sure Erika is protected at all times."

Peter was quiet for a moment. Michael knew he was processing information like a human computer, trying to find a more acceptable alternative.

"You're in love with her," Peter stated softly and truthfully. Michael nodded.

Erika prowled in the library. She remembered thinking how big this room was when she first ran into it. Carlton had caught her arms and stopped her. He was big, too. Now the room was smaller. She felt caged in, and wanted to throw open the French doors at the end of the room and make the space larger.

The rain stopped her. It beat against the panes like steady

smacks. Yet the smacks didn't blot out what had happened earlier, when Michael had touched her, kissed her.

Could he be the one? she asked herself. *The man who would want her, love her? Was there any man who could fall in love with her?* She'd asked herself that question for years, ever since her mother told her she'd never find anyone who'd really love her. Each time Erika had been asked on a date or met a new man, she'd ask herself if he was the one.

Then she'd met Bill Castle. He was the closest she'd come to believing he was the one. Look where that had led her. At first she'd been blinded by his lifestyle; parties every night, mingling with the rich and famous. For a while she thought she could survive in that world, but she knew better now. She didn't like the limelight. She found it too hard to let reporters print lies about her and not respond. The world of pop music was a world in which no one was real. Each person had a mask, and was trying to climb over someone else to get what he wanted. Isn't that what had happened to her? Hadn't Jennifer Ahrends climbed over her to get to her fiancé?

Erika sat down at the desk and stared at the rain. So far, every man she'd ever met had left her, beginning with her father. Michael would be no different. He might have kissed her until she couldn't think straight, until she couldn't distinguish between reality and fantasy, but she knew now, in the cold light of day, that he would be gone in less than a year.

Why should he want her? She wasn't beautiful. She wished she was, but she knew better. Michael was the best-looking man she'd ever seen. Women must fall all over him. The ones at her office certainly would, given the chance. So far she hadn't seen him give anyone a chance—except her. But she was merely convenient. They occupied the same house, met for meals, and found it necessary to talk constantly during the workday.

He didn't really want her, not for the long-term. No one had in the past, and Michael was no different from Bill Castle or any of the other men she'd ever met. When their year was over Michael would go. He'd be a rich man, a very rich man. He could have any woman he wanted. Erika knew she wouldn't be the one he chose.

"Erika."

She whirled around, startled, standing up like a child caught doing something she'd been expressly forbidden to do. Michael walked into the room. He was alone. She'd been thinking of him, and his sudden presence made her pulses beat.

"Where's Peter?" she asked.

"He ask me to say good-bye for him. He had to get back."

Erika was dismayed. She liked Peter and would have liked talking to him again. He'd also provided a buffer between Michael and her. Since this morning she had felt as if electricity flowed around her whenever Michael entered the room. Her heart fluttered out of control when Michael whispered her name. With Peter, she'd be on safe ground.

"I want you to promise me something," Michael began.

"What?" Erika asked.

Michael took the seat in front of the desk. His face was serious, more than when she'd first seen him at the cabin. Erika was suddenly afraid. What had his brother told him after she left?

"Before I ask for the promise, I need to tell you something."

Erika's heart beat fast. Michael was scaring her.

"I was Frank Mason's lawyer. His wife's name was Abigail Mason. She sued him for divorce and I represented Frank in the custody battle over their three young children."

Erika knew this. Carlton's lawyer had given her the overall details, but she didn't tell Michael. She wanted to hear what had happened from him. He'd called Abby's name in his nightmares. She wanted to know how well he knew her and if they had been lovers. It was masochistic, she knew, but she wanted to know, anyway.

Michael got up and paced the floor before the huge fireplace. He dug his hands in his pockets, then took them out. Erika got up and went to stand behind one of the chairs that stood before the fire. The crackle of dry logs was the only sound in the room.

"Frank gave me details about his wife, and I used them. I believed what he said—that his wife was the one who was the unfit parent, that she had a string of affairs, left the children unattended, and was responsible for their accidents."

"Michael, a lawyer is supposed to believe in his client."

"They always lie," he snapped. "At least they omit part of the truth. A lawyer knows that. But I let it go. I let it go, and three children are dead!"

"Michael, it isn't your fault. You couldn't have known what he would do."

"I should have. I should have listened to what his wife's lawyer was telling me, but I was too busy. I had other things on my mind."

"What . . . what other things?"

"I'd been asked to run for state office, and I was considering it. This case was highly publicized. I did my damndest to make Abigail Mason the devil, and she wasn't."

The last two words were almost a cry. Erika's heart clenched at the pain Michael was feeling.

"After the judge awarded the children to their father everything seemed to be in my favor. The political heavyweights courted me, the press followed my movements, the papers hailed me as the next state senator." Michael paused. He wasn't talking to her. He was remembering. Erika had the feeling he'd never talked about this to anyone. She waited, not wanting to interrupt him.

"Then one day Frank agreed to let the children see their mother," he continued. "He called me to meet him for the exchange. He said he didn't want to be alone, didn't trust himself around Abby."

"You agreed to go?"

Michael nodded. "He was to meet her at one of the shopping

malls. I got there and parked. I saw Abby get out of her car and we both got to the entry door at the same time."

He closed his eyes as if he could blot out the memory. "I'll never forget the look she gave me, the vile names she called me. She went through the door before me. The place was crowded with back to school shoppers. When Abby saw the children they were at the end of a long corridor. I saw Frank. He watched her come toward them. He waited until she was close enough to see everything, but too far away to do anything. The children saw their mother and began to run toward her. Then Frank took out a gun, and with the precision of a marksman put a bullet through each one of the children's heads."

Erika gasped, her hand going to her heart. She knew the children had been killed—Steven had told her—but Michael's version was so much more immediate. The impact hit her like a dynamite blast. She could feel the horror of the children dying, of their mother trying to get to them, of knowing that Michael felt he'd been part of the crime.

"I was his witness." Michael hung his head. Erika knew now why he'd retreated to the mountains, and why he never wanted to return to being a lawyer. Hadn't she wanted to do the same thing? What would she have done if her problem had resulted in someone's death? Tears sprang to her eyes and her chest felt hollow.

"Suddenly I was bad news," Michael went on. "No one wanted to talk to me except the press. They wanted to skin me alive." He looked at her. "I graciously withdrew my name from consideration."

"Is that when you left?" she asked.

Michael shook his head. "I testified at Frank's trial, then stayed around until it was over, foolishly thinking I could go on. The day Frank Mason was sentenced I went to court. He swore he'd escape, that no jail or hospital could hold him, that he'd get even with everyone who had made his life miserable."

"That wouldn't include you," she told him, wiping her eyes with the tips of her fingers.

Michael hesitated for a moment. "He looked directly at me when he said it."

"Why?" Her voice was no more than a low rush of air.

"I don't know. The court remanded him to a psychiatric hospital. He blames everyone who had anything to do with his case."

Erika sat, stunned. Then she got up and walked to the fireplace. Frank Mason had escaped. She remembered the reporter at the press conference telling them, and she remembered Michael's reaction to the news. She shuddered as a sudden chill skittered through her. Wrapping her hands around herself, she tried to hold in the nervous tension that knotted her stomach.

"He's been in that hospital for how long? Years? He could have forgotten all about you."

"That's true," Michael said, but he wasn't convinced, and neither was she. If Frank Mason was looking for Michael, he'd be easy to find. Erika suddenly went to him, grasping his arms.

"Michael, you have to leave here," she said.

"That was Peter's suggestion."

"It's a good one."

Michael shook his head. "I've already explained to him the many reasons leaving won't work, only one of which is Carlton's will."

Erika dropped her hands and turned away. She'd forgotten about the will. It seemed that every time they turned around Carlton's will tied their hands.

"Michael, your life could be in danger. Isn't there anything we can do?"

"I'm not the only person in danger."

Erika stared at him. "What do you mean?"

Michael explained what Peter had told him about the families of the other victims.

"We're not related."

"I don't think he's going to stop to check genealogy."

Erika couldn't keep her face straight. She was scared suddenly. Someone could kill Michael and her.

"It's going to be all right, Erika. Let me handle it."

"What are you going to do?"

"Add more security here. And I promise I'll be careful."

"That's all? Shouldn't we call the police or something?"

"What would we tell them?"

"That Frank Mason is trying to kill you."

"We don't know that."

"Yet," she said. "Michael, we can't wait for him actually to—" She stopped, unable to complete the sentence.

Michael came to her. "Erika, I need a promise from you."

She waited for him to continue. Michael told her about the people Frank was alleged to have killed. "I want you to promise me you'll be careful, that until Frank Mason is caught you will take care to always be with someone."

"Someone? Like who?" Erika stared at him. "You think I should get a bodyguard?"

Michael hadn't thought of a bodyguard, but he had to admit it was a good idea. It would solve his problem of how to protect her when he wasn't around.

"Yes," he said, seizing the idea. "We'll hire one tomorrow."

"Michael, I'd feel silly with a bodyguard. Frank hasn't even been spotted near here and we don't even know it's him for sure. With the increase in security, we should be safe enough."

"I'd feel safer knowing there was someone protecting you."

"Me!" she said. "Frank doesn't know anything about me. He'd be looking for you. If anyone needs protection it's you, not me."

"I don't need protection from Frank Mason."

Erika shivered at the coldness in his voice. He spoke as if he wanted to meet Frank. Erika knew there was unfinished business between them. They represented good and evil, black and white, and inevitably they had to meet and take a stand. Erika could only hope that meeting occurred on the opposite sides of a courtroom table and not a .357 Magnum.

Twelve

The clock chimed midnight in the distance before Erika climbed the stairs that night. At the landing that separated her wing of the house from the one Michael used, she stopped and turned back. She hadn't really looked at the house in years. Tonight she turned before the stained glass window and surveyed the bottom floor. Life had been different since Michael had come, but she'd become used to his presence, his habits, even his bouts with nightmares.

Tomorrow they would add different elements to the household. Even though they wouldn't have bodyguards immediately, it was only a matter of time, if Frank Mason really wanted Michael dead. She, too, would have to accept one if she insisted Michael take one on. Erika didn't know how she felt about having a stranger around all the time. She put her hand on the large newel post and stared into the semi-darkness. For so many years it had been Carlton and her. The servants maintained the household, kept the grounds, and cooked the meals. While Erika knew them intimately, they'd been there for years and she was used to their presence. Then Michael had come, on the heels of Carlton's death. Somehow he had a connection to the house. Strangers—she didn't know what to make of them. Someone always with her, protecting her from possible harm. She shivered in the warm air.

She sighed, accepting that change was part of life. Carlton was gone and she never thought she'd be able to get over the hurt his death caused, but she was doing fine. Then Michael had come and her routine had changed. She smiled to herself. She couldn't say she hated the routine. Day by day he'd wormed his way into her heart until the thought of him could take her breath away.

Maybe having more people around would give her something else to concentrate on and she could get her emotions in order.

She glanced in the direction of her room, but she saw something move from the corner of her eye and turned toward Michael's wing. He stood at the top of the stairs dressed in a silk robe. Erika opened her mouth to speak, but her throat went so dry she couldn't. The hallway behind Michael was dark and she couldn't see his face, but something wouldn't let her move, wouldn't let her breathe.

The memory of another night came back to her. She knew the robe—she'd seen it before, lying at the foot of his bed during one of his nightmares—yet she thought she'd never seen him wearing it. Somehow, she had seen that robe on him, contoured to his dark body as he tuned and walked away. It was the dream, what she thought was the dream. Had it been?

"You were in my room," she stated it as fact, as if he knew she meant the night she'd had the dream that he was there.

Michael started down the stairs. Erika took a step back when he reached the bottom step.

"Yes," he said softly. "I needed to know you were safe."

"Safe from what?" she whispered, feeling anything but safe at the moment.

His hands slipped around her waist. Erika didn't think to protest. Indeed, it was the most natural thing that had ever happened to her. Heat swept through her blouse where his hands touched her and instantly her entire body became an incinerator. She didn't know what kept her from dissolving into a puddle of chocolate syrup at Michael's feet.

Michael took a step closer to her. Erika's gaze was fastened on his collarbone. She swallowed and looked up. Light filtering through the stained glass crossed his face with planes of blue and yellow. The garish light turned his features into harsh lines, giving him a sinister look. The dimension increased Erika's excitement. She'd never felt so hungry for a man. His eyes were dark with passion. The heat of his body mingled with hers, cocooning them in a world only they could create. His arms slid around her, pulling her length into contact with his. Every part of them touched—arms to arms, breasts to breasts, thigh to thigh. Everything made contact except their lips.

"If you don't kiss me, I'm going to die," she rasped in a voice she didn't recognize.

Michael stared at her, his eyes reverently memorizing her features. Then his mouth lowered and took hers in a kiss that might have been soft and persuasive, but was hard and hungry and sent the blood rushing to her ears. The ensuing sound was deafening.

Michael's arms pinned her to him. His mouth was greedy in its possession. Erika wouldn't have had it any other way. Her arms went around his neck, the two of them caught in a primal dance as ageless as time.

Michael felt everything about her. His hands had taken on a life of their own. They covered her, touching her everywhere, pulling her into closer contact with him. Her legs lifted against his thigh. Her jeans, rough against his silk-covered leg, sent heat straight to his loins. His mouth couldn't get enough of her. She tasted wonderful, lusty, full of life, and he wanted to touch, feel, learn, every part of her slim body.

Hooking her leg over his, she swung herself into his arms, both legs circling him. Michael lifted his mouth at the boldness of her action. Businesslike, made for the boardroom crowd, Erika St. James was the passionate type. He'd known it, tested her, pushed her until they'd come to this juncture, this charge-building explosive that was bound to detonate this very night.

Michael turned her, taking a step up, never letting his mouth leave hers. It was a slow process climbing the eight stairs to the landing, but it was the most exciting climb he'd ever made.

He wouldn't let her go, wouldn't break the contact as he carried her to his room. Inside, he kicked the door closed and let her slide over his body to the floor.

They stared at each other, both raggedly breathing, heaving air into their lungs as if it were a scarce commodity. Her chest rose and fell in rapid succession. Michael reached forward and undid the top button of her blouse. He felt a quiver run through her when his fingers brushed her skin. In this light she was dark as berry wine, and he wanted to drink.

The second button opened and he felt her tremble. Her bra came into view with the third button. Michael couldn't wait any longer. He pulled her forward, her head lolled back, and he kissed her neck, her cheek. His tongue followed the curve of her ear. The shudder that passed through her pushed him on. He wanted her, he had to have her tonight. Carefully, he peeled her blouse down her arms. Each tender amount of flesh exposed drove him insane with need. His hands went to the snap on her jeans. It came free in his hands. Then he was pulling them down her legs. She stepped out of them and her shoes in one movement, standing before him in only a lace bra and panties. She couldn't have been more sexy if she'd been naked. Michael wanted to look at her, commit her to memory.

She reached for him, taking the knot of his robe in her hands. The silk gave way easily and she opened it. For the longest moment she looked at him. His body was aroused, hard and pulsing. She could be in no doubt of how much he wanted her. The last of her clothes dropped to the floor and, walking her backward, he lowered her to the bed.

Michael joined Erika, threading his fingers through her soft hair. Curling his hand around the back of her head, he kissed her softly, holding himself in check. He felt as if this would be the first time he'd ever made love to a woman. He'd had sex, but tonight he was going to make love. This time would be for keeps. There would be no going back.

Erika had never known herself to be as aggressive as she was with Michael. She pulled him to her, leaving not even enough space for air to get between them. His kisses drugged her and she only wanted more. Quickly, passion gripped them and the last of her control snapped. Michael climbed on top of her and she opened her legs to accommodate him. She groaned as he entered her. Pleasure rocketed through her, feelings so strong, so sensual that she thought the overload would kill her. Her fingers dug into Michael's skin as his body rocked into her. Forces greater than the two of them aligned, setting the pace, the rhythm that culminated into a sexual dance shared by only the two of them.

Waves of rapture rioted through her. "Michael!" she screamed over and over as he dug harder, deeper, into her. Erika abandoned anything that could hold her back. She wanted Michael to have everything. She didn't care if he found out she loved him. She wanted him to know. With her body she told him. She opened the temple, crying out as the pinnacle of allowable pleasure racked her body and together the two of them released in mutual satisfaction.

Michael collapsed onto her, their bodies gleaming with sweat. He craved air, dragging it into his lungs in huge mouthfuls. Sex had never been this satisfying, this rich or poignant. Erika had done this to him. She'd showed him what it was like to be in love. He'd never recover from something like this. He wanted to hold her forever, keep her close and protected and never let anything hurt her. He wanted to live for her, to love her, to be with her morning and night, to make love to her and feel this way for the rest of his life.

The room had the unmistakable smell of sex—sweet, electric, and hot. Erika hugged Michael. He felt her hands on his back, loving the feel of them, loving everything about her. He gathered her close, slipping his weight to the mattress. He gazed into her love-dazed eyes and wondered how he could have come this far in life and never experienced the true meaning of love.

* * *

This was going to be fun, Frank thought. He hadn't been to the mountains since he was a child. His whole family had come—his mother and father, his brothers. Early in the morning they'd get up and go fishing in the stream, just his father and him. The others had been too lazy. They wanted to sleep. But not Frank. Frank could do anything. He and his father caught fish in the small stream and brought them back for breakfast. His mother cooked them and they all ate. In the mountains they didn't have any rules about eating in the kitchen or what constituted breakfast foods.

In the mountains they could explore. Frank liked exploring. He'd climb the hills, better than his brothers. He could get to the top of any cliff long before his two brothers could reach him. And his father praised him. Those were the only times Frank could remember his father giving him praise.

He'd make his dad proud today. Frank touched the gun concealed under his jacket. It was a new revolver—he'd ditched the one he'd used on Abby's lawyer—automatic with chambers for eight, brass-encased bullets. Each chamber was filled, although Frank didn't expect to use more than one. He was a neat man and he liked things tidy. Killing the judge and his wife had been messy business. Blood seeping into the carpet. The entire room would have to be replaced. There was no way to get that kind of a stain out.

Today Frank wouldn't have to think about carpets. He had the entire outdoors. Today he was on a hunt, and he had the upper hand. The prey didn't even know about him. Frank grinned. Adrenaline pumped through him. He'd be finished before morning and he could join Abby and the children. Maybe they'd go camping, fishing with his girls. Abby would cook the fish they caught, and they could eat them for breakfast, too.

Tomorrow, Abby, he thought. *We'll do it tomorrow.*

Michael jerked awake. Sweat poured off him. His knee hit something and he stopped. Something warm. His eyes snapped open. Erika was there. She stirred next to him, her short hair mussed, her features relaxed. Memory came back and he went still, not wanting to awaken her.

He'd had a dream, not the nightmare that usually disturbed his sleep, and it was morning. The nightmares usually came in the middle of the night.

Michael lay back, his arm propped under his head, the other hand gently holding Erika's. It had been a long time since he'd awakened next to a woman. He savored the moment. He wanted to kiss her awake, make love to her again, but the dream was nagging him. Erika had been there, smiling at him, her arms open and inviting. He'd been running toward her. Then she'd suddenly disappeared. Nothing awful had happened. Dreams often dissolve into nothingness. Yet Michael had the unnerving feeling that there was danger in the dream. Danger for Erika.

He watched her sleeping. Her dark skin contrasting against the whiteness of the bedcovers touched him in an elemental way. He wanted her safe. He wanted to know that she wouldn't be harmed for anything he'd done. Hadn't they spoken about Frank Mason? Hadn't Peter shown him films of crime scenes? Wouldn't it be natural for him to have such a dream? Michael knew the answers to all these questions. It was natural that he should have a dream that might include all the conversations he'd had in the past few hours, but he couldn't shake the feeling that Erika was somehow involved, or would be involved, and he'd be unable to help her.

She stirred again, her hand groping for him. She ran it across his bare belly and the first intoxicating thrill of arousal warmed his loins. Abandoning the dream, Michael ran his hand over Erika's arm and pulled her against him. He held her as if she were a baby. She was safe for the time being, and he'd get her a bodyguard, someone who'd make sure nothing happened to her.

And he'd be there whenever he could.

* * *

Erika opened her eyes. Fear made her heart beat fast. She looked around. She was alone. She could hear the sound of water running in the bathroom shower. Michael must be in there. Erika sat up quickly. The sheet covering her nakedness fell away. She grabbed for it as if someone would see her. She had to get out of there. Pushing the sheet away, she got out of bed. Seeing Michael's robe lying on the floor, she grabbed it, stuffing her hands in the overly-long sleeves. Her clothes were strewn over the floor. She snatched them up as she practically ran from the room. At the landing, she skipped steps going down and up the other side.

In her own room she slammed the door and pressed her back against it. How could she have let last night happen? She remembered standing on the landing and deciding to go to her room. Then Michael was above her, looking into her eyes, and from then on everything became a dream. But it wasn't a dream. She'd actually slept with him. The stiffness in her body told her, and her mind remembered. Her nipples got hard at the flash of memory that went through her mind of them making love. Nothing had ever happened like that before. She'd never abandoned herself so freely, demanded so much of a partner, wanted to please so desperately, and been so fulfilled.

What would happen now? He'd leave her, like all the rest. This time would be worse. At least in the past she hadn't had to see them day in and day out. But Michael lived there, worked with her. There was nothing she'd be able to do except die a little each day.

Hot tears spilled from her eyes and rolled over her cheeks. She could never let this happen again. If she did, it was unlikely she would survive when he left. Erika slid to the floor, pulling her knees to her chest and resting her head on them.

She wept.

"Michael, I'm so glad to see you," Malick said when he came into the room. Malick sat in a huge chair next to the hospital bed which had been installed on the first floor of his house. A uniformed nurse smiled at him and left the room carrying a tray with medicines on it. "I've been watching the news and—"

"Malick, this is not good for your blood pressure. I'm going to have that television removed."

"Michael, have you heard that Judge Baldwin and Angela Gilford are both dead?"

"I know that."

"You know? Have you called the police?"

"No," he said. Malick was obviously distressed. Michael sat down on the chair opposite him and explained everything that had happened in the past few days, except the night he'd spent with Erika. That he was keeping to himself. He wanted to hold the memory like a stolen piece of art, that only he could take out and look at. "I want to call Connie Forester."

"Hand me the phone," Malick said, his hand reaching toward the instrument. "She's one of the best. You couldn't do better."

Michael picked up the cordless instrument. "I want her to protect Erika." He paused. "But Erika can't know about it."

"That won't be a problem for Connie, but what about you?" Malick held the phone, no dialing.

"I'll need someone else. Someone discreet Erika won't notice or think is following either of us." He didn't really want anyone. He could handle Frank if he showed up, but he knew if he didn't take a guard Malick would spend time worrying over him. He also thought the two of them could work to protect both him and Erika, if need be.

Malick dialed. "I know just the person."

Malick had been a force in his day. Many people owed him favors—more than a Capitol Hill politician. When he finished one call he immediately dialed another. At the conclusion of the call he smiled and looked at Michael.

"It's all set. Connie will arrive tonight to guard Erika and Adrienne Dantley will be your guard."

"Adrienne?"

"She's just as good as Connie. Don't worry. Until Frank is caught I need to know you're all right."

"I can take care of myself—"

"Don't assume that's true," Malick interrupted. "We've had many assassinations of people who thought they could take care of themselves." Malick smiled. He looked more relaxed than when Michael had first seen him. "How is Erika?"

Michael tensed, hoping Malick didn't notice. He couldn't even think of Erika without remembering last night. It was incredible, what had happened between them. Yet when he'd returned from his shower she was gone. He didn't get to see her before coming here. His thoughts continually returned to the most spectacular night of his life. "She's fine," he said. "I left the maids looking after her and told the guards to admit no one."

Michael felt better, now that he knew Connie would be coming and that Erika would be protected. He'd seen Connie's work. She was expensive, and often sought after, yet Malick had been able to get her to drop whatever she was doing and come to do him a favor. Michael wondered what Malick had done to make her indebted to him.

"Michael," Malick called his name. While Michael had been wondering about Malick, his friend had obviously been observing him. "What about Highland Hills?" Malick paused, giving him a steady gaze. "Have you changed your mind about returning there?"

Erika's face immediately popped into his mind. Michael didn't know when it had happened, but recently he'd been thinking of the future. Whenever he did, his thoughts always came back to her. And after last night he knew he couldn't imagine spending his life on that mountain without Erika. She'd gotten into his blood and he was happy to have her there, but at the moment he wasn't ready to admit it, even to Malick.

"I haven't decided," he finally answered.

Thirteen

Fresh air. Frank expanded his lungs, filling them with the cold mountain air. He wore no shirt or shoes, only his pants. The dirt and gravel under his feet cut into his flesh, and the dew-misty morning cloud glistened on his skin. Frank bent one knee while extending his leg backward and stretching. He loved mornings in the mountains. He'd been camping for a week, climbing the mountains and jogging through trails that only animals saw. It made him tough, like his father had wanted him to be.

Grabbing two large stones, Frank used them as weights, extending his arms backward to flex his triceps and rolling upward to strengthen already developed biceps. He sucked oxygen in and pushed out used air. His father couldn't have survived the past week outdoors but Frank had, and he'd be able to survive more. The police were looking for him, but they'd never find him. After he was through with Michael Lawrence he and Abby would disappear. No one would ever interfere with them again.

Finishing his morning routine, Frank picked up a sweater and pulled it over his head. He slipped his arms into his jacket and cleaned his feet before clothing them with socks and hiking boots. Frank was hungry. His food supply was nearly gone. He had no choice but to go to the store and get more. He'd be discreet. If anyone asked, he was a businessman, spending a few days in the mountains before the weather got too cold for camping. He pulled a baseball cap on his head. He didn't want to be recognized. He'd make sure he didn't look directly at anyone, so they couldn't identify him.

Frank went to the edge of the hill on which he camped. It appeared Michael Lawrence had taken a vacation. Frank had been to the cabin. The place was clean, but there were definite signs that he was still living there. No smoke came from the chimney, and Michael was too soft to stay up here without heat. Frank felt safe in leaving to get more supplies. Michael could take his time. Frank could wait. Abby could wait. Soon it would be over, and then they'd have their whole lives together.

The general store wasn't far. At this time of morning, only mothers needing diapers and true mountain men would be out. Frank didn't think there were too many mountain men running around in November, so that only left mothers.

There were no standard aisles of food, canned goods, or cosmetic products. The place was a mess. There didn't seem to be any order to the products for sale, just a mass of items sitting haphazardly about the floor or littered about on tables. Frank took a wire basket from a stack by the door and forced himself to leisurely walk about in the disorder, putting things in it. In five minutes he had everything he needed and started for the counter.

A white-haired man wearing a black sweater and wool trousers waited for him. Frank bent his head as if checking out possible items to add to his basket on his way to the front of the store. He set the basket on the counter, continuing to check out the space in front of him. His purpose was to keep his head down and his face away from the store owner.

"Anything else?" the man asked.

"That'll be all," Frank said. He reached in his back pocket for his wallet.

The old cash register clanked as the man rang up his purchases.

Frank noticed the wall behind the man. He almost laughed out loud. *Serves me right for not being a reader,* Frank told himself. There, on the wall, was a yellowing newspaper article and Michael Lawrence's picture.

"Used to live up here," the man said.

Frank was so startled he looked directly at the store owner. "Used to?"

"Moved back to the city, must be two months, almost three now," the man supplied.

Frank tried to read the clippings as the ancient cash register went through its designed purpose.

"She come up, and a few days later he followed her back to Philadelphia."

Frank didn't say a word, just continued trying to read the newsprint.

"Can't say as I blame him. She's a looker."

Frank had to agree with that. "Graves Heiress," he read in hopes of keeping the store owner talking.

"She inherited the fortune after Carlton Lipton-Graves died. Then what do you think?" The man stopped long enough to scratch his head. "His grandson turns out to be living right here with us."

"That must have been a surprise."

"Yep," he confirmed.

Frank paid his bill and said good-bye. Outside he dropped the bag in the jeep and climbed inside. So Michael Lawrence wasn't away on vacation. He'd permanently left the cabin to go and claim his fortune. He and Erika St. James.

Frank threw the gearshift into reverse and backed down the drive. He turned the jeep down the mountain and headed toward Philadelphia, abandoning his campsite. There was nothing he needed there. He sought Michael Lawrence. The groundhogs could have everything else.

Erika closeted herself in the library. Papers covered the desk in front of her, but as far as her comprehension was concerned they could have been written in Chinese. Her thoughts were on Michael. She was going to have to face him sooner or later. How was she going to act? she asked herself. They were both adults. There was no reason she should feel uncomfortable. People met and fell into bed together all the time. But not her. And it wasn't as if they had just met. Michael had lived under the same roof with her for almost three months. Then last night had happened. She'd looked up and he'd been there. She didn't know how to explain her feelings, even to herself. She wasn't in love with Michael, was she? Yet their time in bed had been so . . . overwhelming. She swung around to stare at the door of the library. Her body was suddenly hot, flashing heat, the way she'd felt when Michael had held her in his arms.

What would she say when she saw him? They'd spent the night in bed, making love. She couldn't pretend nothing had happened. Something had definitely happened. Her life had been changed, irrevocably. Had his? She didn't think so. He was up and gone before she'd dressed and come down to breakfast. Maybe he didn't want to face her, either.

What were they going to do? They couldn't live here for the next nine months tiptoeing around each other. She certainly couldn't let herself fall under his spell again. She knew where that would lead. She'd be left virtually at the altar again. Reporters would hound her, she wouldn't be able to concentrate on Graves Enterprises, and she'd never be able to raise her head or appear in public again. It was much better if she adopted a more professional attitude. She could control her thoughts, her feelings, and she'd never let herself be pulled into fantasy again, even if the fantasy was the best one she'd ever felt.

Erika turned back to the papers on her desk. It took a while but she immersed herself in the work and forgot about everything else.

When the outer door opened and closed she knew he was back. Her hands shook slightly, her breath went shallow, her mouth dry. She anticipated his approach and stood up, but his footsteps on the tile floor passed her by.

Quickly she went to the door and flung it open. Michael turned at the base of the staircase.

"Hello." He smiled. "I missed you this morning."

His smile was dazzling. She felt herself falling for it. What was it about him that made her all soft and jelly-like inside? She'd just made a decision and now she was considering forgetting it and running into his arms.

He came back toward her. Erika wanted to move but her feet were rooted to the floor. He took her chin in his hand and bent to kiss her. Erika's eyes closed. She refused to fight the fingers of pleasure racing through her. *Just this one time,* she thought. She'd remember later to stop him, but just this one time she wanted to feel his arms around her again.

Stepping into the space separating them, she molded herself to him. Her arms circled his neck and he crushed her to him and kissed her passionately, like he had last night. Erika kissed him as if her life depended on it, as if it were the last time.

Hard bodies. That was the only term Michael could think of to describe Connie Forester and Adrienne Dantley. Even through their clothes he could see the strength of their outline. They shook hands in a small restaurant where the grease smelled old, but the Philly steaks were unmatchable.

Both women had strong grips, but only Adrienne looked as if she could handle a man of Frank Mason's height and weight. She was only a hair shorter than Michael with toned muscles and skin the color of aged teak. Her hair was short and her features angular and hard, but when she smiled every part of her seemed to soften.

Connie, on the other hand, couldn't be more than five feet tall. Her hair was long and fine and she wore it pulled back in a ponytail that hung to her shoulder blades. Streaks of grey strands ran through it like snow trails. She looked about forty. She was compact, muscular, and dressed in pants and a sweater. The sweater had a dragon on it made of gold sequins.

"I know this is a little too cloak and daggerish, but I couldn't meet you at the house. I don't want to upset Erika more than necessary."

"We understand," Connie said in a voice as soft as cotton candy.

"I got these pictures from my brother." Michael handed them both a news photo of Erika. He went on to explain the situation. He told them nothing was certain and he wasn't prone to jumping to conclusions, but two people involved in the case were now dead and he didn't want any surprises if Frank Mason did have something to do with these recent murders.

Connie leafed through the folder. "I'll need more if I'm to be properly prepared. I want to know everything there is about him, from the time he was born until yesterday," she said.

"I'll get you everything I can."

"Transcripts of his trial and the custody battle, where he grew up, his neighbors, church groups, if any, everything."

"I'll have my brother send you everything you want," Michael told her. "Just make sure Erika is kept safe."

Connie nodded. "She'll never know we're around," Adrienne told him.

"Good," Michael said, and finished his steak and cola. He didn't even see them following him back to the mansion. Security had been notified of their presence and given photos of them, so if they needed to get inside there wouldn't be a problem.

He felt a lot better letting himself into the house after meeting the two women. Erika would be safe. He could sleep well.

He was wrong. The dream stole into his sleep like a filmy cloud. Everything was shrouded behind it. He couldn't see clearly, but he recognized Erika. They were in the gym. She climbed the ropes, up and down, hand over hand, pulling herself up. Then the room dissolved into the mountain. Erika ran up the hill, behind bushes and trees. Frank pursued her, cutting the distance between them with his wider gait. Michael screamed to her, hoping she would hear him in time to protect herself. Her motions were slow, yet Michael couldn't get to her, couldn't scream loud enough for her to hear, couldn't reach Frank in time to stop him.

Frank stopped. His face swirled toward Michael in a grotesque mask of determined horror. Then he turned back. Erika ran on. Frank took aim, both hands holding onto the gun. The sound deafened Michael as Frank fired.

The bullet hit Erika in the back. Her hands opened out on impact. The bullet pushed her off balance as she ran. Michael could hear her scream, yet he could do nothing to stop the horror unfolding in front of his eyes. He screamed loud, anguished, gut-wrenching cries until someone began speaking to him. He could hear the calming voice, but not distinguish whose it was. It was a woman. She smelled sweet and felt soft. He grabbed her and held on, wanting it to be Erika, wanting to change the events he'd just witnessed, knowing he had no way of doing so. He buried his face in her neck, ran his hands through her hair and took long, hard breaths. He held on, gasping the air.

Michael came awake holding someone. He opened his eyes, telling himself she was part of the dream, but she didn't disappear. He smelled her perfume and felt the sheer fabric of her nightgown. "Erika!" he said in surprise. Pushing himself back, he looked at her. "You're here?" He hauled her close, hugging her to him.

"You were screaming my name," she said. Her voice was no more than a whisper and Michael loved it. He felt her feather light breath on his neck.

"I'm sorry," he apologized after a moment. "I didn't mean to wake you. I have bad dreams." He released her and fell back against the pillows, one arm covering his eyes. He needed to get control of his breathing and the thudding of his heart. The dream had caused part of it, but finding Erika in his arms was the part that had him unnerved.

"Are you all right?" she asked, leaning toward him.

"Yes," he said.

Erika pushed herself off the bed and stood up. Michael

thought she was leaving, but she came around the bed and sat next to him. "Do you want to tell me about the dreams?"

He moved his arm and looked at her. Moonlight flowed through the windows, the only illumination in the room. It turned her gown into a shimmering robe of silver, making her skin golden in contrast. Michael wanted her. He'd made love to her once, and she had been all he could think of since. He wanted her again and again, thinking he could never get too much of Erika St. James.

"Are they always the same?" she asked.

"Most of the time."

"They're about Abby?"

"How did you know?" He wondered if he'd had a dream the night they were together. He remembered waking after one, but she was asleep, and he hadn't cried out.

"At the cabin," she told him. "You had a dream there. Since you came here there have been two other times that I know of."

He stared at her, hoping she didn't know, that she hadn't heard him calling her name more than this one time.

"Is that why you picked this room, the last one in the wing, so I wouldn't hear you in the night?"

Michael knew she was perceptive. He nodded, but didn't think she could see him in the dim light. "They don't come often," he lied. Since he'd met her it seemed the dreams had accelerated, but then Frank Mason had come back into his life at the same time. Erika had been the messenger. Michael assumed that was the reason she often appeared in the nightmares instead of Abby.

"How often is not often?"

"Erika, you're not a psychiatrist."

She reached for his hand and slipped her smaller one into it. "I hope I'm a friend."

Michael stared at her in the darkness. He closed his hand around hers and urged her forward. She came without hesitation. He pulled until she lost her balance and fell against him.

Slipping his hand around her head, he threaded it through her short curls, staring at each minute part of her face—her eyes, her forehead, her nose, her lips. At the distance of a kiss he whispered, "You're more than a friend."

Michael closed the millimeter separating them, taking her mouth in a searing kiss. Her mouth was hot, wet, and demanding. Michael felt like a man of fire and Erika an oxygen source. His mouth ate up the life-giving air, consuming it, until the two of them were part of the singular.

Erika's gown, under Michael's hands, was cool against her hot body. He ran his palms over the fabric as if it were a liquid. Her mouth opened to him, giving him her taste as their tongues met and mated. Sensations flashed through Michael. He pulled Erika over him, then turned her over his body until he lay on top of her. Her arms reached for him, caressing his back with long fingers that drew trails of fire over his skin. Michael took in a long breath, raising his head to gaze down at her. Erika's eyes were passion-filled, her lips swollen from the impact of his mouth on hers. She was the most beautiful woman he'd ever seen, and he liked seeing her in this light.

She was driving him crazy and he liked it. Michael had never expected his dream to lead him here. He didn't expect Erika to come to his room. He knew he wanted her here. He wanted her here every night and every morning. What would she think if he told her that?

"Michael," Erika said. The low, sexy quality that entered her voice whenever they made love was there, unraveling him. He'd never heard it so deep and sensual. The one word seemed to wrap around him, pull him closer to her like a haunting saxophone playing in the background.

"Am I too heavy?" he asked.

"Nooo." She stretched the word out, her hands sliding down his body and over his buttocks. He nearly shouted at the sensations of pleasure that began at his toes and reverberated through every nerve in his body. He hardened against her. Erika seemed to like the feeling against her leg. She shifted, trying to accommodate him. Michael placed his hands on either side of her head and looked into her eyes. Carefully he kissed her eyelids, the tip of her nose, her mouth. Erika opened like a rose to rain water. He'd begun slowly, but in seconds he was devouring her mouth as if she were his final hold on life.

Erika couldn't help the noises she made. They were natural, as natural as the way Michael made her feel. She was alive and female—all female. To think she could have spent her life, and never known these feelings. Michael pulled the strap of her gown down and kissed her shoulder. Slowly he moved to the other side, removing that strip and kissing the other shoulder. Erika trembled. He lifted her forward until the gown fell to her waist.

"Don't," he said quietly when she went to cover herself. Instead he touched her. Her skin was hot and his hands sent excitement spiraling through her. Her nipples hardened into dark cherries. Her throat was parched, and she had to breathe through her mouth. Erika closed her eyes, letting her head fall back. She arched herself closer to him, closer to the sensations, to the erotic effects of his hands.

She reached for him, needing to touch, needing to feel. He was hot. She didn't understand why he didn't melt, why she didn't melt. He wore nothing. She could see his fully aroused state and knew that she had done this. He wanted her as much as she wanted him. Michael lifted the body of her gown, and inch by inch raised it up her legs. Bending, he kissed her skin. Her muscles quivered at his touch, her stomach clenched, and hot juices flowed to her core. Her breath came in hard gasps, her breasts heaving. Michael reached across her and opened a drawer. Quickly he pulled out a foil-covered condom and covered himself. Erika watched in anticipation and fascination until he pushed her back and kissed her.

His body covered hers, each contrasting the other; her softness against his hardness, her smooth skin against his roughness, each complementing the other; Michael's body beginning where hers left off.

In a smooth effort Michael entered her. Erika cried out as if it were her first time. Her arms flailed a moment at the attack of sensuous pleasure that created bedlam within her system. He set the rhythm and she followed it, her legs circling him, trying to pull him into her, make him a part of her, letting there be no difference between them, letting them merge into a single entity. Erika's body thrashed below him. All thought, rationality, and reason had long since been replaced by the elemental pleasure created by the joining of a man and a woman.

Erika knew she was going to scream. She felt it coming, felt it with the rising level of tormenting pleasure that Michael instilled in her. He carried her toward a pinnacle that had to be the beginning or end of her existence. Together they created the wave of sensation, and in a flash fire of heat and light the two of them crashed through the barrier between life and creation.

Fourteen

"Ms. St. James, your mother is here to see you." Erika's heart suddenly beat like a tom-tom. What did she want? Why did she continually show up, when she'd been silent for years?

"Send her in," she said, keeping the dryness out of her voice.

Alva came through the door in a short, mink jacket and a long skirt. A large smile curved her mouth, and for the first time in her life Erika saw herself reflected in her mother's face.

"Good morning, Mother. Please sit down."

Erika offered her a chair in front of the desk. Alva relinquished the jacket in her usual nonchalant manner, throwing it across the back of an empty chair. She dropped down in the other and crossed her legs.

"Mother, why are you here this time?"

"Erika, aren't you going to be hospitable and offer me some coffee?"

"Of course, Mother." Erika picked up the phone and spoke into it. "Stephanie, would you do me a favor and bring my mother some coffee, black with one sugar—"

"No sugar," Alva interrupted.

"No sugar," Erika repeated. She replaced the phone and returned her attention to her mother. "Now, what is it?"

Alva took a breath and looked around the large office. Carlton had occupied this office, but Erika had made it hers in the last year.

"I want you to spend Thanksgiving with me."

Erika's mouth dropped open. It was the last thing she expected to hear. She and her mother hadn't spent a holiday together since she was thirteen years old. She went there, but invariably they'd get into an argument and Erika would stormed out of the house.

What was she after? Erika had sent her the check and she knew the monthly arrangement was still in effect, although she didn't know why.

"I thought you could bring Michael and we could all spend some time together."

Erika couldn't help her suspicions. Her mother had never wanted her around. Why would she want it now? Was it Michael she really wanted?

"Mother, if you want to invite Michael over, you don't need to drag me along for the ride."

"It isn't Michael I want to spend time with. I only suggested we invite him because he has no relatives here."

Erika didn't ask how she knew that. "It's not as if his family lives on the other side of the world. They're barely an hour away."

"I just thought you'd feel more comfortable having someone else around."

"You want to spend time with me? Why?"

"Erika, I'm your mother. For too long we've been at . . . odds with each other."

Was she saying she wanted to make up?

Stephanie tapped on the door and came in. Alva thanked her politely and sipped the steaming liquid.

"What's going on over at the house?"

Erika stared at her mother. She wasn't used to trading confidences with her mother. "What do you mean?"

"I came by. The place has enough guards to secure Fort Knox."

"You are exaggerating, Mother. We have added a few guards, but there is nothing to be concerned about."

"I'm glad to hear that."

Erika frowned. "Are you, Mother? Do you feel anything for me?"

"I love you, Erika."

Erika felt as if someone had punched her in the stomach. She'd longed to hear her mother say that to her, but she couldn't remember ever hearing her speak those words. She never thought they would have a impact on her life. She never thought she'd even hear them, let alone consider them.

"Mother, are you dying?"

"What would make you ask a question like that?"

"You come here, out of the blue, you make demands one minute, you don't explain anything, and suddenly you're inviting me to a family dinner. I want to know what's going on."

"There's nothing going on. It's a friendly invitation."

Erika hesitated, trying to find some inference, some degree of insincerity, in her mother's expression, but there was none.

"I believe Michael has plans for Thanksgiving," she said.

"Then you come. I'll even cook. You can help me."

For a moment Erika flashed back to a childhood fantasy. She'd wanted to do those things with her mother, but Alva never had time for her. Carlton had cooked with her. They had made a royal mess and the housekeepers had to clean it up, but Erika remembered it fondly. She also remembered wishing her mother had loved her enough to want to cook with her. Even now, Erika wondered whether she would fulfill the fantasy if she went, or would they end up screaming at each other, as they had at every previous encounter?

"Will you think about it?" her mother asked.

Erika hesitated, then nodded.

Alva stood and smiled. "Good." She paused. For a moment Erika thought she saw something flicker in her mother's eyes, something that looked strangely like regret. Did she regret asking her? "I'll call you."

With that, Alva St. James Redford made her exit. She grabbed her jacket and slipped it over her shoulder, then opened the door and went through it with all the panache of a seasoned actress knowing when to end a scene.

That walk was unmistakable. Michael saw Mrs. Redford walking toward the elevators at the end of the hall. Even with a daughter over thirty, she could still turn a head. Michael wondered if Erika knew how similar the two of them were. He smiled as she stepped into the elevator. He turned to Erika's office. She was usually put out when her mother visited. Michael thought he'd go console her. He'd been thinking of her since they woke up this morning. She was there when he woke, and he couldn't help making love to her again.

He knocked, then opened the door. Erika stood by the window. She didn't turn when he entered. *This one must have been bad,* he thought. Michael knew Erika refused to let her mother reduce her to tears, but the effort took a lot out of her.

Quietly he went to her, stopping close enough to feel the heat coming from her body. He wanted to hold her again, share her pain, make love to her again. Would this feeling ever go away? He hoped not.

"She invited me to cook with her."

"What?"

Erika turned around, leaning against the sill. "She invited me to Thanksgiving dinner. You, too. She asked me to come early so I could help her cook."

"Erika—"

"I told her you already had an engagement."

Michael wanted to spend Thanksgiving with her. His brothers had told him to bring her to dinner, but he'd never asked her. Now she was going to her mother's.

"I told her I'd think about it," she said.

Michael could see she was nervous. He didn't know what had happened between the two women. Every time they approached each other the electricity between them could singe hair. Michael knew it wasn't a good idea for the two of them to be alone.

"How do you feel about it?"

Erika waited a moment, composing herself. "Kind of numb."

"Do you want to go?"

Her gaze was direct. "To tell you the truth, I'm scared."

"Are you going?"

"I don't know. My first instinct is to say no."

"But—" he prompted.

Erika walked back to her desk. She leaned against the carved wood frame and stared at the carpeting. Michael waited, not wanting to rush her. He wanted to know what caused the rift between mother and daughter. He had the feeling Erika didn't talk about her mother, but he knew Alva Redford had a profound impact on her daughter.

Erika moved again. She sat down on the chair in front of her desk and looked up at him.

"In all the years and all the fights we've had, I always wanted my mother to love me."

"Erika, I'm sure she loves you." Michael didn't know that for sure, but he couldn't believe Alva Redford couldn't be proud of and love her own daughter. Erika was a wonderful person and he knew how much love she had to give. He couldn't believe she could have been a terrible child. People didn't change that drastically. If her mother had never loved her, it couldn't be because she wasn't a lovable person.

"She's blamed me all my life for my father," Erika said.

"What about your father?"

Her eyes were glassy, but she smiled. "He was the best father a child could ask for, and we did everything together." Erika spoke in this room, but Michael could see her gaze. It went past the windows and out into her childhood. "He'd take me to work on Saturdays. We'd go to the zoo and the movies. I suppose we did all the things normal kids and fathers do, but with us there was a special relationship, one in which my mother didn't participate. When my father died she blamed me."

"You! What did you do?"

"Nothing. He was in a car accident while he was on a business trip. He'd gone to buy me a teddy bear, and a drunk driver hit him while he was crossing the street. She told me if I hadn't asked him to bring me something back, he never would have been in that store and the drunk driver wouldn't have hit him."

Michael took the chair next to her, drawing it close enough to take her hands in his.

"Erika, you have to know you had nothing to do with your father's death."

"I never asked my father for a teddy bear. I didn't even know he was bringing one. It was my birthday, and we'd seen a movie about a bear. I guess that's where he got the idea."

"Did you ever tell her this?"

She shook her head. "What good would it have done? She didn't listen to me. She'd scream that it was my fault we were poor, that no man would look at her because of me, that I was an ugly child, and no man would ever want me. And she was right."

"That's not true," Michael said. "Don't you know the effect you have on men?" Didn't she understand how he felt? Hadn't their time together proved to her the depths of his feelings, the power she had over him?

"Yes," she laughed. "I know it. Look what happened in California. That time I went as far as getting engaged, and look how that turned out. My fiancé ran off with another woman." She stopped again. Michael still held her hands. "All my relationships turn out like that. I'm simply not cut out for the married with children lifestyle."

"God, are you wrong. You just haven't found the right man."

She stared at him then.

Dropping his hands, she continued, "I don't think he's out there. But we were talking about Thanksgiving."

"You don't have to go."

"What if she's trying to make up for the past?" Her confusion showed. "I don't know that I want to be the one slamming the door."

Michael smiled. After all the years and verbal argument her mother had given her, Erika was still willing to give her the benefit of the doubt. Michael had never known a fully beautiful person before, but Erika St. James had that inner beauty he'd read about but never expected to find.

"You want to go?" he asked. Confusion marred Erika's features. "I'll go with you," Michael said.

"You will? What about your family? Peter said you were all getting together for dinner."

"I'll send my regrets. This is obviously important to you, and I'd like to be with you."

Michael didn't know if she heard the emotion in his voice, but he'd suddenly gone soft inside and he couldn't do anything about it. Erika did that to him, and when he thought of her soft body pressed against his he didn't want to do anything except be with her.

She wanted her mother's love. It was natural to feel like that. He'd grown up in a loving family and couldn't imagine the life Erika must have had. Michael didn't want anyone to hurt her again, not even her mother. He'd be there to protect her. If Alva Redford had another agenda, Michael wanted to be there. If she had other plans, she'd have him to deal with.

Wanamaker's Department Store opened its downtown store at Thirteenth and Market Streets decades before any of the mall stores opened. Erika liked the Market Street store best. The building was old and distinctive, with chandeliers and huge display cases. Carlton had taken her here on her first shopping trip. The salesclerk had made her feel comfortable as she bought several pairs of jeans, three sweaters, and a jacket.

Today she needed a dress for dinner with her mother on Thanksgiving. Although she had a closet full of dresses at home, she needed something new to wear, something that would make her feel comfortable, less nervous. Dinner wasn't for another week, yet she was nervous already, and it didn't help that Michael had insisted on coming with her. He'd gone everywhere with her for the past few days. She admitted she loved being with him. All her vows of staying away from him, never allowing him to make love to her again, turned to water the moment he looked at her.

Erika checked her reflection in the three walls of mirror before her. She'd tried on seven dresses, and had narrowed her search to two—a black, straight gown covered with sequins and a green velvet. The one she had on was Christmas green with simple lines. It had a stand-up collar and long sleeves, and fit her to the waist, where it flared out into a full skirt that stopped short of her knees. She turned, inspecting the back. Her pearls would look great with this. She opened the door and stepped out of the dressing room. Michael waited for her in the dress department.

"What do you think?" she asked moments later. He had his back to her, walking near the after five dresses like a man lost in the lingerie department. His eyes opened wide when he saw her.

"You're . . . it's beautiful," he said.

"Do you think it looks all right?"

The look on his face gave her his answer. He came close to her so no one could hear what he said and whispered, "You look go good I could make love to you right here."

Erika blushed, bowing her head and feeling the rush of excitement that coursed through her at the prospect of making love. "I'd better change," she said, going back to the dressing room.

Ten minutes later Michael took her box under his arm and led her away from the department. Erika noticed him looking around.

"Michael, stop doing that."

"Doing what?"

"Looking over your shoulder as if you're expecting someone to be there."

"I'm just being cautious. If Frank Mason has traced me here, I want to be prepared for him."

"If he did kill the judge and the lawyer, then he's probably miles away from here by now."

"You'd think any sane man would be, but Frank Mason isn't sane."

Erika didn't want to discuss Frank Mason. She wanted to have a good time shopping and spending the afternoon with Michael. "Let's go to the shoe department," she said, changing the subject. Michael didn't argue. He led her to the elevators and together they found shoes and other accessories she'd need for her monumental dinner.

When Michael had added three additional boxes and several bags to his load they went to the restaurant for lunch. They were shown to a quiet table in the back, away from the view of the entrance. Michael seemed to approve of the table, b͟ he sat facing the room.

"You're enjoying this, aren't you?" Michael asked.

"I'm having a wonderful time."

Michael could see it. Her expression was anima͟ happy. He only wished he could feel just as carefr͟ did. Erika had the advantage of never having met Fr͟ Michael had seen the destructive nature of the m͟ that he didn't care about killing in public.

The police had found nothing more to con͟ the two deaths, but Michael didn't like coi͟ escaped and the judge and lawyer associate͟ both been gruesomely killed.

"Michael," Erika said, calling him͟ "You're ignoring me."

"I couldn't ignore you if I͟

The four-wheel drive jeep, with mud covering it from his mountain trek, would have looked out of place on the quiet street where Michael Lawrence now lived. Frank knew that, and drove down the street in a rented Lexus. He saw the towering iron gates that protected a house too far from the street to be seen. He smiled. *Neither the gates nor the guards will save Michael Lawrence,* Frank thought. He and Michael had unfinished business, and they were on a collision course in which Frank knew he'd be the victor.

He drove several miles until he found a place to eat, then stopped to kill time. He ordered a short meal and ate it leisurely before turning back toward the house again. He took in the six-foot stone wall that stretched for a mile before reaching the iron gates. The wall was easy enough to scale. The very length of it made it difficult to guard. Although there could ⁿamera surveillance, Frank knew he could get around it. Lawrence's time was coming.

ⁿg soon.

ⁿ other business. He needed to talk to some-
as the mansion wall disappeared from

ⁿme into view within half an
ⁿ to Chestnut, then headed
ⁿremium there, espe-
arby lot and walked
ⁿramped houses along

ⁿw the timing, knew the
ⁿone. He sat in the living

e eyebrow at the unexpected

d be unnecessary," he paused.
here for you."

"What the hell do you want?" Wainscott's face turned redder than its natural ruddy color.

"I have a message for Michael Lawrence, and I need you to give it to him."

"Do I look like a delivery boy?"

Frank thought the old man had guts. He was too incapacitated to do anything to protect himself if it had been Frank's intention to harm him, but he held his ground—or his chair, Frank thought.

Frank wasn't angered in the least, although there was a time he would have beaten a man into submission for making a comment like that. Today he didn't need the old man's heart giving out before he'd completed his mission.

"Michael Lawrence. You know him." Frank stated fact, but the old man nodded, anyway. "He went to the mall today. Little shopping expedition. I guess they're getting a jump on the Christmas crowd."

Malick Wainscott's face gave nothing away at the news Frank had just given him. Frank had never seen him in court, but he thought he must have been awesome. Frank had watched the lawyers. It was a hobby of his, people watching. He'd studied his own lawyer and Abby's and the lawyers pleading other cases, cases he knew nothing about. He'd become an authority on who would win, who had the better argument, and who could keep their cool even when surprises were presented. Which one was getting through to the judge, and which one had only part of his attention. Malick Wainscott was the kind of lawyer who would win nine times out of ten.

"What's the message?" he asked.

"Tell him I know where he is and he can't escape me. Adding guards to the estate won't save him or that pretty little heiress."

"Why do you want to harm Michael? He represented you."

"I'd love to stay and debate the pros and cons of Michael Lawrence's ability to represent me, but I have a previous appointment and your nurse should be back in . . ." He consulted his watch. "Five minutes," he finished. "Don't forget to give Mr. Lawrence my message. You have a nice day, now."

"Appointment where? What are you planning to do?"

Frank smiled. He loved seeing the strong grovel. It wasn't something he thought he'd see in Malick Wainscott, but then he was a loyal friend to Michael Lawrence, and Frank held loyalty high in his estimation of a person's worth. He liked Malick Wainscott.

"Don't worry. I'm not ready for Michael Lawrence yet, but soon. Soon." Frank saluted him and retraced his steps to the front door.

Malick reached for the phone the moment he heard the door close. Checking the window he saw Frank Mason walking down the street. His steps were even and unhurried. Malick may have had a reasonable doubt before, but it was gone now. Frank was definitely stalking Michael, and he had to let him know.

Dialing Michael's number he reached the maid, who told him Michael and Erika had not returned yet.

"I need them to call me the moment they return," he told her, unable to keep the excitement out of his voice. "No matter what time. I have to talk to Michael."

"I understand, Mr. Wainscott," the maid said.

Malick said good-bye and replaced the phone receiver. Frank Mason had a lot of nerve. He'd killed four people in the last three weeks and he walked around the streets as if he had a perfect right to mingle with law-abiding citizens. He didn't, and he had no right to leave messages for Michael. Malick felt his heart accelerate and he grabbed for his pills. Taking one, he waited for the pressure to calm down. Then, remembering his duty, Malick lifted the phone and dialed 9-1-1.

The blue and red flashing lights on the cars with Philadelphia Police Department written on the sides like a huge blue stencil caught Michael's attention the moment he and Erika turned the corner. Within seconds he was running toward Malick's house, Erika in tow.

He didn't stop to knock, but burst through the front door and looked around quickly.

"Is he all right?" he asked the nurse who stopped as he'd made his entrance.

"Yes," she said. "He's in there with the police." She pointed toward the living room area.

Michael immediately headed for it. Malick sat up in his favorite chair. Three uniformed policemen and two detectives stood in the room.

"Michael!" Malick called when he noticed him.

"What's going on here?" Michael addressed the question to the room.

"Are you Michael Lawrence?" one of the plainclothes men asked him in a voice that told him he was the leader of this small assembly.

Michael nodded.

"Mr. Wainscott here tells us he had a visitor this afternoon. It appears Frank Mason has been here."

"Here! Malick, are you all right?"

"I'm fine. He didn't harm me. He wanted me to deliver a message to you."

Erika, still holding his hand, squeezed it tighter.

"What message?"

Malick related the details of Frank's earlier visit while the policemen checked their notes to see that the story remained unchanged.

When Malick finished, one of the detectives said, "The murders referred to by Wainscott are out of our jurisdiction, but we'll be reporting the details of this incident to the New Jersey authorities."

"Is that all?" Erika spoke up.

"No, Ma'am. Mr. Mason is an escaped convict and we'll do everything we can to find him, but we don't have much to go on."

The second detective addressed Malick. "Do you have any idea where he might have been going when he left here?"

"No," Malick answered. "But he told me he was going to kill Michael. I suggest you give him some protection."

"We'll add more patrol cars to the areas around your house and your estate." He glanced at Michael and Erika. "But that's about all we can do."

"Thank you, Officer," Michael said. He knew there was little the police could do. They had budget problems, huge case loads and the size of the city were all public knowledge.

"If you remember anything you haven't told us," the detective went on, "please call." He handed Malick and Michael cards, then said good day.

"I'll see them to the door," Erika said. She led the way and the officers followed. Michael sat down across from Malick when they were alone.

"You look tired," he told his friend. "It must have been a long afternoon."

"It has been," said a voice from the door. The voice was strong and authoritative. Both men turned. The nurse, holding a small tray, stood there. Erika stood next to her. They came into the room.

"Mr. Wainscott has had too much excitement for one afternoon."

"Don't mind her," Malick said. "She's just feeling a little guilty. Frank came while she was out having the prescription filled."

The nurse looked hurt for a moment. Then she regained her composure and handed Malick a glass of water, followed by a small white cup with two pills in it. Malick took them without comment and drank the water.

"He's going to take a nap now," she said, leaving no area for argument by any of the room's participants. "I'll have to ask you to leave."

"We understand," Erika said. Michael stood and she came to him, taking his arm.

"I don't think she'll ever leave me alone again," Malick said.

"Malick, I think you like the attention," Erika told him. She bent and kissed him on the cheek.

The old man smiled.

Fifteen

Erika turned in front of the mirror in her bedroom. Finally Thanksgiving had arrived, and they were going to dinner at her mother's. She wore the green velvet dress, a single strand of pearls, and pearl drop earrings. Her hand went to her belly and she took a deep breath. The butterflies had greeted her when she woke this morning and threatened to stay all day.

For the past week she hadn't had time to think about her mother, with Frank Mason at the top of her mind. Every day she and Michael had gone to see Malick. Each time they stepped outside the house or the office Erika had the uneasy feeling of being watched. Although she never saw anyone, she knew someone's eyes were always on her.

She shrugged it off, telling herself she had transferred Malick's experience to herself. She hadn't seen anyone and if Frank Mason knew what was good for him, he'd be long gone by now. She hadn't told Michael. It was just a feeling. There was nobody there.

Erika took one last look in the mirror and picked up her coat from the bed. Leaving the room, she went down the staircase. Michael met her at the bottom.

"You look grand," he said. "Your mother will like the dress."

He was the most perceptive man she'd ever met. He knew even more than she did that she wanted the dress for approval.

"Did you talk to your brothers?" she asked as he took her coat and held it while she slipped her arms inside it.

"They all send their love, and said you are missing the best walnut stuffing in the world."

Erika smiled. "It's not too late, Michael. I can go to my mother's alone. You can spend the day with your family."

"I spoke to my mother, too," he said, ignoring her comment. "She's still with my aunt and will not be returning until the holidays. We can miss one Thanksgiving, or if we leave early we can always show up for the sweet potato pie."

Michael held the door open for her and Erika walked out into the cold November afternoon. The wind hit her and she pulled her coat closer around her. Michael closed the door and they got into the car.

The staff had been given the day off except for the guards, so they drove themselves. Alva Redford lived in Springfield, a distance of about forty miles from central Philadelphia. Traffic was slow going through the city. Michael took Route 95 to the Blue Route. The road, a superhighway of rolling hills, generally packed with commuters on any other Thursday, was surprisingly deserted. Michael relaxed and the needle on the speedometer edged up a notch.

Erika was too nervous to talk. She sat quietly next to him and watched the scenery whiz by. What was going to happen at her mother's? Did Alva have an ulterior motive in inviting them to dinner, and what was it? Every other time Erika had been with her mother the results had been disastrous. Why shouldn't she think they would be the same today? And be prepared for them? Yet she couldn't think of anything her mother would want from her. Alva had plenty of money, with the checks that Graves Enterprises sent to her each month.

Could she want her love? Erika shivered at the thought. At this stage in her life, could her mother really want to make amends? A numbness went through her. If that was her mother's intention, Erika didn't know if she could handle that. She'd never had any practice. Her mother had been out of her life since she met Carlton. His wife was already dead when they met. The only women in the household were the maids and cooks. Erika had gotten to know some of them, but none of them took on the role of substitute mother.

Erika's attention came back to the car and Michael's driving. She felt, more than saw, the change in him. Panic caught in her throat as she watched him pump the brakes and felt the car accelerate.

"What's wrong?" she asked stupidly.

"The brakes aren't working."

"Try the emergency brake."

Michael stepped on it. Nothing happened. The car careened forward at an extraordinary speed. The road had been sparsely travelled, but now there were cars everywhere. Michael weaved in and out of traffic, avoiding one collision after another. Erika's heart beat like a drum. The guardrail sailed past her in a silver blur.

"Erika, I want you to climb over the seat and get into the back."

"What are you going to do?"

Michael didn't answer. He shifted onto the shoulder past an eighteen wheeler, then shot back onto the paved road. The truck blew its airhorn in protest of such a foolhardy act.

"Put the seatbelt on and lie down."

Putting her trust in him, she didn't waste time arguing, but climbed over the seat and fell into the back. Righting herself she put on the seatbelt.

Looking up she saw a stream of traffic coming in at Exit Two. Both lanes ahead had cars in them. They had no place to go.

"What are you going to do?" she whispered.

Michael switched to the fast lane, cutting off cars and eliciting a blare of horns. Reaching the left shoulder, he sped past a parked highway patrol car at ninety miles an hour. The car immediately began following him. The blue and red flashing lights did nothing to help slow down the car. More and more traffic seemed to come into the roadway.

"Lie down Erika. I'm going to stop this thing."

"How?" she asked. "How are you going to stop? There's nothing in front of us but other cars."

"I'm going to use the wall. Now lie down."

Erika looked to the side. The sound wall built alongside neighborhoods to cut down on the traffic noise stretched ahead. Michael cut in front of a truck and got on the opposite shoulder. The police car followed them.

"Michael, do you know what you're doing?"

"No, but I don't have a choice!" he shouted. "Now get down."

She huddled behind Michael and waited. The car seemed to go faster when she couldn't see what was happening. Then she heard the sound of metal again stone. Erika had never heard anything more frightening in her life. She clenched her teeth and squeezed her eyes shut. The car bumped and grated against the wall, then it appeared to strike something. She rolled against the restraint, bumping her head on the back of Michael's seat. She heard the "whooshing" sound of the air bag being released. The car bumped over uneven ground, throwing her around like a rag doll. Finally, it came to a halt.

For a moment she didn't move. While the air had rushed by the car, creating a harsh sound, all she heard now was the faint ticking of a crushed engine.

"Michael," she called. He didn't answer. Erika released her belt and sat up. Through the windows she saw only sky. The car had passed the sound wall and hit the guardrail. It teetered there. Michael lay unconscious against the air bag, which had opened and pushed him back in his seat.

She shifted to see if he was all right.

"Don't move!"

Erika faintly heard the shout from outside the car. She turned her head, but it was too late. The car pitched forward. She gasped as it went over the railing and picked up momentum as it careened through the brush. Erika screamed as she was thrown back and forth over the seats. She didn't think the car would stop. When it did, she felt like a crash dummy. Her body was thrown against the window. A blinding pain ripped through her head, bringing tears to her eyes. Reaching up, she tried to touch her head. Everything hurt, and she groaned. She felt blood in her eye and tried to wipe it away. Everything was a blur. She blinked, trying to focus, but her head was heavy and she couldn't see. Resting her head, she fought to remain conscious, but she felt her head spinning. She wanted it to stop, but she couldn't stop it. Then she was falling, falling down a long tunnel. She couldn't fall, she told herself. Michael needed her. She needed to know that he was all right. She fought the darkening light closing in around her. It hurt and the dark felt good, cool, and welcoming.

"Michael," Erika moaned.

She lost the fight and fainted.

Michael groaned at the pain. He tried to open his eyes, but the pain was too much. Moving his hand, he found something restraining him. He forced his eyes open. The hospital room was unmistakable. Then it came back. The car, the accident, Erika.

Where was Erika? He searched the bed for the bell that would summon a nurse. The pain made him groan again.

"Michael," he heard his name.

Michael opened his eyes again. This time the pain was worse. He thought he saw Malick, but he couldn't. Malick wasn't here. Then the darkness came. He couldn't remember what he'd been thinking of, just that the darkness felt good and he let it take him away.

When Michael woke again, it was daylight. It hurt even more to do anything—open his eyes, raise his arm, clear his head so he could think clearly—but he forced himself.

"Peter?" he called, squinting. The man sleeping in the chair by his bed looked like his brother.

The man in the chair moved and was instantly at his bedside. "Michael, you're awake." It was Peter. "How do you feel?"

"Like I fell off a mountain."

Peter laughed. "You aren't far from the truth. Do you remember the accident?"

He tried to nod, immediately realizing that it wasn't a good idea. "Yes," he said. "Erika? Is she all right?"

"She'll be fine. She has a concussion, some cuts and bruises. Otherwise she's as good as new. Malick and her mother are with her."

"Her mother?" Michael touched his head. "Oh, yes, we were going to have dinner with her tonight."

"I'm afraid that was last night. We got the news just as we were sitting down to eat. Everyone picked up and left."

"They're all here?"

"Including mother. She flew down last night."

Michael looked around, wondering where everyone was.

"They're in the waiting area," Peter explained. "I'll let them know you're awake."

"Not yet." Michael knew his brother well. Even though yesterday was Thanksgiving, he knew Peter would have found out something about the accident. "What happened to the car?"

"It had so little brake fluid in it, it might as well have been empty."

"That's why they didn't work." Michael found the control for the bed and raised himself to a sitting position.

"That was only part of it," Peter explained. "The brake line had also been slit. If the low fluid didn't give out, pumping it onto the ground surely would have."

"What about Frank Mason? Has anyone spotted him?"

"No luck there. I talked to the policeman who took the report. At my insistence they checked the car for fingerprints. We only found yours and Erika's."

Michael was beginning to feel better. "I suppose that means Frank is confident that everything is under control. He was always like that, knowing he had the upper hand."

"He doesn't have the upper hand here," Peter said, anger in

his voice. "Michael, you've got to hire someone to look out for you."

"I've already done that. I hired two bodyguards."

"Where are they?"

"I don't know. I had them tailing Erika. I haven't seen them in a while, but I know they're close by."

"They surely aren't doing their job."

"I still have confidence in them," Michael said. "Erika is all right and they were hired to guard her person, not to check on the vehicles. In fact, they are rarely on the estate."

"Why?"

"Erika didn't want a bodyguard. I hired them without her knowledge."

"She's going to have to find out now."

"I don't think that will be a problem after the accident."

Peter became very quiet for a moment. Michael was getting tired, but he wanted to see Erika, see for himself that she was fine. He checked the IV in his hand and followed the clear tubing up to the plastic bag hanging over his head. He didn't think he could get out of bed.

"Michael, have you considered that there might be another person, other than Frank, behind this?"

"What? Peter, you were the person who noticed the connection between the judge and the lawyer's deaths."

"I know, but I want to make sure we're not focusing so much on Frank Mason that we overlook someone else."

"Who?"

"I have no idea." Peter spread his hands. "Maybe someone in Erika's past."

Alva Redford's face came to mind. She'd come from nowhere and invited her daughter to dinner. While the two of them had been estranged for years, she suddenly decided to break bread with her daughter. When Michael had first met her, she and Erika had been in the middle of an argument. One other time that he knew of, Alva had appeared and an argument resulted. Then she invited them to dinner.

"Peter," Michael finally said. "I want you to check out Alva St. James Redford."

"Erika's mother?"

"The two of them don't get on." Michael told him his concerns and Peter agreed to check into the files and see what he could find. "Also, find out what connection Alva Redford had with Carlton Lipton-Graves."

Michael yawned and closed his eyes. His eyelids grew heavy. The effort to keep them open taxed his energy. Peter didn't speak and soon Michael entered a warm, fuzzy world where Erika waited.

"Malick, you should be in this chair," Erika admonished.

"Shhh," he quieted her. "This is against all the hospital rules and if we get caught they'll probably keep our dinner from us."

Erika snickered behind her hand. Malick wheeled her through the hospital corridors toward Michael's room. Erika hadn't seen him since they were brought in, two days ago. She didn't remember the ambulance ride. She was afraid Michael was seriously hurt, that Malick hadn't told her the truth and he was unconscious, in a coma, unable to speak or see. Malick stopped the wheelchair in front of a door that looked much like the door to her room. He turned her around and pulled her into the room. When he wheeled her around, she saw that Michael stood near the window.

His room was the same as hers, with standard hospital furniture, but every space in hers was covered with flowers. She wondered how so many people could have heard about the accident so quickly and immediately sent flowers. A lot of them were from people in the office, but several were from her friends. She felt a little guilty that she hadn't had time for them in the past, and resolved to correct that in the future.

Michael wore a blue velour robe, matching the pink one she wore. Malick's nurse had followed instructions in buying them something other than hospital nightclothes, even if she had dressed them like His and Her bookends.

Michael turned as the door closed.

"Erika," he said, coming to her and kneeling next to her chair. "I've been going out of my mind with worry."

Erika didn't notice Malick leaving them. She'd completely forgotten him when she saw Michael. His face had brush burns from the air bag. His skin was raw in places and looked painful. Other than that, his features were as handsome as she remembered. Then she thought of her own state. Without makeup and bruised, her hair flat to her head, she must look like a monster.

"How's your head? Peter told me you had a concussion." He touched her. Erika's hand covered his.

"He came to see me. Your whole family came in one by one. They're very nice people. I liked them."

"I hope they weren't too overwhelming. They can be."

She smiled. "They were concerned about you."

"I was concerned about you."

Erika's heart swelled large enough to lodge in her throat. "The doctors say the headaches will go away in a few days. I'll be as good as new before you know it. And you, what have they said about you?"

"I'm being discharged tomorrow morning."

Erika's heart dropped. "They haven't told me when I will be able to leave."

"It will be soon."

Michael stood up. He opened his hands and she put hers in them. With him helping her, she stood up. He led her to a chair and sat her down. Then he took the other chair.

"Erika, it's time for the bodyguards."

"I agree," she said.

Michael thought he was going to have to argue with her, but she eliminated the need for his well-planned speech. "Two of them will be here when you're discharged, and from then until Frank Mason is caught."

Erika began to shake. She gripped his hands tightly. "I've never been so scared in my life. When I saw you . . ." Her voice cracked. "I thought you were—"

"Erika, stop. We're both fine. And nothing is going to happen to us."

She took a deep breath. "I didn't really believe it could happen until we were in the car. Even Malick's house seemed unreal, but you pumping that brake made me think I was going to die."

Michael left his chair. He pulled her into his arms and held her. Erika trembled against him. He cradled her head against his shoulder. He was angry. Frank had made her scared, and Michael didn't like that. He didn't like him putting her in danger. She could have been killed. He had to do something. He had to find Frank. This cat and mouse game had gone on long enough.

It was time for them to have their stand.

Frank laughed, threw his head back and bellowed. Michael Lawrence was as predictable as night falling. He'd played right into his hands, as if he didn't know the cards were stacked against him. Of course, Frank had thought he'd only have an accident in town. Going over a ravine and spending a couple of days in the hospital was a far better script than the one he'd written. And he gladly accepted the revision.

Michael's little accident had forced his family to join him. From the smallest child to the oldest adult, they'd all run to his rescue, like they could do something. And they must have left in an incredible hurry. From the looks of things, they took only enough time to clear the dinner dishes.

Frank walked about the dining room, a sneer on his face. This looked like a lawyer's house. He hated lawyers. If he could have one wish in life it would be to eradicate the world of lawyers. If he was lucky, by this time next week there would be at least one less in the world, maybe two if they came home together.

Frank looked around, went through the kitchen. The door to the garage was unlocked and the car was missing. He looked up. The garage door was controlled by a remote. More than likely they would enter through this door. To be on the safe side, he wired both doors.

He went to work then. The wires matched the molding, as if he'd had a blueprint of the interior of the house. No one would notice it if they came in, but they weren't going to get the chance. Opening the door would arm the device. Ten minutes later, when everyone was safely inside the folds of their own home, it would blow. The ensuing explosive would travel through to the other door, either by wire or heat, and it, too, would flare up like an exploding rocket.

He was sorry he wouldn't be here to see it. This kind of an explosion was a work of art, and Frank enjoyed art. But he knew better than to be anywhere near this when the candles were lit. This wasn't his primary target. He needed to concentrate on Michael Lawrence. It might not be as easy to penetrate the grounds of that estate, but he could certainly draw him out into the open. The two of them knew they had to meet sooner or later, and Frank wanted it to be sooner. This was his method. His family had run to him when he was hurt. Michael would certainly return the favor. Would he be surprised at his welcoming committee.

"Kaboom," Frank said, then laughed, laughed to the heavens. The sound echoed off the furniture, the woodwork, the kitchen sink, and gleaming refrigerator. It was a wicked laugh, the kind that Frank had given the judge when he'd sentenced him to a mental hospital. Well, the judge was certainly not laughing now. His time had come. Now it was Michael's time, and it was almost out.

Sixteen

Erika's discharge came twenty-four hours after Michael's. The company limousine came to pick her up and drive her to the house. Stiffly she got out of the backseat, leaning heavily on Michael for support.

"I don't think I'll be able to return to work for a few days," she joked.

Michael turned around and swung her into his arms. "Michael," Erika said in surprise. "You shouldn't be carrying me. You were in an accident, too."

"I had on a seatbelt and from what the officers told me, you didn't."

Erika placed her head on his shoulder and hugged him. He smelled good and she wanted to kiss him at that moment. She settled for holding him close.

Inside, Michael took her directly to her room, but he didn't lower her to the floor. "I'm not very tired," she said.

"Is that an invitation?"

Erika blushed, lowering her head.

"As much as I'd like to oblige you, I'm sure it would delay any healing you have yet to do."

He set her on her feet and kissed her briefly. Erika didn't believe she'd said that. She did feel giddy, but then she felt that way each time Michael came near her. He'd been here for months. She should be used to his presence. Yet she couldn't control her emotions whenever he was around.

"If you need to rest before lunch I can have it postponed," Michael said.

"There's no need," she said.

"We have guests." Michael raised his eyebrows.

"We do?" She braced herself for the news that her mother was downstairs. At the hospital Alva Redford had acted as if her own life was in danger.

"My family and Malick. They refused to go home until they knew you'd be all right."

Erika smiled. She wasn't sure if she was relieved or upset. "They probably wanted some time with you." He hadn't really spent any time with them since he returned from Maryland. She was just an excuse for them to get to see him. Erika had wished for brothers and sisters when she was a child—she used to imagine her life with many relatives—but her mother never had any other children.

"I'll clean up and come down in a few minutes."

Michael kissed her on the forehead and left the room. Moments later Tess came in and helped her shower and change. She was stiff, and the effort took a lot out of her.

"Would you like me to call Mr. Lawrence?" Tess asked when they stood at the top of the massive staircase. Erika heard voices coming from different areas of the house. It had been a very long time since they had guests. Certainly not in the year since she'd returned and Carlton had been sick. Only Carlton's lawyers and an occasional friend dropping by, nothing like the sounds she could hear now.

"I think I can make it down if you let me lean on you." Erika didn't want Michael knowing how stiff she still was. She had the feeling he'd confine her to bed if he knew.

At the bottom of the steps she thanked Tess, and the young maid went toward the kitchen. Erika went to the salon. Hoping it was empty, she needed a moment to prepare herself. She went inside.

She thought she'd been lucky until a strong, musical voice said, "Hello."

Erika turned toward it. Sitting in one of the reclining chairs was a brown-skinned woman with soft features. She nursed a baby in her arms.

"I'm Catherine, Bobby's wife. You must be Erika."

Erika nodded and went to sit next to her.

"I couldn't come to the hospital with the baby, but I'm glad you're all right."

"Thank you," Erika said. She couldn't help looking at the child in Michael's sister-in-law's arms, dressed in a pink outfit. Erika assumed it was a girl. "How old is she?" she asked.

"Three weeks."

"I've never seen a baby that small," Erika said in wonder.

Catherine leaned forward, adjusting her clothing. The child was asleep. She looked like a small doll.

"Can I touch her?" she asked cautiously.

"Sure," Catherine said. "Would you like to hold her?"

Erika's eyes opened wide. "I'd love to . . . but . . . I never . . . I never held a baby."

Catherine looked at her kindly. "You must have been an only child."

"I was," Erika said.

Catherine slid forward in the chair, then stood up. "I had three brothers," she told Erika, "and I was the oldest. I got to hold many babies."

Catherine took a step toward her.

"What do I do?" Erika asked, scared but wanting the experience.

"Didn't you ever have a babysitting job?" Catherine asked her.

"No." Erika suddenly felt as if she'd missed out on something.

"Just be sure to support her head." Catherine laid the baby in her arms. Erika held her breath.

"She's so light," Erika said, staring at the sleeping child. "Will she wake up?"

"She's a good sleeper. She won't wake for at least an hour."

Instinctively Erika rocked the baby. She put her finger in the tiny hand. The child curled her perfect little fingers around it, and Erika smiled as if a miracle had occurred. "What's her name?"

"Roberta Ellen," she said. "After her two grandmothers."

Erika glanced up. "They must be very proud."

The door opened and Michael came in. He'd changed into grey slacks and a fishermen's-knit white sweater. He came forward and kissed Catherine on the cheek, then sat next to Erika on the sofa.

"Is lunch nearly ready?" Catherine asked.

Michael nodded. "As soon as everyone gets here we can go in."

"If you'll be all right, I'll go hurry them up."

"I'll be fine," Michael answered.

Catherine laughed at him.

Erika nodded to her and she left the room. As soon as the door closed Michael took her chin and turned her to face him. He kissed her on the mouth. "I missed you."

"I missed you, too."

He kissed her again and was still kissing her when the door opened.

"Excuse me, but you two keep that up and you'll have one of those of your own." Erika and Michael looked up. Peter walked over with a smile on his face. "How do you feel?" he asked.

Before she could answer, the rest of the family arrived—Bobby, Catherine, and Michael's mother, Ellen—all of them asking the same question. Erika had met them at the hospital. Ellen Lawrence was shorter than anyone in her family. She was a petite woman who reminded Erika of a college professor she'd had her freshman year in college who was stern and competent. Ellen Lawrence had the same manner, and Erika thought she didn't like her.

Michael stood up. "We're all here now. Why don't we go in?"

"I'll take her," Michael's mother said, scooping the baby from Erika's arms as if she were more competent than Erika. She turned and led the assembly toward the dining room. Michael helped her up and they followed everyone into the room.

Lunch may have begun on a strained note, but it quickly turned to fun and laughter. The brothers began with stories of small accidents in their childhood. Most of the incidents included things they hadn't told their parents about. Soon everyone was laughing, including Ellen Lawrence. Her face was marked with laughter at the antics of her children. The only time it changed was when her eyes were shining with love over her grandchild, still sleeping in a bassinet near her mother, and when she looked at Erika.

Erika couldn't help looking at Ellen. The woman didn't like her. Erika could tell by the way she never made eye contact. She looked away each time Erika's gaze found her. Did she blame her for the accident? Was it her fault that Michael's life was in danger? They both could have died in the accident. Didn't she see that? Erika didn't think so.

When everyone was nearly through with the coffee, Erika was visibly tired. Malick noticed it and suggested she go to bed. At that point, everyone decided they needed to begin their trips home, and the party broke up.

"There's no need for you all to leave," Erika said. "I'm sure Michael would like you to stay for a longer visit."

"I have to go, anyway," Bobby said. "There's work tomorrow."

The rest of the party echoed his excuse and soon they were kissing each other good-bye.

Catherine came over to Erika as she stood at the door. She carried Roberta. "I enjoyed myself," she said.

Erika looked at her and at the baby. "I'm so glad you came," she told her. She liked Catherine. "Thank you for letting me hold her." Erika ran her hand lightly over the baby's arm. The child's hands were covered, but Erika let her grasp her finger, anyway. Tears gathered in her eyes at the tiny hand holding hers. Catherine kissed her on cheek, whispering good-bye and going to the car where Ellen Lawrence already sat. Michael leaned over his mother and kissed her. They seated the baby in the child's seat and waved as they started down the driveway.

"Good bye, Erika," Peter said. "I hope to see you soon."

She waved and he, too, left.

Michael came back to her. "You're dead on your feet," he said. "Come on." He pushed her inside and closed the door. They walked to the steps before Michael lifted her and carried her to her room. This time he didn't send Tess in to help her. He unzipped her dress and took it off. In moments he had her in a gown and under the covers. The bruises on her body were dark patches of blue blemishes. Michael didn't mention them. He got her some water and two white tablets.

Leaning her against him, he watched her take the painkillers and drink the water.

"Sleep now," he said, laying her back. Michael turned the lights off and left the room, but she didn't sleep. She wondered about his mother. She had come to her hospital room the day Erika woke up, but she'd hardly had a word to say. What had she done? She wasn't trying to marry her son. Some mothers found that a threat. She was friendly toward Catherine, but Catherine had given her a grandchild, and that could be the difference.

Smiling, she thought of the baby. She hardly weighed anything. Erika loved holding her. She'd never wanted to have a child. At thirty-four, she'd never held a baby in her arms before. She hadn't wanted to give the child up. If Ellen Lawrence hadn't taken her, Erika would have been content to hold her the rest of the afternoon.

How could a mother hold her child, then not want it around? Erika thought of the way her mother had treated her as a child. A single tear formed in her eye and fell onto the pillow.

When Erika woke it was dark. The house was quiet and she felt much better. Getting up she had a slight headache, and took a pill for it. She went downstairs. Voices came from the living room. She recognized Michael's deep voice. Erika wondered who else was there. She went to the door.

"Here's Erika now," Michael said. He stood and came toward her. "Let me introduce Connie Forester and Adrienne Dantley. They're the bodyguards I've hired."

"Hello," Erika said.

"We know about the accident," the shorter woman, Connie, said. "We'll make sure nothing like that happens again."

Erika sat down. "What will you do? I mean, what do bodyguards do?"

"One of us will be with you at all times," Adrienne replied. "We'll make sure the cars are checked, and that no one gets in to see you that you don't want to see."

"What about Michael?" She glanced at him.

"I'm your bodyguard," Connie told her. "Adrienne is Michael's."

Erika didn't know if she liked that arrangement. When she'd agreed to bodyguards, she'd expected men; big, muscular, bouncer types. Not two women, two pretty women.

Michael could see that Erika looked uncomfortable. He understood. Even though it was for her own good, she was giving up her freedom, her ability to come and go as she pleased without the need for a third party looking over her shoulder.

"Has Michael shown you to your rooms?" she asked.

They nodded.

"You were asleep, but I need to get into your room now so I can check out alternative accesses," Connie said.

"Alternative access?"

"Windows, balcony, even vines on the outer walls," she translated.

"Why don't you do that now? You know where the room is?"

She nodded and the two of them left.

"I'm going to hate this," Erika said the moment the door closed.

"Give it time, Erika," Michael said calmly. "We both know this is necessary."

"I don't know that," she argued.

"Erika, you can barely move after that accident. You could have died, because Frank Mason tampered with the brakes of that car." Michael paused to come around to her. "Erika, it will be all right. After a while you won't even notice they're there."

Erika sighed. She knew they needed to protect themselves, but she hadn't expected to have to account for her time to another person, and that's exactly what she'd have to do.

"You'll be home for a few days. The two of you will have time to become friends."

"While you and Adrienne become . . . *friends,"* she said, sneering.

"You're jealous," Michael stated.

"I am not," she denied.

Michael came around the sofa and stood in front of her. It made him feel good that she was jealous. "You have no need to be," he said. Placing his hands on either side of her head, he leaned over her, and her head fell back against the sofa. "I'm already in love with you."

Michael kissed her, hard and deep. Erika reached for him, and his hands went to her waist and he pulled her forward. The two of them fell back and ended on the soft carpet. Michael raised his head to look at her.

"Am I hurting you?" he asked.

She took his face in her hands and pulled him close to her. "Yes," she whispered just before their mouths melded. Michael lay across her, and even though her answer meant he wasn't hurting her, he didn't want her to carry his full weight. He shifted, slipping his arms around her and pulling her close to him. His tongue swept inside her mouth and he felt himself trembling in the wake of the rapturous love that poured from him. She wasn't like any woman he'd ever known. She made him think of families, of loving, of wanting nothing more than to please her for the rest of his life.

"Michael," she said against his mouth.

"Hmmm," he said, refusing to break contact. He couldn't. She tasted too good. And she had him. His mouth left hers and he kissed her cheek, her chin, her bottom lip.

"Michael, if we don't stop—"

He took her mouth again, cutting her speech. He knew he should listen, but he was too far gone. He wanted her too much. She'd frightened him when she'd been in the hospital, and this afternoon when she looked so weak. She didn't look weak now, and she didn't feel weak. She felt wonderful and her perfume drove him crazy. He reached for her sweater and slipped his hand under it.

"Stop," she said, pushing herself back. "Michael! The guards. They could walk in on us at any moment."

It wasn't the guards that came in, but Tess, the maid. She sized them up. Michael checked Erika. The blood in her face colored it a shade darker.

"Did you fall?" Tess asked, coming to her.

Michael helped Erika to her feet.

"Yes, Tess, she fell." He could hardly keep the laughter out of his voice.

"I'll help her, Sir." Tess took hold of Erika's arm. "Your brother is on the phone. There's been in explosion."

The two of them looked at each other for a moment, then quickly got up and rushed to the library. Erika got there only a second behind Michael. He was on the phone asking all the newspaper questions—Who? What? Where? When? Why? How?

Erika didn't interrupt him with questions. She studied his face, looking at his expressions, trying to read what was being said at the other end of the phone.

Michael replaced the receiver and hung his head in his hands. He expelled a long breath and looked up at Erika. He sat at the office desk in the library. She moved to sit on the floor in front of him. Taking his hands, she waited.

"Everyone is all right. They've gone to Mom's house, and the bomb squad has been there to check it out," he told her. "Apparently, Bobby's house was wired. Two doors. They were set to go off ten minutes after the doors were opened."

"Enough time for everyone to get inside," Erika deduced.

"If it hadn't been for a neighbor calling to them when they arrived, they would all have been inside the house when the bomb went off."

Erika shivered. She raised herself up on her knees and put her arms around him. "Michael, I'm so sorry. I never thought when I came to see you that I'd draw you into a world where someone is trying to kill you."

He leaned against her, kissed the top of her head. "It's not your fault. Frank's been planning this for years. Just as I had time on the mountain to think, he's had the same amount of time, and now we're running toward each other. He tried to kill my brother and his family tonight."

Erika shivered. Just a few hours ago she'd held a baby in her arms. And this man, this crazy lunatic, had tried to kill that innocent child. How could anyone want to hurt someone who'd never done anything to anyone?

He kissed the top of her head again. "It won't be long, Erika, before he finds his way here."

"Michael." Erika looked up at him. "When I was trying to find you, I hired an investigator. Why don't we hire one now? If the police don't have the resources to track Frank's movements, we do. It's time we started thinking like rich people."

Erika returned to work three days later. The first thing Connie Forester did was to change the methods they used to get to work. Erika and Michael no longer occupied the same car. For the past three days she'd barely seen Michael.

Erika entered the offices to a chorus of "Welcome back"

from everyone she and Connie passed. Her office had a huge bouquet of flowers and a card signed by the entire corporate office staff. Connie checked it for bugs, explosive devices, and poisonous containers. Erika imagined she also checked it for timing devices, electrical charges, and exploding ink. By the time she finished, the surprise of finding a present sent to her was gone.

"We had to get a big card," her secretary told her, and she looked in surprise at what Connie was doing.

"Thank you," Erika said. "I appreciate all your kindness. Please pass that along. I'll take a walk this morning and try to thank everyone, personally."

"Connie, security has been alerted in this building. My staff will feel truly inhibited if you search every piece of paper that comes across this desk."

"This is a big package. You can't imagine the things that could be hidden in there."

"You're right, I can't, and I'm sure I never want to know anything about those kinds of devices, but I also don't want my staff feeling like they're suspects."

"I'll be more considerate," she said.

"There's a small office through that door." Erika went and opened it. "You and Adrienne can use it while you're here."

Connie went through it and Erika sat down at her desk. Separate stacks of reports and mail waited for her. She searched the stack for the report from Jeff Rivers. What had been the activity of the stock over the past week? Thankfully the market was closed on Thanksgiving and the weekend. Jeff's report showed no additional unusual activity. She breathed a little easier. Maybe they had jumped to conclusions, and there was no attempt to gain access to the board or to undermine the market share.

She went on to the competitive reports. Nothing out of place there. She felt better. Maybe they had been chasing their tails in the past few months. Erika hoped that was true, but she knew she'd keep monitoring the reports.

"Good morning." Michael came through the door the way he did every morning about this time. He had two cups of coffee. Handing her one, he sat down.

"How come you're enjoying this so much and I'm having the worst time with it?"

"I've always wanted to be followed around by a beautiful woman." He sipped his coffee. "You probably haven't."

Erika picked up one of the letters in front of her and threw it at him. He put his hand up and blocked the shot, laughing at her.

Picking up the envelope, he handed it back. "What are these?"

"More requests for my hand in marriage," she told him.

Michael got up. "Turn them down," he said. "I've got a meeting. I'll see you soon."

He left and she began her usual day of meetings, reports, and market strategies. By five o'clock she was dead tired and ready to go home. She and Connie rode without speaking in the limousine back to the estate.

Erika opened the door to hanging wreaths and garlands. The staff must have been working all day to make the place ready for Christmas.

She went to her room. She felt guilty. It wasn't like her to be angry with someone for no good reason, and she certainly had no good reason to use cross words with Connie Forester. She didn't dislike her. What she disliked was having her ability to move freely curtailed. There were times when she wanted to be alone, and with Connie lurking about she wasn't given that opportunity.

She should feel grateful for her presence. It allowed her to keep her vow of staying away from Michael. But she'd long ago abandoned that vow. Now she wanted nothing more than to be in his company, to be free to make love without someone knowing where she was.

Erika changed into jeans and a sweater and headed down to the library.

"Excuse me!" She heard her mother's voice from the top of the staircase. "I will not be searched."

Erika ran down the stairs. "It's all right, Connie. She's my mother."

"Ms. St. James—"

"I know, Connie," her voice was a little harsh. Erika let her shoulders drop, and the anger she felt went out of her. "I apologize," she said in a quieter voice. "Let her in."

Alva Redford walked past the guard.

"Don't look so smug, Mother, or I will let them search you." Alva followed her to the living room. A tree that reached near to the ceiling stood fully decorated in front of the window. The fireplace mantel held a scene from the Dickens Village lit with small lights. Everything about the room was merry. It should have made Erika happy.

"What's going on?" her mother asked the moment they were in the room. "Who was that?"

"She's my bodyguard."

"You're kidding." She stared at her for a moment. Erika stood with her arms crossed. "You're not kidding?"

"The accident was caused by someone tampering with the car."

Alva's mouth opened and she clamped her hands over it. Erika could only think of her mother and drama in the same breath. "We've added some extra guards, including the woman you met at the door."

Erika took a seat and waited. Her mother sat down, but said nothing. This time she was determined to wait her mother out. It didn't take long. Alva looked around the room several times. Eventually her gaze came back to her daughter.

"The staff is fully awake, Mother. Should I order you coffee?"

"No, dear. I'm cutting down on my intake of caffeine. It isn't healthy to drink too much caffeine."

"So you're becoming health conscious?"

"It wouldn't hurt any of us. We all need to take care of ourselves sometimes."

Again they lapsed into silence. It stretched about the room like a tight rubber band.

"You know, you look a lot like me when I was your age," Alva said.

"I don't think you want to begin any discussion that goes along that line," Erika said.

"Why not?"

"Because, Mother, you know I don't look like you. I look like my father."

Erika watched her mother. Alva had mastered a flinch that would in the past have been invisible to the naked eye.

"I don't want to talk about your father," she said.

"You never want to talk about him. Why?"

"Erika, I didn't come here to argue with you."

"Why did you come? Each time we get within ten feet and two minutes of each other, we're ready to scratch each other's eyes out. Why is that, *Mother?*"

Alva hesitated a moment. Erika didn't know which of them she wanted to calm down.

"Where's Michael?" she asked calmly and sweetly, as if they hadn't been about to explode.

"He teaches tonight," Erika told her. "Except for the guards, we're alone."

"Your injuries, from the accident," she said. "Are they completely healed?"

"Completely," Erika lied. She still had bruises on her arms and legs, but her headaches were gone. "Mother, you're trying to get to a point to ask for something. Come straight out with it. We get on much better when we're honest with each other."

"All right, Erika." Alva leaned forward in her chair. "I want to borrow some money."

"For what?"

"I can't tell you that."

"How much money?"

"Fifty thousand."

"You have to be kidding."

"I assure you I never kid about money."

"You want me to loan you that much money without knowing what you're going to do with it?"

Alva's head bobbed up and down.

"You have got more nerve than a . . ." She couldn't think of an adequate metaphor. "Give me one good reason why I should lend you anything."

"I'm your mother."

"That's not a good enough reason."

"The reason is personal. That's all I can tell you."

"If I give you this money, is there a chance at all that it will be repaid?"

Alva stared at her daughter for a long time. Her face didn't change. Not one thing about her changed except a narrowing of her eyes. "No," she finally said.

"Yet you think I should give it to you, anyway?"

She nodded. "If you ever in your life felt anything for me. I need the money."

"Why don't you go to a bank? You obviously have assets."

"I need it faster than a bank could process it and they would insist on knowing its purpose, and I couldn't tell them that."

"Whatever you're doing, is it legal?"

"Of course," she said, astonished that her daughter would even consider she'd do something illegal.

Erika had never written a check for that much money, not a personal one. She'd had the need to write few checks at all. Carlton had paid her expenses while she lived here, and when she went to school he paid the bills. After her graduation she got a job and lived on her salary. Carlton insisted she have an allowance, but Erika had never used it. The money had been in the bank for eight years, collecting and compounding interest. Writing a fifty thousand dollar check wouldn't even dent it.

"Mother, I'll give you the money." Alva's shoulders dropped in relief. "On one condition," Erika finished.

"What is it?"

"I want to know what the trust fund was set up for, and why it's been paying you since I moved into this house."

"The establishment of that fund was an agreement between Carlton and me. I promised him I'd take its reason for being to my grave." She stared directly at Erika. "You understand a promise, don't you?"

Erika surely understood promises. They were not to be broken. Alva had broken many promises to her, yet she threw up a curtain when it came to this fund.

"Do I get the money?"

Erika didn't move. She thought about her mother. There was no earthly reason why she should give this woman a penny. She'd mentally abused her as a child. She'd given her no moral support or guidance during her entire life, and now when she could go nowhere else she'd came begging for money—money she wouldn't even tell the purpose for. So why was Erika getting up and going to the library to write her a check?

Seventeen

The University of Pennsylvania School of Law was a brightly lit modern building. Michael looked down from his window on the second floor. His class had ended fifteen minutes ago, and Peter was right on time. Adrienne waited for him nearby. Moments later his brother came into the room and closed the door.

His features were grim, not at all like his anchorman look from the six o'clock news.

"What have you found?" Michael asked.

"Your suspicions were right. Alva St. James Redford does have a secret, but it had nothing to do with stock manipulations."

"How can you be sure?"

"Using sources you don't want to know about, I checked the dates of the checks she received from the fund against the surges in stocks. They coincide closely enough, but the funds don't go for stock."

"Are you sure?" Michael didn't want Alva to be behind anything that affected Graves Enterprises. He knew how much it would mean to Erika to discover her mother really loved her, but if Alva had secretly been buying stock, what could be her purpose, other than to force her daughter to do something? But what?

"All my sources say there isn't any stock problem. The increased activity surrounded Erika and you being named copartners of a vastly successful business. The analysts think the stock is levelling off."

"If there's not a stock problem, what is Alva using the money for?"

Peter looked directly at him, in the same way he did each night when the camera transmitted his face to an unseen audience. Michael waited.

"Medical treatment," he said. "She's dying."

Michael remembered seeing her walking toward the elevator that day she invited Erika to Thanksgiving dinner. He'd never have thought there was anything wrong with her.

"She has a rare disease that causes an imbalance in the chemistry of the brain. It causes mood swings. One minute she can be normal and talking and the next she'll be screaming and shouting. The addition of alcohol accelerates the process."

"Oh my God!" Michael said. "That's why she treated Erika so badly. Her bouts of shouting and screaming. Her moods changing. For a child that would be unbearable."

"It's not inheritable," Peter assured him. "It is longterm, however. Most people who develop it don't even know they have it. To them, their actions are completely normal. It's everybody else who is irrational."

"How long has she got?"

"No one knows."

"Can she be treated for it?"

"She has been. For the past twenty-five years she's been taking medication to control the imbalance."

"And now?"

"I don't know. Maybe she only takes it at times, or maybe the imbalance has grown worse with time. It's such a rare condition that not much is known about it." Peter reached across to his brother and squeezed his shoulder. "I'm sorry, Michael."

Michael nodded. "What about Bobby and Catherine? Are they all right?" He moved the subject to other avenues.

"They're fine. Mom is having the time of her life with Roberta, and Catherine is supervising the building of the new kitchen."

"She's not alone, is she?"

"No," Peter said. "The guard you hired is always with them. Until this maniac is caught, none of us travel alone. Even Mom has agreed to the terms."

"Good," Michael breathed. At least he didn't have to worry about them.

He told Peter about the firm of investigators they had hired to track Frank. He hoped they could find him and turn him over to the authorities. Then everyone could go back to a normal life.

Michael didn't know if his would ever be normal again. It hadn't been normal in years. He'd thought he was on the right track after he'd met and fallen in love with Erika, but he wasn't sure. The night he'd told her he loved her, she hadn't returned the sentiment, and she still hadn't. He knew she was attracted to him. He knew she satisfied him in bed, and he satisfied her. He'd seen the way she looked at him when her eyes were unguarded and filled with passion. Yet he didn't know how she really felt, or what it would mean to her when he delivered his news.

"I have to get back, Michael. Will you be all right?"

"Sure," Michael said. They both stood and put their coats on. Michael picked up his briefcase, and they met their guards in the hall. Outside the law school they separated and went to their waiting cars.

Michael rode in silence to the mansion. Erika always waited for him. Tonight he had news she probably wouldn't want to hear. He didn't want to tell her. He wanted to make love to her. Tomorrow would be plenty of time to give her bad news. He didn't want to spoil her night. He wanted it to be the most wonderful night in the world.

"Good-night, Mr. Lawrence," the limo driver said as he got out of the car. Michael and Adrienne came through the door. Erika stood in the doorway of the library. She looked beautiful.

Michael dropped his briefcase on the hall table and left his overcoat on a chair.

"I have to talk to Erika," he told Adrienne. "We don't want to be disturbed."

Michael came to her. She didn't move. He didn't try to conceal anything from the bodyguard behind him. He took her in his arms and kissed her thoroughly. Then he took her hand and led her up the stairs. At the landing they turned toward his rooms and she followed him, looking back to see if Adrienne was standing in the hall watching. She wasn't. She had discreetly disappeared.

Michael closed the door to his bedroom and locked it. He turned back to Erika, who stood before him. The room was dark except for the firelight. He smelled pine and noticed that Christmas accents had been added to the suite. Then his gaze came to rest on the woman he loved. Her short curls glowed with a red tinge as she watched him. Neither of them moved. Only the hammering of his heart through his shirt was visible. Michael slipped his jacket from his shoulders. His tie followed it before he took a step toward Erika.

"Touch me," he said.

Erika's hands reached his chest. Through the material he felt her slim fingers. Heat speared through him. Nimbly she opened the buttons on his shirt and slipped her fingers inside. When she'd opened it completely she kissed his brandy-hot skin. His muscles contracted. Her tongue tasted him, working a slow, hot magic on his nipples. She circled them in long, rapturous strokes. The flat surfaces hardened into sand pebbles.

Michael groaned at her action. He took hold of her head, his fingers softly digging into her hair. He brought her mouth to his in a hard, fervent kiss. She came up on her toes, her arms circling his neck as she held on, pressing her body into his, devouring his mouth as their tongues danced in a wet, warm, erotic dance.

Moving his hands, Michael caressed her back, slowly sliding

his long arms down her spine and up again, pulling her hips into his and reveling in the carnal excitement that tingled about them.

Michael found the hem of the sweater and pushed his hands under it. Pushing it upward, he stepped back, breaking contact only long enough to pull it over her head. He gasped at the touch of her hot skin. He slipped his thumbs in the top of her jeans and made a ceremony of sliding them around to the front snap. Erika expelled air into his mouth when his hands touched the core of her being. He opened the snap and slid the zipper to the bottom.

The mounting heat in the room threatened to incinerate them. Erika pushed his shirt down his arms, and one by one he pulled it free of his arms. The white silk floated to the floor, joining the clothes. Her hands were small as they touched his ungarnished skin, bringing it to fiery life. Her mouth again touched his chest, open and wet, seeking, persuading. Michael clenched his teeth at the pleasure she caused to rocket through him. Opening his pants, she slipped her hands inside. He groaned at the bliss that shot through him, the hardness that pulsed in her hands and the sheer need to have her continue the torturous thrill she'd begun. His pants slipped down his legs and he stepped out of his shoes and the material with no effort.

Lifting Erika, he carried her to the bed and laid her on it. In seconds he'd removed her jeans and shoes. He pulled her to a sitting position and kissed the swell of the breasts still encased in the lacy cups of her bra. Her hands drew widening circles on his back. He unhooked the bra, freeing her breasts. He took them in both hands, his thumbs padding over nipples that hardened to his touch. Erika moaned, asking for more. His fingers moved faster. Her breath caught in her throat, and his mouth took it on the exhale.

He never wanted to be separated from her again. He didn't care about bodyguards or family or business meetings. He wanted Erika to himself for the next hundred years or more. Michael slipped his hands inside the matching lace panties and was rewarded by finding her wet and ready for him. Her mouth bit into his shoulder. He slipped the last scrap of fabric down her long legs and pushed her back onto the bed.

Quickly finding his condom and securing it, he looked into her eyes.

"Say you love me," he said.

"I love you," Erika repeated. "I love you." Her words were full of emotion, and they touched a part of him that had never been reached before.

"I love you, Erika," he said, and slipped inside her.

Her eyes closed on a moan of pure pleasure. Michael moved and she moved with him. He touched her shoulders and she arched into him. He touched her breasts and she grasped his arms. Her legs circled him, giving him greater access as the two of them found their rhythm, found that place where light and dark come together, where man and woman merge into one being, and where the two can no longer control what happens. Michael lunged into her, his body strong, hers stronger, as she took his powerful strokes. Need gripped them, and they fed on their mutual selves, gratifying and consuming. Wet and hungry they continued, pushing, pulling, taking, giving, until Michael thought he'd die of joyous satisfaction.

Erika pushed him on. Guttural sounds came from her throat as she held onto him, as time after time they met, separated, and met again. His heart raced, his lungs fought for air, and his body filled with her and his need to go higher until there was nothing to do but fall. Michael reached for that place, that one place that no other couple could find. His voice sounded in his ears like the wind rushing over dry leaves. Groans and deep, incomprehensible words flowed from him as he reached for the light above him, and the world shattered.

Together they collapsed. Michael held onto Erika, knowing that if he let go they'd fall off the world. Slowly, they came back to reality. He turned her into his arms and kissed her.

"I love you, Michael."

"I'll always love you, Erika."

* * *

Erika woke up reaching for Michael. He'd filled her dreams, her bed, and her arms. She cradled herself in his arms and snuggled closer to him. Strong arms circled her, drawing her to him and keeping her safe. She wanted to never get up. She wanted to stay here in his arms and let the world take care of itself. Inside his embrace there were no Graves Enterprises, no market shares, no Frank Mason. There were only the two of them, two lovers who'd shared heaven together and selfishly wanted to keep it for themselves.

"We'd better get up," Michael said from above her head.

"I don't want to," she said, sliding her smooth leg over his rough one. "Isn't today Saturday, or something?"

"I'm afraid it's Friday."

Erika groaned.

"I have an idea," Michael said, drawing her hair back to kiss her forehead.

"What?"

"We play hooky today." He paused to kiss her cheek.

"Hmmm, that sounds good." She felt as feline as a stretching cat.

"We could go and get a blood test, and get married on Wednesday."

Erika froze. Michael continued to nibble on her, placing featherlight kisses on her cheeks and her lips, but Erika had ceased moving, feeling.

"What?" he asked. "What's wrong? You want a big wedding with a white gown and penguin suits?"

Erika couldn't find her voice. She was stunned, too surprised by his declaration to speak.

"Erika, we can do that. We can do—"

She put her fingers to his lips to stop him. She'd made him nervous, and she knew it. Her silence had made him keep talking, staving off what he feared she might say, but Erika had to say it.

"Michael, I can't marry you."

He grabbed her wrist and moved her hand, then turned her on her back and imprisoned her against the mattress. "Didn't you say you loved me?"

She nodded.

"Were you lying?"

She shook her head.

"Then why won't you marry me?"

She felt boxed in. Michael's elbows dug into the mattress on either side of her head. "I told you," she began. "I'm not good with man woman relationships."

"Erika, that's bull and you know it."

She didn't know it. "Every relationship I've ever had went sour."

"And I'm no different, is that it?"

"Let me up." She pushed his arm aside and turned over, swinging her feet to the floor while she held the sheet to her. She looked about for Michael's silk robe.

"Where's your robe?" she asked.

"In *your* room. You took it the last time we made love." His soft words made her flinch. Her sweater lay on the floor halfway across the room. She dropped the sheet and walked to it. Her entire body grew hot at the eyes she knew bore into her back. Drawing her arms into the sweater, she pulled it over her head and down her body. It stopped halfway to her knees.

"If you think that covers you, you're dead wrong," Michael said. "You're more sexy now than when you were naked."

Undaunted by his own nakedness, Michael left the bed and walked toward her.

"I should go now," she began.

"Not on your life," he told her. "We've started a conversation and I'm not postponing it."

"What about Connie Forester? She might discover I'm not in my room."

"You really think she doesn't know where you are?"

Erika hung her head. She was sure she knew. Neither of

them had eaten dinner last night. After Michael came in from teaching, neither of them had been seen again by their new houseguests.

"Can we get back to my question?"

"Aren't you going to put on some clothes?" Erika found it hard to talk to a naked man. Especially a man as good-looking as Michael. Instead of talking, she wanted to go back to bed. Her body was already hot, and he was deliberately throwing her thinking processes off.

"Do I make you nervous?"

"Yes," she said.

"Good," he whispered and caught her, pulling her close. "Marry me and I'll get dressed."

"Michael, listen to me." He ran his hands down her back, over the sweater until he reached the hem. Then he ran them up under it. "Michael," she whispered, "there's too much we have to think about." Her body burned like a two-alarm fire. Michael bent his head and leaned toward her mouth. She moved back. He followed her until she couldn't go any farther without falling. His mouth hovered above hers. His tongue traced her lipline. Erika felt the heat in the pit of her stomach and knew she was lost. Each time he reached for her, she had no resistance. She didn't want to resist. She was in love with him. She had been since almost the first moment she'd seen him. Her heart told her to forget her head, forget everything except the fact that her insides had turned to pudding.

She moved closer to him, coming up and joining him in the passion he created. She was weak and she knew it. She wanted Michael. On her toes, she pulled him closer to her, hugging him, aggressively taking his mouth and trading kiss for kiss. Erika stopped thinking. She no longer had the ability. The burning in her belly flashed white and hot. She stood against Michael, pressed into the hard structure of his body, liquefying in the heat of their combined fervor.

Breathing raggedly, Erika and Michael separated but remained in each other's arms. Michael squeezed her as hard as he could without crushing her.

"You've got to marry me, Erika. I love you."

She heard the emotion cracking his voice, making it warble in his throat. Her defenses began to crumble. God, she loved him. She wanted to marry him, to love him the rest of her life.

"I don't want anyone else," he said. "I want you to complete my life, mother my children, share my rewards. You could make me the happiest man alive. And I'll die trying to make you happy."

Tears rushed into Erika's eyes. Hot and salty, they rolled over her cheeks. She shifted and Michael pushed her back.

"What's wrong? Why are you crying."

"Micha—el." His name cracked as she said it. "I can't have children."

The time is now, Michael. Frank had failed in his attempt to kill Michael's brother, rid the world of another lawyer, but he'd sent the message, anyway. It was Michael's time now. Frank had to get home for Christmas. He needed to shop for his children, and Michael was the only thing standing in his way.

Frank saw the police car and slipped down in the driver's seat so he couldn't be seen. He was parked far enough away on a hill, several miles, but from here he had a clear vision of the estate. He couldn't see the house, but he could see over the wall and for several yards beyond it. With a high-powered rifle he'd have a clear shot at any car that came in or went out of the gates.

Every morning two limousines left the estate. They never left together, and their times varied. Frank knew they were trying to throw him off, but he was no fool. He'd planned this for a year but he wasn't locked into a precise date and time.

Still, he wanted to get home. Christmas with Abby and the kids would be especially happy this year.

Then he saw it. Frank tensed. He lifted the binoculars and peered through them. Two women in a car. One of them was Erika St. James. The other he didn't recognize, but by the look of her and the way she checked the streets, she had to be hired help. Frank smiled. Adrenaline rushed into his system, his breath came in gasps, and sweat broke out on his skin. This was his chance.

The driver turned left out of the driveway. She wasn't going to the office. Frank spied the license tag and make of the car. Then he started the engine and headed down the hill. He gripped the steering wheel, hoping he'd have time to get there before they turned off or got too far ahead for him to follow.

The time is now, he thought, and began humming "It's Beginning To Look a Lot Like Christmas."

Facing the office was something Erika couldn't do this morning. Michael would undoubtedly want an explanation and she wasn't up to it. She couldn't marry him. She wouldn't be able to defend herself against his insistence. All he had to do was touch her and she'd fall into his arms. This was what real love was like, not what she'd felt for Bill Castle. He'd done her a favor by running off with Jennifer Ahrends. She now knew what it was like at the creation, when the stars were flung into the dark void and the earth was set among them. Michael had taught her that. It was up to her to live with it.

She felt like dying. Erika had a brain, but it was having a difficult time explaining to her heart what she knew was the right decision.

After Erika tore herself from Michael's arms she stumbled from his room, falling on the steps, but pushing on to get to her room. She showered and dressed in record time, fighting the clock to get out of the house. She needed to be alone, but that option had been taken from her. She had Connie Forester as her constant companion.

The limousine waited for them, but Erika wanted to drive herself. Connie refused her request. Erika was in no mood to argue with the woman, but she was going to have her way. She passed Connie and went to the garage. Connie rushed in and stood in front of her.

She tried to make her see reason. "Erika, think about what you're doing. Obviously, you and Michael had a fight. That's no reason to put your life in danger."

Erika stared at her for a moment, then burst into tears. She cried for Michael, for herself, for the love they shared that would die, for the children they would never have, for the babies she would never hold.

"Get in," Connie said. The bodyguard opened the door and pushed Erika into the passenger seat. "You're in no condition to drive."

Erika sat still while Connie quickly did a check of the car. When she was satisfied everything was all right, she got into the driver's seat and started the engine. Connie drove expertly. She turned the car away from downtown Philly and headed west. Erika didn't ask where they were going. She didn't care as long as it was away from Michael.

Fresh tears pooled in her eyes and spilled down her face. She let them run unchecked, no longer caring that Connie was there, she guessed that Connie knew she'd spent the night with Michael. They had argued, argued over getting married. They were in love with each other. Shouldn't that be the easiest decision in the world? Maybe for someone else, but not for her. It wouldn't last, and then she'd die. She could never hold a man. She wasn't pretty. She didn't have what it took for the long run. And children. He wanted children. She couldn't risk it.

Erika didn't notice where they were going. The traffic on the other side of the road was thick and backed up. Connie drove competently and quietly. She hadn't said anything since they left the garage. Erika let her head fall back and her mind go blank, numb. Her fatigue after a night of lovemaking, coupled with the steady rhythm of the road, lulled her to sleep.

The sudden cessation of motion woke her. "Where are we?" Erika looked around, disoriented.

"Strasburg," Connie said. "I was born here."

Erika got out of the car. The air smelled of horses. On the road she saw a small black carriage, pulled by a single horse. Lancaster County. She remembered. This was Pennsylvania Dutch country. Erika looked at the house. It was a white clapboard structure with black shutters.

"It was my mother's house," Connie explained. "She died six years ago, but I still keep it."

Erika heard the catch in Connie's voice. Everyone spoke well of their parents. Why hadn't her mother given her the love that could produce that kind of emotion even after death? Why hadn't she taught her the forever kind of love? Why hadn't she prepared her for a man like Michael? Erika's eyes clouded again, but she brushed them away.

"Come on in."

Inside the place was spotless. Dark, sturdy, handmade furniture filled every room. Not enough to crowd, just to provide places to sit or work. The kitchen chairs were hard and without cushions. Erika sat down on one of them while Connie made coffee in a percolator that sat on the woodburning stove. While the coffee heated, Connie busied herself making breakfast. Erika felt useless. The house reminded her of the dirty cabin where she'd found Michael. She'd cooked there under less than ideal conditions.

Connie's food was delicious. Erika ate hungrily and drank two cups of the hot, steaming coffee.

"We can stay here as long as you like," Connie said, sipping her second cup of coffee. "But your problems aren't going to go away because you do."

Erika agreed with her. She knew she had no choice but to return. She had to go back and face him. She just needed some time alone to think and decide.

"Do you think it would be all right if I went for a walk?" She meant alone, and she could tell Connie didn't like the request. "I promise I'm not trying to make things difficult. I just need some time by myself."

For a moment Connie didn't say anything. Erika was sure she was going to refuse.

"It's not a good idea."

"No one followed us," she said.

"You were asleep most of the way," Connie told her.

"Didn't you check?"

"Of course," she said. "I'm pretty sure we weren't followed. But it's my job to be with you all the time."

"How could anyone track me here? Frank Mason doesn't know about you. He couldn't possibly know about your mother's house. And I'll be within shouting distance," she paused. Connie looked as if she wanted to refuse. Erika knew she was asking her to compromise her principles, but she needed the space.

"When I needed to be alone, I used to go up to that tree over there." Connie pointed through the window. On a hill stood a huge oak. "There used to be a tire swing hanging from it. I'd swing for hours."

"Thanks, Connie." Erika smiled for the first time since she'd left Michael.

Connie smiled back at her. "I'll tell you what," she said. "We'll stay here all night. I'll make us an authentic Pennsylvania Dutch dinner, and we'll drive back in the morning."

"Connie, you're an angel." Erika hugged her.

"Go on," Connie said, probably a little embarrassed.

"While you're communing with nature, I'll be at the grocery store."

Erika left by the back door and started up the hill. The air still smelled of horses, but she liked it. She pulled her coat around her, continuing toward Connie's tree. She saw the car leave the driveway. She waved at Connie and saw her arm waving from the car window. She headed in the opposite direction from the one they had come. Was Connie trying to gain her trust? She hadn't been the best client a person could work for, but she was warming to the short bodyguard.

She looked up the hill toward the tree. She remembered Michael lying by the stream with the mountain in the background. Where was he? Did he go to the office? Should she call him? She hadn't seen a phone, and from the look of the furniture and kitchen nothing invented after 1700 would be in the house, except that ancient coffeepot. Erika thought about Connie. There would be a phone at the grocery store and surely she carried a cellular unit, although Erika had not seen it. Would she call Michael to let him know they were safe? She hoped Connie would. There was no need for him to worry needlessly.

Erika continued toward the tree. She saw a man on another hill and waved. He stood up and waved back. On the other side was a whole family. Erika again raised her hand in the universal salute. Two small children smiled at her. Then the family, all dressed in black, got into a buggy and rode away. She wondered where they were off to this sunny December morning.

She remembered her morning. She'd reacted badly. Michael had surprised her with his proposal. The night had been beautiful, filled with love and magic and an array of color that comprised their own private world. It was the most wonderful night of her life. She should have seen where it was leading. Hadn't he asked her if she loved him? Hadn't she admitted she did? What else could she say when he looked at her with his own love shining in his eyes? She couldn't have lied if she'd wanted to. Then morning dawned and the magic was gone. Reality was back.

The wind picked up and Erika pulled her coat collar closer to her ears. She'd go back now, and when Connie returned she'd ask to call Michael.

Erika turned, then gasped. Pointed at her heart was the barrel of a black gun. Holding it was Frank Mason.

* * *

Where was she? Michael paced the office. She hadn't come here, and Connie hadn't called. At least he knew they left together. Connie was good. She could take care of her. But Erika was headstrong, and she'd fought Connie since she arrived. They weren't in the limo with bulletproof glass, but in the Mercedes, which had regular windows.

Calm down, Michael, he told himself. *You're in love, but this is a time for rationality.* He picked up a letter opener, then dropped it. The phone rang and he snatched it up before it completed the first ring.

Shouting into it, he said, "Lawrence."

"Michael, it's Connie."

"Where the hell are you?" His voice was angry, but he was relieved to hear hers.

"We're in Strasburg at my mother's house. Erika's fine. There's no cause for alarm. She just needed some space."

Michael knew Connie well enough to know she'd held her tongue over why Erika needed space.

"I told her we'd stay the night and return in the morning. Is that all right?"

"Do you think that's wise?" He didn't want them staying overnight. He wanted Erika back so he could talk to her, make love to her. If she didn't want to get married, they didn't have to. If she couldn't have children, they could adopt. He didn't care. All he wanted was her.

"No, I don't," Connie replied. "I'd much rather be at the estate with the added guards, but I kept a close check on the drive up here. We weren't followed."

"Where's Erika now?" Michael played with the letter opener. "I'd like to talk to her."

"She went for a walk. I'm calling from a local grocery store. We left so fast, I left my cellular unit in the limo."

"Is there a number where you can be reached?"

"I'm afraid not. My mother was a Quaker, remember. She didn't believe in telephones."

Michael sighed.

"Do you want me to tell her anything?" Connie offered.

"Yeah," he said. "Tell her I love her."

Eighteen

"Where are you taking me?" Erika asked.

"Shut up and drive."

Frank Mason sat next to her in the jeep. She drove according to his directions. He'd forced her to go with him. Connie hadn't returned, and Erika didn't even get to go into the house. They'd immediately climbed into the black Cherokee and taken off.

Friday afternoon traffic was light and Erika couldn't count on it to give her any time to get away or at least call for help. They bypassed Philadelphia and headed north along Route 1. A heavily trafficked route that ran from Maine to Florida, it was sometimes a four-lane highway, sometimes a normal city street. When they connected with it it was a highway, but soon it would go through the business district of central New Jersey.

Frank had her switch to Route 95, then the New Jersey Turnpike. They got off at Route 18 in East Brunswick and went to a quiet neighborhood with manicured lawns. She stopped in the driveway of a pretty yellow house on a cul-de-sac, with vinyl siding.

"Don't try anything stupid," he told her. "If I have to I'll shoot you here and now."

She believed him. Michael had told her how he killed his children. The man was psychotic. He'd kill her in a minute. Inside, he tied her hands and feet to a chair. Erika's breaths came too fast. She forced herself not to hyperventilate.

"What are you going to do?"

"Don't worry, Sister," he said. "Your time isn't right, yet. I need Michael Lawrence. You're the bait."

"Why?" she asked. "What do you want with Michael?"

"I want him dead."

"Why?"

"No more questions," he said, and tied a scarf around her head, cutting her mouth and forcing her to remain quiet. She nearly gagged on it. It tasted of perfume and powder. "I have to go out now," he said. "You wait here."

Erika didn't move until she heard the jeep drive away. Then she tried to free her hands. The knots were too tight and the more she moved, the more they seemed to tighten.

She wondered what Connie had done when she came back and found her gone. Had she called Michael? Were they looking for her? Tears sprang to her eyes. They would have no idea where to look. She didn't even know where she was.

Think, Erika, she told herself. *You're alone for the time being. How can you get away?* Phone. She needed to call someone, the police, 9-1-1. There was a phone on the wall in the kitchen. She could see it from the chair he'd tied her to. It was too high. She'd never reach it to get it off the wall. There had to be another one.

Trying to stand, she found that the ropes cut into her ankles and wrists. It hurt to move. She couldn't walk with the chair tied to her, but maybe she could scoot along in the chair. She tried it, and found pain shooting up her legs and arms. Still, she had to try. There had to be a phone in the other room. Inch by painful inch she moved the chair until she got to the door of the room.

If Erika could have made a sound she would have screamed at the top of her lungs. All she could do was suck on the wet scarf in her mouth. Lying on the floor, in a pool of blood, was a man of about sixty. His eyes were blank and staring at the ceiling. One side of his head had been bashed in, and near him was a bloodstained baseball bat. Tears formed in Erika's eyes and she cried, making guttural noises and choking on her own saliva.

A key stuck in the door and Frank came through the kitchen. "Going somewhere, Ms. St. James?" He grabbed the back of her chair and pulled her back into the dining room. The shades were down in all the rooms except the living room. The house looked lived in, especially with Frank coming and going as if he lived there.

"Getting to the phone would have done you no good," he told her. "The line is as dead as Mr. Thompson." He glanced at the doorway. "Now all we have to do is wait for Michael to come to the rescue."

Erika couldn't speak. She could only use her eyes to question him.

"I sent him a message," he answered. "Your purse."

Erika looked blankly at him. Her purse had been inside Connie's house. They hadn't gone in.

"I got it while you were enjoying the morning air. Black bag, with a gold clasp. Inside was a wallet with your initials on it, a comb, lipstick, more credit cards than any one person ought to have, a checkbook, and a set of keys. I sent him everything . . . but this." He pulled the Christmas picture of Carlton and her from his pocket and showed it to her.

Fear caught in Erika's chest. What would Michael do? Would he come to save her? Did he love her enough to risk his own life?

Oh God! she cried silently. *I love him. Don't let him come.*

Michael had spent the worst twenty-four hours of his life. He couldn't seem to be still, calm down. He'd paced the library practically all night, waiting for the phone to ring, willing it to ring to give him some relief. He needed to know Erika was alive, that Frank had not done anything to her yet. He'd thought seeing the Mason children killed and Abby's suicide had been enough trauma for a lifetime, but now Erika missing was driving him insane. What had Frank done to her? Michael's stomach was tied up in sailor's knots. His imagination brought pictures of Erika killed in grotesque ways. What could he do? What could the police do? They hadn't heard a word. Was she all right?

Connie came in looking as bad as he did. "Has there been any word?"

"Nothing," he said.

"Michael, I'm sorry—"

"It's not your fault, Connie," he cut her off. It was his fault, Michael told himself. He'd been the one to make her angry. He was the one she wanted to get away from. If he'd kept his thoughts to himself she'd be here now. But he hadn't. He couldn't know a marriage proposal would cause her pain and anger. He hadn't thought about the effect her mother had had on her. Alva Redford had abused her, never giving her the complete love she needed, and even though Michael offered it, she couldn't accept that he wouldn't treat her the same as she'd been treated in the past. If she'd just stayed home or gone to the office, he'd have had a chance to explain. She'd gone off in a rage and now he might never see her again.

Michael wrung his hands, wishing he had Frank Mason's neck between them. His back ached with pent-up tension. What should they do now?

"Michael," Connie said. "She'll be all right. The police are looking for Frank. You've got an agency tracking him, and now the FBI is involved. They'll find her."

Michael squeezed Connie's shoulder. They had to find her. He felt helpless. The room had been full of people for the entire day and most of the night. The only person who hadn't arrived was Alva Redford.

"This package was just delivered," Adrienne said, coming into the room. She carried a familiar red, white, and blue Federal Express box. "It has a return label bearing Frank Mason as the sender."

Michael shot across the room, heading straight for her.

"Wait," Connie stopped him. She had to physically restrain him from taking the box and ripping it open. "Has it been swiped?"

"Yes," Adrienne said. "As soon as I saw his name."

Michael had sudden images of finding an ear or a finger inside the box. "Open it," he said, clearing his throat.

Adrienne pulled the paper tape. A rough, ripping sound exploded in his head. She dumped the contents on the desk. Erika's purse fell out, its clasp striking the polished surface. For a moment no one moved. Then Michael grabbed the bag and opened it. "It's hers," he said. He let his breath out slowly, not wanting to reveal that he'd expected a body part to roll out of the box. Looking at Connie, he saw that her face was as pale as his own. She must have had a similar thought.

"What's this?" she asked, picking up a cassette.

"I don't know," Michael answered.

The label read "Play me."

"Where is there a cassette player?" Adrienne asked.

He led them to the salon. There was more music equipment than he'd had as a college student there. Slipping the cartridge into the deck, he turned on the many switches and a voice boomed into the air. Connie reached around him and turned the sound to a more comfortable level.

"No police, Lawrence," the voice said. Michael hadn't heard Frank speak for over a year, yet he immediately recognized the inflection in his speech patterns. "If you want to see your little heiress again, do exactly as I say." There was a pause. "First, no police or she'll be the first one to drop. Second, no bodyguards. If you're not getting this . . . I'm saying I want you, and you alone."

Michael understood. He'd constantly had to school Frank on being precise, leaving no interpretation for his words except the ones they intended. The man had learned quickly.

"Now, you're to go to the old Rutgers boathouse along the Raritan River. The one near the tennis courts off Route 18, just before you get to Commercial Avenue. You know where they are. You played there as a child."

Connie looked at Michael, and he nodded. He knew where it was.

"The boathouse used to be new, but like all things that age it's rundown and boarded up now. There will be a package for you there near the back door. Lawrence, don't try to cross me on this. Come alone. If I even *think* I see a cop, Erika St. James won't live out the day." He paused again. Michael heard him take a breath. "According to Federal Express, this package should arrive before ten thirty Saturday morning. You've got until two this afternoon to get to the boathouse, or her death will be slow and painful."

The tape ended there. The three of them stood in the salon staring at the machine and hearing the dead, mechanical air of the rolling tape. Michael checked his watch. Eleven-thirty. The delivery had been late. Michael started for the door. Adrienne's hand on his arm stopped him.

"Michael," she began. "Don't even consider going alone."

"I don't have a choice," he said. "The area he picked is across from a high hill, with Douglass College sitting at the top. The boathouse and tennis courts are open. Nothing covers them. Any place you could think to hide is visible."

"We need to call the police."

"We can't do that," he said too fast, too forcefully. "Adrienne, he's in New Brunswick, not here or New York. The New Brunswick Police Department might be good for traffic tickets and breaking up a student party, but they're no match for Frank. I have to go alone if there's any chance of getting Erika back."

He pulled loose from her hand.

"Then we call the FBI," she said.

"There isn't time," he told her. "It's Saturday, nineteen days till Christmas. The day is sunny and warm for this time of year. The roads will be mobbed. I'll be lucky to get there on time, and I'm not waiting around for the FBI to come blundering in and get her killed."

"Michael!" Connie shouted. Both women followed him as he started for the front door. He stopped to get a coat and put it on. "Think about what you're doing. You don't want to be the cause of getting her killed, do you?"

That stopped him. "What are you talking about?"

"What are you planning to do when you get there?"

"I don't know. Follow his instructions, I suppose."

"And if he's on that hill with a high-powered rifle pointed at your head, what will you have accomplished?" Connie stopped for a breath. "How will that help Erika? All you'll do is provide him with the ability to kill both of you on the same day."

She got through to him. Michael dropped down on one of the chairs in the hall. "What do you suggest?"

"First, we call the FBI. We can do that from the car. And then we let them take it from there. They're the experts in this. Let them do what we pay them for."

"All right," Michael agreed after a moment. He wasn't sure they should completely put Erika's life into the hands of strangers, but he had to admit Connie's plan made more sense than his did.

The two women got jackets and put them on. "We can't leave together," Adrienne said. "We don't know if he's watching the house or not. If he sees us all together, he'll know something is up."

"Michael—"

"I'm going to drive myself," he said, not accepting an argument. Michael knew the streets of New Brunswick. They could be small and narrow. If he needed to maneuver, he wanted something small and fast.

"Use the front entrance. Connie and I will go out the back. He can't watch them both at the same time. When you get to New Brunswick, pass it and meet us at the beginning of River

Road in Highland Park. I want a good look at that area before we let you go into it."

Michael nodded. "I know where it is." He remembered the interchange well. Twenty years ago River Road had been the easiest method of accessing one of New Jersey's highways. It sat on one side of a two lane bridge spanning the Raritan River. Traffic backed up into the center of Highland Park and the heavily traveled Albany Street on the New Brunswick side. In recent years the roads around it had been redone. A bypass had been added on the New Brunswick side, leading to Route 287 and relieving the small towns of snarling traffic jams.

"Ready?" Michael asked.

"Ready," Adrienne said.

At the garage Michael got into his Porsche. It was small and maneuverable, and he'd once compared its hidden power to Erika's underlying passion. He started the engine. It roared to life at the slight turn of the key. He hoped that before this day ended they would be reunited.

Connie came over to his window. He lowered it. "We're going to find her, Michael," she said. "All we have to do is keep a cool head and remember our purpose."

"Connie, I'm playing your way." He wanted her to know he wasn't planning any cowboy tactics. Erika's life was the one thing he was concerned about.

"Then we're going to put this bastard away where not even his mother could find him."

Connie was angry. Frank had ruined her perfect record and she really wanted him. Michael saw it in her eyes. Yet, she was cautious, and not apt to overplay the role. She wanted to make sure he didn't, either.

The food on her plate smelled delicious, and Erika was weak with hunger. Frank had kept her tied up all night. Her arms and legs were numb. He'd only allowed her up one time, to go to the bathroom.

This morning he'd cooked her breakfast—bacon, scrambled eggs, fried apples, rolls, and coffee. He'd untied her and brought her to the table, then tied her left arm to the chair. Erika ate with her right hand. The food tasted as good as it smelled. Her mouth was sore from the scarf, but she ate, anyway.

Erika ventured to talk. She wanted to try to reason with him. "You move about as if you live here."

"I do live here," he told her. "This is my house. Mine and Abby's."

She stared at him. Frank ate normally. Nothing seemed out of place to him. Suddenly, Erika knew this *was* his house, at least it had been before the divorce and his wife's death. He knew his way around, but Erika had attributed that to his being there for a while.

He seemed in a rational mood, and Erika might not get another chance to question him. Frank could seem so normal. Last night he'd talked to her about politics, what was happening in the East Brunswick area, how global warming was affecting life on earth. If Erika's hands hadn't been tied behind her back and her ankles fastened to the chair she sat in, and if she hadn't known there was a dead body only a few feet away, she would have had to rethink her decision about his sanity.

"How long are you going to keep me here?" she asked.

He stopped eating and looked her directly in the eye. "If I'm lucky it should all be over today."

The intensity of his gaze sent a chill down Erika's back. How long did she have? What had he done?

"What are you going to do to me?"

"I'm going to kill you."

Erika shivered. Every part of her trembled. She could feel every organ, every cell, every nerve and blood vessel vibrating. Frank continued to eat as if he'd told her they would take in a movie after breakfast.

"Why?" she asked when she could find her voice. It was breathy and weak.

"So Abby and I can live without enemies."

"You and Abby?" Erika asked. Unconsciously she tried to raise her left arm. The restraint forced her to remain where she was.

Frank nodded.

He was crazy! Didn't he realize Abby was dead?

"Where is Abby, Frank?"

Frank looked up, and lightning seemed to flash in his eyes. Suddenly, his glass sailed across the room. Erika had only enough time to shift to the side before it sailed past her. Orange juice splattered her as the glass clipped her shoulder and fell to the floor.

"You don't care about Abby. You don't even know her. But he does, and he'll pay for what he did to her."

"Frank, Abby's dead."

Erika knew she'd stepped over the line. Frank stood up slowly. He glared at her, towered like a giant over his kingdom. Every line of his body was granite hard, menacing. She bit down on her lip to keep from screaming. Fear choked her. He was going to kill her now. She tried to stand, but the chair restrained her. She couldn't run, couldn't get away from him.

Erika had nothing to protect her. If she was going to stay alive, she had to convince him not to kill her. She racked her brain, trying to think of something to say. *How do you talk to a crazy person?* she asked herself.

He moved away from his chair and started for her.

"Frank," she said. "It's Abby. What are we going to get the children for Christmas this year?"

Frank stopped. He stared at her, but she knew he wasn't seeing her. She breathed heavily.

"I've looked in the malls and I can't find anything for . . ." *Who?* she thought. *What were the children's names?* She'd never heard anyone call them anything except the Mason children. "For them," she finished. "I thought a doll for our baby."

She gauged his reaction. He stopped, but she didn't know if the rational Frank had returned or the crazy Frank was still standing in front of her.

"Melissa would like a doll," he finally said. "She told me when I put her to bed last night."

Erika let her breath out. Frank's anger seemed to be going. He turned away from her and checked his watch. "I have to go out," he said.

"Where?" she asked before she could stop herself. He'd told her it would be over today. Had he called Michael when he left her yesterday? Had they agreed to meet somewhere? Was Michael coming here? She had to know.

"I won't be long," he said, ignoring her question. He didn't move, but stood facing the hall door. Erika followed his gaze. The dead body still lay on the floor. She wondered who the man was, and why no one came by or called him. Frank had said the phone was dead. Wasn't there anyone who knew this man? Did he live alone? He wasn't that old. Did he still work? Why hadn't the people from his job called to check on him? Why didn't the neighbors think it strange that the jeep came and went at will?

Frank turned back to her and Erika froze. He came toward her. She pushed herself back in the chair as far as she could go. Her hands and feet went dead cold. Frank grabbed her free arm and pulled it behind her. Her back hurt from the strain of sitting in an unnatural position. He untied her other hand and pulled it behind her, securing the two together.

"I'll be back . . . with Michael," he added.

Nineteen

The Raritan River spanned about a hundred yards at the point from the boathouse to the opposite shore. A string of apartment buildings that had been converted to condominiums sat above a run of trees hugging the shoreline. Michael crouched on the ground with a pair of binoculars. The area was teeming with FBI agents. Michael agreed that they were concealed, and even if Frank were looking from the other shore he'd see nothing.

Michael panned the hilltop, the busy roadway, and the boathouse. From his position he saw no sign of Frank. The day was cold and few people walked on this part of Route 18. Cars pulled in and out of the gas station at Commercial Avenue and the one just across from where Michael lay on the ground.

Frank knew what he was doing when he picked this place. There was nowhere to hide, to conceal himself from attack. Frank could pick him off from a number of places and he'd never know which way the bullet had come. Michael checked his watch. He had only half an hour left. He had to go now to get over the bridge and into the yard before the two o'clock hour.

"It's time," one of the agents he'd met, but couldn't remember, said next to him.

Michael pulled back and stood up under the cover of the leafless trees.

"Are you sure you want to do this? We can still put a double in your place."

"He'd know in seconds I wasn't there, and we don't know what he'd do to Erika," Michael said. "I'm going."

"You have the vest?"

Michael touched his chest. Under his coat he wore a bulletproof vest, but he didn't think it meant much if Frank wanted to kill him. Frank's history called for bullets through the head, and they had no vest that would protect him there.

"We have the car bugged, and we can track you through the vest."

Michael nodded. They walked through the trees to the condos and into the parking lots beyond. Michael got in his car and started the engine.

"Good luck," the agent said. "You'll be picked up by our people on the other side."

"Thanks," Michael said, and drove away. He'd never felt so alone in his life.

Frank saw him coming. He recognized the car. It was the same one he'd driven day in and day out during Frank's trial. Small, sleek, powerful. It wouldn't help him today. Neither would the FBI. Kidnapping was a federal crime. The local police would have little to do with it, if he were caught. Frank had no intention of being caught.

Checking around him he saw no one anywhere, but he didn't expect to. Michael was a letter-of-the-law man. He'd follow directions. The two women guards were a different story. They would call the FBI no matter what he'd told Michael. Frank was prepared for that.

Michael came across the Highland Park Bridge and took the ramp for Route 18 South. He stopped at the light and waited for it to turn green. He was going to have to pass the boathouse and go to the Paulus Boulevard jughandle to turn around and get on the north side of the highway. That's where Frank would make his move.

He saw him coming. He drove fast and took the curve at

an easy angle. The light was red when he got to it, and he stopped. Frank had concealed himself in the branches that hung from the top of the hill. The ground beyond the rough vines was a ten foot drop to the ground. He took it easily, landing directly next to the car. His gun pointed at the glass, he said, "Open it."

The automatic door locks clicked and Frank got in the car. "Run the light. Make a right," he said, pressing the cold steel against Michael's neck. "Now!"

Michael did as he asked.

"Take the ramp to 1 South," he commanded.

The first exit took him down to Route 1, heading toward Trenton and South Jersey. At the bottom of the hill, they immediately exited into the Sears parking lot. Frank directed him to the back, where he'd parked his jeep. He estimated they had about three minutes before the FBI agents scrambled and converged on them.

In moments they were out of the car. He pushed Michael to the jeep, grabbed his coat and pulled it down his arms, restraining any movement.

"I know they're on their way. You got one minute to strip to your shorts." Michael didn't move. Frank jabbed the gun into his throat. "Fifty-nine seconds," he shouted. "Do it as if you were trying to get to Erika as fast as you could. Or I'll put a bullet through your head and save myself the trouble of dragging you home."

The FBI offices had been set up in an office building at George and New Streets, across from The State Theater. Connie stared out of the window at the main street of the City of New Brunswick. The agent assigned to Michael and Erika was a tall, blond man of about thirty, but he looked younger. He had a cellular unit pushed up against his ear, listening. "Did they get him?" she asked, looking anxiously at the FBI agent.

"I'm afraid not," he said. "They got to Mr. Lawrence's car, but it was empty."

"What about the bug in his vest? Can't you track him?"

"His clothes were lying in a heap next to the car, including the vest."

Connie turned away. What could they do now? There was no way to determine where they had gone. Leaving that lot by the back gave Mason access to all four directions, and they had no idea what kind of vehicle he was driving.

"What about the transmission before they left the lot? Did they say anything that could help us?"

"They weren't close enough for a clear tape. We'll have to send it to the lab for amplification."

"I want to hear it," Connie commanded.

"It's garbled. You won't be able to make out anything."

"Look," Connie told the blond man, "I know more about Frank Mason than his father does. Let me hear the tape. I might understand something you don't."

The agent turned on the machine and she listened. The first time through she heard nothing but background noise. Connie hit the rewind button and listened again. This time she heard something that sounded like "men" but it was too fast. When it ended she played it again, and again and again.

"If only we could filter out the background noises."

"I told you it wouldn't yield anything," the agent said. "The sooner we get it to the lab, the faster we'll get an answer."

"We don't have time for that. The closest lab is in Newark. Frank Mason has both of them now. He isn't going to wait around for us to analyze a tape. We have to do something now."

"I'm open to suggestion," he told her, spreading his hands.

Adrienne, who had been quiet to this point, spoke. "Give me the tape. I can filter the noises."

"You can?" the agent asked. "How? We need equipment we don't have."

"We have the equipment," she said. She pointed to the window.

Connie and the agent looked out. Then Connie looked at Adrienne and smiled.

"Let's go," she said.

"Where?" the agent asked.

"The State Theater. They've got sound equipment."

The automatic garage door mechanism closed the door completely before Frank got out of the car. He unlocked the cuffs on the jeep door and cuffed Michael's hands behind him.

"Get out," he commanded.

Michael stepped barefoot onto the cold concrete floor. Debris and small pebbles cut into his skin. Frank pushed the gun into his bare back and urged him forward. They went into the house. Michael knew where he was. He'd never been here before but he recognized the street address. This was the house Abby had received as part of the settlement, where the couple had lived as man and wife, and where Abby had committed suicide. Frank had told him he was taking him home.

A jab to his kidneys had him stumbling forward. He went through the kitchen and into the dining room. Erika sat there, tied to a chair. It was tied to the decorative column that separated the living and dining rooms.

"Erika!" he called and rushed to her. "Are you all right?"

She had a gag in her mouth, but she grunted his name. Tears formed in her eyes and spilled down her face.

"Don't," he said, dropping to his knees. He moved his hands, but they were confined. Unable to touch her, he leaned forward and kissed her cheek.

Erika dropped her head to his shoulder and sobbed.

"Take the gag off her," he ordered Frank.

Frank went behind her and untied the scarf. Her mouth was bruised when he saw it, and he wanted to kill Frank. Erika kissed him as soon as she was free.

"I love you, Michael," she said. "I didn't think I'd ever see you again."

Michael didn't want to tell her how much that fear had weighed on his mind. He kissed her again. "Are you all right?" he asked a second time.

She nodded and leaned to kiss him, her wet face brushing against his.

"This is a sweet reunion," Frank sneered. "Too bad I'm going to have to break it up." He got Michael a chair and put it next to Erika's, keeping him in line with the gun in his hand. "I got you some clothes," he told him. "Put them on."

Michael looked at the neatly folded pile of clothes on the living room sofa. "Whose are these?" Michael asked.

"The man who owned them no longer has a need for them," Frank said.

"Michael, there's a dead man in the hall." Erika looked over her shoulder at the doorway to the center hall. Michael followed her gaze.

"His wife's upstairs," Frank explained.

Michael stepped into the pants. Everything was there, down to the socks. Only shoes were missing from the pile.

"What was their crime, Frank? Why did you kill them?"

"This is my house," he said. "They tried to say it was theirs."

Erika groaned. "Frank, I need to go to the bathroom."

"Not yet," he shouted. "First I do him, then you."

Michael pulled on a white shirt and buttoned the front buttons. The shirt fit, but the pants pooled at his ankles.

"Sit down."

Michael did as he was told. Frank bound his arms to the chair back.

"Frank, please," Erika pleaded. "I can't wait any longer."

He looked at her. "You're as bad as one of the children," he scolded.

"Please, Honey."

Michael stared at her, but said nothing. What was she up

to? Frank also looked different. His mood swung like a fast pendulum. He went to Erika and untied her legs, then her arms. She pulled them around the chair and massaged the flesh. Michael saw the bruise marks the ropes had left on her skin.

She tried to stand, but fell.

"Let me help you, Abby," Frank said. He pulled her arm around his shoulder and supported her while she limped across the room. Whet had happened here, Michael wondered. What kind of game was Erika playing, and would it get her killed?

Erika used the toilet, then massaged her wrists and ankles. She couldn't stand like this—her circulation had cramped long ago and her foot and hands were numb—but she wasn't going to get another chance. She'd discovered Frank's weakness. She could keep him thinking she was Abby, and everything would be all right. If he lapsed back into normalcy, he'd kill them.

Wiggling her toes hurt, but it was the only way to get the blood back into her feet. Pins and needles the size of ten-penny nails felt as if they were sticking into her feet. Her wrists weren't as bad. She ran cold water over them to slow down the rush of blood, giving her fingers the effect of the bends.

Gingerly she tried to walk in the confined space. She could do it. Buying herself time to let her body repair itself, she stayed in the bathroom for as long as Frank allowed. Which turned out to be just a moment more.

"Let's go," he said from outside the door.

Erika opened it and walked out. He grabbed her arm the moment she came out. He knew she was Erika again. He pushed her back to the chair and sat her back down.

"Frank, no," she cried. "Please let me have a little exercise. My skin is red from the ropes, and my fingers are so swollen I can't open and close my hands."

"Too bad," he said, yanking her hands behind her. He set the gun on the floor next to him while he tied her up again. Erika looked at Michael. On the floor next to his chair was the rope that Frank had used. He hadn't taken the time to tie him as tightly as he had her, and he'd gotten free, or almost free.

"Frank," Michael said. "Why are you doing this? It doesn't make sense."

"It doesn't have to make sense," he told him.

"Why do you want to kill us?"

Frank stood up when he'd tied her hands. He left her ankles free.

"You killed *her*," he accused.

"Killed who?"

"Abby . . . my wife."

"Frank, Abby committed suicide."

Erika didn't like this. When she'd confronted Frank with Abby's death he'd acted as if he was going to kill her right then. She tried to get Michael's attention, but Frank stood between them.

"Why Erika, Frank? She didn't even know Abby."

"Erika?" He said her name as if he didn't remember who she was.

"I'll do what you want, Frank. Let Erika go and you can do anything you want with me."

"Michael!" Erika said.

"Why should I let her go? I have you both. I have all the power now. I'm the judge."

"This isn't a court."

"This is your court, Counselor." Frank glared into Michael's face. He swung the gun nonchalantly in his right hand. "This is the last court you'll ever see."

"All right, since this is court," Michael tried another tactic. "What is it you want to tell the court?"

Frank actually looked like he wanted to address the invisible body. "That they're wrong."

"Wrong about what?"

"About separating my family. They have no right, no juris-diction over taking what's mine."

"Who has that right, Frank?"

"I do."

"What about Abby? Does she have the right to care for her

children, to protect them from anyone who tries to harm them?"

"She's their mother. Mothers protect their children."

"From whom?"

"From anyone, everyone who tries to hurt them."

"Even their father?"

Frank thought about that. "It wasn't my father!" Frank shouted. "My father would never hurt me."

His voice had changed, and he sounded like a younger version of himself.

"My father taught me everything. Not my brothers. They were wimps, sissies, but not me. I could kill the little deer, gut it, carve it up, and eat it."

Erika frowned at the picture he was drawing.

"My father didn't have to make me do it. Not like he did my brothers. I was a good boy. I was a man. I did it."

"Your mother, Frank, what did she do when she saw you were doing what your father did? Did she help you?"

"No, she scolded me. She told me it wasn't good to hurt the animals. That if I didn't want to eat the Bambi deer I didn't have to."

"But you were a man, Frank. You couldn't let your father see that you were afraid of the deer, that you wanted to pet the deer, not eat it."

A coldblooded rage entered Frank's eyes. He was no longer a little boy. He'd turned into a soulless killer.

"I lifted my rifle." Frank demonstrated with the gun. He clasped it in both hands, spread his legs and aimed it directly at Michael's heart. "She stood in the misty morning dew, dazed by my silent appearance. I closed one eye and lined her up." He cocked the trigger. "She waited . . . I held my breath. She lifted her head . . . I squeezed the trigger."

"No, Frank!" Erika shouted, breaking the haze he'd worked himself into. She could see Michael had freed the rope from the chair, but his hands were still tied. "You don't have to do this. It's Abby. I didn't die, Frank. We can be together."

Frank turned his head and looked at her.

"We can be a family. We'll take the children and go wherever you want. We'll stay as long as you like. No one ever has to find us again."

"Do you mean it, Abby?"

She nodded, her face wet with tears. Frank rushed to her, hugged her. "Abby," he said, pushing himself back. "What have you done to your hair? Where is that long, beautiful hair?" He combed his fingers through her nearly straight mane.

"It fell out when I was sick, remember?" Erika had to think fast. "It will grow back. The doctor said it might take a few months, but it will be as long as it ever was."

"Yes," Frank said, more to himself than to her. "It will grow back."

"Frank?" she began. "Can we go now? We can pick the children up from school and leave right away."

"We'll need clothes," he reminded her pragmatically.

"We have clothes in the car. We packed yesterday." Erika made her story up as she went along. As long as she kept Frank diverted, Michael could work on the bands restraining his hands.

"Release my hands, Honey, and we'll go."

Frank reached around her. She felt his hands on hers. The first knot slipped, then he stopped.

"What is it?" she asked.

"Him." He turned back to Michael. "I'll never be free as long as he lives."

"Why, Frank? He's just the man who helped us. We don't want to hurt anyone who helped us."

"He didn't help us."

The old Frank was back. The psychotic Frank. The Frank who remembered she was Erika and he was Michael. The man pointing the gun at Michael's heart.

Oil and water had been Connie's first thoughts about the FBI agent assigned to this case. Yet she had to revise her opinion when she saw them mobilize outside the yellow-sided house on an East Brunswick cul-de-sac. They'd evacuated the neighbors without a single sound to tip off the inhabitants that anything was going on. The place was surrounded on all sides, and there was confirmation that Frank had gone inside separately with a man and a woman.

Connie and Adrienne huddled behind an open car door directly across the street from the yellow house.

"What do we do now?" Connie whispered to the agent.

"We wait," he told her.

She looked about the other houses. Men crouched on rooftops of neighboring residences. The street had been closed to traffic. There was only one way in or out.

"Can we find out if anyone in there is alive?"

He nodded and sent a signal to the agent in a van parked at the end of the opening that started the circle.

"Put your earphones on."

She plugged them into her ear.

"Frank, that's not true." Erika St. James's voice came through the wire and into her ear. She breathed a sigh of relief that she was still alive. Now they just had to get them out of there.

"Lawrence." Frank tested the name. "Michael Lawrence, my lawyer. A man who defamed my wife. Told the court lies, half truths, made my Abby cry." Frank assumed the position for a point blank hit.

Erika saw Michael was still working with the ropes.

"He didn't, Frank. You did." Her voice was strong, authoritative, challenging.

This was their only chance. She needed to buy them some time for Michael to get free. If she could keep his attention on her, Michael could surprise him from behind.

"You killed them. You killed them all. The children, Abby, the judge, the lawyer. It isn't their fault. It's yours."

Connie glanced at the FBI agent. They both pressed a hand to their ear.

"It's going down now," she said.

He nodded. Another hand signal passed to the other cars. Men begin closing in on the house.

"Admit it, Frank. You're a scared little boy, and you're hiding it. The others aren't the wimps, are they, Frank? You're the wimp. You're the one who can't sleep at night because of the things you have to do during the day."

"Stop it!" Frank cried.

"You're the one who can't tell your father that you don't want to kill Bambi. That you don't want to eat the deer meat. Your brothers, they told him, didn't they, Frank?"

Frank whirled around. He pointed the gun randomly. "There he is." Frank aimed an shot. The explosion made Erika's heart stop, then beat fast as an escaping bandit.

"Now!" the FBI agent yelled. Men started running toward the house.

"There." Frank shot again. "Die!" he shouted and sent a third shot into the lamp. "Die." A chip of wood jumped up and hit Erika on the side of the face.

"Stop it, Frank!"

Michael's hands came free just as Frank leveled the gun at him. Erika saw the flash of light in her mind, knowing she had to move now. Michael lunged for Frank, the shot rang out, and Erika charged, chair in tow, split seconds apart. Using her head, she tackled Frank, hitting him low in the stomach. The two of them crashed against the doorway. Erika heard the breaking of wood as they went down. The gun fell from his hand and landed on the carpet.

She hung sprawled on top of Frank, unable to move, her legs free, her arms wrenched and painfully clasped behind the back of the chair. Then Connie appeared in front of her. Suddenly there were voices, commands being shouted. Someone calling for a medic. A blond man, obviously in charge, stepped in front of Connie and pulled her and the chair easily to a sitting position.

"Untie her," he said with all the authority of an army captain.

"Where's Michael?" Erika asked Connie. "Is he all right?"

Connie didn't answer. Erika turned as far as she could. Michael lay on the floor. Blood stained the carpet near him. Men in white blocked her view. "Is he all right?" she shouted.

Her hands came free and she bolted from her position. Pushing people aside, she got to him.

"Michael," she pleaded. "Please be all right. Michael, I need you. I love you, and I want to marry you. Michael!"

She looked at the medic. Connie and Adrienne pulled her to her feet to let the medics take him to the waiting ambulance.

"He can't die, Connie," she cried. Connie pulled her into her arms and let her cry. "I love him. I told him I wouldn't marry him, but I will, Connie. He's got to be all right."

"Come on," Connie said. "We'll follow the ambulance to the hospital.

Erika started to move. Frank Mason stepped into her path. This time *his* hands were cuffed behind his back. Erika stared into his eyes. Raw hatred clear as glass assaulted her. She'd never hated anyone in her life, not even her mother, as much as she hatred Frank Mason at this moment.

"If he dies," she told him. "You'll have me to deal with me, and I'm no Abby."

Twenty

Erika stepped out of the limo in front of Robert Wood Johnson University Hospital. Her heart sang at the prospect that Michael was coming home today. She had on a new dress, the house was festively attired, and she couldn't wait to have him all to herself.

She thought of the day when Frank Mason's stray bullet had hit him in the chest. If his hands hadn't come loose at that moment and she hadn't lunged for Frank, Michael might well be dead. Putting her hand over her heart, she thanked God things had worked out differently. The medics working on him had looked grave, and there had been so much blood.

Since Michael had come through the surgery and they'd been told he'd recover completely, there had been a steady stream of family visitors each time she'd come. They hadn't been alone for the entire week he'd been here. She looked forward to having him home, alone. She didn't want any visitors. The two of them had so much to talk about, so much to explain.

She looked down the hill at the new section of the hospital. Michael's room was in the old section. Snow kissed her nose and she stuck out her tongue to catch a snowflake. It was going to be a beautiful Christmas.

Erika turned and put her foot on the first step. Then she turned back. A woman wearing a red coat turned the corner and began walking uphill. Erika scrutinized her. She'd recognize her mother's walk during a sandstorm. *She must have come to see Michael,* Erika thought, but when Alva Redford reached the glass doors to the new section of the hospital she went inside.

It was possible to get from the new section to the old without walking up the hill, she told herself. But her mother had walked with a purpose, as if she'd intended to go through those doors.

Michael hadn't mentioned her coming to see him before. If this was her first time, why would she look as if she knew where she was going? On impulse Erika walked down the hill and entered the area with glass doors. Inside, the place was airy and light, not like the old section which was brick and mortar instead of glass and steel.

She walked up the stairs, checking each floor to see if she could spot her mother. On three she saw her being shown into a room. Erika stepped into the carpeted hall and went to the desk.

"My mother, Mrs. Redford, just went through that door," she told the nurse.

"If you'll have a seat over there I'm sure the doctor will want to speak to you."

Erika opened her mouth to speak but decided against it. She turned around and sat down, facing the door through which her mother had gone. Erika wanted to know what she was doing there.

Ten minutes later a woman doctor came out and briefly stopped at the nurse's station. Erika saw the woman look at her, then back at the nurse. She came over. "Ms. Redford?" she said.

"No," Erika hesitated. "My name is Erika St. James. My mother remarried."

"Would you come with me?"

Erika followed the woman. She was young, probably in her early thirties. She had clear brown eyes and skin a shade lighter than her eyes.

"I'd hoped Alva would bring someone with her," she began

when they were seated in her office. Erika looked at the degrees covering the wall behind Dr. Megan Bruce. "Until today she's always come alone."

"She never said she needed—"

"I know she wouldn't," the doctor said. "She's been that way for years. But things are changing now, and you'll have to help her."

"I don't understand, Doctor. Exactly what is wrong with my mother?"

The doctor went on the explain Alva's condition while Erika sat in wide-eyed horror. She left the doctor's office holding her stomach and feeling as if she needed to sit down. *Dying?* Her mother was dying. All those years when Erika had fought with her mother, Alva had had a condition that forced her mood swings. She couldn't control them, and wasn't responsible for them. The medication had helped in the beginning, but Alva had built up a tolerance to it over the years and her ability to control the moods grew shorter and shorter.

Erika found a seat in a waiting room and sat down. She felt bereft, full of grief. She'd never expected to feel anything. Why did she? Was this why she'd tried time and again to get her mother to love her? Because all along she'd thought there was an explanation for why her mother acted the way she did? She could be lying to herself, setting herself up one more time for her mother to come in and stomp on her feelings.

"Erika?"

She looked up as the door opened.

"May I come in?"

Alva Redford stood in the door. She looked unsure of herself, not the competent, always right actress Erika was used to seeing. She sat down opposite her daughter. Her hands fidgeted for a moment.

"I never expected to have to tell you. I didn't want anyone to know."

"Not know, Mother? Not know that all these years you've been trying to control something that was a medical condition?

You let me think you hated me, that the two of us were like champagne and beer, incompatible, at opposite ends of the spectrum. When the truth would have been so much easier to understand."

"I didn't want you to know."

"Why?"

Alva looked away from her. She checked the walls and the other seats in the room before she answered. "You've always been so strong, so sure of yourself. Even as a child you were decisive, knew what you wanted to do from the beginning and went after it no matter what anyone . . . what I said about it. You frightened me."

"Me?"

"When your father was alive, he took care of me. Then he died, leaving us with so little money. I couldn't afford the medication, and my moods killed any love you might have had for me."

Tears gathered in Erika's eyes.

"You were running from me that day you met Carlton. You ran fast and long and kept going until I couldn't see you anymore. I got in the car and came after you, but you disappeared. I found out you went to Carlton's."

Erika nodded. "We had tea together."

"When you went to live with Carlton, I signed the papers allowing him to be your guardian, it was to protect you from me. I loved you, Erika, and I couldn't go on hurting you."

Hot tears scalded her cheeks.

"Carlton set up the trust fund to pay for my medication. If he died, he didn't want you to find yourself in the same position you did when your father died. The money I borrowed from you is for a special operation. It's scheduled for January fifth."

"Mother . . ." Her voice cracked.

"I know I'm dying, Erika . . . but before I do I want us to forgive each other for the things we've done and said to each other. I love you. I've always loved you."

Erika sobbed aloud. The floodgates opened and tears cascaded over her face.

"Erika?" Alva Redford stood up and opened her arms. Erika let out a loud sob and rushed into them.

They held each other for a long time, both crying, neither wanting to let go.

"Come on, Honey. Let's fix our makeup. My future son-in-law will be upset if he sees you looking like this."

Erika laughed through her tears. Her mother loved her, had always loved her. She wouldn't think about the time they had left. It was good to know they did have some.

Erika's eyes were bright and shining when she walked into Michael's room. She wore winter white pants and a navy blue jacket. A Christmas tree pin with sparkling diamond lights adorned the lapel.

Michael stood at the head of the bed wearing jeans and a light blue shirt. His left arm was folded in a blue and white sling. At the foot of the bed sat a small canvas bag she'd brought with his clothes and toiletries.

"I'll be in class Tuesday night," he said into the phone. When he saw her he opened his good arm and she walked into his hug. "Don't worry, Malick. I'll be there." She kissed him on the mouth. "Good-bye." He hung up and pulled her closer. She kissed him, tenderly and sweetly. He wanted her so much. If the hospital door had a lock he'd consider claiming her here.

"You look awfully happy," he told her. "I hope I'm the reason."

Her smile grew larger. "You're always the reason," she said. "But I have other good news, wonderful news to tell you."

"What?" He pulled her down on his lap and kissed her cheek.

"I'll tell you later. I have a million things to tell you, but let's go home first." She stood up and pulled him with her. Michael clamped his arm around her waist and pulled her to him.

"Just tell me you'll marry me," he said, his voice emotionally charged. "I can wait for everything except that."

"Yes," she replied. "I'll marry you." Erika lifted her mouth to his. She felt lighter than air. Michael loved her and he wanted to marry her, and she wanted to marry him. She knew there was no guarantee that things would last forever. She knew love meant sharing and risking. She'd work at loving Michael, and he'd work at it, too. As long as they shared Carlton's legacy, they had a chance for the forever kind of love.

"Ready to go home?" she asked.

"Ready."

Erika handed the canvas bag to the driver when they reached the front door. Michael got out of the wheelchair the hospital had insisted he ride in for being discharged. Alva Redford came to stand next to them. Michael tensed and grabbed Erika's hand. She looked at him with a smile.

"Hello, Michael," she said. "I'm glad to see you're better." She kissed him on the cheek, then hugged Erika. Erika returned the open display of affection. When she pulled back, her eyes were bright. Both women looked at each other as if they shared a remarkable secret. Michael wanted to know what it was. He remembered what Peter had told him about Alva. He'd intended to tell Erika the last night they were together, but never got around to it. Since then he'd had no time with her.

"She told you?" he asked when the limo pulled away from the curb and joined the traffic on Somerset Street.

"You know?" Erika said.

"I know she has a disease that causes mood swings, and that she'd had it for a long time."

"It's incurable," Erika said, her voice hoarse. "She's going to die."

He put his arm around her and pulled her close. She smelled of flowers and spring, and the promise of a better time.

"She told me this morning," Erika went on. "How long have you known?"

Michael explained his request to Peter that they check out

the possible stock manipulations. The unexplained trust fund payments coincided with the dates for stock activity. It turned out to be coincidental, but in doing one he found the other.

"Are you all right, now?" he asked.

Erika looked up at him. "I've never been happier," she said. "I know my mother is dying, but I also know why she treated me as she did. I won't say I totally forgive her, but at least we have some time to work things out."

Michael smiled and kissed her. He loved her ability to take the best from people, even those who treated her badly.

"If she'd told me years ago I could have helped her, taken care of her."

"She didn't want you to become her nurse."

"I didn't want to be her nurse. I wanted to be her daughter." She paused. "We could have had some good times together. Some of my fears would never have been."

"You're no longer afraid, are you? You understand that she said things she didn't mean?"

Erika nodded. "Some of them cut deeply. I don't know that I'll be able to forget them for a long time."

"Erika, you are a desirable woman. I love you. Don't let that doubt creep into your mind."

She put her fingers over his mouth. "It isn't you. I know you love me and I love you. It's the children."

"Whose children?"

"Yours . . . mine . . . ours."

"We can adopt children. If you don't want them, we don't have to have them. I'll be content—"

"Michael, I *can* have children," she said, stopping his argument. "I mean, no one has ever said I couldn't."

"Then, why—"

"I was scared. I was so afraid of everything my mother had told me." She stopped to smile at him. "I'm not afraid anymore. I'd love to hold my own child. When I held Roberta in my arms, I felt like a miracle had happened." Erika's voice choked.

Michael understood her fears. In time they would all be

removed. He'd feared leaving the mountain, returning to the world that had rejected him. Night after night he'd run in his dreams, trying to get away from the things that hurt him. He was no longer afraid, either. He'd put Abby to rest in his mind and he'd help Erika find out she'd be the kind of mother Alva Redford never was. She'd never do to a child what her mother had done to her.

"A miracle has happened. Sharing is a miracle. Your mother only acted like that because of the disease, and her inability to share her concerns with you. You're not that kind of person. We'll share everything, just as Carlton's legacy required. It won't happen to you."

"I know," Erika said. "I know mother leaned on my father. When he died, Carlton was the only person she told about her condition, and he helped her."

Michael cradled her in his arms and held her. "He must have been a wonderful man."

"He was. I'll tell you about him one day. You're a lot like him," she said.

"I love you," Michael said. He shifted around on his sore arm to take her fully against him. The kiss told him everything he wanted to know. All the doubts were gone. He could feel it in her, feel the softness of her body as they united for now and all time. She was free of the fear, free to love him with all her heart and know that she had his love and they would share this legacy.

Erika loved him, too. She loved him more than she'd ever loved anyone, and if it hadn't been for her mother's condition she'd never have run away, never met Carlton, and Michael might not be part of her life. She shuddered at the thought. Michael tightened his arm around her. He didn't know the legacy Carlton had left them. Money might be one of life's true burdens, but with Michael to share her life, whatever burdens came their way were conquerable.

Dear Reader,

Life has often been likened to the concentric circles that form when we drop a stone into a pond. Each ripple touches the next, altering and changing them in some way. Erika and Michael were two stones thrown into the same pond and they couldn't prevent the effect they had on each other, the love that grew and developed, just as the circles widen and grow. The *LEGACY* left to them brought them love, understanding, and the ability to heal. I hope you enjoyed sharing in their story and learning that we are all given a *LEGACY* by those people who touch our lives.

I receive many letters from the women and men who read my books. Some of them contain plot ideas, Version II of the book they've just read, or casting calls for the movie version. Thank you all for your generous comments and words of encouragement. I love reading your letters as much as I enjoy writing the books.

If you'd like to hear more about *LEGACY,* other books I've written and upcoming releases, send a business size, self-addressed, stamped envelope to me at the following address:

Shirley Hailstock
P.O. Box 513
Plainsboro, NJ 08536

Sincerely yours,

Shirley Hailstock

ABOUT THE AUTHOR

Shirley Hailstock, a short-story writer and award winning novelist, has been writing for more than ten years. Holding a bachelor's degree in Chemistry from Howard University and an MBA in Chemical Marketing from Fairleigh Dickinson University, she works for a pharmaceutical company as a systems manager. She is a past President of the New Jersey Romance Writers and is a member of Women Writers of Color and the International Women's Writers Guild among others. She lives in New Jersey with her family.

SPICE UP YOUR LIFE
WITH ARABESQUE ROMANCES

AFTER HOURS, by Anna Larence   (0-7860-0277-8, $4.99/$6.50)
Vice president of a Fort Worth company, Nachelle Oliver was used to things
her own way. Until she got a new boss. Steven DuCloux was ruthless—and the
most exciting man she had ever known. He knew that she was the perfect VP,
and that she would be the perfect wife. She tried to keep things strictly professional, but the passion between them was too strong.

CHOICES, by Maria Corley   (0-7860-0245-X, $4.95/$6.50)
Chaney just ended with Taurique when she met Lawrence. The rising young
singer swept her off her feet. After nine years of marriage, with Lawrence away
for months on end, Chaney feels lonely and vulnerable. Purely by chance, she
meets Taurique again, and has to decide if she wants to risk it all for love.

DECEPTION, by Donna Hill   (0-7860-0287-5, $4.99/$6.50)
An unhappy marriage taught owner of a successful New York advertising
agency, Terri Powers, never to trust in love again. Then she meets businessman
Clinton Steele. She can't fight the attraction between them—or the sensual
hunger that fires her deepest passions.

DEVOTED, by Francine Craft   (0-7860-0094-5, $4.99/$6.50)
When Valerie Thomas and Delano Carter were young lovers each knew it
wouldn't last. Val, now a photojournalist, meets Del at a high-society wedding.
Del takes her to Alaska for the assignment of her career. In the icy wilderness
he warms her with a passion too long denied. This time not even Del's desperate
secret will keep them from reclaiming their lost love.

FOR THE LOVE OF YOU, by Felicia Mason   (0-7860-0071-6, $4.99/$6.50)
Seven years ago, Kendra Edwards found herself pregnant and alone. Now she
has a secure life for her twins and a chance to finish her college education. A
long unhappy marriage had taught attorney Malcolm Hightower the danger of
passion. But Kendra taught him the sensual magic of love. Now they must each
give true love a chance.

ALL THE RIGHT REASONS, by Janice Sims   (0-7860-0405-3, $4.99/$6.50)
Public defender, Georgie Shaw, returns to New Orleans and meets reporter Clay
Knight. He's determined to uncover secrets between Georgie and her celebrity
twin, and protect Georgie from someone who wants both sisters dead. Dangerous secrets are found in a secluded mansion, leaving Georgie with no one to
trust but the man who stirs her desires.

*Available wherever paperbacks are sold, or order direct from the
Publisher. Send cover price plus 50¢ per copy for mailing and
handling to Kensington Publishing Corp., Consumer Orders,
or call (toll free) 888-345-BOOK, to place your order using
Mastercard or Visa. Residents of New York and Tennessee
must include sales tax. DO NOT SEND CASH.*

WARMHEARTED AFRICAN-AMERICAN ROMANCES
BY *FRANCIS RAY*

FOREVER YOURS   (0-7860-0483-5, $4.99/$6.50)
Victoria Chandler must find a husband or her grandparents will call in loans that support her chain of lingerie boutiques. She fixes a mock marriage to ranch owner Kane Taggert. The marriage will only last one year, and her business will be secure. The only problem is that Kane has other plans for Victoria. He'll cast a spell that will make her his forever.

HEART OF THE FALCON   (0-7860-0483-5, $4.99/$6.50)
A passionate night with millionaire Daniel Falcon, leaves Madelyn Taggert enamored . . . and heartbroken. She never accepted that the long-time family friend would fulfill her dreams, only to see him walk away without regrets. After his parent's bitter marriage, the last thing Daniel expected was to be consumed by the need to have her for a lifetime.

INCOGNITO   (0-7860-0364-2, $4.99/$6.50)
Owner of an advertising firm, Erin Cortland witnessed an awful crime and lived to tell about it. Frightened, she runs into the arms of Jake Hunter, the man sent to protect her. He doesn't want the job. He left the police force after a similar assignment ended in tragedy. But when he learns not only one man is after her and that he is falling in love, he will risk anything to protect her.

ONLY HERS   (07860-0255-7, $4.99/$6.50)
St. Louis R.N. Shannon Johnson recently inherited a parcel of Texas land. She sought it as refuge until landowner Matt Taggart challenged her to prove she's got what it takes to work a sprawling ranch. She, on the other hand, soon challenges him to dare to love again.

SILKEN BETRAYAL   (0-7860-0426-6, $4.99/$6.50)
The only man executive secretary Lauren Bennett needed was her five-year-old son Joshua. Her only intent was to keep Joshua away from powerful in-laws. Then Jordan Hamilton entered her life. He sought her because of a personal vendetta against her father-in-law. When Jordan develops strong feelings for Lauren and Joshua, he must choose revenge or love.

UNDENIABLE   (07860-0125-9, $4.99/$6.50)
Wealthy Texas heiress Rachel Malone defied her powerful father and eloped with Logan Williams. But a trump-up assault charge set the whole town and Rachel against him and he fled Stanton with a heart full of pain. Eight years later, he's back and he wants revenge . . . and Rachel.

Available wherever paperbacks are sold, or order direct from the Publisher. Send cover price plus 50¢ per copy for mailing and handling to Kensington Publishing Corp., Consumer Orders, or call (toll free) 888-345-BOOK, to place your order using Mastercard or Visa. Residents of New York and Tennessee must include sales tax. DO NOT SEND CASH.

LOOK FOR THESE ARABESQUE ROMANCES

AFTER ALL, by Lynn Emery (0-7860-0325-1, $4.99/$6.50)
News reporter Michelle Toussaint only focused on her dream of becoming an anchorwoman. Then contractor Anthony Hilliard returned. For five years, Michelle had reminisced about the passions they shared. But happiness turned to heartbreak when Anthony's cruel betrayal led to her father's financial ruin. He returned for one reason only: to win Michelle back.

THE ART OF LOVE, by Crystal Wilson-Harris (0-7860-0418-5, $4.99/$6.50)
Dakota Bennington's heritage is apparent from her African clothing to her sculptures. To her, attorney Pierce Ellis is just another uptight professional stuck in the American mainstream. Pierce worked hard and is proud of his success. An art purchase by his firm has made Dakota a major part of his life. And love bridges their different worlds.

CHANGE OF HEART (0-7860-0103-8, $4.99/$6.50)
by Adrienne Ellis Reeves
Not one to take risks or stray far from her South Carolina hometown, Emily Brooks, a recently widowed mother, felt it was time for a change. On a business venture she meets author David Walker who is conducting research for his new book. But when he finds undying passion, he wants Emily for keeps. Wary of her newfound passion, all Emily has to do is follow her heart.

ECSTACY, by Gwynne Forster (0-7860-0416-9, $4.99/$6.50)
Schoolteacher Jeannetta Rollins had a tumor that was about to cost her her eyesight. Her persistence led her to follow Mason Fenwick, the only surgeon talented enough to perform the surgery, on a trip around the world. After getting to know her, Mason wants her whole . . . body and soul. Now he must put behind a tragedy in his career and trust himself and his heart.

KEEPING SECRETS, by Carmen Green (0-7860-0494-0, $4.99/$6.50)
Jade Houston worked alone. But a dear deceased friend left clues to a two-year-old mystery and Jade had to accept working alongside Marine Captain Nick Crawford. As they enter a relationship that runs deeper than business, each must learn how to trust each other in all aspects.

MOST OF ALL, by Louré Bussey (0-7860-0456-8, $4.99/$6.50)
After another heartbreak, New York secretary Elandra Lloyd is off to the Bahamas to visit her sister. Her sister is nowhere to be found. Instead she runs into Nassau's richest, self-made millionaire Bradley Davenport. She is lucky to have made the acquaintance with this sexy islander as she searches for her sister and her trust in the opposite sex.

Available wherever paperbacks are sold, or order direct from the Publisher. Send cover price plus 50¢ per copy for mailing and handling to Kensington Publishing Corp., Consumer Orders, or call (toll free) 888-345-BOOK, to place your order using Mastercard or Visa. Residents of New York and Tennessee must include sales tax. DO NOT SEND CASH

ROMANCES THAT SIZZLE
FROM ARABESQUE

AFTER DARK, by Bette Ford (0-7860-0442-8, $4.99/$6.50)
Taylor Hendricks' brother is the top NBA draft choice. She wants to protect him from the lure of fame and wealth, but meets basketball superstar Donald Williams in an exclusive Detroit restaurant. Donald is determined to prove that he is wrong about him. In this game all is at stake . . . including Taylor's heart.

BEGUILED, by Eboni Snoe (0-7860-0046-5, $4.99/$6.50)
When Raquel Mason agrees to impersonate a missing heiress for just one night and plans go awry, a daring abduction makes her the captive of seductive Nate Bowman. Together on a journey across exotic Caribbean seas to the perilous wilds of Central America, desire looms in their hearts. But when the masquerade is over, will their love end?

CONSPIRACY, by Margie Walker (0-7860-0385-5, $4.99/$6.50)
Pauline Sinclair and Marcellus Cavanaugh had the love of a lifetime. Until Pauline had to leave everything behind. Now she's back and their love is as strong as ever. But when the President of Marcellus's company turns up dead and Pauline is the prime suspect, they must risk all to their love.

FIRE AND ICE, by Carla Fredd (0-7860-0190-9, $4.99/$6.50)
Years of being in the spotlight and a recent scandal regarding her ex-fianceé and a supermodel, the daughter of a Georgia politician, Holly Aimes has turned cold. But when work takes her to the home of late-night talk show host Michael Williams, his relentless determination melts her cool.

HIDDEN AGENDA, by Rochelle Alers (0-7860-0384-7, $4.99/$6.50)
To regain her son from a vengeful father, Eve Blackwell places her trust in dangerous and irresistible Matt Sterling to rescue her abducted son. He accepts this last job before he turns a new leaf and becomes an honest rancher. As they journey from Virginia to Mexico they must enter a charade of marriage. But temptation is too strong for this to remain a sham.

INTIMATE BETRAYAL, by Donna Hill (0-7860-0396-0, $4.99/$6.50)
Investigative reporter, Reese Delaware, and millionaire computer wizard, Maxwell Knight are both running from their pasts. When Reese is assigned to profile Maxwell, they enter a steamy love affair. But when Reese begins to piece her memory, she stumbles upon secrets that link her and Maxwell, and threaten to destroy their newfound love.

Available wherever paperbacks are sold, or order direct from the Publisher. Send cover price plus 50¢ per copy for mailing and handling to Kensington Publishing Corp., Consumer Orders, or call (toll free) 888-345-BOOK, to place your order using Mastercard or Visa. Residents of New York and Tennessee must include sales tax. DO NOT SEND CASH.